Starting Eleanora

Chapter One

Eleanora huddled on the wide, chilled windowsill of her bedroom window. Knees pulled up to her chin, she stared meditatively at the empty street below, contemplating the small section of Little Italy her family called home. Her shadowed bedroom felt protective in the semi-darkness. Occasionally, her mother's cough or the scrape of a chair on the kitchen linoleum reminded her she wasn't really alone. A glance at the luminous dial of the windup clock on her dresser informed her that it was 2:00 a.m. Her father almost never came home before 2:30, when the bars closed and he and the other musicians packed up their instruments and said goodnight.

She wasn't sure why she waited up for him — or if her mother was waiting for him to come home as well. Eleanora didn't understand why her mother would wait up for her father — they barely talked to each other, nor did they sleep in the same bed together. When her father came home he'd put away his trumpet, fix himself something to eat, read the paper for a while, then retire alone to the spare bedroom, the window shade pulled down. Her mother never slept. All she ever appeared to do — if doing was what you'd call it — was sit with her feet up on a chair, a cigarette dangling between her fingers and a half-empty glass of wine within reach.

Sometimes, Eleanora would sit with him while he ate eggs or leftover pasta. With a little encouraging, he'd share what had happened during the evening or — what she looked forward to most — talk about the music: how he or Milton, the pianist, had created a totally new melody line, or played off each other in such an intimate and intuitive way that it was almost spiritual. Or he'd regale her with gossip about Jimmy, the drummer; Henry, the bassist; or Buster, the saxophonist, who was her dad's closest friend. But mostly, it was the talk of music that brought energy and vitality to her father's voice. "You should have heard us," he'd say wistfully. "We were beautiful, like magic. I tell you, sweetie, having you and creating music are the only things that make my life worth living."

1

But tonight, the street remained deserted. No moon — at least not in the sharply angled piece of sky visible from her perch — only a dark void. Shivering, she decided to give in to her fatigue. The idea of curling up in bed was comforting, like being held in protective safety from something ominous.

Later, awakened from a deep sleep, she became aware of voices — her parents. He was home. She opened her eyes to see 4:00 a.m. displayed on the bedside clock. She listened. It was easy to hear through the thin door.

"How come you never have anything to eat in the house?" Silence. "You're pathetic, Eva. You know that? What's the matter with you?" Her father spoke the way he played — in fast, choppy rhythms.

"Nothing's the matter with me." Her mother's voice was a soft, low monotone. She always spoke in Italian. It wasn't that she didn't understand English, she simply refused to speak it.

"Oh no? Nothing's the matter with you? You don't sleep. You don't eat. You call this a life? You think this is normal? You're a fucking vegetable."

"You think what you do is normal?" her mother countered. "Staying out all night, hanging around in bars with whores — that's normal? Who are you to criticize me? At least I believe in God. At least I go to church, not out gallivanting all night. What are you, a gigolo?"

Eleanora heard the metallic sounds of a fork in a pan and guessed that her father was at the stove, maybe making scrambled eggs. She wondered if she should get up, but remained frozen. She heard her father sigh deeply and then hum a few notes, a snatch of a song.

"Eva," he said, "you know what my work is. I'm a musician. As long as we're here in the city, these clubs are where I'm going to play. I'm damn lucky to work as steady as I do, so don't go making a big deal about my being out at night. I'm not cheating on you."

Her mother ignored this last thought. "Give me some more wine while you're up," she muttered.

Eleanora heard the clunk of the half-gallon jug on the table. The scrape of a chair signaled her father sitting down. His jacket would be slung over the back of the chair, his collar undone, tie loosened, glistening black hair slicked back. She thought he was handsome.

"If we moved out of this neighborhood, if we moved to Jersey, we could have a life," he said. "There's plenty of jazz clubs in Jersey. I could get gigs easy. All the guys are open to it. I'm the one holding things up. Eva, we could have a life there. It would be good for Ellie."

"No." Her mother was adamant. They had been arguing about this for three or four years, maybe longer. "This is my home. Everything I need is here. I'm not moving anywhere. There's nothing for me out there. What's in New Jersey?

There's nothing. Nothing. All they've got is swamps and mosquitoes."

"What are you talking about?"

"Giuseppi, they have nothing Italian, no Italian markets, no fresh meat, no fresh bread. Here I have everything I need. The food is fresh, like in my village. I have my family, my friends. Everybody speaks Sicilian. This is my home. I'm not going anywhere. No. Never."

"Sure, your family is here, but what friends? You have no friends. You hardly even speak to your parents. When was the last time you saw your grandmother? Or your aunt or cousins?"

"I see them."

"Yeah? When?"

"I saw them today. I went to my mother's."

There was silence. Ellie imagined the look on Daddy's face. She didn't believe her mother and guessed that her father didn't either.

"You went to your mother's today?"

"Yes."

"You went dressed like that? In that housedress? The same housedress I've seen on you all week? You went to your mother's without taking a bath? Smelling like that?"

Eleanora pictured her mother's glare. Silence.

"You know what? I've had it. I've put up with this crap long enough. I've pleaded with you for what, 15 years? I've begged you to get a life. Go to school, get an education, learn the fucking language. For Christ's sake, Eva, we're in America, not Sicily. And for 15 years you put me off. Maybe, you say. Maybe next year, when Eleanora is older. Excuses. All the time excuses. Now, you finally admit that you have no intention of ever changing, of ever becoming American."

He waited, but was met with more silence. "I can't even talk to you," he plowed on. "You don't know anything. You know nothing except the stupid gossip from your family and the Italian markets. Now, on top of everything else, you have the nerve to sit here and lie to me? Well, I'll tell you what, Eva. *I'm moving to Jersey. I'm getting out of this goddamned ghetto of yours.*"

Ellie heard her mother's sharp laugh, the bitterness and derision in her voice.

"You think because you went to college you know everything, don't you? You know nothing! You think you're American? You think you're going to be accepted in New Jersey? To them, you'll just be another dumb guinea like me."

"I'm not a guinea," her father said calmly. "I'm American and so is my daughter."

"Ha! You'll see. You think you're so smart. Big man. A real *pezzo grosso*. Go

3

on. Go to your New Jersey if you think it's paradise, if it's so important to you. But Eleanora stays here — and you will pay our support. It's the law. I know."

"Son-of-a-bitch," her father said in tone that sounded like amazement. "You've been preparing for this, haven't you? Is this why you stay up? To provoke this? To get me to leave?" A few moments of silence passed. "Answer me," he said more firmly. More silence. "Fuck you," he said quietly. "All right. You want me out? I'm out. I'm leaving."

Eleanora heard their bedroom door open and knew he was gathering his clothes together. Rising from her bed, she opened the door to the kitchen. Her mother looked up from the table and flicked her cigarette ash into a saucer.

"Ciao, *bambina*," she addressed her daughter wryly. "I guess you heard. Your father is leaving us to go to New Jersey where there are no Italians, only Americans who speak English and eat food from cans."

Eleanora crossed the kitchen and leaned against the doorjamb to her parents' bedroom. Her father was stuffing clothes into a small suitcase.

"Papa?"

He shook his head. "I'm sorry, princess, I really am. I just can't do this anymore. I'll crash with Buster for a couple of days."

Eleanora didn't bother to argue with him. A part of her wanted him to go, like a caged bird flying away to freedom. But another part would miss him terribly.

"Am I going to see you?"

"Of course you'll see me. I'll be in touch, we'll work something out. Don't worry — this has nothing to do with you. I love you. You know that. I'll get a place and you'll visit. You'll stay with me. It'll be all right, I promise."

She stood paralyzed, her mind blank as she watched him pack. She turned and looked at her mother sitting at the Formica table, the half-gallon of red wine an ugly centerpiece on the table. Eleanora gestured to her mother, but she made no response. Her father emerged from the bedroom and kissed her on the forehead.

"I'll talk to you soon," he said.

Then he turned to address his wife, the growing distance already evident.

"I'll send you money every week, so don't go spreading stories that I've abandoned you." He paused to give her an evil look. "I hope you're happy, Eva," he mumbled as he walked out.

Eleanora stared blankly at the closed door, the thump-thumping of her father's steps on the stairs echoing as he fled.

Chapter Two

Eleanora became aware of the silence. Total and complete, it struck her like an invisible wave. Tears trickled down her face as she cupped the cold mug of tea in her hands. *Funny how that scene from over 20 years ago is still so alive for me. And yet here I am in 2005, a married woman living in Leonia, New Jersey, no longer that young girl in Manhattan's Little Italy.*

Pushing herself up from the upholstered rocker, she carried the mug to the kitchen and rinsed it out. Three o'clock. Julie and Zach should be home from school soon. Or was Julie working today? *That reminds me, I have a rehearsal tonight.* Eleanora started getting things ready for dinner. She would have to leave by 6:00 to get to the church for choir practice on time. If she didn't have something ready for dinner, Aaron would be angry and Eleanora didn't want to have to deal with that again.

She was in the kitchen when Zachary came in and headed straight for the refrigerator, sticking his head in and finally deciding on orange juice.

"Hi, hon," she said, hoping to prompt him into acknowledging her existence.

"Oh, hi Mom."

"Anything interesting happen at school today?"

Snatching a glass from the dishwasher, Zach poured his juice without giving any indication of responding.

"Yoo hoo! Zachary," she called, "over here. There's a mother in the room talking to you."

"Huh? What?"

"I asked you if anything interesting happened at school today. It's really not nice to ignore someone, Zach, when they're speaking to you."

"I'm sorry, Mom. I didn't hear you." His look somehow managed to convey that it was her fault.

"Well?"

Zach shrugged his shoulders in puzzlement. "What?"

"Forget it, Zach. Drink your juice."

Eleanora returned to breading chicken cutlets. The harder she tried to break through her son's wall, the more she failed. He was just like his father in that respect. It was as if they were hermits living within themselves, only emerging when necessary and then befuddled by an unfamiliar world. When she looked up again, he had vanished, ghostlike — the empty glass on the kitchen table the only evidence of his having passed through.

A short while later, Julie entered the house like a windstorm. Breathless, she blew into the kitchen, having already deposited books and clothes in her wake.

"Hi Mom. What's for dinner?" She peered over her mother's shoulder to see what she was doing, depositing a kiss on Eleanora's cheek in the process. "Umm, cutlets. Good. Don't forget I'm working late tonight," she interrupted before her mother could answer. "I'm on the closing-up team. What time are we eating?" A purse, a scarf, a hat were dropped onto a chair while she headed for the fridge.

"You're so full of life, you don't even give me a chance to answer. Yes, cutlets and carrots and mashed potatoes and we're eating at 5:30 because I have to leave by 6:00 for my rehearsal. What time are you going to work?"

Julie looked up from the fridge as she withdrew a container of soymilk, which only she and her mother drank. "I'm working 7:00 to 11:00, but I probably won't be home until close to 12:00 by the time we clean up and everything."

Eleanora frowned. "I thought there was some kind of law that said you school kids weren't allowed to work that late during school days."

Julie shook her head as she gulped her milk. "I don't think so, Mom. Besides, technically, I'm only working four hours and only to 11:00, so I don't think there's anything wrong with that. Besides, it's fun and I enjoy it. So," she raised her shoulders and smiled her broad smile, "no problem, right?"

"Just make sure you're getting enough rest, OK?"

Julie gave her mother a hug. "You're such a worrywart. Relax. I'll be in my room. I've got a ton of homework. Call me when supper's ready."

"Count on it." Eleanora felt an upwelling of pride as she watched her daughter, a fully grown young woman, head for the stairs. Julie was her treasure.

Around 5:15, Eleanora heard the garage door go up and then close. A few moments later, Aaron came through the kitchen door.

"Hi," she said, "how was traffic?"

Aaron made a tiny motion with his head as he came toward her, leaning his head forward for her to kiss his cheek.

"What's for dinner?" he asked, as he headed to the front hall to hang up his coat.

"Chicken cutlets," she called to his back. Then, waiting for his return to the kitchen, she added, "We're eating in 10 minutes. I have to leave for rehearsal by 6:00."

"Again?"

She stopped what she was doing and looked at him wide-eyed. "What do you mean?"

Aaron was rummaging around the kitchen counter looking for things to put into his mouth. "You just had rehearsal."

"Every Wednesday and Friday."

"And then there's Sunday," he corrected her.

"Of course there's Sunday. That's what we rehearse for."

"Sounds like a lot," he said disapprovingly, his scowl pushing onto his face like a mask.

Eleanora felt scolded. Wanting to strike back, she imagined picking up the cast-iron frying pan that had been her mother's — in which the cutlets were turning a wonderful golden color in the bubbling oil — and smashing it over his head. But in her imagination, everything would go wrong: Hot oil would splash onto her own arms; the cutlets, the supper for her children, would end up wasted on the tiled floor; and the frying pan itself would be too heavy to swing. It would all be in vain. She felt defeated and hopeless. Instead, she turned away from him and proceeded with dinner.

"I don't understand why you continue to do this when you know exactly how I feel," he said. "They hardly pay you anything for all the time you put in. It's not even your church, for God's sake. They're just taking advantage of you, Ellie." When she didn't respond, he persisted. "Answer me. Why won't you quit this nonsense?

"I've told you, Aaron. I've got to. Playing for the choir is my only outlet. I'm not doing it for the money. I'm doing it so I can breathe. I'd pay them if I had to. I'm sorry, I know you want me to stay home all the time, but I can't."

Aaron glared as she turned her back to him again. "Can't or won't?"

"What?" she asked, half turning to him.

"Is it that you can't stay home or that you won't? You make it sound like it's beyond your control. It's not. You can stop anytime you want to. You're only doing this to humiliate me."

Eleanora spun around, a long fork clenched in her hand. "Humiliate you?" She stared at him, speechless.

"It makes me look like I can't support my family and I have to send you out to work at this less-than-minimum wage job to help put food on the table."

My God! God help me contend with this stupidity. With this selfishness. Give me strength to cope.

She took a deep breath.

"Aaron," she said slowly, "I am not doing this to humiliate you. My music doesn't have anything to do with you. So please don't get it into your head that I have to stop playing or anything else connected with my music. I couldn't stand that. If you tried to make me stop, I would die. Please." She said all of this as calmly as she could, but her hands trembled as she spooned the carrots into a bowl and transferred the cutlets to a platter.

"Please call the kids for supper," she said in a half whisper as she carried the food into the dining room, where the table was already set.

Chapter Three

When choir practice was over, Pastor Peter Van Houten stood in the door-way of the church until he caught Eleanora's eye. With just a glance he indicated that she should come to his study when she was finished. Eleanora hurriedly gathered her sheets of music and grabbed her coat. When she entered his office, her eyes were wide.

"What's wrong?" she asked.

Peter chuckled. "Why do you always assume there's something wrong?" Smiling weakly, Eleanora sat in the chair he gestured to. "You always look frightened," he told her, "like you expect to be punished for something."

"You mean I'm not?"

He laughed. "Good lord, no. What on earth could I ever punish you for? You of all people! No, what I wanted to tell you was — you know Bethann Winters, of course."

"Of course," she said, leaning forward, "she's in the choir, but she didn't show up for practice tonight. Is she all right?"

The pastor nodded and then got up to close the door. He sat down again in the chair next to her.

"She's pretty shook up." He paused, looking down at his hands. Eleanora waited, barely breathing while she searched his face for some clue of what was to come. "Do you know her son, Kevin?"

She shook her head. "Not really," she said, picturing the shy 15-year-old who more resembled his short and pudgy father than big-boned Bethann.

"Well," Peter said, unsure how to continue, "I'm not sure I should be telling you this, but I need to share it with someone and I don't know who I trust more than you."

Eleanora's hand went to her chest. "Me?" He nodded. "My God, Peter. Why me? What are you talking about?"

"Don't be upset, Ellie. I mean it as a compliment. I need to bounce this off someone who knows the people involved — me, the Winters. Can I talk to you?"

"Of course you can talk to me, Peter. You know that anything you tell me in confidence will be safe with me. But what's happening? What's this about?"

"I received a note from Kevin yesterday. It was a love note. Apparently Kevin is gay and he thinks he's in love with me. He said life wouldn't be worth living, and he threatened suicide if I couldn't accept his love."

Somehow Eleanora wasn't shocked by this revelation. She'd long had an impression that gender issues were somewhat confused in the Winters family — Toby Winters, the unphysical, pudgy aesthete married to robust Bethann, a former field hockey star in college.

"The poor boy," she said half to herself.

"I wasn't sure what to do, but I finally decided I had to let his parents know. I went to their house last night and talked with Bethann. Toby wasn't home and, fortunately, neither was Kevin. Beth was absolutely blown away. She felt that this was an aspersion on her and if people found out, they'd blame her. I'm not sure I understand that. At any rate, I implored her and Toby to get some professional help immediately, and indicated that I'd talk to Kevin and try to let him down gently."

"How awful for you. Have you seen him yet? Kevin?"

"Tomorrow morning. I left a note at his house asking him to come by. I figured we could take as much time as necessary and if anything happened, if he flipped out or threatened suicide, we'd be able to, you know, get him to a hospital or a doctor or something." He paused to look at her. "What do you think? You've got teenagers. You know the Winters. What do you think?"

Eleanora's head was swimming. She imagined Bethann feeling overwhelmed with nameless guilt and shame and fear. For some reason, she pictured Toby as emotionally disengaged, trying to deal with the facts as some kind of intellectual abstraction, like interstellar gravitational waves. Her heart went out to Kevin, an introverted loner who reminded her of Zachary as well as of herself — and to Peter, sitting patiently and quietly beside her, wanting to be told he had behaved appropriately.

"What do you plan on saying to Kevin tomorrow?"

"I'll tell him that he's a fine young man and I'm proud to have him in my congregation, but that I'm not gay, despite what he might think. I'll be happy to be his friend and pastor but there's no way I can be his lover, and he has to accept that without feeling there's nothing more to live for." He paused. "Something along those lines, I guess."

Eleanora nodded, then looked at Peter. She saw fear in his eyes.

Peter turned away and looked up at the ceiling. "I'm not gay, if that's what you're thinking," he said, standing up and walking to his desk. He turned and looked at her. "Ellie, you know I'm not gay, don't you?"

"I never thought you were. You've been married, so I never really thought about it."

"Well, I'm not gay. And you're right. I was married. Happily married, too. But Amy's been dead for six years and I don't know if people forget or not. My God, I don't want people to think I'm gay."

"I don't think anybody does."

"But what are they going to think if this gets out? Isn't there some kind of saying that homosexuals can tell if someone is gay or not?"

"I don't know. I never heard that." Her ignorance did not reassure him.

"Peter, people know you, they respect you. Everybody thinks the world of you. You're a wonderful model for all of us."

He regarded her with a level and steady gaze. "You hardly know me, Ellie. I'm not perfect."

"None of us is. But being imperfect and being unacceptable are two different things, aren't they? What's the line? 'Let he who is without sin cast the first stone.'"

"Yes, but that doesn't stop people from judging each other. We do it all the time."

An image of Aaron flashed through her mind. "Nobody is judging you."

"What if Kevin kills himself? What then? People will judge me as having failed as a minister. They'll say I should have been able to prevent it. They'll ask why Kevin was attracted to me in the first place. Why me, for God's sake? Why did he have to pick me to be attracted to?"

It was as if he were imploring her to think about it, so she did. It wasn't that Peter was particularly handsome. In his late 30s, he was thin and trim at slightly under six feet. He was patient, good-natured, nurturing, generally friendly. All of these were reasonable virtues that might attract someone in need of comfort.

"There are a number of reasons why someone might find themselves attracted to you," she concluded.

He looked at her questioningly.

"You're a good person, Peter. People like you, they look up to you. Perhaps Kevin hasn't received the kind of love he's been looking for. Why not you?"

There was a moment of silence, then suddenly she reached for her coat and got up to leave.

"What's the matter?" Peter asked.

"It's getting late. I have to get home. Aaron will be wondering what happened to me."

"Of course. It's just that you looked frightened."

"I have to get going, that's all." Then almost as an afterthought, "Let me know what happens with Kevin. Do you want me to stop in on Bethann tomorrow? See if she's all right?"

"That's a good idea. She might welcome the opportunity to talk to you." He hesitated, "But it probably wouldn't be a good idea if she knew I told you about Kevin's note."

Eleanora thought for a moment. "I'll just say I missed her at practice tonight and stopped by to say hi."

Peter took her hand in his. "I don't know how to thank you, Ellie, for not going all freaky on me." She smiled and impulsively hugged him. "I'll let you know what happens with Kevin," he said.

"Good," she said, "I'll talk to you tomorrow."

Eleanora was deep in thought when she entered the house and she jumped at Aaron's voice close behind her.

"I was getting worried," he said, standing in the doorway to the living room, papers in his hand. "I expected you home hours ago. What were you doing?"

She used the time it took to hang up her coat to compose herself. "Nothing. Peter wanted to talk to me about one of his parishioners who's in the choir, that's all. I didn't realize I was that late."

"What's the matter with you? You're all flustered."

"Nothing. You just startled me." He looked at her piercingly and she turned away, heading into the kitchen.

"What was so all-fired important that the reverend had to keep my wife an hour late?"

Eleanora closed her eyes and rolled her head around to ease the tension in her neck. He always did this to her. She felt beat up and bruised. She hurt all over.

"What the hell is the matter with you?" he demanded, following her into the kitchen.

"What?" She looked up, startled again, surprised to find herself grasping the edge of the sink.

"What the hell is wrong with you, for Christ's sake? I talk to you and you don't answer. You go off in space somewhere. I hate it when you do that. I'm talking to you, goddamnit! The least you can do is answer me. I at least deserve that from you."

"I'm sorry, Aaron. I didn't hear you."

"Of course you didn't. You don't listen to me. How dare you shut me out when I'm talking to you."

"Aaron, I'm sorry. It's just that when you come at me ..."

"Come at you? I asked you a question! Are you so damned sensitive that I can't even ask you a simple question? I can't ask what you've been doing? Almost an hour late coming home at night? You might have been in an accident. I was worried. Am I not allowed to have a normal conversation with my wife?"

"I told you where I was tonight." She felt her gathering fear converting into anger. Eyes blazing, she clenched her fists unconsciously. "Peter wanted to talk to me about one of the women in the choir. Stop hounding me."

"Who?"

She looked at him, puzzled.

"Who did he want to talk about?" he challenged.

She shook her head in disbelief. "What difference does it make? This doesn't concern you. You don't know these people."

"If it keeps you out late at night, it concerns me. There's no reason to keep secrets, is there? So tell me. Who was so important that you chose not to come home?"

Ellie felt torn and paralyzed. "I'm sorry, Aaron, but I can't tell you. It's a confidential matter."

Aaron glared at her, head shaking. He walked back into the living room and threw his papers onto the coffee table where he had some work spread out. She took advantage of his absence to put a kettle on for tea. Aaron came back into the kitchen and poured himself some wine.

"Come," he said to her, motioning to the table. "Come sit down while you're waiting for the water to boil."

She walked obediently to the table and sat down, hands in her lap, eyes averted. Aaron sipped his wine.

"I'm sorry," he said. "I don't mean to hound you. It's just that I have this feeling, more and more, that you're shutting me out. It feels like we're hardly ever alone. You're always out of the house and even when you're here, you're not here. I talk to you and you don't respond. You make me feel like I don't exist." He paused, but she made no attempt to respond.

"We hardly ever make love anymore," he said more softly. "Ellie, I don't know what's going on. Sometimes I feel like you hate me. Ever since Todd died things have been different with us. What is it? Do you want a divorce? Is there somebody else? Tell me, Ellie. Help me understand."

Eleanora just stared at her hands. She knew what Aaron said was true. She often felt immobilized around him, as if her body went into lockdown. Sometimes she found herself holding her breath, her body rigid with anticipation of his impending slap. Realizing that her silence might provoke him, she made an effort to nod her head, a signal that she had heard. She struggled to meet his gaze, eyes round and wide. She swallowed. The apology, the explanation, wouldn't come. Instead, she rose to pour the boiling water into her mug.

"Please, Ellie. Talk to me."

She took a breath. "I'm sorry, Aaron. Sometimes everything just goes blank and I don't know what to say." She returned to the table and sat down.

"Please, Ellie. Just take your time. I need to know."

"There's nobody else," she whispered, making the effort to find her voice. "Divorce? I never thought about it."

He waited for her to continue, but she said nothing more.

"Ellie, do you love me?"

Her breath caught. Staring at him, she shrugged her shoulders. "I don't know," she said, looking away. She paused and furrowed her brows in thought.

"Do you love me?" she asked suddenly.

"Of course I do," he stated brightly.

Eleanora looked at him intently. "Are you sure?"

"Of course I'm sure. You're my wife. We have two kids, two teenagers, one headed to college soon. We have a wonderful home, everything. Of course I love you." Eleanora continued to study him without changing her expression. "Aren't you happy here?" he asked. "Don't you love our kids? Our life?"

"Are you asking if I'm happy?"

"Yes. Aren't you happy with our life? God, what more could you want? How could you not be happy?"

Eleanora's head spun. It was as if they were speaking two different languages. The conversation felt futile. Aware that she had never permitted herself to think these thoughts, she also knew Aaron wouldn't understand even if she could articulate her feelings. He'd shame her for even thinking about her own happiness.

Did she want a divorce? Questions suddenly bombarded her. What about the children? How would she survive without his financial support? Where would she live? Would she have to move out of this house? Would he stay here with the children? Was it even possible? Avoiding his gaze, she remained lost in a swirl of uncertainty.

Was she happy? When was the last time she had been aware of feeling happiness? She thought of an organ recital she had attended in St. John's Cathedral in New York. The music had filled her with joy and wonder and hopefulness. But that had been over 20 years ago, before her marriage, before Todd, before anything.

"Do you think I'm happy?" she asked, as if his opinion could settle the issue for her.

Aaron sighed and raised his hands hopelessly. "I guess I don't really know,

Ellie. I thought you were. I assumed you were. But maybe you're not. I don't know anymore. I don't understand you anymore. You're an enigma." He drained his glass of wine and wearily stood to put it in the dishwasher. "I'm going up to bed. I can't do this anymore."

Eleanora remained lost in thought as she heard him climbing heavily up the stairs to their bedroom.

Chapter Four

The next morning, Eleanora drove to Bethann's house and parked in the doublewide brick-paved driveway. She took a small pleasure in the melodious, two-tone chime of the doorbell. No one came to the door. Impatiently, she rang again and waited. Turning to leave, she spotted Bethann peering out from behind a curtain. Eleanora waved and smiled and, a moment later, Bethann opened the door.

Eleanora was shocked. Bethann looked like she hadn't slept for days. Her eyes were red and raw and her usual robust and rosy cheeks were sallow and lifeless.

"Beth, are you all right? I missed you last night and thought I'd stop by on my way out shopping. You look — are you OK?"

Wincing as if the morning sun was too bright, Bethann gave a hardly noticeable shake of her head. Eleanora thought she detected a slight odor of staleness, as if Beth had been closed up indoors for too long.

"Is there anything I can do? Anything you need from the store?" She looked at her friend imploringly, wanting desperately to do something helpful.

"I'm sorry, this isn't a good time," Bethann said, her raspy voice barely above a whisper. She shook her head as if to make everything go away. "I can't talk to you now."

Eleanora thought she detected the smell of alcohol. "I understand, Beth. All right," she said, trying to appear nonchalant. "If there's anything you need or anything I can do, just give me a call. All right?"

Beth nodded. Eleanora had not yet turned to leave and the door was already closing. She hurried to her car, head down, embarrassed at having witnessed this deterioration in her friend. She imagined that a bomb had gone off in the Winters' home, an explosion that shattered everything, blown it all to bits. She decided to call Peter later that morning.

Sitting alone in the car reflecting, she had a sudden impulse. Beth's death-like mask had reminded Eleanora of her mother. Instead of driving to the supermarket as she had planned, she headed for the George Washington Bridge. It had been a while since she had seen either of her parents. Her father was tied to his bar in Newark and rarely visited — which was fine with Aaron, who discouraged any contacts with her family, or his own for that matter. Still, whenever she and her father were together, she felt a special closeness, a sense of protection in his presence. It was a cozy feeling and she felt her face spreading into a smile.

In contrast, her mother was a constant source of agitation and annoyance. But for whatever reason, she had always felt responsible for her mother and it was that sense of duty that pulled her toward lower Manhattan, to what had once been Little Italy but was now being swallowed up by an ever-expanding Chinatown.

Eleanora enjoyed the views along the East River as she drove down East Side Drive toward Canal Street. When she arrived at the familiar apartment house on Broome Street, she rang the bell and was buzzed in. The heavy glass-paned door closed behind her, sealing her in the dimly lit hallway of the ground floor. She looked up from the bottom of the stairwell and climbed the worn wooden treads to the third floor. Her mother's door opened and Aunt Velia peered out.

"Ah, Eleanora, what a surprise. *Ciao.* Come, give me a kiss. Let me look at you." The plump woman with the angelic face held her at arm's length and gave her the once over. "Oh, *bambina*, what's wrong? Your eyes, they look so sad."

Eleanora tried putting a smile on her face. She hadn't realized her eyes would give her away. Zia Velia was always the most perceptive member of her family.

"Come in, come inside," she ushered Eleanora by the elbow into the apartment. It was like entering the past: the same sheer lace curtains, overstuffed furniture, and worn linoleum; the same tarnished, gaudy brass lamps and religious pictures; the familiar smell of olive oil, garlic, and spices. Seated at the table wearing a stained flowered apron over her housedress, her mother barely glanced up from the vegetables she was cutting.

"*Sorella*, look who's here," Velia said to her youngest sister. "It's Eleanora."

Eva's face showed no sign of emotion or recognition, and Eleanora felt the usual sting of her mother's rebuff.

"Don't get up, Ma," she said, leaning over to give her mother a kiss on her forehead. "I can only stay a little while."

"Of course," said Eva in her monotone, without even a glance at her daughter. Instead, she looked at her sister who stood somewhat embarrassed behind Eleanora. "Is this some special holiday? What's the occasion that my daughter should make a trip all the way from New Jersey?"

"No special occasion, Ma. I just found myself thinking about you this morning and decided to visit, see how you are."

Her mother nodded while she kept chopping vegetables. "Well, now you see."

Eleanora glanced at Velia, who shrugged her shoulders.

"Eleanora," she said, "would you like some espresso or tea? Perhaps a glass of wine? Will you stay for lunch? We're making minestrone. We have plenty, right Eva?"

Eleanora regarded her aunt. She loved Velia and was relieved that the two sisters had apartments in the same building. Eleanora could see that her mother had dug herself deeper into a pit of angry self-pity. Eva was a black hole, sucking energy from everyone around her and giving nothing in return. Even now, standing across the kitchen table from her, Eleanora felt herself being pulled in — that old feeling of responsibility. Against her better judgment, she wondered how to rescue this woman from the misery of her own bitterness.

"No, I don't think so, Zia. I can't stay that long. Maybe just a cup of tea and then I have to get back."

Velia immediately put some water on and got a cup for her niece. "How about you, Eva? You want some tea?"

"*Vino*," said Eva without looking up. Eleanora sighed as she watched her aunt reach behind the curtain that covered the space under the sink and retrieve a gallon of red wine. She handed her sister a glass and gave Eleanora a resigned smile in the process.

"So how are you feeling, Ma?"

Eva put down the paring knife and wiped her hands on her apron. A shrug of her shoulders was her only answer. She took a sip of wine and lit a cigarette from a pack in her apron pocket.

"You see your father?" she asked, staring at Eleanora through the expelled smoke.

"Not for a while, a couple of months maybe. He's pretty busy with the bar. I don't get to see him much."

"He still with that whore?"

"Irene?"

"I don't know her name. The singer, with red hair you said." Eva was referring to a description that Eleanora had given on a previous visit — a mistake that she'd immediately realized.

"I don't know, Ma. He didn't mention her the last time I saw him. I'm not sure they were really going with each other. They might have just dated a few times. I don't know."

Eva picked a piece of tobacco from her tongue and glanced at Velia, who was preparing tea for herself and Eleanora.

"He give you any money?" she asked her daughter.

"Ma, I'm married. Aaron earns a good living. I don't need Pa's money."

"So he don't give you nothing either. Just like him."

"How's your arthritis?" Eleanora changed the subject.

Another shrug of the shoulders. "Eh. It's arthritis. What are you going to do?"

Eleanora turned to her aunt. "How about you, Zia. How are you doing?"

Velia laid her hand on Eleanora's. "I'm fine, sweetheart. I get out every day. I have a part-time job on Canal Street, selling lighting fixtures. And a couple of times a week I go to the senior center and play cards or bingo. I don't spend all my time down here with your mother."

Eleanora was glad to hear that. She had always adored her aunt. Whatever confidence she had in herself had grown from the love Zia Velia had given her. She blew her aunt a kiss.

"I'm glad you have a life of your own. That's good."

Sipping wine, Eva inquired about the children. Eleanora went on about them, calling up as many details of their lives as she could. It was an attempt to bridge the gap, to construct a relationship between a grandmother and her grandchildren where none existed. Finally, the tea finished, Eleanora gathered herself up. She bent down toward her mother, but Eva did not raise her face to receive the kiss.

Chapter Five

Velia waved as Eleanora started down the stairs, then closed the apartment door. She let out a long sigh as she regarded her younger sister .

"What are you sighing about?" Eva asked reproachfully. Her tone was dismissive. *What problems do you have? I'm the one with the daughter who rarely visits. What are you accusing me of? I haven't done anything.*

Ignoring Eva's question, Velia wiped her hands on her apron and carried the teacups to the sink.

"If you're so tired, go upstairs. I can finish the minestrone myself."

"Oh, come on, Eva. Why be so touchy? You're always ready for an argument."

"I'm not arguing with you, Velia. I just asked a question."

"Yes, like you really want to know why I sighed."

Velia sat silently for a few moments. "Fine, you want to know? I'll tell you. I sigh in exasperation. I love you, *sorella*, but sometimes you are so pigheaded. You know it, don't deny it. We always said it in the family: *Eva is the most stubborn*. You are so ..." she searched for the word, "vindictive. You just want to punish, to hurt. You never give an inch. Where's your heart, Eva? You couldn't even return a goodbye kiss from your daughter? You're like ice. I don't understand you."

Eva watched her oldest sister as she spoke. She put down the paring knife and reached for her glass, draining its remaining wine. Then, her eyes following Velia as she moved about the small kitchen, she lit a cigarette and sat back in her chair.

"I won't deny that I'm stubborn. Some might call that having principles. Am I vindictive with you? Do I try to hurt you? The only one I punish is my daughter, who has hurt me so much." She paused, gathering steam. "Look what she's done with her life. Has she stuck by her mother the way you and I have stuck by each other all these years? The way we stuck by our mother after she took sick? Where's her sense of family? Her sense of decency? No, instead, she got herself pregnant like some common tramp. Then she ran off and got married. Didn't even finish high school. Made us all look like stupid peasants."

"It was better that she got married."

"Better that she didn't get pregnant. What was she doing with that pasty Americano anyway? He's not even Italian."

"He was good looking, you have to admit that. And he went to college."

Eva dismissed her sister with a wave of her hand. "She deliberately got pregnant to get away from me. She made her choice. And God punished her with that child."

Velia was flooded with images of Todd. Born prematurely with a severe case of cerebral palsy, he had been a tremendous burden on Eleanora until his death five years ago. Barely a grown woman, Eleanora had found herself drowning in an unhappy marriage, weighed down with three young children, one of them disabled.

"Eva, that was 20 years ago. Let it go. Can't you forgive and forget?"

"Twenty years and like it was yesterday. Her father run off, leaving us alone in a strange country."

"Eva, you're rewriting history! You practically pushed Giuseppi out the door."

"He left! He chose to leave us — me and his only child."

"Ahhh!" Velia threw her hands up in disgust. "See! That's what I mean about your stubbornness. You're always right. You never admit anything. You never listen. No wonder Giuseppi left — you never listened to him. Always accusing him. Never making him feel loved."

"Oh, you would have done better?"

Velia caught Eva's challenging scowl. She lowered her eyes, not sure what Eva was referring to.

"I'm only saying that a woman has to make her husband feel like a man, like he has some value, like he's more than just a paycheck. Pio felt loved. He knew I loved him up until he died. Giuseppi, I don't think ever felt loved, Eva."

"So that's an excuse for him to go with whores?"

"You don't know that."

Now it was Eva's turn to call her sister's bluff. "Velia, why are you defending him? You know what he was like. He always had an eye for the women. He still does." She paused and smiled at her sister. "He had an eye for you too, *sorella*."

Velia blushed bright red. "That's not true."

Eva laughed. "Of course it's true and you know it. Look how you're blushing, as red as a tomato."

Velia sat down at the table, bringing a glass with her. "Well, if he did, you know I never did anything to encourage him," she said, pouring herself some wine. Eva nodded as she refilled her own glass.

"Like you say, Velia, it was long ago. I knew he was attracted to you and I knew you were attracted to him. And I knew you loved Pio and would never do anything to hurt him or me. I knew that." She reached over and stroked the back of Velia's hand.

Velia covered her sister's hand with her own, her eyes suddenly glistening. Sitting back on her chair, she sighed again. "I miss my Pio," she stammered. "He was such a good man."

"I know. We both miss him."

"I never wanted anybody else. Even though he's been gone all these years, I never wanted anybody else. Yes, Giuseppi was a handsome devil. Any woman could see that. But I never wanted him. I never thought of him that way."

Eva nodded reassuringly, although she wasn't sure she completely believed her sister. But it didn't matter. Giuseppi had left them 23 years ago, when Eleanora was only 14. Eva lit another cigarette and stared out the window, past the fire escape, into history.

Chapter Six

Driving up the West Side Highway toward the George Washington Bridge, Eleanora found herself wondering about how her children would remember her. She hoped she made them feel loved and valued — not invisible.

Once home, she telephoned and left a message for Peter. Waiting for his return call, she put some music on and made a small lunch from leftovers. Later, she drifted off into a light sleep thinking of her father. After he had moved to New Jersey, he telephoned often to speak with Eleanora. But Ma would answer and harangue him about money, holding him hostage until she tired of lashing at him — and only then would she relinquish the phone to her daughter. Of course, he soon stopped calling and took to writing her brief letters instead.

Getting gigs in New Jersey had proved to be more difficult than he'd thought, so he and Buster and the others were forced to endure a fair amount of traveling. When he was going to be nearby, he'd arrange for them to get together, but it wasn't as often as either of them wished. It was a long, chilly rainy season in Eleanora's life, and the first time she remembered having thought seriously about suicide.

She was awakened by the ringing. On the phone, Peter told her that he was ambivalent about his meeting with Kevin. Toby had brought the boy to the church and waited outside in the car. Peter recounted that Kevin had been relatively unresponsive, and he couldn't tell if the boy had accepted the reality of the situation or not.

"To be honest, Ellie, I don't know what he'll do. I just hope Toby and Bethann get him some help."

Eleanora described her encounter with Beth that morning, including her fleeting suspicion that she'd smelled alcohol on Bethann's breath. "Maybe I was mistaken, but I don't think I've ever seen anyone so distraught. This is so unlike Beth. We've been fairly close and she's always been warm and friendly with me — but this morning, I felt like she was another person, a stranger. I'm really concerned about her."

Peter was silent for a moment. "Yes, I really need to follow up on this. I'll stop by this evening and see if there's anything I can do."

Eleanora encouraged him to do that and then they hung up. She stood there for a moment, the ravaged, distorted face of Bethann still vivid to her. The concern in Peter's voice for Kevin remained in her head, but the image of Bethann — that really frightened her. She took a deep breath and pulled herself together. Wandering into the kitchen, she thought about what to make for dinner. After some beginning preparations, she sat down at the kitchen table and called her father.

"Hello," he said when he got to the phone.

"Hi, Papa," she said. "How are you?"

"Hey, Ellie. What a great surprise! I'm fine. How are you?"

"I'm fine. I was just thinking about you. I haven't seen you for a while."

"Yeah, well …"

"I know. We're both leading busy lives."

"So what's happening? How're my grandkids doing?"

"They're fine, Pa. Julie is still working at the burger place and Zach is still in his own world."

"So were you when you were that age."

I had a reason to mope, she thought to herself. "Yeah, teenagers. You still seeing Irene?"

"Oh sure. We're an item. She sings here a couple of times a month. In fact, she's going to be here this weekend. Me and Buster are playing too. Why don't you come out?"

Eleanora thought for a moment. Aaron would never let the kids go on Saturday night, even if they wanted to, and he wouldn't want to go then either. "Are you playing Sunday too?"

"Sure, Sunday is good. Come around seven. Bring the kids and Mr. Jerkoff, too. We'll have dinner, a couple of drinks. We don't start with the music until about nine."

"I'll try, Pa. I have to talk to Aaron, but it sounds like a fun idea. I'll get back to you."

"OK, sweetheart. Give the kids a hug."

"I will, Pa. Love you."

"Love you too, kid. Be good to see you."

"Same here. I'll call you later."

That night at dinner, Eleanora shared her father's invitation with her family. Julie was the first to respond.

"I'd love to," she said, "but I have to work Sunday evening since I have Saturday night off. I'm working lunch on Saturday." She appeared to be genuinely disappointed. "I haven't seen Grandpa for ages and it sounds like it would really be fun."

Zach took his cue from Julie. "Uh, if Julie can't go, then I'm not going. I'd be the only kid there. It would be too weird."

Eleanora tried to persuade him, but he piled excuse upon excuse to defend his decision. She got no help from Aaron, either. Although he remained silent, his facial expressions clearly articulated his lack of enthusiasm for spending a perfectly good Sunday evening in a Newark bar.

Once both children had expressed themselves, he felt freer to dissuade her from going on her own. "Look, if it's so important for you to visit your father, why don't you go in the afternoon? Why spend another night out? Besides, it's not that safe down there and I don't like the idea of your being there alone at night."

"If you're concerned about my safety, then come with me," she said pleasantly. "My father specifically invited you. And I want to hear him play. I haven't heard him for a long time, and I want to hear Irene sing." She noticed his face getting red. "Oh, come on, Aaron. It'll be fun. Loosen up."

"No!" he barked suddenly. "Don't turn this into a power struggle, Ellie. I made it clear that I don't want to go and I don't want you to go. Just call him and tell him no. Make an excuse. We'll go together another time. This Sunday night just doesn't work for us. He'll understand. He doesn't care that much anyway. If he did, he'd have called on his own instead of waiting for you to call him."

Holding their breath at the outburst, the kids glanced from one parent to the other, waiting to see what would happen. Eleanora, knife and fork suspended in her hands, stared incredulously at her husband. She felt like she was floating on the ceiling, looking down at the scene from a detached distance. As if she were watching a movie, she saw her husband's agitation; her daughter's hopeful eyes, eager to see if her mother would challenge her father's assertion of dominance; her son's fear of reprisal. Eleanora watched Zachary timidly push his chair back from the table, as if getting ready to bolt. She saw Julie's cheeks flush in readiness to ally herself with her mother if the need arose.

Still peacefully detached, Eleanora restrained the mischievous smile struggling to reveal itself at the corners of her mouth. Time seemed to creep and, in this strange state of removal, she sensed a shift. The feeling was strange and elusive. What was it?

She wasn't afraid.

"Yes," she said simply, "I understand perfectly how you feel about the subject." She smiled reassuringly at her children and resumed eating. "I made chocolate pudding pie for dessert. Zachary, I think that's one of your favorites."

He nodded to her, still confused by the paradigm shift.

"When you're done with your dinner, would you bring it in for me? And Julie, when you're ready, please bring in dessert plates and forks."

Julie barely concealed a look of relief and puzzlement.

"I'm going to make some tea. Would anybody like something else to drink?"

She looked questioningly at Aaron, who could only shake his head no. "You guys want milk?" she asked her children.

"Yeah," said Zach with some enthusiasm. Julie, too, nodded assent.

Eleanora took a deep breath. "Fine," she said. She finished her meal before getting up and going to the kitchen, soon to be followed her children. Aaron remained alone at the table, his empty plate still in front of him.

Chapter Seven

Friday's choir rehearsal went well. The members had become a relatively stable and warm social group, and some of the women asked about Bethann, who again had not shown up that evening. Eleanora didn't volunteer any information. After practice she went the rectory, where she found Peter engaged in a telephone conversation. She was about to turn and leave, but he motioned to her to stay.

"That was Dr. Cirullo," he said as he hung up the phone, "calling from the hospital." Eleanora's first thought was that Kevin had made good on his suicide threat.

"Kevin?" she asked. "Is he all right?"

"You're not going to believe this," he said. "The whole Winters family is in the ER. Apparently, Bethann put some kind of poison in their dinner. Dr. Cirullo wasn't completely sure of the details, but they're all getting their stomachs pumped. He asked me to come over. For some reason, he thinks my being there might be helpful."

Eleanora was stunned. Bethann poisoning her family? It was too preposterous. "There must be some mistake," she said out loud, half to herself. "I can't imagine Bethann harming anyone — or anything, for that matter. Poisoning her family? Her son, her husband? It must have been an accident. She wouldn't do such a thing."

"That was my first reaction too, but Cirullo sounded pretty definite. Anyway, I better get over there."

Eleanora wanted to go with him, to be a source of support for him and for Bethann, but she anticipated Aaron's reaction if she was hours late getting home. Still, if he knew it was an emergency, he might be more understanding.

"Peter, what do you think of my going with you? I could call Aaron and tell him someone from the choir is in the emergency room, and that I'm going to visit for a while."

"You know, it's probably going to be long hours of boredom with no information and nothing to do. I don't see any point in your coming. You probably wouldn't be allowed to see Beth anyway. I'm not even sure why I'm going. I have no idea how sick they are. I'll call you tomorrow morning and let you know what the story is. Maybe you could visit Bethann then."

"Yes," she agreed, "that's probably a good idea. If you see her, tell her I was asking for her." Peter nodded as he put on his jacket, already lost in thought.

As usual, Eleanora went upstairs that night while Aaron was still in the family room watching TV. As she lay in bed, she could not help but think of her friend Bethann. What could possibly have motivated her to poison her husband and her son? Even in the worst of times, when she felt so hopelessly overwhelmed by the responsibilities of taking care of her own three kids — four-year-old Todd, who was in many ways still like an infant, plus two-year-old Julie and new-born Zachary — could she have ever conceived of something so extreme. They had still lived in the small walkup apartment in Jersey City then, the three cribs crammed into one small bedroom. Aaron, who worked long hours as a beginning accountant, was no help at home. And at 22, Eleanora herself was young and inexperienced. Looking back on those years, both she and Aaron were always irritable and stressed — and they fought a lot.

With no energy left at the end of a day caring for three children, she craved relief and sleep. Aaron complained — understandably — that she didn't pay enough attention to him. Of course, he meant sex. It wasn't that she didn't enjoy sex — in fact, she had been wonderfully surprised to discover how much she did enjoy it. But he always seemed to approach her at the most inopportune times, and she'd inevitably push him away. Rejected, he'd become cold and nasty, wanting only to hurt her in return. But even then — wishing she could run away, or be rescued by some Prince Charming, or immerse herself in music — even then she never entertained the idea of harming him or her children.

She had, however, considered suicide. In fact, she now recalled, she had once taken a whole handful of pills from the medicine cabinet. Not enough to kill her, it turned out, but she had passed out on the bathroom floor. Aaron had accused her of making some grand, dramatic bid for attention and stepped over her prone body, leaving her there half unconscious. When she had awakened before dawn, she crawled into their bed and they never spoke of the incident again.

These thoughts were carrying Eleanora dreamily away from the reality of the day when she heard Aaron open the bedroom door and quietly enter the room. A few minutes later, he slid beside her and pressed up against her. She felt his erection against her bottom and his bare arm came around her waist.

"Still awake?" he asked.

She lay silent as she went through the process of deciding whether to respond to him. Recalling her anger toward him the other night at dinner, she felt decidedly disinterested. Yet here he was, with no warning or buildup, asking for — expecting — her to be the responsive, loving wife. Well, she admitted, it wasn't all that unreasonable, was it? Besides, she knew her own capacity for responding to any minimal amount of tender attention and stimulation. Wordlessly, she sat up and pulled her nightgown over her head and lay down again to face him.

Chapter Eight

Saturday mornings were generally pleasant. Everybody slept late and felt more rested. Eleanora usually made pancakes or waffles, which added to the relaxed, easygoing atmosphere. This morning, Aaron was in an exceptionally good mood and during breakfast he suggested taking the kids into New York to see the Yankees play. It had been a long time since Zachary had been to a game and his eyes lit up. Eleanora saw Julie hesitate for just a moment before saying it sounded like a great idea, but she had to work.

Genuinely pleased at the prospect of Aaron doing something with Zachary, Eleanora asked if they wanted her to make sandwiches for the trip.

"No," said Aaron expansively, "we'll get something there — burgers, hot dogs, pizza, whatever. We might as well go all the way."

"You sure we can get tickets?" asked Zachary. "It's September. They could be all sold out."

"There's always scalpers," his father reassured him. "No problem. Ah, this'll be great!"

They left by 11:00 to make sure they'd have time to negotiate the traffic, find parking, and buy tickets. Waving them off, Eleanora felt a lightness she hadn't experienced in days. As she finished in the kitchen, Peter Van Houten called with an update on the Winters family.

"It's a long story," he began, "maybe we can meet for coffee and I'll bring you up to date."

"Why don't you come here?" she suggested. "Aaron took Zach to the Yankee game, and Julie's left for work, so we'll have some privacy."

"That would be great. You sure it's no trouble?"

"No trouble at all," she laughed. "Coffee or tea?"

"Coffee's good. I'll see you soon."

A few minutes later, she heard his car pull up.

"Well," he started, "I hardly know where to begin. Both Toby and Kevin ended up in surgery. Bethann had loaded up their dinners with everything she could get her hands on — pills, cleaning agents — including tiny slivers of bamboo! Cirullo said Beth was completely psychotic. Apparently, she was raving nonsense about people broadcasting stories about her and Kevin on the TV and the radio, saying they were homosexuals. As you thought, she'd been drinking heavily, apparently going through more than a fifth of scotch a day."

Eleanora couldn't comprehend what had happened. Bethann always appeared so stable, so strong, so self-confident. Such a dramatic change in just a matter of days? It made no sense at all. "How is she now?" she asked.

"Well, she was pretty wild to begin with. Actually, she called 911 and told them she'd murdered her family. When the police got there, of course, everyone was alive, but Toby and Kevin were unconscious. Bethann wouldn't let anybody touch her. She just kept screaming crazy things at the cops and paramedics. Nobody knows how much of the poisons she might have consumed herself, so they couldn't put her in a psych ward until they checked her out physically. I think they're all in intensive care now, but Bethann is under police guard and can't have visitors."

"Oh, my God. Do you think they'll all live?"

"Toby and Kevin are still in critical condition, although Cirullo sounded optimistic."

"How about you?" she asked. "How are you handling all of this? You were concerned you'd be blamed if anything happened to Kevin."

"I'm OK. I thought about what you said and you're right. People do like me and respect me and I think they'll give me the benefit of the doubt."

Eleanora nodded. "Is there anything to be done?"

"I'll stay in touch with Dr. Cirullo and let you know if there's anything we should be doing." Peter put on his jacket and started toward the door. Eleanora walked with him.

"Well, see you tomorrow morning in church," he said distractedly.

"Yes," she said, "see you in church."

It was a little after 6:00 when Aaron and Zachary got home.

"How was the game?" Eleanora asked her son as he glided through the kitchen.

"Good. It was a good game."

"Well, who won? Did the Yankees win?"

He nodded as he bounded up the stairs to his room. A few minutes later,

Aaron sauntered into the kitchen from the garage.

"I hear the Yankees won," she said.

Aaron grumbled, "Yeah, seven to five. But they were lucky to pull it out."

"You sound disappointed."

Ignoring her comment, Aaron hung his jacket in the closet. "Where the hell's the paper?" he yelled.

"Did you look on the porch?" Aaron didn't answer as he strode through the kitchen toward the rear of the house. A minute later he returned with the paper in his hand, then walked wordlessly to the living room.

Eleanora put on some music while she prepared dinner. *Why is he always so grouchy and sulky? Would it cost him so much to be pleasant? You'd think he'd want to talk about his afternoon with Zach, what they did.* It was as if he were Ali Baba's cave, filled with hidden treasures that she was supposed to make every possible effort to extract from him — even while he resisted all of her efforts. *Screw him! I'll be damned if I ever ask him another question about what he's thinking or feeling. Let him choke on his damned treasure.*

She had planned to make pasta with sundried tomatoes, olives, and goat cheese, but she reached for a can of plain tomato sauce instead. *To hell with it! They don't notice the difference anyway*, she said to herself as she slammed the can on the counter.

"What's the matter, Mom?"

Eleanora turned to see Julie standing in the doorway. "Dinner isn't ready yet," she said defensively.

"I know. I just came down to help. I heard Zach clomping up the stairs."

Eleanora stopped where she stood and took a deep breath. "I'm sorry, honey. It's just that sometimes ..."

Julie looked back over her shoulder toward the living room and then came further into the kitchen. "I know," she said confidentially, "Dad can be a pain sometimes."

Eleanora frowned. "He's your father."

Julie rolled her eyes. "I know." She began taking plates from the cabinet. "I'm just glad that I had to work today. Can you imagine if I had to spend hours with him in the car, stuck in traffic at the bridge, finding parking, haggling with scalpers, complaining about the price of everything?"

"It was nice of him to offer. I'm glad he and Zach got to do something to-gether."

"So am I," said Julie, "I just wish he would lighten up."

Eleanora had the sudden realization: *This is a bright young woman. She's got a good head on her shoulders, and she sees how he is too. It's not just me. It's not my imagination.*

Chapter Nine

Eleanora left the house early Sunday to play piano at the three morning services. The church was buzzing with news about the Winters family. A number of women in the choir asked if Eleanora had seen the morning paper or the local TV news. Speculations about Bethann's motives flew through the congregation and, as the gossip spread, she was portrayed as having become a homicidal maniac. Eleanora noted with relief that no mention was made of Kevin's note to Peter.

After the last service was over, Peter approached her. "You heard the gossip, I gather?" he asked, lifting his eyebrows.

"I couldn't help but hear it. Everyone is talking about it. But I haven't seen the papers or the TV yet myself," she answered.

"Well, I don't imagine there's much to be done right now. I'll let you know if I hear anything."

"Yes," she said eagerly, "let me know if there's anything I can do." She finished gathering her things and left. It was a beautiful September day. The sky was deep blue and cloudless, and the low hills to the west beckoned. Imagining a peaceful ride up into Sussex County, she fell into the usual questions about the pros and cons, and finally chose to return home.

When Eleanora entered the house, Aaron was in the living room reading the paper. "Did you hear the news?" he asked. The question sounded like a challenge. She looked at him questioningly as she hung up her jacket. "A woman in town tried to murder her husband and son. Poisoned them, it says."

"I heard about it at church. They're members," she said offhandedly.

Aaron lowered the paper and stared thoughtfully at her. "Does this have anything to do with Wednesday night? With whatever was so important that you couldn't talk about it to me?"

Eleanora knew Aaron would never stop tugging at this until he had it all out — and she was determined not to let that happen. "No," she said simply, shaking her head. She felt badly for lying, but she didn't have a choice.

"Can I see the paper?" she asked. Most of the article was about Toby and his position as a professor of astronomy at a local college. Few details were given about Bethann — and Kevin was left unnamed, although that would not provide him with any protection at school if and when he returned. She couldn't begin to imagine the notoriety of having a mother who tried to murder him. And for what? To protect them all from the embarrassment of Kevin's homosexuality? *My God, could it possibly be that big a deal? To die for? To kill for?*

When she finished the article, she looked at Aaron, who was reading the sports section. "I've decided to go to my father's this evening. It would be nice if you changed your mind and came with me."

Letting the paper fall into his lap, Aaron looked up and shook his head. "Why are you doing this? We have so little time together. I work all week, you're out nights. You were out all morning. Why can't we have a nice Sunday evening at home together for once?"

"We have this afternoon together," she countered. "Let's go for a ride. It's beautiful outside."

Aaron sighed with exasperation. "The Yankee game starts at 1:00 and the Giants are playing later this afternoon. Besides, I just want to relax. I work all week."

"You went to the game yesterday."

"Don't remind me," he rolled his eyes.

"Why? What was wrong?"

"Believe me, you don't want to know."

Eleanora waited for him to explain why he hadn't enjoyed going to the game with Zach, but he ignored her and resumed reading. *Is this what it was like for Beth? For my father? This coldness. Being shut out. An image of her mother flashed through her mind. What am I doing here? Why am I trying so hard?* She glanced again at her husband, recalling his question from earlier in the week: Was she happy?

"Well," she said as she got up from her chair, "I'll fix some dinner for you and Zachary. I won't be leaving for a few hours. I should be home by 11 or so."

Aaron mumbled something that sounded like "Fuck you," but she wasn't sure. Deciding to ignore it, she went out to the porch to read. But the book lay in her lap and her mind drifted. *We are all prisoners*, she thought. That's how she felt now, and it's how she remembered feeling growing up — like a prisoner in the small, dark dungeon of her mother's depression, chained to her cell by obligation. How had she become responsible for her mother's well-being and happiness? How did her father escape, but not her?

She hadn't deliberately gotten pregnant while she and Aaron were dating, but once she discovered her condition she knew it was her only chance to get out. He had been furious and initially insisted on an abortion, but she had refused. At the time she had used her Catholicism as a shield, but the truth was she wanted something, someone who would return her love. After the parents were told, Aaron relented and agreed to marry her.

But soon after Todd's birth, she realized she had only exchanged one prison cell for another. Throughout his short life, Todd's handicaps made the relationship with her son just another one-way street of responsibility. He was almost 14 when he died of pneumonia — 14, but still a baby. Julie and even Zach had helped with his care, and Julie, especially, loved him dearly. But Eleanora had to admit these last five years without Todd had been easier.

She had planned to return to school after Todd's death, but Aaron was so adamantly opposed that it wasn't worth constantly fighting him. He had even complained about her taking music lessons, claiming they deprived him and the children of her time and attention when they needed it most. But she had paid for the lessons herself. Her defiance had never been forgotten, but she had persevered. And she continued to persevere. She continued to defend her need for music, a core part of her — an essential part.

A smile of recognition crossed Eleanora's face: *I'm still having the same fight, but I can make a life for myself. My father did. If Bethann was that unhappy, she could have done something about it. I don't have to resort to suicide and murder. I won't give up like Bethann or my mother. I don't have to. I don't.*

She repeated the phrase over and over to herself: *I don't have to.* At first she felt like a spoiled child — willful, spiteful, defiant. But soon a sense of empowerment emerged. She intoned the mantra slowly and deliberately: *I don't have to.* Calm and rational, it felt like an epiphany. It was liberating.

Lifting her head, she looked out onto her back yard, where pine trees formed the rear border. Her vision rose over the trees to the deep blueness of the sky and the dark violet of space beyond. As the breath expanded within her, Eleanora felt both exhilarated and peaceful. She realized at that moment, with a keenness she had never before appreciated, that her life was a function of her own choices — and she was free to make *different* choices. She was not imprisoned against her will. It was her choice to be there, her choice to be passive and submissive, to be afraid, to be *the good girl.* But now she reminded herself: *I don't have to.*

Chapter Ten

Julie left for work later that afternoon and Zach was at his best friend's house shooting baskets. Eleanora made some sandwiches and fried potatoes, which she brought to Aaron in the recreation room, where he was watching the Giants lose.

"I should be home around 11:00," she said calmly. With no verbal acknowledgment from her husband, she decided to leave earlier than she had planned. Driving alone to Newark as dusk approached felt eerie and strange — like she was running away from home. But she also felt exhilarated and free. The enveloping darkness held the promise of something new and possibly dangerous. Slightly giddy at the thought, Eleanora let herself enjoy the experience. It was as if she had never driven alone before. Everything felt new.

Parking on a Sunday evening was simplicity itself. She ended up practically in front of the entrance to her father's club, the B&J Restaurant and Lounge. A few people were talking at the bar while the TV, muted, showed the Giants game. A few diners were seated in the long, narrow dining room that extended beyond the bar area. Buster spotted her from his perch at the end of the bar.

"Hey, darlin', how you doin'? Long time no see."

"Hi, Buster," she said, leaning in to his embracing hug.

"Your father said you'd be coming. No kids this time, huh?"

Eleanora smiled. "No, my daughter is working and my son's at that age. No way he's going anywhere with his mother."

Buster laughed. "Yeah, I know how it is. Here, have a seat. I'll let your dad know you're here."

She hoisted herself up onto one of the stools and ordered a glass of white wine. In a few moments, her father emerged from the kitchen.

"Ellie," he said cheerfully, approaching her with outstretched arms, "you came early. Good."

"Hi, Papa. It's good to see you," she said, kissing his cheek and enjoying the pleasure of his embrace.

"You're alone, I see." She shrugged and rolled her eyes. "Well," he continued, "it's just as well. We'll enjoy ourselves more without Mr. Beancounter. But it's a shame the kids couldn't come."

"Julie wanted to, but like I told Buster, she had to work and Zach won't go anywhere if it's just the two of us."

Her father nodded. "When he turns 21, he'll be down here by himself, believe me." He took her glass and led her to a table near the raised platform that served as a stage. "So, how's it going?"

Eleanora saw the concern in his eyes, the furrowed brows. "I don't know, Papa. The kids are OK. At least, I'm pretty sure Julie is. They're doing well at school and we're not having any problems with either of them. But who knows? I'd be a fool to think I know everything that's going on in their lives. But me? I'm not too sure about me."

He touched her shoulder. "What is it, sweetheart? What's the matter?"

Eleanora smiled weakly and took a sip of wine before answering. "It's hard to put into words. Part of me is irritable and angry, part is scared, and part of me feels excited. I'm confused. I don't know what I'm thinking. Don't pay any attention to me." She sipped more wine and tried to manage a self-deprecatory chuckle.

"What is it? That husband of yours? He causing problems?"

"Aaron's just being Aaron." She caressed the glass in front of her. "But I don't know how much more of him I can take." She glanced quickly at her father. "I'm depressed most of the time, but I don't know what to do about it. I could never leave the kids, but I don't know if I can stay. And if I left, how could I afford to take the kids with me?"

Her father looked at her, his hand consolingly on her shoulder.

"If I left alone, I suppose the kids would be all right," she went on. "They're old enough, so they can pretty much take care of themselves — and Aaron would be there for them. But I'd miss them so. I don't know if I could do it. And how would I survive financially? What would I do? How would I live? It all feels so hopeless."

"Listen, things have changed in these last 20 years or so," her father said reassuringly. "The laws are different now. Why don't you ask a lawyer what your options are? You're not helpless. You have rights. Aaron has to support you and the kids, especially if you got him to leave and you stayed put with the kids. Have you thought about that?"

Eleanora made a face. "Aaron would never leave. You know him, how controlling he is. He'd never leave. Never."

"Well, I'm just saying, you never know. Anyway, if you want, I can hook you up with my attorney. I'll put it on my tab, a birthday present, OK? My treat."

She raised her eyes to look at him, his mustached smiling face. "You're serious?"

"Sure, I'm serious. If there's anything I can do to help make you happy, of course I'm serious. Ellie, you know you never belonged with that guy. He was never right for you."

Eleanora nodded. No one in the family had liked Aaron, but the situation was problematic. On one hand, having an out-of-wedlock child was just not acceptable. On the other hand, Aaron was older, he wasn't Italian, he wasn't Catholic, and he was a cold, controlling miser. Her mother called him *Stingyguts* — one of the few times she attempted English.

"He was always a cheap bastard," her father went on. "If you leave him and get a divorce, he won't make it easy for you. But listen, I've got some money put aside. I can help you out, if it comes to that."

Eleanora could only nod silently in response. This was all going too fast. She had only just begun to allow herself to think of the possibility of a life without Aaron. Now her father already had her in a lawyer's office, suing for divorce. She felt sweaty and reached for the cooling glass of wine.

"My God, Papa, I don't know. You're way ahead of me on this."

"Well," he said calmly, "I'm just saying what's possible. If that's the way you want to go, then I'm here for you. Think about it. It's your life. You choose. You decide what you want."

She took a deep breath and relaxed. "You're right, Pa. I'll think about it. Thank you. That's a real comfort to me, to know you're willing to do that for me."

"Yeah, well, I wasn't always there for you when you were younger. Maybe if I had stayed, you never would have had to marry that jerk. You could have gone to school. I know you wanted to."

"Who knows, Papa? I'd have had to get away from Mama anyway."

"Yeah, but you could have done it the way so many young people do, by going to college."

"We couldn't afford it then."

"There's always scholarships. You were so bright. You could have gotten one."

"Maybe," she admitted, "but that's all over and done with. I have to deal with the situation as it is now."

He was about to reply when he saw Irene come through the front door. He strode rapidly to the front of the bar and embraced her. Eleanora watched them, their faces lively and full of expression. Eleanora rose to greet her.

"Hiya, honey. It's so good to see you again," said Irene, extending her fleshy body to kiss Eleanora on the cheek. Despite his 69 years, her father's eyes twinkled as he looked admiringly at this attractive woman. Eleanora didn't know how old Irene was — she guessed between 55 and 60 — but she was still quite curvaceous.

"I'm glad to see you again too, Irene. You look beautiful."

"You're as bad as your daddy. But thank you anyway. At my age, I take all the compliments I can get."

Irene's presence brought a festive energy to the evening. Eleanora had never heard her sing, but had always enjoyed the smooth, low, musical quality of her speaking voice. Buster joined them for a while, but then the room got crowded and he left to tend to business. After they had finished dinner, her father left to give Buster a hand.

"How are the children, if that's the right word to use?" Irene asked when the two women were alone at the table. Eleanora beamed as she brought Irene up to date on their latest doings.

"You must be very proud," sighed Irene. "That's the one regret of my life, not having any kids. I know your pop misses seeing them. He mentions them all the time."

"Does he?" Eleanora was genuinely surprised.

Irene pulled herself back on her chair. "You didn't know that? He talks about you all so much. I bet I could describe the inside of your house — and he hasn't been there in what, almost two years? You still have that picture of him with your two children, at a zoo or something? On your fireplace mantel? Am I right?"

Eleanora shook her head in disbelief. "You know my dad, maybe even better than I do, so you know he doesn't show his feelings that much. I had no idea he gave us that much thought."

Irene cocked her head and leaned forward. "Oh, Ellie. He thinks about you all the time. Of course," she said in mock seriousness as she leaned back, "he's not all that enamored of your spouse."

"I know," Eleanora sighed. "In fact, before you got here, he said he'd help me financially if I want a divorce."

Irene leaned forward again. "Divorce? Are things that bad? Is he hitting you?"

"No, nothing like that. It's just that …" she fumbled for words, not sure how much she wanted to say. She saw the concern in Irene's face.

"It's never been a love match," Eleanora admitted. "There's never been any romance. It's been all about duty and obligation and responsibility. I guess we've each done what we were supposed to, but over the years — 20 years now — resentment has built up, like sludge in a drainpipe. It's just getting harder and harder to make it work, to get through a day or a meal. We don't talk anymore. We shoot zingers at each other, pecking away at old hurts, trying to wound. I feel like I'm bleeding to death. But," she turned up her hands helplessly, "he doesn't cheat or drink or gamble or — like I said — he's not beating me. He's a decent father. He works hard. He's there. He cares about the kids. He tries. Do I have the right to upset the status quo? Am I being selfish or unrealistically romantic to want something different?" Tears came to her eyes. "I don't know, Irene. I don't know what I'm supposed to think or feel. You know?"

Irene nodded. "I do know. I've been there. Your father isn't the first man in my life, you know. Of course, nobody can tell you what to do. I can tell you this, though: Feelings don't lie. Your head can fool you, words can fool you — but feelings are real. They're information and you have to respect them. If you're unhappy — and honey, you sound downright miserable to me — then that's something you can't deny. That's your starting point." She paused to gather her thoughts. "Now, I know you have other feelings too: love for your sweet children, and fear of what will happen if you do something to bust things open. Those feelings are real too, and you have to pay attention to them as well. Balancing them all out, deciding what's the realistic or constructive thing to do, that's what life is all about. But don't ever question your right to feel what you feel. Don't go burying that reality or you're done for."

Eleanora felt propped up. It had been a long time since she'd confided in another woman and received such support. An image of her Aunt Velia came to mind. Eleanora reached across the table and took Irene's hand in both of her own. She felt a surge of love and her eyes moistened.

"Oh, here's Connie," said Irene, breaking the intimate silence between them. Eleanora looked over her shoulder toward the front of the bar and saw Buster and her father talking with a tall, well-dressed African-American man.

"I don't think you've met Connie yet, have you?" asked Irene. Eleanora shook her head. "He often plays for me when I sing, especially here, since he lives nearby." The three men approached the table.

"Ellie," said her father, "I want you to meet Duke Chermant. Duke, this is my daughter, Eleanora."

Eleanora looked up into laughing eyes and a bemused smile. He had a handsome face with a thin manicured moustache, and close-cropped salt-and-pepper hair that looked so soft she wanted to touch it. His voice was strong and confident, yet softened with drawling southern rhythms. He had an air of educated refinement.

"Ah, the famous Eleanora I've heard so much about," he said to her.

Eleanora's eyes widened in surprise.

"Your father speaks of you often. You play piano, right?" Eleanora could only nod in response. "So do I," he said with a smile. "At least, I do the best I know how."

"I guess that makes two of us," she managed.

Her father and Buster went over some last-minute details about the upcoming sets. Irene would be accompanied by Duke on piano and a couple of young, local musicians on bass and drums, then Buster and her father would join them for the last three or four numbers of the set.

A few minutes later, her father mounted the platform and addressed the room: "Good evening, ladies and gentlemen and special guests" — casting his gaze at Eleanora — "welcome to the B&J Restaurant and Lounge. I'm Joey Albanese, one of your hosts. We are very fortunate this evening to have with us once again a special favorite of ours, a wonderful song stylist and successful recording artist who has sung with many of the leading musicians, and who has graced our stage on numerous occasions. I know you will very much enjoy listening to her this evening. Please give a warm and welcoming hand to Miss Irene Duffy."

Irene stood and, with a hand from Eleanora's father, stepped onto the stage. She introduced the trio behind her, making a reference to the distinguished recording history of her pianist, Duke Chermant. Irene opened the set with "Body and Soul," then covered a number of standard jazz ballads, some in up-tempo, some slow and mournful, like Billie Holiday's "Black Fruit." Eleanora was mesmerized by the range of Irene's voice and the emotion with which she imbued the lyrics. But she was also keenly aware of Duke's light, facile, and intelligent support, the intricacy of his improvisations and the complexity of his techniques. She had sufficient training to hear and perceive all of it at once, but she was torn — wanting to concentrate exclusively on each of the performers.

When Joey and Buster joined the group on stage, she focused more on her father. Hearing him brought back memories of her childhood, when she loved listening to him practice. Now, as an adult, she appreciated that both her father and Buster were accomplished and talented musicians, and she found herself feeling a deeper respect for him.

When the set was over, Buster returned to the front of the bar and her father mingled among the tables.

"I loved hearing both of you," Eleanora said to Irene and Duke. "I wanted to concentrate on what each of you was doing, but couldn't satisfy myself. I can't wait to hear more."

"Thank you, sweetie," Irene said graciously, bowing her head slightly. "I'm delighted that I finally got to sing for you."

Eleanora turned to Duke. "And you — I'm sorry, what do I call you? Duke or ..."

"Connie," he said, laughing. "Duke is an old nickname and, of course, it conjures up the great Mr. Ellington. But among friends, I'm Connie."

"Connie, then — what you were doing up there was amazing. You reminded me of Oscar Peterson and John Lewis, too, but even more classical …"

Connie bowed his head slightly. "I thank you very much. That's good company, indeed. I had no idea you were such a jazz buff. But yes, I did study classical piano and still play a great deal of it."

"You studied classical piano?"

"Yes, yes I did. Don't be so surprised. I graduated from Juilliard and was a budding concert pianist until I discovered jazz."

"Juilliard?" she exclaimed. "How wonderful to be exposed to that level of training. Oh, how I envy you. I've been very limited in who I've been able to take lessons from. Juilliard! It must have been heaven."

"Not quite. I imagine heaven, if such a place exists, as being all positives — although that would probably be boring as hell — and Juilliard was definitely not all positives. It was stimulating, I'll grant you that, but it was constant pressure and, surprisingly, very rigid constraints. To tell you the truth," he spread his arms and looked around the club, "this is more like heaven. This is paradise enough, at least for me. I have all the contrasts of life, the yin and the yang. I have beautiful women," looking deliberately at her and Irene, "good and loyal friends such as your father and Buster, and most importantly perhaps, the opportunity to do what I do and be who I am."

Irene agreed. "Right on!" she said enthusiastically. "I think what Connie is saying, Ellie, is that each of us, and your dad and Buster too, is living exactly the kind of life we choose to live. Musically, we do only what we want and only when we want. We're at a point in our lives where we don't have to sell out in order to get by. We have what we need and aren't enslaved by any system or any person."

"Amen to that," chorused Connie.

Eleanora reveled in their sense of freedom. What a blessing that her father was finally able to enjoy this mixture of contentment and exuberance.

Returning to the table, her father pointed to his watch. "Meter's ticking," he said to his star performers. "Time for the second set."

Again, Eleanora was torn between listening keenly to Irene's skilled use of her voice and life experiences, which added depth and range and humor to her performance, and to Connie's virtuosity on the keyboard. When the set was completed and they returned to the table, Eleanora could hardly contain her excitement. Connie and Irene both retreated to the restroom after their long set, leaving Eleanora alone with her father.

"So what do you really think?" he asked deadpan.

At first, she thought he was serious, then realized she had been so effusive it was obvious what she thought.

"Now I realize why you love Irene," she said softly. "She really is a soulmate, isn't she?"

His eyes glistened a bit. "Yeah. Isn't she something? Sometimes, I don't know how I got so lucky. How did I ever end up with such a beautiful, intelligent, and talented woman as Irene? And to think, it wasn't until I turned 65 that I met her."

"And what about Connie?" She was curious what her father might have to say about him. And she was surprised to realize how eager she was to hear his reply.

"Duke? Isn't he something? A wonderful man, a real gentleman. And what a talent. We try to get him here as often as we can, but he's often out of the area, performing or recording."

"He seems very nice."

"What the Jews call a *mensch*. A real stand-up guy. A piece of bread," he said, repeating one of the greatest compliments her mother ever made about anyone.

She saw Connie stop to chat with some people at the bar. It was obvious they wanted to buy him a drink, but he declined and approached Eleanora's table. Feeling her skin grow hot, she realized she had drunk more wine than she was used to.

"My goodness!" she exclaimed, "it's after 11:00. I should be home by now."

Connie heard her remark. "Don't tell me you'll turn into Cinderella, doomed to a life of cleaning out stoves and fireplaces."

"Nooo," she laughed, "but I do have a family to make breakfast for in the morning and ..." she hesitated, not wanting to refer to her husband, "I did tell them I'd be home around 11:00."

Her father put his hand on her arm. "Why don't you have a cup of coffee first, before you go? Another 20 minutes won't make much difference. Call and let them know you're running late. I'm sure Julie is still awake."

Eleanora glanced sideways at her father. Was she imagining it, or was he being complicit in omitting a reference to Aaron? She gave him a little smile and thought she detected a subtle hint of understanding in his eyes.

"All right, a cup of coffee and a telephone," she said playfully. Connie pulled a cellphone from his pocket and handed it to her. She looked at him, an amused smile still on his face, his eyes merry and twinkling — but intense all the same. She looked at the phone, puzzled.

"Here," he said, taking the phone. He pushed a couple of keys and then said, "Just punch in the number and push this button." She thanked him and entered her home number. She told Aaron she'd be home within an hour and reassured him that all was fine.

Eleanora looked around the table and saw Irene and her father watching her knowingly. Connie caught her eye for an instant, then discreetly looked away as he returned his phone to his jacket pocket.

Irene reached into her purse and pulled out a card. "Eleanora, anytime you'd like to talk, I hope you'll feel free to call me." She handed the small, engraved card to Eleanora.

"Thank you. I'd like that. I'll definitely take you up on that."
Irene gave her a kiss on the cheek. "I'll look forward to your call, then."

Connie leaned across the table to shake her hand. "I'm delighted that I finally got a chance to meet you. I hope I'll be able to see you again sometime."

"Yes," she said, "I do too."

Her father introduced Irene for a third set on stage, then returned to the table.

"This was a wonderful evening, Papa. I hate to leave."

"I'm always here, princess. You never need an invitation. You know that."

"I know," she moaned, "but it really isn't all that simple."

"Then come out during the day sometime. Come for lunch."

Her face brightened. "Yes. That might be easier."

"It's settled then," he said, squeezing her hand.

"I don't think it's the wine," she said smiling. "I really didn't have that much, but I feel high and happy. It's a good feeling."

"Yes," he agreed, "happy is a good."

Chapter Eleven

It was well past midnight when Eleanora arrived home. A lamp had been left on in the living room, as well as a light in the kitchen — as a courtesy or a rebuke, she wasn't sure. Hanging up her coat, she only then realized how tired she felt. As Eleanora undressed and put on her nightgown, she found herself hoping Aaron was asleep. She slid into their bed as quietly as possible.

"What time is it?" he mumbled suddenly, startling her.

"I thought you were asleep. I guess it's about a quarter to one."

"That's kind of late isn't it?" The edginess in Aaron's voice revealed his wakefulness.

"Yes, I guess it is. That's why I called, so you wouldn't worry."

"I have to get up early in the morning and go to work. It's not right, Ellie, to make me stay up late worrying about your getting home safely."

"You didn't have to stay up," she said, regretting the edge in her own voice.

"I would think you'd want to apologize."

"For what?" She turned toward him, although he was facing the wall, his back stiff.

"You were in Newark, Ellie. At a bar. Don't pretend that it's a safe place to be. Then you come home long after midnight and I'm not supposed to care? I'm supposed to just go to sleep as if everything is all right? It's not right, damn it."

"Aaron, if you decided to stay up and worry after I called you, then I'm sorry, I really am. But that was your decision, not mine. I didn't expect you to wait up for me." She glared at the back of his head. "I'm not Julie," she added as an afterthought. "I'm a grown woman."

She rolled over again, and turned her back to his. Her heart raced and her chest was about to explode. She felt caged and strained to burst out. Tears of frustration filled her eyes. Her jaw clenched. Her whole body was tense. She held her breath, trying to calm the wild fluttering within. As she slowed her breathing, she realized that Aaron's reaction had not been unexpected. She had

51

known from the moment she decided to visit her father that Aaron would find a way to scold her for not obeying him. Yet, in her excitement, she had failed to prepare herself for his punishment. Eleanora took a deep breath and let herself remember the time at her father's club. Slowly, she relaxed the hold on her rage and let it float away. Gradually, her body relaxed and she drifted into a deep sleep.

The next morning, Eleanora was in the kitchen preparing breakfast. Both she and Aaron felt strongly that the family should eat together whenever possible. Aaron and Zach were the last ones downstairs. At the table, her husband cleared his throat and announced, "By the way, Reverend Van Houten called last night while you were out."

"Peter?" asked Eleanora. "What did he want?"

"It was about that family, the woman you know who poisoned her family."

"The Winters?" asked Zachary.

Eleanora looked at her son. "You know Kevin?"

"He's in a couple of my classes. His mother tried to poison him. Do you know them?"

"I only know Kevin and the father slightly, but I'm good friends with Mrs. Winters." She turned to Aaron. "What did Peter have to say?"

Aaron lowered his eyes momentarily before looking up at her. "He said to tell you that both Toby and Kevin passed away."

"Oh my God!" she exclaimed. "Oh, dear Lord!"

"I don't know any of the details. He asked me to tell you — they died shortly before he called."

"When was that?"

"Soon after you called last night, maybe about 11:15 or so. I was still up," he added after a beat.

"Kevin's dead?" Zachary's voice reflected both disbelief and excitement. "Murdered?"

Aaron nodded. "I'm afraid so. Was he a friend of yours?"

Zachary shrugged. "I don't know that I'd call him a friend. But he was all right. Quiet. He was OK, I guess. You know, he'd lend you stuff, like paper or something, if you needed it. God, his mother murdered him and his father?" He turned to look at his mother. "And you know her? What kind of woman murders her own son and her husband?" He looked from her to Aaron and back again.

Eleanora took a moment to regain her composure. "Mrs. Winters is a very nice woman, a good woman. But recently, she suffered some sort of breakdown. If it's true that she did this, she couldn't have been in her right mind. She was the last person you'd expect to do anything hurtful to anyone. Obviously, what happened to Kevin and Toby, Mr. Winters, is a tragedy — but don't be so quick to judge Bethann. She's a good person and a terrible thing has happened to her as well. She must be suffering horribly."

Eleanora had spoken quietly, but it was clear that Bethann should not be judged harshly or prematurely because only something extraordinary could have made her act as she had.

Zach avoided her gaze. "Maybe, but you would never do anything like that."

Julie had remained silent during the entire exchange, but Eleanora noticed her daughter nodding slightly as if to affirm her stance. Eleanora smiled back, suddenly aware that she had expressed herself in a manner that was, if not rare, at least infrequent. Aaron had continued to eat his breakfast. Looking at his wife over the rim of his coffee mug, he said nothing. If it hadn't been for Julie's supportive look, Eleanora would have felt that she was out on the proverbial limb.

"Well," Aaron said finally, "I've got to go. Either of you kids need a ride?"

Grabbing backpacks, the family was off to school and work — and Eleanora found herself alone in a quiet house. She finished her tea, then called Peter.

As a member of the clergy, he had been allowed in Bethann's room at the hospital, which remained guarded. She was heavily medicated, both for her physical condition and her emotional state, which was agitated and psychotic.

"I feel like I was there more for me than for her," he said. "The truth is, she wasn't making a lot of sense. Her wrists are restrained because she's been scratching and tearing at her own skin. You can see the bloody lacerations on her arms and cheeks. Anyway, one of the detectives informed me that Toby had died, so now she'll face a murder charge. Christ, that's all this woman needs. And not a half-hour later, the same detective came back and told us that Kevin had passed away. Poor kid's body just gave up. Bethann was so out of it, I don't think it even registered with her. I don't think she realizes what she's done. Ellie, I felt so helpless."

She heard his voice crack. "Peter, if you need to talk, I could come over. Or you can come here if you want to." There was a pause.

"I'd like that, Ellie, if you're sure that it's all right."

"Of course it is."

Eleanora put on a fresh pot of coffee and cleared the breakfast dishes. She was still loading the dishwasher when the doorbell rang. Peter looked haggard and weary.

"Come in," she urged. "I've got fresh coffee on. Let's sit on the porch where it's sunny."

In the kitchen, he took off his jacket and laid it across the back of a chair.

She saw a boy, sad and confused. Putting the coffeepot down, she went to him, arms outstretched in a maternal hug. With a deep sigh, he fell into her embrace. Eleanora was relieved to share her grief for Bethann and her family. She felt his warm breath on her neck, and then he kissed her there, gently. Confused, Eleanora shivered and reflexively nestled in closer. Peter kissed her neck, her throat, her earlobe. She responded to this affection even while her mind was unsure what was happening. She pulled back a bit, her hand on his cheek, and saw the intensity in his eyes. Peter leaned forward and kissed her lips. She returned his kiss despite her own uncertainty. She pulled her head back and held his shoulders at a distance, feeling the pressure of his growing erection against her.

"No," she finally managed to whisper, "we shouldn't be doing this." Recognizing the desire in his eyes, she felt tempted. Being hugged and kissed and wanted felt good. It had been so long since she had felt her body respond this way, since she had been aware of feeling hungry for something. She pulled away, busying herself with the coffeepot.

"I'm sorry," he said.

Eleanora shook her head. "No, don't apologize. It's all right. Nothing happened."

"Maybe I should just go."

"No, don't go. Please," she said, pouring a mug of coffee and extending it to him. She immersed herself in making tea. By the time they were seated on the porch, Eleanora had regained her composure. Safely hemmed in by the arms of her chair, she cradled the hot mug protectively in her lap.

"Ellie, I'm so sorry. I never should have done that."

"I know. Me too. I'm sorry if I led you on in some way."

They remained silent for a while. Finally, Peter spoke.

"Let me ask you something." He took a sip of coffee and continued, "I want you to be honest with me. Do you think I had any responsibility for what happened with the Winters? Because I feel like I'm the cause of it all — that if it weren't for me, nothing would have happened."

She thought for a moment. "Peter, it would be easy for me to reassure you that none of what happened had anything to do with you. I could sincerely believe it just because I know you, because I like you. But I really don't know if you did anything to encourage Kevin. Assuming you didn't, then you have no responsibility whatsoever for anything Bethann did. And even if you had encouraged Kevin — and I don't believe you did — you're still not responsible for what she did. My goodness, Peter, I don't even know if Bethann is responsible for what she did." A nervous laugh escaped her throat.

"I guess it's true that if Kevin hadn't written that note to you, none of this would have happened," she went on, "but that doesn't mean you caused it. If not you, then Kevin would have developed a crush on somebody else. Maybe once Beth found out about his homosexuality, something tragic was bound to happen. It just happened to involve you. I don't see what you could have done differently."

Peter listened carefully. "Thank you," he said. "Part of me knew that, but I needed to hear it from somebody else." He sipped his coffee, then let out a sigh. "So that's not why you pulled away from me?"

"No, the reason I pulled away ..." she searched within herself, wanting to be honest with him and wanting to understand what had transpired between them. "It had more to do with me than with you. I've never even thought about kissing another man. You're the minister of the church where I play for the choir. I've never considered you — or any man — in that way. It never occurred to me that I'd be capable."

Eleanora suddenly realized that, until that moment, she'd had no idea that being held, being kissed, being wanted could feel so natural. Aaron was the only man she'd ever been with. He was the only man who had ever seen her naked, who had touched her. She never considered the possibility that she could be loved or desired by anyone else.

"I understand," he said. "That comes with the territory. No one thinks of me romantically or sexually, as if ministers are some kind of sexless android. But at least I'm glad I didn't repulse you," and this time it was he who emitted the little nervous laugh.

"To be perfectly honest," she said, "I should thank you. As far as I know, no one other than Aaron has ever thought of me that way. I'm flattered. It's actually reassuring to know that someone finds me attractive."

"I can't believe that no other man has ever found you attractive, Ellie. My God, you're a knockout."

"A knockout?" she laughed. "That sounds so old-fashioned! Is that what the young people still say? Even so," she chuckled before he had a chance to answer, "I am grateful. No one ever called me a knockout before."

"Seriously, Ellie, you're a very attractive and desirable woman. What I did was wrong. I'm glad you're OK, that you're not offended. But still it was wrong of me. I mean, not only am I your employer, but you're a married woman. I just wasn't thinking, that's all. I hadn't planned for that to happen. Really."

"I know," she said. "I know. Maybe we each needed a little solace, that's all."

Peter nodded. He raised his empty mug toward her, as if in a toast, "Solace in the solarium."

"Amen," she laughed.

Chapter Twelve

After Peter left, Eleanora was practicing the piano when the phone rang. "Hello?" she said, wondering who it might be.

"Hi," said a not unfamiliar voice, "it's Connie Chermant. How are you?"

"Connie? What a surprise. How did you get my number?"

"The wonders of modern technology," he said, laughing. "You punched it into my cellphone, remember? These little gizmos keep track of all the outgoing calls. Listen, I just wanted to know if you made it home all right last night."

"Yes, I did. Thank you for asking. I really didn't have that much wine. I was fine. I was more high on emotion than anything else."

"You did look like you were enjoying yourself."

"I'm glad you called. I meant to ask you last night, but I didn't get a chance — I was wondering why you called me Eleanora. Nobody calls me that except my mother and my aunt."

"That's your name, isn't it?" he asked teasingly.

"Yes, but most people call me Ellie."

"Well, that strikes me as a shame. Eleanora is a beautiful name. I like the way it sounds and the feel of it in my mouth when I say it. It's a musical name. It has rhythm and melody and so much more personality than Ellie."

"My goodness," she said, "you make me blush." *What a day! A minister kisses me and gets a hard-on and calls me attractive, and now this flattery.*

"Eleanora," he said, pointedly, "let me ask you a question. I was wondering if I might attend the service where you play — I'd like to have the opportunity to hear you?"

"What?" she said incredulously. "You want to hear me play?"

"I do. Would you mind?"

"No, I guess not. Why would I mind? I just don't understand why you would want to hear me play."

"That's no mystery. Music is the center of my life and I think the same might be true for you. Am I right?"

She knew he was right. True, she had her children and a whole host of topics she was passionately interested in, but music was the core of her being and everything else revolved around it. "Yes," she admitted softly, "I think so."

"Well, then, I'd like to experience that part of you."

Eleanora couldn't believe her ears. Her chest heaved as if she were about to sob, and she looked for a place to sit down. Her vision blurred and she let herself slide down the wall until she sat, knees to her chest, like she had seen Julie do on so many occasions.

"Eleanora? Are you still there?"

"Yes," she said hoarsely, "I'm here, Connie, Duke. I don't know what to say."

He was quiet for a few moments and then said softly, "I didn't mean to upset you. Listen, let me give you my number and you can think about it. If it's all right with you, give me a call and let me know where the church is and what time the service is. If you don't feel comfortable with it, for whatever reason, that's fine. How's that?"

She managed to whisper, "All right."

She wrote his number on the back of an envelope from the morning's mail. After they hung up, Eleanora remained on the floor, the phone in her hand. Had she imagined the call? Was Connie really interested in her piano playing — was he interested in her? How was this possible? She had no idea, but the experience of two men — in one morning! — showing an interest in her was so alien that she had no framework for thinking about it. She felt disoriented. The only way she knew how to cope was to put it out of her mind.

She returned to the piano and resumed practicing, working to lose herself in the music. But a nagging refrain kept flitting around in her head among the notes: *He knows you, Eleanora. He knows who you are.* It felt exciting, though also vaguely threatening, and Eleanora tried to hide from her own thoughts. Later, she copied Connie's number onto the back of Irene's card and stuck it in her wallet. The thought occurred to her that she might give Irene a call to discuss the confusing conversation with Connie. Flooded with the swirling currents, she struggled to put the morning's events out of her mind. *I'll wait until I can talk with Irene*, she told herself, and went back to the piano.

———

When Zachary returned from school, he found his mother in the kitchen, the warm smell of baking in the air. "What did you make?" he asked, approaching her at the counter.

"Carrot cake," she said, picking up a spoon and scraping the bowl. "Want some frosting?"

His eyes widened. Licking the spoon, he asked, "Can I have a slice?"

"I'm just finishing the frosting, but if you pour yourself some milk and get a plate, I think I can spare a slice."

By the time he approached her, beggar-like, plate held out, she had cut a nice big wedge for him. He smiled appreciatively.

"Thanks, Mom. Carrot cake is my favorite."

"Really?" she asked ironically.

Mouth full, Zachary mumbled something unintelligible, but she saw the look of pleasure on his face. When Julie come into the kitchen, she saw her brother eating a piece of cake.

"Have a seat, honey, I already cut a piece for you."

"Not too big, I hope."

"I know," she said, "just a small piece. Get yourself something to drink."

As she cleaned up, Eleanora enjoyed listening to her children talking and laughing together. Glancing out the window above the sink, she saw the sun shining on the lawn and shrubs. The old swing set still stood in the corner of the yard, as if waiting patiently for kids to come and play. The kitchen, heated from the oven, had a warm, spicy smell. Eleanora wanted to hug the moment, to draw its comfort into her heart for safekeeping.

The carrot cake loosened Zachary's tongue and he jabbered excitedly about the buzz at school. Rumors had spread fast about Kevin Winters' death. Julie appeared somewhat subdued, making a reference to her current boyfriend as a "Neanderthal." Eleanora reminded them that she was available to talk if they wanted.

Eleanora was sitting on the porch with a glass of iced tea when she heard the garage door rumble open. A minute later she heard Aaron's deliberate footsteps enter the kitchen, then into the front hall to hang up his coat.

"I'm on the porch," she said loudly enough for him to hear, and a moment later he stood in the doorway.

"Hello," she said, "how was your day?"

Ignoring her question, he sifted through the day's mail. "Whose number is this?" he asked, holding up the envelope with Connie's number on it.

"Oh," she said, "I didn't have any scrap paper handy to write it down. I didn't mean to mess up your mail."

"You didn't mess up my mail. I'm just asking whose number this is."

"A pianist," she said, "I got a call from a pianist."

"A pianist?"

"Yes," she said firmly. Aaron stared at her. She returned her gaze to her book and he walked into the kitchen. A few minutes later, he returned with a glass of wine in his hand.

"So," he said, "who is C. Chermant?"

She stared blankly at him for a moment then, putting her book down, she said, "I told you. He's a pianist. He plays classical and jazz piano. He was at my father's club. He knows I'm a fellow pianist and was interested in hearing me play. That's all."

"You know, if that's all there was to it, you'd have told me right off. By playing cat and mouse with me, you let me know you're hiding something. So why don't you just tell me what that is?"

Her eyes widened and, for a moment, she felt paralyzed. In a flash, she imagined the entire argument with him: his relentless, smug pursuit of her secret, bullying her into confessing that she had already or was planning to betray him. And she realized in that instant — it was true! She was planning to betray him. She hadn't admitted it to herself, but that's what she was doing. The realization emboldened her. Her gaze came back in focus and she saw that Aaron was waiting for a response — for what she couldn't remember.

"Thank you," she said, rising from her seat.

"Thank you? For what?"

"For being such a perfect jerk," she said, leaving the room.

"Wait a minute," he shouted, following her into the kitchen. "Don't walk away from me like that." Ignoring him, Eleanora began setting the dining room table. Aaron stood in her way.

"I demand to know what's going on. What are you hiding from me?"

She handed him the plates and turned to get the silverware.

"Don't turn away from me!" he shouted and threw the stack of plates onto the tiled floor. The shattering made her jump. Alarmed by his unexpected violence, she recoiled from him, her eyes wide with fear. Aaron froze, speechless. He shook his head and threw up his hands, then left the room. A moment later, jacket in hand, he got into the car and drove off. Julie and Zachary ran down the stairs and burst into the kitchen.

"Jesus!" said Julie, looking at the scattered fragments of dishes, "how did that happen?"

"Your father dropped them," said Eleanora quietly. "Help me clean up, will you? And be careful not to cut yourself."

Zachary got the broom and dustpan. "Where did Dad go? To buy new dishes?"

Eleanora didn't know what to say.

Chapter Thirteen

It was as if Aaron's ghost presided at the head of the table where the empty place setting silently called attention to itself. Julie and Eleanora made strained attempts at conversation. Finally, Eleanora put her fork down and addressed her two children.

"I suppose you have a right to know. You're not little children anymore. Lately things have been more tense than usual between your father and me. I don't know if either of you has noticed it." She looked questioningly at each of them, but neither said anything. "Anyway," she continued, "I've been thinking of possibly leaving your father."

It was out and could not be taken back. The kids looked stunned.

Both shot questions at her: "Why? When? Where would we live? Would we stay here? Would we have to change schools? Would Dad move out?" Eleanora slumped back on her chair and shrugged her shoulders under the barrage.

"I don't know, guys. I've just started to think about it. I really don't know how it would work. I don't even know if it's possible. Maybe I shouldn't have said anything, but after tonight I knew you would notice something was wrong. I haven't said anything to your dad yet. It just feels so impossible between us."

How could she convey to them what was still so unclear within her? Was being unhappy sufficient reason to disrupt everyone's lives? Did she have a right to even think this way?

Zachary interrupted the long silence. "Why?" he asked painfully. "Why do you have to do this? It's not fair."

Julie gave him a sharp look. "Don't be a jerk. You know how Dad is. You're always complaining about how he won't let you do stuff, how he's too over-protective."

"You do too!" he yelled. "It's not just me. You complain too."

"Exactly," she said, "that's the point. He's that way with all of us, including Mom. If we can't wait to get away from him, why should it be any different for her?"

Eleanora wanted to calm the building tension between them. "Come on, kids ..."

"No," Julie said, interrupting her, "Zach has to understand." She turned back to her brother and lowered her voice to a more reasonable tone. "You're 15 and I know that you understand this. If Mom and Dad separate, we're all going to have to sacrifice in some way. That's just the way it's going to be. So don't be a whiner. This isn't about you or me. It's about Mom and Dad. Mom's got rights too, Zach. It's not just about you and me."

Chastened, Zachary stared down at his plate. Eventually, he asked quietly if Aaron would come home again. Eleanora shrugged her shoulders, but said she assumed he'd be home soon.

He looked at his mother. "If Dad isn't home soon," he said in a serious voice, "can I have his share of the cake?"

Eleanora burst out laughing and the tension broke. But then, surprising herself and the kids, her laughter turned to sobbing. It was as if her body wasn't under her control, and she couldn't stop the flow of tears. Julie and Zach tried to console her. Neither had ever seen her so disconsolate, although they were used to her high-intensity emotions.

In silence, both kids cleared the table. They returned with three plates filled with carrot cake, plus a cup of tea for their mother. Their tender thoughtfulness brought a fresh gush of tears from Eleanora, but this time accompanied by a smile.

Later, when Julie and Zachary had gone upstairs, she heard the low murmur of their discussion. Eleanora dug out Irene's card from her wallet and dialed. She briefly described the events of the day and asked if they could meet for lunch. Irene was comforting and sympathetic, and they set up a luncheon date for the next day.

Later, Eleanora sat propped up in bed, but she couldn't concentrate on her book. Ruminating on Aaron's whereabouts, her imagination conjured up frightening scenarios. Finally she turned out the light, though she was still too agitated to asleep. The moonlight shone through the sheer curtains of her bedroom. She felt no relief when the low vibrations of the garage door signaled that Aaron was home. Her whole body stiffened and her breath caught. She turned on the light and waited.

Aaron's face wore the usual glum demeanor. He avoided eye contact with her. She felt his diminished sense of control, which allowed her to relax somewhat. He dropped down into the easy chair by the window and pulled the chain to light the lamp. Sighing, he bent over and untied his shoes and then, huffing, slumped back. Eleanora was the first to speak.

"The kids were concerned. They wondered if you were coming back."

"Of course I was going to come back. I live here, don't I?"

"Yes, you do. I'm just telling you they were upset by your leaving like that."

He tossed his head as if to dismiss such nonsense. "I was too upset to stay. I had to leave or ..." he let the implications drift ominously in the room.

"Or what?" she asked, goading him.

He glared at her. "Or I might have done something I'd be sorry for later on," he said matter of factly.

"Like hitting me?"

He nodded his head as he continued to glare at her from his reclining position across the room. "Yes, like hitting you."

"It wouldn't be the first time." She thought of one occasion, years before, when he had lost his temper and slapped her sharply.

"It's not the first time you've provoked me."

"If I don't kowtow to you, to every moody suspicion, then I'm being provocative?"

Aaron's lips spread into a sneer. "You're doing it again, Ellie. Those insipid insinuations, that I'm some monster control freak and you're the innocent victim. Jesus, you're so fucking neurotic. Ellie, the poor wounded bird, can't even protect herself. Cheep, cheep, cheep, poor helpless Ellie," he mocked. "You're about as helpless as a terrorist. You fight a guerilla war, Ellie. With you, everything is sneaky and hidden. No wonder you wops can't be trusted. You say one thing and mean another."

"Aaron," she broke in, "what are you talking about? Have you been drinking?"

"I'll tell you what I'm talking about, little miss goody-two-shoes. I'm talking about your playing the innocent, wouldn't-say-shit if you had a mouth full."

"Aaron," she pressed again, "have you been drinking?"

He waved his finger at her. "Oh no you don't. Don't go turning this back on me. This isn't about me. This is about you, Mrs. Eleanora Hoffman, the slut of northern New Jersey."

"Aaron!" she shouted. "How dare you. You're out of your mind. You don't know what you're saying." Eleanora drew back the covers and put on her robe, as if more modesty was required in the presence of this stranger.

He pushed himself up and lunged across the room. "You're not going anywhere," he growled. "Sit down!" Pushing her back onto the bed, "You want to know where I went tonight? I was checking up on your Negro boyfriend."

"You what? Are you crazy?"

"Me? Crazy? Like a fox, I'm crazy. You're the one who must be crazy, thinking you could have an affair with some colored junkie musician and get away with it."

"Aaron ..."

"Shut up! I don't want to hear any of your lies. I looked him up. I did my research. Oh, he's a very successful pianist," he taunted. "You can really pick 'em, El. Moving up in the world? A partner in a major accounting firm isn't glamorous enough for you? Not artistic enough?"

She heard the slurring of his speech. It was clear to Eleanora that there was no possibility of a rational discussion with him. She had been concerned the kids would hear him and believe his accusations, but she gave up on that too. She'd deal with it later. Clearly, Aaron had jumped the gun and decided she was having an affair with Connie. He was understandably hurt and angry. The fact that she had been entertaining the same fantasy made her feel guilty — as if she had, in fact, already committed adultery.

Aaron slumped back in his chair.

"Well," he said, breathing heavily and spreading his hands wide, "what do you have to say for yourself?"

So he thought she was cheating on him. Maybe that was just as well. Maybe this was the excuse they both needed to call an end to their charade. This gave her the confidence to assert herself. She massaged her face and tightened the belt on her robe.

"What do I have to say for myself? Do you really want to hear what I have to say?" Aaron smiled contemptuously. "Just this: You're a stupid, arrogant bastard. Your accusations are preposterous. I know you're drunk, Aaron, so you're not totally responsible for the horrible things you said. Even so, I don't think I'll ever be able to forgive you. You've always treated me as if I'm a non-person, like I'm invisible."

Aaron started to rise, waiving a pointed finger.

"Don't you dare dismiss what I'm saying. I exist, Aaron. I am a person. I deserve respect. I don't deserve this kind of treatment from you. I've never deserved it and I won't take it anymore. You think you're so damn superior, but you're not. You're not even human, just some kind of android. Maybe you're part human, Aaron, but not enough for me. I'm leaving you. I won't put up with your sneering, arrogant selfishness any longer. Not one day longer than I have to." Eleanora stood up. "There is no way I'm going to sleep in this bed with you ever again."

Aaron clapped his hands slowly. "Big fucking speech. You finally got it out, didn't you? You've been aching to say that ever since we got married, haven't you? All these years, 20 goddamned years, nothing from you but one big act. You never cared about me. You never gave me the respect I deserved — speaking about what one deserves. You only married me because you had to, because you were knocked up and wanted to get away from that stupid mother of yours. All these years I busted my goddamned hump to earn a good living for you, buy you a nice house," he extended his arms wide and gave an appreciative look to the spacious master bedroom, "a nice car, nice clothes. You never had to work. We go on nice vacations, go into New York to see a show. Never, Ellie, never do I hear a thank you, a word of praise, some appreciation for how good you've got it — for taking you out of that fucking guinea ghetto. Talk about selfishness! You have raised selfishness to a fucking art form!"

"In that case," she said sarcastically, "you can have the bed and I'll go to the guest room."

"You're goddamned right I can have the bed. I paid for it! I paid for all of it. It's all mine. You leave, Ellie, and you leave with nothing. Understand? Nothing. Nada. El Zippo," he said snapping his fingers. He stepped closer to where she stood hugging herself, shivering, her eyes wide, her jaw set.

"Let me tell you something else, you stupid guinea whore. You're not fit to be a mother. You leave and you leave alone. You understand? The kids stay here, where they belong, in their home. You don't deserve them," he sneered, jabbing his finger deliberately into her chest.

Eleanora had an impulse to spit in his face, but she knew it would only provoke a more violent retaliation. She moved toward the door, but he grabbed her tightly by her arm.

"One more thing you stupid bitch — you really think you're going to leave? Where the fuck do you think you'll go? You're going to leave your kids? Don't make me laugh. You leave and you'll never see those kids again. Look at me, damn you."

She stared him in the eye.

"Do you hear what I'm saying? Do I look like I'm kidding? You go, Ellie, and you'll be sorry. I promise you. You will be forever sorry."

She pried his fingers from her arm and stepped past him without a word.

Chapter Fourteen

The next morning, Eleanora was making breakfast when her children came down. Julie asked if she was moving out that day or if she'd be there when they returned from school. Eleanora responded to the sad, confused look in her daughter's eyes and gave her a hug. "I'm pretty sure I'll be here when you get home," she assured her daughter.

When Aaron came downstairs, he greeted the children, pointedly ignoring his wife. "I've got to go in early," he announced. "I'll grab something at the office."

Eleanora was grateful to be spared the awkwardness of having to make his breakfast. She had purposely not brewed any coffee, but he appeared not to notice. All three breathed a sigh of relief when Aaron left.

"I'm sorry," Eleanora told her children quietly. "I have to leave. There's no way I can stay with him any longer."

Both Julie and Zach nodded in resignation, but they kept their eyes on her, waiting for clarification. "I'll move in with Grandpa or Zia Velia for a while if I have to, but I can't stay here."

"Are you going to get a divorce?" Julie asked.

"I don't see any alternative," she said.

Zachary looked glum. "Can we go with you? Or couldn't you stay here and Dad move out?"

"Not for now," she said, trying to soften the bad news. "Maybe later on, when I get settled. I don't know. We'll have to wait and see what happens. In the meantime, you kids will stay here and your lives won't change that much. He's a decent dad. You'll be OK with him, although you both may have to do more around the house." Her eyes filled up. "I'm sorry, guys. I truly am."

"We know," Julie said consolingly.

"Will we get to see you?" Zachary asked, his eyes glistening.

"Of course," she reassured him, suddenly recalling her own father's attempt to comfort her so many years ago. "Your dad and I will work something out. Don't worry about that. I'm not leaving you. You know that, don't you?"

Tears spilled from the corners of Zach's eyes, and he nodded.

"Come on," she said, "you'd better get a move on or you'll be late."

As she rinsed the dishes in the sink, she looked out the window and noticed the leaves were beginning to change, the birches a deepening yellow, the oaks a rich shade of brown.

Autumn is starting, she thought, a new season. Or is summer ending? Tears welled up in her eyes. *If my mother made it on her own, then damnit, so can I.* Anticipating lunch with Irene, she smiled hopefully at the thought of sharing everything, even though she hardly knew her. It also occurred to her that she should tell Peter what was happening.

Both kids made a point of giving her a hug and kiss goodbye before going off to school. After they left, she called Peter.

"Good morning," she said, "it's Eleanora Hoffman."

"Of course it is," he said warmly. "You think I don't recognize your voice? How are you?"

She paused for a moment. "Actually, a little discombobulated. I've had a major fight with Aaron and I've decided to leave him."

"Wow," he said, sounding shocked, "I had no idea things were that bad."

"Well," she found herself shrugging her shoulders helplessly. She didn't want to go into the details — 20 years of being erased, dismissed, taken for granted.

"Are you sure this is what you want to do?" he asked.

"I'm sure, Peter. It's time."

"Where will you go? Are you staying in town?"

"I don't know yet. There's the whole economic thing. I'll need support from Aaron, which I know he'll fight tooth and nail."

"What about the choir? I know the pay is minimal, but do you still plan to play?"

"Of course. I couldn't give that up. Besides, now the money will be more important than ever, little as it is."

"Yes," he said, drawing it out as if pondering something, "I hope there's no problem."

"No matter where I'll be, Peter, I'll make sure to get in for the rehearsals and the services."

"Actually," he said slowly, "I was thinking about the board."

"The board? What have they got to do with it?"

"It's this whole Winters affair — one of our parishioners becoming a homicidal maniac and murdering her family. It puts the congregation in a bad light. We got some negative publicity and some of the board members are upset."

"I don't understand. What's that got to do with me?"

"Don't get me wrong, Ellie. I'm just thinking out loud here. I wonder how they'll react to our pianist separating from her husband. They might be skittish about it."

"Peter, first of all, I'm not a member of your congregation. I'm an employee. And second, I'm certainly not the first person there to be separated. My goodness, you have plenty of divorced people who are church members."

"I know, Ellie," he said soothingly. "I wouldn't worry about it. I was just trying to anticipate how some of the board members might think, that's all."

"Well, if there were any nonsense like that, I'd certainly hope you'd stand up for me."

"Of course I will. Like I said, it probably won't be anything at all. Forget I even said anything about it. Of course, if anything does come up, you can count on me. Don't give it another thought."

Eleanora stood holding the phone and shaking her head. "OK, Peter. I just wanted to alert you, but I'll be there Wednesday evening as usual."

"Good. I'll see you then."

"Oh, by the way, what's the latest with Bethann?"

"I guess you didn't hear. They transferred her to Trenton State Hospital for the Criminally Insane."

"What?"

"Yes, somehow she got hold of a pair of scissors from one of the nurses or technicians and stabbed herself numerous times. They're just not equipped to handle her at the local hospital. Obviously, she's not competent to stand trial or go through any sort of legal proceedings. It's probably for the best," he concluded, his voice full of resignation.

"Bethann in Trenton State? That had to have been built back in the 1800s."

"Probably," he agreed.

Eleanora didn't know what else to say. "All right, Peter," she said with a sigh. "Thanks for telling me. I'll see you tomorrow night then."

After she hung up, Eleanora made another cup of tea and sat on the porch thinking about her options. She decided to wait until after her lunch with Irene before making any decisions — but first, she wanted to make one call. She dug Irene's card from her wallet and dialed Connie's number. With no answer, she left a message that she would try him later but that he was not to call her, she'd explain when they spoke. Then she showered and dressed.

Getting ready for lunch, she thought about how rapidly her life was changing. It felt as if she were in a canoe heading for a waterfall, being swept through the rapids and heading for a precipitous plunge. Scared and shaky, she also recognized excitement at the possibilities, unclear as they might be.

On the surface, she had imagined that just being apart from Aaron would make life better, but now she thought about practicalities: Where would she live? How would she earn enough for rent and food? Could the children live with her? What did Aaron mean when he said she'd never see them again? She had assumed that his warning was only the angry bluster of alcohol and wounded pride — but could there be anything to his threat? Could he really cut off access to her own children? Would he?

And was Peter actually suggesting that if she left Aaron she might be out of a job? Was that possible? Could people be that small-minded? Then she remembered Bethann, who had opted for her own death, and that of her son and husband, rather than face the prospect of scandal and social censure. Obviously Bethann believed people could be that petty. What would she do if she lost her job playing for the choir? She had never done any other kind of work. She felt like a child — helpless, vulnerable, and confused. Maybe talking with Irene would help. And her father — she would let him know as well. She knew he'd want to help, but what could he really do?

Heart racing, it was difficult to concentrate. She kept forgetting little things and had to retrace her steps from the bathroom to the bedroom and back again. Not yet 10:30, she realized impatiently — still an hour before she had to leave. She decided to play the piano to calm her nerves, and realized suddenly that wherever she ended up living, she would be without a piano. How would she practice?

Thoughts swirled as panic ensued. Was giving up everything — her children, her work, her music — the price she had to pay for surviving? Was life really that cruel? Is that what survival was all about — the absence of living?

Distraught, she let her hands fall randomly upon the keyboard, her fingers instinctively seeking chords. Unconsciously, she found herself playing a melancholy piece by Lizt and then works by Chopin and Brahms. When she finished, she sat back on her bench and stared at the piano, a sense of peace enveloping her. All of the seemingly insoluble problems were still there, still as frightening and intimidating. Yet, she felt calmer. Perhaps she was not totally helpless; perhaps she could control her own frame of mind no matter what the external realities were. For a moment, at least, she felt a breath of hope.

Walking into the small restaurant in Edgewater, Eleanora was surprised to find herself in such a busy place. Nestled into the Palisades, the old stucco building was out of the way — even isolated — but the charming, intimate atmosphere buzzed with conversation. Spotting Irene, she waved, and the two shared a hug. Eleanora noted the marvelous view of upper Manhattan.

"What a view!" she exclaimed. "How much did you have to tip the maitre d' to get this table?"

Irene laughed. "Robert is an old friend and always gives me this table whenever I come here."

"But how did you ever discover such a place?" Eleanora wondered. "It's like being in another country, it's so out of the way. The whole atmosphere feels so …"

"European," Irene chimed in. "I know, it's been here forever. I think this is the third or fourth generation that's running it now. In fact, Robert is the nephew of the owners. He's the one who introduced me to the place."

Eleanora felt overwhelmed. Photographs of celebrities, both current and past, adorned the walls, and family heirlooms and antiques added a touch of history.

"It's like being in a museum or a gallery," she gushed.

"The owner and his wife are great collectors. It's wonderful, isn't it?"

"I've never seen anything like it," she declared, thinking what a far cry this was from the diners and chain restaurants she usually frequented with Aaron and the children. Irene ordered an Old Fashioned on the rocks. After some encouragement, Eleanora agreed to a white wine spritzer.

"I'm not used to having alcohol in the middle of the day," she explained.

"I think today is an exception," Irene reassured her. "So, tell me, what's going on?"

Eleanora pulled herself together. "So much is happening so fast," she began. "I feel like Dorothy in *The Wizard of Oz*, being tossed around in a tornado. When I first called you, I don't even remember what day that was or what I wanted to discuss with you, but everything has already changed. Last night I decided," she paused, as if reviewing the pros and cons in her mind before saying it out loud, "I made the decision to leave my husband. I can't live with him anymore, Irene." She paused and Irene remained quiet. The waiter brought their drinks.

"Connie called me the other day," Eleanora continued. "He said he wanted to hear me play piano and asked if he could come to the church. I didn't know what to say. It was so unexpected and," she stumbled for words, "he made me feel like he saw into me." She looked at Irene almost imploringly. "I don't know if anyone has ever made me feel so …" she searched for the right word, "real, like I truly existed. I was confused. I didn't know what I was feeling, but I knew it was profound. I didn't respond," she went on. "So he gave me his number and asked me to think about it. I guess that's why I called you."

She brushed her hair back and sipped her wine. Irene watched her, still quiet.

"Aaron saw Connie's phone number where I had scribbled it, and of course he questioned me," Eleanora explained with a resigned shrug of her shoulders. "I guess he could tell I was uncomfortable, so he left. I don't know where he went, but he said he did 'research' on Connie. Anyway, the bottom line is that when he came home he was drunk and accused me of having an affair. We had a big fight and I decided then and there that I wasn't going to put up with his nonsense anymore."

She looked at Irene with moist eyes. "I don't know what to do. I don't know where I'm going to live, or how. Aaron said if I leave I'll never see the kids again. And how am I going to exist without a piano? Am I crazy to do this? I don't know who else to ask."

Irene took a deep breath. "Whew! Oh, honey, you do have a whole lot going on. Let's take one thing at a time. First, no, you are not crazy to want out of that relationship. It's obscene to even call it a relationship. It doesn't sound like a relationship at all to me. From what you told me on Sunday, you've been unhappy in your marriage for a long time. Maybe you're finally allowing yourself to realize how miserable you've been all along."

Eleanora nodded. "Yes, I think so. It's been a long time. Years ago I tried to kill myself." Irene grimaced. "I only tried it that once, but it wasn't the only time I thought about it." Eleanora had a flash of Bethann standing in her doorway, her eyes red and raw, her face haggard and drawn. She recognized that look of wild desperation and felt a kinship with her sad friend.

"I don't want to go there again," she said. "There has to be another way."

"Leaving your husband is always a difficult decision," Irene admitted. "Economically, you'll take a beating. Believe me, you'll have to make some very real financial sacrifices. But most of the time women say it's worth it. In the long haul, you'll probably feel better off." Eleanora nodded and tried to smile.

"But it won't be easy, Ellie. Make up your mind to that," Irene warned.

"What about the kids?" Eleanora asked. "I can't bear the thought of leaving them, but I don't know how I can take them with me. I have no idea what I'm doing."

"He's not going to hurt them, is he?"

"No, Aaron may be a real jerk, but he's not a bad person. He'd never do anything to hurt them."

"Then he's just trying to intimidate you. He's bluffing. Legally, he can't keep the kids from seeing you, so don't waste one minute worrying about that. If you have to leave them with him temporarily, don't worry too much about it. You'll be able to get them back. Even if you had sex with Connie out on your front lawn, Aaron still couldn't keep you from your kids."

At the mention of Connie, Eleanora blushed a deep crimson. "You're sure?"

she managed to ask.

"Oh, absolutely," Irene reassured her with a dismissive wave of her hand.

The waiter appeared. Eleanora ordered a bowl of avocado soup that came with a small salad, and Irene ordered a Portobello mushroom and eggplant panini with a glass of red wine.

"Now," Irene continued after the waiter had gone, "what about Connie?"

"That's what I wanted to ask you. Why do you think he really wants to hear me play?"

"You mean, could he have some personal interest?"

Again, Eleanora felt the heat rising in her face and she nodded in embarrassment.

"Ellie, you may be married and have two grown children, but you are a beautiful woman. Of course he's interested in you. But if I know Connie, he's not — what should I say — obsessed about it. Connie is a mature man. He's been around. He knows who he is and doesn't have anything to prove. My guess is that he genuinely wants to hear you play, to see what it tells him about who you are."

Hearing Irene's explanation made it sound more reasonable — almost natural. She smiled and relaxed a bit.

"My father said he'd help me if I decide to leave Aaron. I thought he was jumping the gun, but now it doesn't look that way."

"I know for a fact that your father will want to help you. Since Sunday night, he and I have talked about the possibility of your leaving Aaron. Your father refers to him as Herr Hoffman. Anyway, I spend most nights at your father's now, so why don't you stay at my place for a while? I have a condo down in Hoboken. It's small, only one bedroom, but it's convenient to everything. It's only about a half-hour to your dad's place and you could be back in Leonia in 45 minutes or so."

"You're sure?"

"Of course I'm sure. Your dad and I already discussed it, like I said. Actually, I've been slowly moving into his place as it is, even though we haven't actually made anything official. It's just sort of happening naturally." Irene sat back with a dreamy look on her face and took a long sip of her wine.

Eleanora pictured the two of them in her dad's little house in Nutley, having breakfast in his cozy kitchen or sitting in his living room reading or listening to music.

Music!

"Irene, do you have any ideas about a piano? Anywhere I might be able to practice?" As she asked the question, the thought occurred that she might be able to use the piano at church — if she could keep her job.

"Job!" she blurted out. "What am I going to do about money?"

Irene was laughing again. "Oh, girl, you don't give your daddy near enough credit. First, about the piano, I have an electronic keyboard at my condo. I don't really need it at your father's because he has that wonderful upright downstairs in the rec room. But there's also the piano at the Lounge, and you could work there as a hostess or waitress or something."

Eleanora practically squealed with delight. "I could? You mean it?"

Relieved of the mounting tension, Eleanora ate with gusto. She felt celebratory, full of excitement and energy. Irene ordered another glass of wine and Eleanora joined her. Reveling in her good fortune, she was now confident that everything would work out all right. Eleanora asked a variety of questions and Irene enjoyed midwifing the long-delayed emergence of this beautiful young woman.

When they finally walked out into the sun, Eleanora took in the view of the Hudson River, the grace of the George Washington Bridge to her left and the magical Manhattan skyline stretching south. "This is a beautiful spot," she sighed. "Thank you so much, Irene. I feel like you've saved my life."

Irene hugged her. "You're a sweetheart, Ellie. You have no idea what pleasure it gives me to help you. Joey loves you so much. How could I not love you too?" She handed Eleanora a key to her condo. "If there's anything you need, just call."

Entering the Lounge, Eleanora spotted her father at the end of the bar, sipping a cup of coffee and going over some paperwork. She strode past a couple of men nursing their beers, engaged in sports conversation.

"Hi, Papa," she called out.

His face lit up. "Hiya, kiddo. How're you doing?"

"Oh, Papa, Irene was such a help." She told him about their conversation, about her decision to leave Aaron. Without saying anything, he took out his phone and made a call.

"Rose? Hi, it's Joey Albanese. Is Mr. Byrd in? Thank you." He raised his eyes to hers and mouthed, "My attorney."

"Herbie? It's Joey. Good, thank you. Listen, I'm here at the Lounge with my daughter, Eleanora Hoffman. She's in the process of leaving her husband — finally, after 20 years. No, it's a good thing, believe me. Anyway, she needs a really good divorce lawyer." He took a pen from his jacket pocket. "OK, shoot. Yeah, I got it. Will do. Thanks, Herbie." He handed the number to Eleanora.

"She works with Herbie. He said to call her this afternoon and set up an appointment. Listen, baby, this is on me. Whatever it costs. You just put yourself in her hands."

"I don't know what to say. You have no idea what this means to me."

"Yes, I do. I know exactly what it means to you. I'm sorry to talk badly about your mother, but anytime I think of what my life would have been like if I had stayed with her ..." he shook his head in disbelief. "There's no way I could have made it. No way. I'd have suffocated to death. So," he said, grasping her arm, "I have a pretty good idea of how desperate you are to get out of that cage he has you in."

"Irene said I might be able to work here?"

"Of course you can."

"I'll have to do something to earn money. I may not be able to keep my job playing for the church choir." She told him about her conversation with Peter.

"And this is a friend of yours, this minister?" He shook his head in disbelief.

"There but for the grace of God go I," he muttered. "Well, anyway, I've been thinking about what it would be like if you were here. Suppose you start out being a hostess, seating people who come in for lunch or dinner. That would be the easiest way to learn the business, get to know the clientele." She nodded her head. It sounded interesting, exciting even.

"If it's busy, you can help with setting up the tables, taking orders, whatever. If it's slow, you can provide some background piano music." Her eyes lit up and she imagined playing popular music, standards, and show tunes.

"We'll play it by ear, you know, see how it goes," he went on. "If you like it, who knows?"

"It sounds great, Papa. Thank you."

They talked more about the details and she made arrangements to start her new job. Everything was happening so quickly! For now, she suggested a schedule that would permit her to continue playing at the church, just in case her fears there were unfounded.

Before she left, she called the lawyer, Carmella Rotundo, and made an appointment for the next morning. The attorney was adamant that Eleanora should not move out until they had talked. When she kissed her father goodbye, she saw that his eyes were moist — and in that instant, she felt so special, she knew everything would be fine.

Chapter Fifteen

The kids were overjoyed when she pulled into the driveway. They helped her in the kitchen as she shared the day's events with them. When Aaron arrived home, he was his usual reticent self, but Eleanora was determined to have a constructive family discussion during dinner. When they were all seated, Eleanora made her announcement.

"Aaron, I've already told the kids that you and I will be separating. Also, you should know that I have an appointment to see a divorce attorney in the morning."

"What?" he glared at her and looked questioningly at both kids for confirmation. "I wish you wouldn't have done that, Ellie. Jumping the gun like that. I think you should have discussed this with me first. This is between us. It doesn't concern them."

"Of course it concerns them. The breakup of our family concerns them. They have a right to know what's happening, what's going to happen, and how it will affect them."

"You should have talked to me first," he repeated, shaking his head in disbelief. "You don't know about these things. You're going to end up giving them the wrong impression."

"Dad," interjected Julie, "we're right here. Don't talk about us as if we don't exist."

"I don't recall asking for your opinion, miss," he said sharply. "This is between your mother and me. In fact, I'd appreciate it if the two of you would take your plates and go to your rooms and let your mother and me discuss this privately."

The two children looked at Eleanora for direction.

"It doesn't make any difference," she said to her husband. "If they don't hear what we say now, then I'll fill them in later. For my part, I'd rather have them here. As I said, it's not just about us, this concerns them too."

Aaron lowered his head and his jaw muscles worked furiously. Finally, he looked up. "All right," he said through clenched teeth. "So you have an appointment tomorrow with a divorce lawyer. Are you going to tell him that you've been having an affair with a black man?"

Eleanora saw from her children's faces that they had heard their father's ravings the previous night. Deliberately, she took a forkful of salad and chewed it slowly.

"What I will tell my attorney is that my husband suffers from a delusion that I've been having an affair with a 'junkie Negro musician.'"

Aaron's face turned beet red. "How dare you throw my words back at me like that."

"Come on, Aaron. Now who's playing the victim? You accuse me of having an affair, not only last night in the privacy of our bedroom, but now in front of Julie and Zach, for the express purpose of trying to turn them against me. That's really cheap. But if you're going to accuse me, then I have a right to defend myself."

She looked directly at her children. "In spite of your father's beliefs, I have never had a relationship with any other man, ever, in my entire life. But," and she returned her gaze to her husband, "that is not going to stop me from leaving you. And," again she turned to Julie and Zach, "regardless of what you may have heard last night, there is nothing your father can do to stop me from seeing you — wherever I live." She sat back and deliberately took another forkful of food. "So don't worry about it."

"This isn't accomplishing anything," Aaron said under his breath and withdrew into his study.

As he left the room, Eleanora stared at his retreating image and stuck out her tongue. Both kids giggled nervously. Eleanora quickly raised her finger to her lips, but winked at them.

"It's going to be all right," she said quietly. "You'll see."

That night, Eleanora sat propped up in the guest room bed, making lists: clothes and mementoes to take to Irene's condo, chores for Julie and Zach to do in her absence, probable living expenses she'd need to cover, questions to ask Carmella Rotundo, assets she and Aaron co-owned — the lawyer would want to know those. She began to grasp just how little she knew about her own life: the value of their house, the monthly mortgage payment and the balance, were just a few. Frustrated by her own ignorance, she put the pad down. She felt afraid, but she was also angry with herself for having relied so thoroughly on Aaron these past two decades. Still a teenager when they'd married, she had naturally fallen into a pattern of letting him handle all the responsibilities and decision-making, while she — like her mother — reared the children and kept house. Now she realized how that subservient role had kept her dependent and undeveloped.

Looking around, she recognized pictures and objects that had outgrown their usefulness elsewhere in the house and were exiled to the guest room — *like me,* she thought. Pictures of the three children when they were young, a generic painting of New Jersey sand dunes, a vase of dried flowers — they all brought back memories. Some, like those of the children and their big St. Bernard, were happy — but she was shocked by the visceral, seething anger unleashed by images of her and Aaron.

A soft knocking on the door startled her, and Zachary and Julie poked their heads in to say goodnight. She reassured them that she'd be home for supper the next day, before she had to go to choir practice. After they retired, she was about to turn out the light when the door opened and Aaron entered into the room.

"What are you doing in here?" she asked, reflexively drawing the covers over her.

"We have to talk, El. This craziness has gone too far."

"I'm not sure what you mean."

"I mean this business of seeing a lawyer. We should be able to work out our differences by ourselves. It's nonsense to bring other people into this. You have no idea how expensive attorneys are." She assumed he was making an enormous effort to appear reasonable and conciliatory.

"You don't want me to see a lawyer?"

"Of course I don't want you to see a lawyer."

"Don't you want a divorce?"

"I never said I wanted a divorce. Why would I want a divorce, for Christ's sake?"

"Because you think I've had an affair with a junkie Negro musician."

He shook his head and sat down on the edge of the bed. Eleanora drew her knees away from him.

"OK, maybe I was a little out of line. Maybe I put two and two together and came up with five, but you've got to admit …"

"I've got to admit what, Aaron? That I've done something wrong? That you were right to treat me the way you did, to say those things, to threaten me the way you did? What is it you want me to admit, Aaron? That I don't love you? That you don't love me? Do you want to admit that, Aaron? That you hate this dumb little guinea you never wanted to marry, who saddled you with three kids — including that sweet child you could never bear to look at, never mind touch?"

"Calm down. There's no need to get excited. I said I was sorry."

"No you didn't. You did not say you were sorry. You have never said you were sorry — not for anything, ever."

"OK, I'm sorry."

"Ha!"

"Come on, El, what do you want from me? Do I have to get down on my knees to you? Do I have to grovel? Is that what you want?" He tried to manu-facture a smile to show her how absurd she was.

"Do you want to get down on your knees and beg me to forgive you? Is that what you want to do?"

"Do I want to? No, of course not," he stammered.

"I didn't think so. But that's what you wanted me to do, isn't it? Even though I didn't do anything except to disobey you by visiting my own father? You son of a bitch. Get out! Get out of my room. This is my room now and I don't want you in it."

"Wait, El, I thought we could work this out."

"No, we cannot work this out. You may have second thoughts, you may not want a divorce — but I do. I want one. I'm not staying married to you anymore. I don't have to! Now get out!" She pulled the chain on her bedside lamp and cast the world into darkness.

The kids were almost done with breakfast before Aaron came downstairs. Julie reminded her parents that she would be working late, and Eleanora said she had to leave early for rehearsal.

"There are leftovers in the fridge," she said to Zachary, casting a quick glance at Aaron to make sure he got the message too.

"I'm going in a little late, this morning," Aaron announced.

Eleanora braced herself for a repeat of last night. She wished the kids could stay with her as a buffer. Fearing what Aaron might do if the two of them were alone in the house, she looked desperately at the kids, but no one said a word.

"Hey Dad," said Zachary suddenly, "I was hoping you could give me a ride to school today. I've got a lot of books to carry."

"Sorry, Zach, not this morning. I just said, I'm going in late today."

Zach shrugged and snuck a peek at his mother, who flashed him a weak smile. A few minutes later the kids left. When the front door banged shut, she got up to clear the table.

"Wait a minute before you do that," he said, reaching out to grab her arm. Eyes widened, she withdrew from his touch.

"Relax," he said quietly, "I'm not going to hurt you. Sit down. Please." She sat, her body leaning away from him like a tree in a hurricane. "I just wanted to — it's just that I really believe you're jumping the gun on this, El. We've been married for 20 years. It shouldn't come down to this. We should be able to talk about it. I don't think you've thought this through and I hate to see you take some irrevocable step, where there'll be no turning back."

Eleanora remained silent, staring wide-eyed at her husband, this man who had dominated and controlled her life for 20 years. She had been expected to anticipate and fulfill all of his expectations — and be grateful for having been rescued from a ghetto and spared a life of shame. The message had always been the same: I married you, didn't I? What more do you have a right to expect? The implied answer, of course, was *nothing. I expect nothing. I deserve nothing. I need nothing. I am nothing.*

"Well?" he asked. She stared at him blankly. "Ellie, are you listening to me? I don't think you should see that lawyer today. Cancel the appointment. If you still want to go after we've talked things over, you can always make another appointment. What do you say?"

"What is there to talk about?"

"Well," he stammered, "there are changes we could make. If we have problems, we can solve them. We should talk about what you see as our problems, what changes you would like to see. Maybe we should do more together. Maybe you'd like me to watch less football. I don't know."

Eleanora looked at him quizzically. "Football? You really don't have a clue, do you?"

"I'm not sure what you mean."

"Yes," she said, amazed, "I know."

Aaron waited for her to explain, to give him something he could work with. "Well?" he said finally. "What do I have to do?"

Heaving a big sigh, Eleanora leaned forward, her hands unconsciously playing with her napkin. "You're right, Aaron, we have to talk. But not about what we can do to save the marriage. It's too late for that. But going forward, we'll have to talk about the kids, finances, all sorts of practicalities. Who's going to stay in the house? How much money will you provide for me and the kids, medical and auto insurance, things like that. Practical things that you're very good at."

The color rose in his neck and face. Eleanora saw his jaw muscles clench.

"I'm sorry, Aaron," she said, attempting to ward off an outburst. "I'm really sorry. I can't do this anymore. I won't. Don't act so surprised — we've both been miserable for a long time. It's time." She rose and carried the breakfast dishes to the kitchen. "It's getting late," she said quietly. "I have to get going."

"OK," he said. "You can't say I didn't try. I did my best. I think you're making a big mistake."

She listened to the masculine sounds of his leaving: the metallic clicking of the car door, the heavy clunk of its closing, the slow rumble of the garage door. Only then did she feel herself relax.

Chapter Sixteen

Three hours later, Eleanora fairly flounced into the B&J Restaurant and Lounge, tossing a cheery hello to the bartender and proceeding to the kitchen, where she found her father and Buster.

"Reporting for duty, boss," she said, smartly saluting both men.

"Well," said her father, taking a step back to appraise his daughter, "you're full of vim and vigor today."

"I am. I am. Today I am free!"

"Already?"

"Well," she laughed, taking off her coat, "not exactly. But I feel like a great weight has been lifted off my shoulders. I feel lighter and younger. I'm a new person."

"What happened?" asked Buster, "you win the lottery?"

"No, Buster, even better than that. Thanks to my father, I won a lawyer who is going to get me a divorce."

"I never saw anybody so happy about getting a divorce," he said, somewhat befuddled.

Eleanora's face relaxed into a more serious mien. "I know there'll be some problems ahead, some tough times. But today the sun is shining and I am flying. Anyway," she said, turning to her father, "I'm ready to begin work."

Joe could not stop beaming. He introduced his daughter to the waiters and the busboys, and began some preliminary training. When the lunchtime crowd had thinned, Eleanora filled him in on her consultation with Carmella Rotundo and he gave her a few more practical suggestions. On the way home, she stopped and bought three cellphones. Both Carmella and her dad had independently come up with this idea. She chose the cheapest plan for her and the kids to keep in touch with each other.

Eleanora arrived home in time to throw something together for supper and talk briefly to Julie before she left for work. Both kids were delighted with the phones, but Zach, especially, was saddened to hear she planned to move out the next day. Aaron had not yet come home by the time she left for choir practice.

After rehearsal, Peter wandered over to Eleanora as she gathered up her music. "You look absolutely radiant tonight," he told her. "Did you and Aaron make up?"

Eleanora laughed. "No, Peter, just the opposite. I saw a lawyer this morning. It's such a wonderful feeling to know someone really competent is going to take you by the hand and lead you through the valley of death. Seriously, I have every confidence in her. I feel giddy, like a six-year-old out of school. Liberty, thy name is Divorce," and she laughed again.

"I'm glad it agrees with you. It's great to see you so happy."

"Oh, I'm just starting to flap my wings. I'm more excited about the idea than the reality. I know that will hit me soon enough, but I'm enjoying the moment, anyway." She saw in his eyes that he was genuinely pleased for her, and wondered if she had been wrong to feel apprehensive about their last conversation.

"Any feedback from the board members yet, regarding their wayward pianist?"

"No, I haven't mentioned it to anybody. I think I was overreacting, Ellie. Really. I guess I was still caught up in my own anxiety about the Winters family and let it color my thinking. There's really no reason it should be a problem. Just forget anything I said about that. Please." He playfully hit himself in the side of the head, as if to knock some sense into it. "Don't mind me, I'll be all right one of these days."

Eleanora took his hand. "I'm glad to hear you say that, Peter. You had me worried. Not only that I might lose the job — I really enjoy it and I need the money — but I was concerned that you might be reluctant to stand up for me. I was afraid I was losing your support."

He looked shocked. "Eleanora, I would never abandon you. Never. Don't even think of it, not for one second. You're the one person I trusted and you stood by me. How could I ever not stand by you?"

"I'm sorry," she said. "Maybe that was my own sense of vulnerability. Anyway, I'm glad to hear you say it. It's what I wanted to believe." They gave each other a reassuring hug.

Once in her car, Eleanora got out her new toy and punched in Connie's number. This time he answered.

"Connie? It's me, Eleanora."

His voice was low and relaxed, and she heard a hint of a smile. "Well, well,

well, Eleanora. I was about to give up hope of hearing from you. How are you?"

"Oh, I'm fine. I feel like my life is a three ring circus, so much is going on — but it's exciting."

"Tell me about it," he urged. "I'll get some popcorn."

Eleanora laughed. "Oh, it's way too much for a phone call."

"Then we'll have to get together."

"Yes," she said, surprising herself, "that would be great."

"Are you free tonight?" he asked.

She looked at her watch. "Hmmm. No, not tonight. I just finished choir rehearsal and I shouldn't be getting home too late." She thought for a moment. "How about tomorrow evening?"

"Works for me. How about dinner?"

She thought for a moment. The idea of going out to dinner — with any man — brought her up short. She had no idea what she'd had in mind when she'd agreed to meet him. She hadn't thought it through. This would be a date! Without thinking, she found herself blurting out that she was separating from Aaron — so Connie would know he wouldn't be dating a married woman.

"I'm leaving Aaron," she said, "and I'm moving into Irene's condo tomorrow. I thought you should know that."

"I see," Connie said, "then this is probably an upsetting time for you. Perhaps I was hasty in suggesting dinner."

"No," she said quickly, "I would like to. Where should I meet you?"

After a moment of silence, he said, "I know Irene's place. Suppose I pick you up. Shall we say 7:00 or 7:30?"

"Seven sounds fine. I'll see you then."

"Yes," he said, "I'm looking forward to it."

Eleanora said goodnight and closed her phone. She sat for a few minutes in the dark, empty parking lot of the small suburban church and shook her head in disbelief. Then she started up her car and headed home.

Aaron was sitting in the living room when she got home. After hanging up her coat, she joined him. He put down the papers he'd been reading, and Eleanora noticed the glass of scotch on the table next to him.

"I'm leaving tomorrow," she began. "I'll be staying at Irene Duffy's place in Hoboken. I'll leave her address and phone number in case you have to reach me in an emergency." His face looked weary, as if dulled from battle fatigue.

"You'll be receiving a letter from my attorney tomorrow or the next day," she went on, "informing you that I'm suing for divorce on the grounds of mental cruelty and advising you to get an attorney." His eyebrows shot up at "mental cruelty" but he remained silent.

"I purchased cellphones for the children so they'll be able to stay in touch with each of us. I know you've been against them having their own phones, but I think they'll be necessary now to coordinate things between you and them." Eleanora expected Aaron to squawk at the extra expense, but he didn't utter a sound. "Once I get settled somewhere permanently, we can discuss what items I might need from the house."

She suggested three weekly visitation times for her to be with the kids. Nodding, Aaron reached for his glass and drank from it, sucking on one of the ice cubes.

"OK," he said. He suddenly sounded much older than his 42 years. For the first time, Eleanora observed him with detached objectivity — his thin, receding hairline, the looseness of his facial muscles, his growing paunch — and wondered why she had always ceded so much power to him. In this moment, all she saw was weakness.

Eleanora pushed herself up. "Well, I'll be here in the morning if you have any questions, and I'll talk to the kids about helping to make supper. You guys will have to work something out." There wasn't anything more to say, so she said goodnight and went upstairs to peek in on the kids, who were still up.

She reviewed with them her contact information and her planned visitation times: supper together on Thursdays, breakfast on Saturdays, and lunch on Sundays. "But the Thursday supper will start next week, not tomorrow. And we'll arrange a sleepover as soon as we can so you can see where I'm staying."

Julie tried to put a bright face on it. It was obvious they were unhappy with the turn of events, but Eleanora was deeply touched by their attempt to be gracious and supportive. She hugged each of them tightly.

"You guys know how much I love you. You know this is just temporary, until I get a permanent place. I fully intend that you guys will be with me as soon as I can arrange it. You understand, don't you? It's just that I can't stay with your father anymore." After a moment, she added, "I don't know how, but somehow, I'll make this up to you. I promise."

Chapter Seventeen

Thursday morning Eleanora had lists ready for everyone, including phone numbers where she could be reached and her new work schedule. The kids didn't say much, Aaron lingered at the table and when both children had hugged Eleanora goodbye, he was still at the table drinking an uncharacteristic third mug of coffee.

"Don't you have to be at work?" she asked, clearing off the table.

"I can go in a little late today," he answered, his voice resigned. "Ellie, I wish you would tell me why you're doing this. I really don't understand. We had a misunderstanding. People have misunderstandings all the time. Why blow it up into this? Consulting a lawyer? Moving out? Divorce? I don't get it. Help me out here. I don't know what to do or say to get you to see this more realistically."

Eleanora put the dishes back down on the table and appraised her husband. It was like looking at an optical illusion: Her vision alternated between the handsome 22-year-old college grad who had seduced her when she was 16, and this defeated sad sack across the table from her. There was so much she could say. *I could tell him my whole life story — and for what?*

"You'll make sense of this eventually in your own way. You'll never understand this from my point of view. You don't have to see things my way or agree with me. More importantly," she added, "I don't have to see things your way. Not anymore. So let's just accept that it's over. Let's try to do this without too much rancor, all right? I promise I won't try to take everything you've got. I just want what I'm legally entitled to. We'll work it out, Aaron, and you'll be free. Try to be happy about that, about being free of me. Finally. At last." She rose from her chair and brought the dishes into the kitchen.

"Aren't you going to at least tell me why?" he asked. "You don't just go around breaking up families for no reason, for Christ's sake. You saw the kids. They're miserable. Why are you doing this to us?"

She carried the dishes all the way to the sink without answering him. He got up and followed her into the kitchen.

"Ellie, please, talk to me. Why?"

She turned and stared at him. In a soft, whispery voice, she said, "Because the alternative is too terrible to imagine." Her eyes filled with tears. Avoiding his gaze, she hurried past the dining room table, still littered with the cold remains of their last breakfast together, and ran upstairs. A few minutes later she heard him drive away.

She took the luxury of lying in bed for a while, studying the ceiling. Finally, she showered, dressed, and packed some clothes. After cleaning the kitchen for the last time, she lingered over the last load of laundry, pausing over socks and underwear, tee shirts and jeans, as if they were the children she was parting from. She said a final goodbye to bushes and trees, the yellowing birches, the swing set, the house itself.

"So much to mourn," she said quietly to herself. Starting up the car, she took a long, loving look at her beautiful home. "Christ, I'm leaving this for Hoboken?" she wondered out loud to no one.

Eleanora had never been to Hoboken before. She found her way down a long, descending road from the top of the cliffs to the main street of the old riverfront community. The Palisades towered behind her and the skyline of Manhattan rose, like the Emerald City of Oz, a mile away across the Hudson River. The view was more dramatic than she had expected. The Jersey side was an old enclave of immigrants, and across the river lay Manhattan, full of magic and excitement.

After asking a number of people for directions, Eleanora found Irene's address — an early-1900s three-story bank building that had been converted. A gated parking lot next door required a coded card for entrance and exit. She approached the front of the building. Her key was required for the outside door, an inner lobby, and the small old-fashioned elevator with an accordion-style metal door. Irene's third-floor condo occupied the northeast quarter.

Entering the main room, she was dumbstruck. The sunlit expanse had formerly been an executive boardroom, with soaring 16-foot ceilings. Two outer walls were fully paneled in exotic wood and one wall housed built-in bookcases, which Irene had filled with books, records, pictures, and an astounding variety of curious mementos. The windows reached almost to the ceiling from deep windowsills. But the best part was the view: the Hudson River and Manhattan island stretching northward, and the Verrazano Bridge and New York harbor reaching southward out to the sea.

Eleanora stood transfixed. To her left was a small, modern kitchen separated from the large living space by a granite-topped counter. She immediately spied the keyboard against the northern wall, facing upriver. To her right, partitions, which did not reach to the ceiling, separated the living room from what she assumed were a bedroom, bathroom, and utility room. Large, leafy green plants lent an exotic atmosphere to the space.

After hauling her belongings upstairs, Eleanora made herself a cup of tea and sat on one of the low windowsills, drinking in the exciting view spread out before her. She realized, in terms of actual distance, she was probably only a few miles from her mother's apartment. Taking the PATH train, a short walk away, would transport her to downtown Manhattan in no time at all. So many possibilities! She made an effort to calm the excited flapping in her chest.

When Eleanora finished her tea, she approached the keyboard. With it's own unique sound, it contained many more possibilities than a piano. She experimented with the hymns she would play on Sunday and tried some old standards. She was excited about the possibility of playing at her father's Lounge. Next, she decided to explore the neighborhood. She delighted in spotting restaurants, coffeeshops, art galleries, food markets, laundromats, and a host of other resources. The experience of strolling leisurely, with no preset agenda, on the sidewalks of this old city — so different from suburban Leonia — reminded her of growing up in New York. She welcomed the familiar stimulation of cars and buses, bustling crowds, commerce, even the smell of exhaust fumes. *Strange,* she thought, *it feels so much like home, like where I belong.*

Realizing that her stay in Irene's condo was only temporary made her sad, but reminded her that she'd have to give serious consideration to where she would live. Carmella had asked her if she wanted Aaron to move out so she could stay in the house until the children were emancipated, but — even if it were possible — she didn't think that would be best. Maintaining the house would be expensive and would give Aaron the opportunity to wield power over her by holding up payments. Better that he had total responsibility himself for maintaining it. The children would be better off not being caught in the middle of a power struggle.

On her way back to the condo, her cellphone rang.

"Hi, Mom, it's me."

"Julie? Is everything all right?"

"Everything's fine, Mom. I just got home from school and thought I'd check in with you. What are you doing?"

Eleanora filled her daughter in on her exploration of the area surrounding Irene's condominium. Julie brought her up to date on her work schedule for the week and complained again about how Roy, her boyfriend, was being a jerk, but dismissed her mother's willingness to listen as unnecessary. They talked more about chores that Julie and her brother would have to share: laundry, cleaning, meals, and so on. Eleanora suggested that she and Zach make up a list and ask their father do the shopping.

"He's not going to go for that," Julie moaned.

"Well," mused her mother, "explore it with him. Maybe he has a better idea." While they were talking, Zachary came home and wanted to say hello, which made Eleanora smile. The short exchange was apparently enough to satisfy him, and she reminded him that they had a breakfast date for Saturday.

After practicing some more on the keyboard, she took a long, luxurious bath in Irene's immense tub. She felt like a little girl, using some of the exotic bath oils and lotions Irene had on a shelf. Indulging herself in this way was a totally new experience, something she had only read about in women's magazines or overheard other women talking about. It felt delightfully sinful. By 7:00, she was fresh and relaxed in her new surroundings. A sudden thrill shot through her when the bell rang and, in her excitement, it took a moment to figure out how to use the intercom.

Connie was waiting outside the front door. "I hope I'm not too early," he said, taking her elbow as they went down the steps to the sidewalk.

"No," she assured him, "not at all." He guided her toward a silver Mercedes coupe and opened the door for her. She gulped when she saw the red leather seats and walnut trim on the dashboard, and flashed him a quizzical look.

"It is a little low to the ground, I'll grant you that," he said. "But then again, without that, it wouldn't be the same car, would it?"

Eleanora held onto his arm as she lowered herself to the seat. Then he walked to the driver's side and slid his long, thin frame easily onto his seat.

"It's a beautiful car," she offered.

He smiled easily at her. "You have a way with understatement," he joked. "It's a beautiful machine. I love it. You can drive it later if you'd like."

"Oh, I don't think so," she said, hearing the quiet power of the engine igniting. "I'd be afraid it would run away from me, like a huge dog I couldn't hold back."

"You don't know what you're capable of until you try," he reassured her.

Without effort, Connie spun the car around and roared back up the hill she had descended earlier in the day.

"I thought we might go to a little Cuban restaurant up here in Union City. I imagined you've had a hectic day and a little place where we can enjoy some peace and quiet might be more to your liking than a restaurant with a lot of hustle and bustle."

You're amazing, she thought to herself, appraising him once again. "That's very perceptive of you." She stared at him as he drove. "I have to tell you, it's a very eerie feeling that I get with you, as if you can see right into me. I've never experienced that before."

Connie glanced at her, then returned his eyes to the road.

"No one has ever taken the time to learn who you are? You know, you're not that big a mystery, Eleanora. It's just a matter of paying some attention."

"You make me sound quite simple."

"No," he protested, "not at all. I'm sure you have complexities that will confuse me no end. I only mean that you wear your emotions right on the surface. You're a very intense and emotional woman. There's no way you can leave your home and move into a strange place without it taking a lot out of you. That's not rocket science."

Eleanora blushed. "I guess not. Still, it's not the kind of attention I'm used to."

He nodded. After a minute or so, he said, "I'm interested in hearing why you decided to leave your husband." When she didn't answer right away, he stole a glance at her.

"I'm not sure what to say," she said in response to his look. "Actually, Aaron thought you and I were having an affair." *Oh my God*, she thought, *he's going to see right through that. He's going to know that's what I'm thinking about, as if I'm asking him to have an affair with me.* She shook her head vigorously, as if to erase her thoughts.

Connie raised his eyebrows. "That must have driven him wild." He hazarded another quick look at her. "I'm surprised you're still alive."

"Why do you say that?"

"Oh, I just got the impression that your husband is used to controlling you. For you to have an affair with anybody — but especially with a black man — does he know I'm black?" Eleanora nodded. "Well," he continued, "I would imagine he took that as an ultimate threat to his claim on you. How did he react?"

"He got drunk. He got verbally abusive." After a few moments, she continued, "I decided I didn't need to take that kind of treatment anymore, that I'm entitled to more."

"You didn't waste any time," he chuckled.

"It's been coming for a long time." That image of Bethann standing in her doorway flashed though her mind again, the bleary red eyes, the slight quiver of the lips, the unpleasant smell of fear and alcohol. "I didn't think it was a good idea to put it off any longer."

"I understand," he said.

They looked briefly at each other. Eleanora hadn't been paying attention to where they were going, but suddenly realized that Connie was pulling into a parking lot.

"There's a little place just around the corner from here. Do you like Cuban food?"

"I don't think I've ever had it," she admitted.

Connie helped her out of the car, and they walked arm in arm to Bergenline Avenue, where the unassuming restaurant was located. Seated at a table with a pink tablecloth and a glass top, Connie asked if he could order her a Mojito, a traditional Cuban cocktail. She found the minty flavor delicious and had to exercise some self-discipline to not drink it too quickly.

For an appetizer, they ordered *yuca con mojo*, prepared in a sauce of garlic and lime juice. Connie ordered paella for her and chicken breast stuffed with shrimp and crabmeat for himself, and they agreed on a white wine. In the course of the leisurely dinner, Eleanora told him the history of her marriage to Aaron, the saga of Todd, and her determination to pursue her interest in music, and the piano in particular. She found him understanding and perceptive. He asked probing questions and made constructive comments.

Connie revealed that his father's family had originally been slaves in Jamaica, after having been brought over from West Africa. In Jamaica, one of his ancestors worked on a sugar cane plantation and made rum. Eventually, he had been sold to the Chermant family in Louisiana. There, the family prospered.

"In 1845, when my great-great-great grandmother was about to give birth to my great-great-grandfather, Mr. Chermant gave them their freedom. Of course, they still had to work for the family, but they were considered valued employees; they were able to save enough money to purchase their own land and house. As former slaves of his, they took on the Chermant family name. That was common practice at the time." Connie explained that his ancestors had prospered throughout the generations and had eventually come to own a significant share of a very profitable rum-making business.

Many members of his family were professionals. "What may surprise you," he said with a wry smile, "is that among the black middle class, there can be a prejudice and a racism that is as virulent as any you'll find in white America. In fact, if I'm honest," he said with a slight tilting of his head, "one of the reasons I may have switched from classical music to jazz was as a rebellion against that kind of thinking."

"I'm not sure I understand."

"Well, a couple of things," said Connie. "One, for the last 150 years, my family has striven to be white. The mixture of white genes with our black ones has been highly valued. As you can see," he said, turning his palm up toward his face, "I'm not exactly light skinned. My complexion has always been a source of disappointment in my family, a mark of disgrace. You might say that I'm the black sheep of the family. And because jazz has a historical association with black musicians, by joining them I flipped the bird to my racist family. At the same time, I was welcomed into a community with whom I could identify. It's funny, so many blacks wish they could find acceptance in spite of being black — and I needed to find it because I'm black."

"This whole thing, black, white, I have so much trouble understanding it," Eleanora admitted. "Everybody is different. I don't understand what all the fuss is about."

"I guess you've never been on the receiving end of it."

"I guess not. Oh, Aaron would insult me sometimes about being Italian, but it was just his way of trying to hurt me. I figured he couldn't hate Italians so much if he married one and his own children are half Italian. But my mother never accepted anyone who is different. They not only had to be Italian, they had to be Sicilian, and even then she wouldn't fully accept them unless they came from the same village in Sicily where she was born. I decided early on that I wasn't going to be filled with hate and suspicion the way she was."

"Your father is pretty blind to race," Connie noted.

Eleanora nodded and smiled. "Being a musician, especially in jazz, he always had close friends who are black. Buster has been like a member of the family. Others too, but especially Buster."

By the time they ordered strong Cuban coffee and a deliciously sweet dessert called *bunelo*, much of the restaurant had emptied out.

"So, when am I going to hear you play? I'm assuming it might be problematic if I showed up at your church."

"There's an electric keyboard back at Irene's," she said. "We could go back there."

"I have another idea," he countered. "How would you like to see my place? I have a baby grand."

Her eyes lit up. "You do? A real baby grand?"

Connie leaned back in his chair and laughed heartily. "Oh, Eleanora, I do love your capacity for joy. Yes, I do have a baby grand — a Steinway."

"A Steinway?"

"Yes, and I'd love to hear you play. I'm not all that far from here. What do you say?"

"I'd never forgive myself if I turned down such an opportunity."

Fifteen minutes later, Connie pulled into a cavernous garage under a tall complex that sat atop the Palisades, overlooking the Hudson River and the sparkly Manhattan skyline. They took an elevator to his condo. Connie ushered her in and turned on the lights and Eleanora saw a tasteful, contemporary, expansive space. The outer wall facing the river was all glass and she made out a balcony beyond the sliding doors. The focus of the large room was the magnificent piano in beautiful rosewood. Reflected back by the wall of glass, its majesty took her breath away. The parquet floors were covered with expensive area rugs and the leather and steel furniture lent a modern and masculine atmosphere.

"It's wonderful," she gasped, "and look at the view. I don't believe it. You actually get to see this every night."

Connie took her coat and led her to the piano, where she perched tentatively on the cushioned bench.

"Think of her as a living thing," he said. "Introduce yourself, let her get used to your touch. Ask her about herself. Get to know her. Listen to her voice."

Eleanora did just that. Shy and tentative at first, she was surprised by the responsiveness of the keys, the clarity and richness of the tone. Hesitantly, she began to explore and soon found herself lost in conversation with the instrument. She was startled when Connie returned with a glass of iced tea for her and a beer for himself.

"It has such a wonderful sound," she mused. "I can't believe I'm actually doing this."

"She, not it," he corrected her gently, "and that's her voice, not just a sound. Think of her as alive. She has a personality all her own. She deserves to be appreciated for who she is and not expected to be something she's not."

Eleanora nodded in agreement. "That reminds me of me," she said.

"Yes," he agreed, "now, just let your fingers and the keys interact. There's a reason we call it *playing*."

Connie relaxed into one of the steel and leather chairs and closed his eyes, which gave Eleanora the permission and freedom to explore. Her fingers roamed up and down the keyboard, at first practicing scales and then little snatches of a variety of pieces before she found herself getting into something longer and more demanding.

"You have a very nice touch," he said quietly as he sat down on the bench to her left. "Let's try something together." He started playing some chords in a slow, leisurely rhythm. She looked at him with a puzzled expression. "Just interact," he coaxed. "Let your fingers play with mine."

Maybe it was because she knew he was a jazz pianist. Maybe it was the insistence of the repetition of his chords, but she started to hit notes almost randomly until she was reminded of a song. Before long, she was playing the melody and he was playing the rhythmic chords, but in a way that disrupted the melody and forced her to improvise.

"Yes," he said excitedly, "keep going." Eventually, they hit a point that felt like a natural ending and Connie reached across her to add a final flourish.

"Wow!" she exclaimed. "That was incredible!"

"I think you just played your first piece of jazz," he said smiling, and patted her on the shoulder.

She shook her head in disbelief. "I don't believe this. I played jazz? On a Steinway baby grand?"

"Life is full of surprises, isn't it? It's just so damned hard to predict what we're going to do."

"This whole evening has been amazing. That dinner — and now this. Connie, how can I ever thank you?"

He looked into her eyes and took her hand. "I don't want you to thank me. I didn't give you anything that you didn't give me tonight."

"I don't feel like I've given you anything," she protested.

"But you have. We each contributed something completely new and unique and unexpected. And we did it together, spontaneously. I couldn't have done it without you, nor you without me. The whole evening was that kind of experience, a little jazz riff — unplanned, unscripted, requiring two free and independent people to make it happen."

Eleanora was mesmerized by his words. His face was close to hers. She smelled the beer on his breath, saw the little pores above his trim moustache. She looked into his eyes and saw gentleness there, but also something else. She became aware of his hand holding hers. She knew she was going to kiss him even before he leaned in to her.

It was as if her mind had abandoned her — she was all sensation and feeling: his hand lightly cupping her face, his lips on hers, her body yearning toward his. There were no thoughts. He kissed her eyelids, her eyebrows, her neck, her throat. Her hands felt the texture of his shirt, the back of his neck, his hair.

She felt him pull back slightly and she opened her eyes.

"Are you sure you want to?" he asked.

"Yes," she said.

Connie took her by both hands and led her into his bedroom. It was a large room with one glass wall facing the river. He led her to the bed. Looking into her eyes, he cupped her face in his hands and kissed her more ardently. Eleanora returned his passion, frustrated at not being able to kiss him intensely enough. She felt her excitement mount as Connie began removing her clothes, unbuttoning her blouse, unzipping her skirt, unhooking her bra. She made a half-hearted attempt to undress him as well, but let herself dissolve under his experienced hands. Connie laid her back upon the bed and knelt over her, kissing and sucking her breasts, taking her nipples into his mouth. She felt his teeth stimulating them with gentle nibbles. He slid his hand under her panties and she felt his fingers inside her. She felt how wet she was, her pelvis already thrusting involuntarily against his hand. In her mind she kept repeating: oh, Connie, oh, Connie.

He rose up onto his knees and pulled her panties off, throwing them aside. She reached up and undid the front of his pants, and soon he joined her naked on the bed. A dim light slanted in from the living room and starlight shone through the wide wall of glass.

Eleanora's hunger grew. She wanted to devour him. Her hands couldn't explore him enough. His body was so different from Aaron's — lean and muscular compared to Aaron's softness. She was amazed at how light and delicate his touch was in spite of his obvious passion — and yet, the softness of his caresses was electric and scintillating. Her whole being shuddered. With delightful abandonment she gave herself to him, his kisses flowing lightly across her body like a warm spring shower, her throat and neck, her breasts, her belly. (*Oh*, she thought, *my stretch marks! He'll see them and be repulsed!*) Then she was aware that his mouth was on her, his tongue licking her. She couldn't believe he was doing this — she had read about this in novels, but Aaron had always been adamant: Oral sex was disgusting, the mother of his children could never even think about such a thing. But here was Connie kneeling over her, loving her whole body, making love to her with his mouth.

Eleanora lost track of how many orgasms she had. He spread her legs open wide and entered her. She clasped herself to him and held him tight, contracting around his erection and squeezing it as she returned his thrusts. Then she felt a change and recognized that he was about to come. Squeezing his buttocks, she pulled him deeper into her and felt him throbbing. She clamped down and held him within her, feeling his spasms until he came to rest upon her. They lay quiet and spent, wrapped together.

"You OK?" he asked.

"Um hmm," she answered.

"Are you getting chilly?"

She nodded. "But I don't want you to move. I want to keep you inside me."

"I don't want to move either." He reached out and pulled the bedspread toward them, covering them against the coolness.

"This evening has been one surprise after another," she sighed.

"Were you really surprised that we made love?"

She turned her head slightly to see him better, and extended herself for a kiss.

"Not really. If I'm honest with myself, I was hoping we might, though I never thought it would be anything like this."

"Neither did I."

"What you did before, going down on me ..."

"Yes?"

"That was the first time for me."

"Nobody ever went down on you before?"

"Aaron's the only man I've ever been with. He wouldn't even consider it. He thinks oral sex is disgusting."

"Even if he is on the receiving end?"

Eleanora nodded.

"So you've never performed fellatio?"

Eleanora shook her head. "I've thought about it. Would you like me to?"

Connie laughed so hard that he slid out of her. He rolled over onto his back and pulled her onto him, rearranging the blankets so they remained covered.

"What's so funny?" she asked, afraid she had done something wrong.

"Oh, Eleanora. You're so precious. You ask me if I would like you to suck my dick? Sweetheart, no man is ever going to say no to that kind of invitation."

"Aaron has. More than once."

"Aaron must have some kind of major mental illness. I'm beginning to wonder what kind of man he is. Listen, Eleanora, I want you to feel free to just do whatever you want to do, whenever you want to do it. And I don't only mean going down on me. I also mean telling me what you'd like me to do to you."

She kissed him again and let herself luxuriate in their bodily smells. She became aware that the musky smell on Connie's moustache was from her own juices.

"Do you like the smell of me?" she asked.

"I like the smell of you, and the taste of you, and the feel of you, and the ...
"

"I'm serious," she said, poking him.

"So am I."

"I'm not a young woman anymore. I've had three children."

"So?"

"You're not going to forget about me tomorrow, are you? I'm not just a one-night stand, am I?"

He took her by the shoulders and raised her up so they could look into each other's face. "Eleanora, I'm going to be 51 years old soon. I don't go chasing after schoolgirls anymore. In fact, I don't go chasing after women, period. Life is slowing down for me. I'm more mellow now than I used to be. Nothing is as urgent as it once was," he paused. "You came along. We met. There was an instantaneous attraction — on both our parts. I would never do anything to insult or hurt your father. He's been a decent friend for a long time and he's been wonderful to Irene, who's been a dear friend of mine. I'm saying this to reassure you that I did not pursue you lightly. I hoped that you'd be available for some kind of relationship. I hoped we'd have enough in common to form a relationship of some substance, but I didn't need us to end up in bed together. When you left your husband, that only made it easier for us to explore whether there's anything here for us. It gave us a chance to discover if we could make some good music together."

She smiled at his reference to her first effort at improvisation. Connie continued in a serious tone. "I'm not going to tell you that I love you — not until I know you well enough and I'm sure that's what I really feel. But, bottom line? This is not a one-night stand. You are not just a roll in the hay. I am very attracted to you — and I was even before you asked me if you could give me a blowjob."

Chapter Eighteen

The first thing Eleanora did when she awoke on Friday morning in Irene's luxurious queen-size bed was call Julie.

"Where have you been, Mom? Are you all right?"

"Of course I'm all right. What do you mean?"

"Zachary and I were trying to reach you all last night. We left messages on your voicemail. Didn't you get them?"

"I'm sorry, honey. I must have turned the phone off by mistake. I'm not even sure how to check the voicemail. Why were you calling? Is everything OK?"

"Nothing major. Zach and I just had some questions about the laundry. We finally figured it out. We're OK, but Dad isn't doing too well."

"What happened?"

"Oh, I don't know. More irritable than usual, giving orders, you know," she lowered her voice, "and I think he's drinking."

Eleanora thought for a moment. She didn't want to overreact, but didn't want to ignore a potential problem either. "Let's give him some time to adjust. It's natural for him to be upset. But if you're concerned, call me. I promise I won't turn the phone off again."

"OK, Mom. Zach wants to say hello."

"All right, honey. Love you."

Zachary got on the phone and they chatted for a few minutes. Her heart went out to him. At 15, he still needed his mother — even if he tried to deny that to himself. She apologized again for having turned off her phone and reassured him that she loved him.

"I can't wait until I see you guys for breakfast tomorrow," she said. "I really miss you."

After closing her phone, Eleanora lay back in bed, delighting in the reflected sunlight shimmering on the ceiling. Images of Connie flashed through her mind, and she marveled at the sudden about-face her life had made.

Eleanora glided into the Lounge with an enthusiastic greeting for everyone. Working made her feel like an adult. When the lunch crowd thinned out, she sat down with her father and Buster.

"I have to tell you, Papa, I went out to dinner last night with Connie."

"Duke?"

Eleanora nodded, a smile on her face.

"I guess you had a good time, judging from that smile on your puss."

"We had a wonderful time. I just wanted you to know, that's all."

"Hey," her father said, "you're a big girl. You see who you want. Like I told you, Duke is a good person. Just use your head. Take your time. You know what I'm telling you? Don't rush into things. That's all I'm saying."

Buster put a hand on her arm to get her attention. "I know I don't have any business butting in here, but your Daddy's right. It's been a long time since you went out with a man. Duke is as good as you can find. I'd be thrilled if any of my nieces went out with him. Just don't be too quick to give your heart away, that's all. Give it time, you understand?"

"I know," she reassured them both. "It may be a long time since I've gone out with anyone, but I know what you're saying. Please don't worry. I just wanted you to know."

"Well," her father said, "for both your sakes, I hope it works out. If it does, I couldn't be happier. Just don't feel that it has to. Don't try to make something happen."

"OK, Papa. I'm 37, not 17. I'll be all right."

"I know, pussycat. It's just that I want you to be happy, and I wasn't around all that much when you were 17. I'm just getting my two cents in, that's all." He gave her a hug and a kiss. Eleanora glowed inside. She felt comforted having their stamp of approval.

That evening, as she was leaving for choir rehearsal, she received a call on her cellphone.

Aaron's voice surprised her. "I wonder if you can come over tonight after choir practice. I'm going to see an attorney tomorrow morning and wanted to talk to you first. I think it's important."

Eleanora thought. She had hoped to see Connie, but they had no firm plans.

"Let me think about it, Aaron. I'll call you when practice is finished."

"It won't take long — 15 minutes tops. What do you say?"

"I want to think about it. I'll call you in a couple of hours and let you know."

At the rehearsal, two of the choir members said they'd heard about her split-up and offered to help if she needed anything. Eleanora marveled at how quickly word had spread, and suddenly wondered if anyone knew she had gone out with Connie — and what they'd say if they knew. She expected shock and horror, especially from her kids, who would have a great deal of difficulty accepting her dating somebody other than their father. What would they think of her being held or kissed by another man — let alone an African American? Would they accept the possibility of their mother actually having sex with another man? Eleanora pondered it for a moment. Did she know anyone — outside of her father, Buster, and Irene — who would be comfortable with her dating Connie? She didn't think she knew such a person, and the idea astounded her.

She would take her father's advice and go slowly, but she had no doubt that at some point she'd have to tell her children — not only tell them, but introduce them to Connie. And how would *he* deal with that? How would he feel having them as a new part of his life? It dawned on her that she had no idea if Connie had children or even if he'd ever been married. There was a lot she didn't know, and she was only becoming aware of the extent of her ignorance.

After practice, Peter asked how she was doing. She shared that a couple of the choir members already knew of her separation.

"I know," he nodded, "three or four people must have called me today, asking if it was true and cluck-clucking about what a shame it was. Don't worry about it. Some people don't have anything else to do. Just ignore it." Then he thought for a moment. "But don't be surprised if people start acting differently around you." Eleanora looked at him quizzically. "You are now an available woman," he said. "For some men, that translates into a loose woman — and for some women, it means competition."

"Right!" she gave a wan smile. "Me as the *competition.*"

"I'm serious," said Peter. "Don't be surprised at some of the looks you may get. And don't let it bother you. That's just the way some people are."

Eleanora nodded as she gathered up her things. "Thanks for the advice," she said.

"You've got a place to stay?"

"Luckily," she said, getting her coat on, "a friend of my father's is letting me use her place until things settle down. For now, it works great."

"Good. Take care," he called after her as she left. In the car, she tried Connie again, but got no answer, so she called Aaron and told him she'd stop by.

It felt odd to stand outside her own front door in the chill night air and recognize that it was no longer her home. Awkwardly, she rang the bell. She heard running feet and Julie appeared, giving her a big hug and welcoming her into the familiar space. Aaron stood in the living room doorway and merely nodded in her direction before returning to his chair. Eleanora let herself enjoy the long hug with her daughter, then entered the living room and sat down on the sofa opposite her husband.

"You want a cup of tea or something?" he asked, making no effort to rise.

"There's no need to bother," she said, waiting for him to proceed.

"I've been thinking," he began, "if we're going to separate, we'll have to come to an agreement about how to manage money ..." his voice trailed off and he glanced up at her from the sheaf of papers in front of him.

"Yes?"

"Well, I've written some things down that we should be able to agree on. I thought it would save time and expense if you'd look them over and sign them so I can bring them with me to the lawyer tomorrow."

"You want me to sign off on your suggestions tonight?"

"Yeah. It'll save us both some time and money. They're reasonable things, Ellie. There's no reason for you not to agree."

"Well," she said, shrugging her shoulders. "I'm just thinking what my attorney would say. She'd wonder what I was paying her for."

"That's the whole point, El. We don't have to let other people tell us how to run our lives. We're two intelligent people. We're perfectly capable of deciding these things on our own. Why should we pay them to write letters back and forth to each other when we can do it ourselves?"

"I tell you what, Aaron. Give me a copy of what you've written and I'll bring it with me when I see my attorney on Monday. I'm not signing anything without her approval."

Aaron shook his head. "Ellie, you're not listening to me. Just read them and you'll see how logical and fair they are. There's no reason for you not to agree."

"And I may very well agree to them, Aaron. I'm not saying they're not fair or reasonable. I'm just saying they could be written on clay tablets and brought to me by Moses and I wouldn't sign off on them until my lawyer says it's OK."

"But, El ..."

"You'll just have to respect my wishes on this," she said firmly. "I'm not signing anything without my attorney's approval. Period. Now, if you want to give me a copy, fine. Otherwise your lawyer can send it to my lawyer." She gathered her coat and stood up.

"You're being unreasonable and disrespectful."

"What?"

"You heard me. Once again you're putting me down, implying that either I'm stupid and incapable of knowing what's best for us, or that I'm devious and trying to screw you."

"I'm not implying anything. I just don't feel comfortable signing anything without the approval of my attorney. That's not an unreasonable position, Aaron. I'm not going to let you bully me into doing something I'm not comfortable with. Give me a copy and I'll review it."

As he shook his head in frustration, it was clear to Eleanora that he had only the one copy he'd expected her to sign. She was amazed at his arrogance, his sense of entitlement.

Aaron disappeared into the kitchen and it registered with Eleanora that he might be making himself a drink.

"Don't forget," she called to the kids as she left, "my phone is on. Call if you need me, and I'll see you tomorrow."

She had just climbed into bed when her phone rang. It was Connie.

"Hi," she whispered, forgetting for the moment that there was no one else with her, no kids or husband to be awakened. "I tried calling you earlier."

"I know," he said. She heard noise in the background. "A friend of mine asked if I could fill in for him on a gig in New York. We're on a break and I thought I'd try you. How are you?"

"So so," she answered. "I had a little to-do with Aaron, but I'm OK." After a moment, she added, "I miss you."

"That's my kind of girl," he joked.

"I was hoping I'd get to see you tonight." Connie was silent and Eleanora heard only background chatter and laughter. "Connie?"

"I'm here. I was just thinking. Of course I'd love to see you too, but I'm not sure how. We won't finish here until early in the morning."

"Oh," she sighed. She was disappointed and worried that he might be losing interest in her. "How about tomorrow afternoon? I don't have to be out to my father's until about 5:00."

"Wonderful. That works out perfectly."

"Should I come over to your place?"

"Yes, indeed," he said, the customary smile evident in his voice. Eleanora turned out the light, imagining that he was in bed with her. She fell asleep smiling.

Chapter Nineteen

As Eleanora pulled into the driveway, Julie and Zachary burst out the front door and into the car, arguing as usual over who had the front seat. The transformation in her son made her anxious. While she relished the attention, she worried that he might be feeling abandoned.

"Smooches!" she yelled. "Mama wants smooches." And smooches she got.

"Where are we going?" Julie asked.

"I was thinking about The Forum," she said. "Unless you guys have someplace special in mind."

"Forum's great," Zach volunteered.

"Dad left before you came," Julie confided. "He said he was going to the lawyer's."

"How is it going at home?"

Zachary and Julie appeared reluctant.

Finally, Zachary spoke. "Dad and Julie had a big fight last night after you left."

Julie rolled her eyes. Eleanora looked at her daughter questioningly. "What happened? Tell me."

"He was just letting off steam," Julie told her. "It was no big deal."

Eleanora waited for more, but Julie remained quiet. "If there's an issue, then I need to know so I can deal with it. Now tell me what happened."

Julie relented. Aaron had been drinking — she didn't know how much — and he started berating her about her mother.

"What did he say?" Eleanora wanted to know.

"I don't remember exactly. Just some crap about how you were going to try to take him for everything and you weren't really interested in us, you just wanted to get even. It was crazy. I didn't pay attention really."

Zachary practically jumped out of his seat. "What do you mean, you didn't pay attention? You were screaming at him like crazy! I thought he was going to knock you through the wall."

Eleanora interrupted them. "Wait a minute, guys. Hold on."

Overwhelmed by the scene the kids were describing, Eleanora pulled the car into a nearby parking lot. "This is more serious than I had realized," she began. "Your father's drinking too much and taking out his anger on you. I don't like this one bit."

She thought for a minute, trying to calm down. The firmness in her voice got the kids' attention. "I remember one of the women in the choir had a husband who physically abused her. She was advised to have an escape plan ready in case of an emergency. I don't want to blow this out of proportion, but it's better to be safe than sorry." They nodded.

"I want each of you to pack a small bag of clothes — underwear, socks, sweats, whatever. Always keep your phone with you. Keep 10 or 20 dollars stashed away in case you need it for anything. And talk to your best friend — find someplace you can run to in the middle of the night if you have to." They agreed.

"I'll talk to your father. Maybe he'll agree to move out and let me back in. I don't know. I never thought he'd react this way." Eleanora looked at her children. "Will you do what I said?" They nodded. "Good. Maybe none of it will be necessary, but just in case, it's good to have a plan, right?"

They sat silently for a few moments. "I'm proud of you both, for standing up for yourself and for each other. I'm sorry that I've caused such a mess. I didn't mean for you guys to have to deal with anything like this."

Eleanora started the car up again and pulled out into the traffic.

"Mom," Julie ventured uneasily, "what's this with the musician Dad keeps going on about? I don't understand that at all." Julie looked pleadingly at her mother, as if willing it not to be true.

"When I went to dinner at Grandpa's last Sunday," Eleanora said calmly, "I met one of the musicians, a jazz pianist. His name is Duke Chermant, but his friends call him Connie." She told them how Aaron had seen Connie's phone number and jumped to conclusions. After she'd moved out, Connie asked her to dinner. "That's the first time I've been out with him — or anyone. And yes, he is black and he's very nice. And your grandpa likes him very much, and so do I."

It was Zachary who responded first. "So you're dating this guy?"

"We went to dinner. If that means I'm dating him, then I guess I am." After a moment's silence, she turned to Zachary.

"How do you feel about me going out with someone other than your father?"

He made a face. "It feels weird, Mom. I guess once you and Dad get divorced it would be OK, but I don't know. It doesn't feel right."

"It is strange, Mom," Julie added, "but kind of cool, too. I like the idea of you maybe finding someone who really loves you."

Eleanora pulled into the parking lot of the diner. "But what about my going out with a black man?"

Julie shrugged. "Personally, I never met a black guy who I wanted to go out with, but if I did, I don't see the problem. We have all these Asians in school. Half of Leonia is Korean or Japanese. I don't have a problem with it. If the guy is cute, what's the problem?"

Eleanora smiled at her daughter's priorities. Connie was more than just cute. He was handsome and educated and talented and sexy.

"How about you, Zach? Does it make a difference to you whether I go out with someone who is not white?"

He shook his head. "I don't believe the two of you. It must be a girl thing or something."

"Oh, Zach," his sister chided him, "you mean you don't have any fantasies at all about any of those Korean girls in your classes? They're adorable."

He blushed and sat up defensively. "That's different!" he yelled. "We're talking about our mother."

"OK, OK," Eleanora said, reaching between them. "Look, it's far too early to talk about my dating. I just went out with Connie once. Who knows what's going to happen? But I promise you guys, I'll take things slow and I'll be discreet. I don't want to do anything to embarrass you or make you uncomfortable. Meanwhile," she added, "I don't see any good coming from your mentioning this to your father."

"That's all he'd need," said Julie.

After a moment, Zachary shook his head. "I don't even want to think about it."

During breakfast, Eleanora luxuriated in watching her children — young adults, really — bantering easily without the tension their father's presence usually engendered. It was obvious that they felt more free. Would it have been possible, she wondered, to have been more assertive with Aaron? Could she have stood up to him, pursued a career, advocated more effectively for their children?

"You know, guys, this business of your Dad and me separating — I think all of us, including him, will learn a lot from it. You'll see — we're going to be stronger for it."

"I don't think Dad needs to get any stronger," said Zach, deadpan.

"I know what you mean, Zach, but you're wrong. I don't think your father really feels strong — that's why he's coming down hard on all of us. He's got to prove something."

"Well," said Zach, shaking his head, "he doesn't need to prove it to me. Let him find someone else to prove it to."

"I don't know, Zach," said Julie quietly. "You stood up to him pretty well last night."

Zach smiled at her, puffing out his chest. "That's true," he said, nodding thoughtfully.

Eleanora made plans to pick them up for lunch the next day after she finished playing at church. They hoped this could become a regular schedule: breakfast on Saturday, lunch on Sunday, and dinner on Thursday. Hopefully, Aaron wouldn't object.

Julie asked if she had plans to go out again with Mr. Chermant. Eleanora fudged.

"No," she answered, "we'll just wait and see what happens."

It was a little before 11:00 when she dropped her children off. She made one stop before driving to Connie's. When she exited the elevator on the 18th floor, he was there to greet her. She looked into his smiling face and stretched up to kiss him, one arm around his neck, the other holding a little white box.

"What have you got there?" he asked, as curious as a child.

"Just something I picked up at the bakery on the way here."

"Umm, sweets for your sweet."

"Something like that," she laughed.

They were naked within minutes. Making love in the middle of the day was a new experience for her. The bright daylight flooding in through the expansive windows made her feel exposed, as if she was on display for all of New York City — and she was surprised to discover that she enjoyed flaunting her sexuality to the world.

The openness also made her more keenly aware of her body's imperfections: stretch marks on her belly, thighs turning flabby, a softening of her breasts, skin imperfections like moles and discolorations. But after a few moments, these self-conscious doubts were washed away by Connie's impassioned caresses.

This time, as he worked his way down her body from her mouth to her throat, her breasts, her belly, he swung himself around to straddle her head, then finally lowered his mouth to her wet and swollen clitoris. His erection hung over her and she reached for him, kissing and sucking just as she had read about. Having him in her mouth felt like an accomplishment! She was finally experiencing something she had always been curious about, and it felt like an initiation, like losing her virginity. She moved against his tongue, echoing his rhythmic thrusting between her lips. She felt his buttocks tighten and knew he was about to come in her mouth. After a momentary hesitation — what would it be like? — she let herself be carried along by her passion, her own orgasms leaving her too weak to worry.

She grabbed his buttocks and felt him gush into her mouth. Swallowing reflexively, she continued licking his penis even as it began to lose some of its hardness. After a few moments, she crawled up to nestle in his arm. Eleanora discovered that she liked their smells and tastes. Just to be sure, she inserted a finger into her vagina, swabbing up some of her own juices, and brought it to her own mouth. She not only liked the taste and smell of it, but was surprised that sucking her finger felt good.

"What are you doing?" he asked.

"I was curious what I taste like."

"What do you think?"

"I like it," she giggled. "God, does that make me weird? Am I some sort of pervert?"

Connie chuckled. "You're wonderful, you know that? You're so open to new experiences. No, I don't think you're weird. You do taste and smell good. Not every woman does."

She raised her head to look at him. "I guess you've had a lot of experience."

"Well, we don't need to get into a numbers game here. Let's just say I've had my share and everybody is different."

After a moment, she asked, "Did I do it right?"

"You mean did you do a good job of sucking my cock?" She blushed and nodded. "You can say it, you know. *Cock* is a good word. It has that hard, heavy sound of an engorged penis, doesn't it?"

She nodded. "So, did I do a good job of sucking your cock?"

He laughed out loud. "Yes!" he shouted. "Yes you did."

They both fell into laughing. "Listen," he said, more seriously, "there's nothing magic about words. I certainly don't want to tell you how to speak. I just want you to be yourself, and tell me if there's something you're not comfortable with."

Eleanora hugged him. Snuggled against his chest contentedly, she reveled in his kindness. Aaron was often grumpy and sullen, argumentative, overbearing — which left her feeling stupid or neurotic. Connie gave her the space to participate, to observe her own experience. The thought aroused her again, and she glanced at Connie's flaccid penis. Smiling to herself, she took hold of it and watched it grow, feeling it swell, expanding to fill her hand and coming to full bloom. She looked at Connie and saw the smile on his face. Rising up, she straddled him and slid him into her.

Eleanora was sitting at the glass kitchen table, his robe swimming around her like an exotic caftan, when Connie emerged from the bedroom in a sweat suit, fresh from a shower.

"What's this?" he asked.

"Just some Italian pastries I picked up. I thought we might want a snack."

"You mean you thought we might work up an appetite?"

She grinned. "I didn't want to go rummaging around your kitchen, or I would have made you some coffee."

He produced a pot and began making espresso. "Listen," he said slowly, "I hadn't thought about it until I was showering, but I've got a recording date next month in Paris. How would you like to go with me?"

"What?" Eleanora's eyes widened in disbelief. She tried to talk but could only sputter.

Connie smiled as he brought two small cups to the table. A sliver of lemon peel rested in each saucer next to a small demitasse spoon. Her mouth was still open in disbelief as he brought the brass espresso pot to the table and filled their cups.

"Paris? Are you serious?"

"Of course I'm serious. I didn't think of it before because it's still a few weeks away. But yes, I'll be in Paris for three or four days and then I thought I'd hop down to Florence for a couple of days — maybe seven or eight days all together."

"But how could I?. My job — jobs actually — and my kids. And I could never afford it ..."

"Well, it would be no cost to you, unless of course you decided to pick up some souvenirs for your kids. And it would only be for a week. Wouldn't you like to see Paris? Florence?"

"Of course I would," she stammered, "but I couldn't — could I?"

He put some sugar into his coffee and stirred, then took a bite of one of the pastries.

"Umm. This is good. Does it have a name?"

Eleanora shook her head. "No. I mean yes, probably. I don't know. I can't think. Connie, are you sure?"

"That I'd like to have you with me in Europe? I'm quite sure. How about you?"

"Oh, Connie, I'd love to, but it just feels like such a big — I don't know. It's like it's too much, something I'm not supposed to accept. I can't grasp it yet."

"OK. Just think about it."

"Everything is moving so fast," she mused. "My whole life feels so different, so new, like I'm just coming alive. It's raw and overwhelming."

The faces of Julie and Zachary flashed before her and she thought of their conversation earlier that day. Could she really go traipsing off with Connie to France and Italy? Could she keep that a secret? Should she? What if Aaron found out? How would that affect their separation agreement, or her chance for joint custody? She'd have to talk to Carmella — she didn't want to burden Connie with any of these concerns. Maybe they would amount to nothing.

"Connie," she said, sitting back after finishing the pastry and espresso, "do you have children? You haven't spoken much about your past."

"No," he said, "no children and no ex-wives. My mother and father live down in Louisiana, and so do my older brother and his family. My baby sister and her family are just across the river there," he said, pointing with his chin to the Upper West Side of Manhattan.

He looked at her inquisitively. "You concerned about your kids?"

She looked away, toward the city where he'd indicated his sister lives. Eleanora remembered now that he'd mentioned her — a physician, living on West End Avenue with a view of the Hudson. She had a fleeting image of her looking out her window and watching them make love.

"Can you and your sister see each other's places?" she asked.

"I don't think so. Maybe with a telescope, but there are probably buildings in the way." She nodded thoughtfully. "So," he continued, "what about your kids?"

"I don't know," she said softly. Suddenly she felt sad. She knew he could see her eyes filling up. "I don't know," she shook her head. "I was so happy a minute ago. Now, all of a sudden, reality is flooding in on me."

"Does it all have to do with your kids?"

"Maybe," she acknowledged, "maybe that's it."

Eleanora recalled what Julie and Zach had told her about their confrontation with their father. *Another thing to discuss with Carmella.* She was reluctant to discuss Zach's discomfort about her dating Connie.

"The kids had a confrontation with Aaron last night," she confided. "I'm worried that he could get violent."

"You think he'd hurt them?"

"I wouldn't have thought so before, but I think he's drinking more than he should. I don't know."

"Well," Connie said as he carried their plates to the sink, "worrying about their physical well-being is understandable. But that's not what's making you feel sad, is it?"

Eleanora had trouble maintaining eye contact. She shook her head and felt her eyes fill up again. "Oh, Connie! This is all so new and already I'm afraid I'm going to lose you," she said. He handed her a clean handkerchief. As she unfolded the big, white square, it reminded her of when she was a little girl. Her father's handkerchief always looked so big and protective, so different from her mother's delicately embroidered useless ones.

He reached over to hold one of her hands, but she pulled it back.

"I'm sorry. I'm just too sensitive or something."

"Are you afraid that your children are going to come between us?"

Her eyes filled up again and her lips began to quiver. She gathered the courage to look at him. "They're concerned — well, mostly Zach, I think — about me dating. I know it's something they'll get used to. But Aaron has been harassing them with so much bullshit, pardon my language, about you and me having an affair, that he's got them focused on it. I told them that you and I went out to dinner once, but if I go away with you — to Paris of all places — then won't it look like Aaron was right? That I really had been cheating on him?"

She threw her hands up in frustration. "I don't want to embarrass the kids and I don't want to give Aaron anything to use against me, but I also don't want anything to come between us." These last words came out haltingly in sobs. Connie came around the table and pulled her up to an embrace.

"Hey, everything is going to be all right. Relax. One step at a time. You and your kids come first. That's the priority. If it doesn't work out for you to come with me this time, there will be other times. Don't worry."

She wiped her eyes. His arms felt strong and reassuring. She looked up and he bent to kiss her.

"My God," she gasped when their mouths parted, "you're getting me all excited again."

"Hold on," he said smiling, but with a strained look on his face, "I'm not as young as I used to be."

Eleanora laughed. "I didn't really mean we should make love again. At least I don't think that's what I meant ..." She felt more calm. The idea of her being too much for Connie to handle buoyed her spirits. She had never felt so sexy, so full of power, so much a woman.

While showering, Eleanora visualized the two of them at the famous Paris tourist spots: bridges over the River Seine, the Eiffel Tower, the Arch de Triumph, the Louvre. She saw herself strolling along the Champs-Elysee arm in arm with Connie. She thought of photographs she'd seen of Florence — the red-tiled roofs, the rolling Tuscan hills — and imagined picnics of cheese and olives and fresh loaves of Italian bread with local wine. She saw them wandering through museums, along the historic Po River, over the ancient Ponte Vecchio — and all of it in the company of Connie. She imagined making love in romantic *pensiones* overlooking the ancient city.

But what about Zach and Julie? How would they react if they knew she was going away with Connie? Of course they'd know that she and Connie were sharing a hotel room. How could she deny that? And how would Aaron react? What would he do to punish her?

But if fear of reprisal from Aaron and her children was going to keep her from living her own life, then why endure the hardships of divorce? *And if I'm afraid of upsetting the kids or Aaron, will I be able to maintain a relationship with Connie — or any man?*

Emerging from the shower, she heard Connie playing at the piano. Again, she marveled at his skill, and shook her head in embarrassment at how amateurish her playing must sound to him. Who was she kidding? She'd never be able to improvise like that. Compared to him, she was just a naïve, no-talent beginner. Eleanora plopped down on the bed and bent over to slip on her shoes. If she was consumed by fearful doubt, who would want to spend two minutes with her anyway — especially a free spirit like Connie? By the time she entered the living room, she had sunk into hopeless dejection.

Connie was playing "Our Love Is Here to Stay."

He winked at her. "You've got me thinking of all these wonderful old romantic love songs," he said.

"Really?" she asked somewhat listlessly.

"Eleanora, she always wants some *more-a*," he sang.

"Don't," she said.

He looked at her more seriously. "What's the matter? Still upset about Paris?"

"Not just that," she said, leaning against the piano and caressing its lustrous rosewood finish. "It's everything. I've got so much baggage, so many problems to work out. You're free — you can fly off to wherever you want, whenever you want. I feel like I've never been out of my front yard, except twice to Disney World with the kids. I just know you're going to tire of me."

He patted the bench beside him. "Here, sit down next to me," he said. "Now, I'll grant you, some of what you say is true. You and I are in different stages of our lives. You've got shit to contend with that I don't. I've deliberately lived my whole life so I would never have to deal with that shit. I grew up with so many rules, you wouldn't believe. Your Catholic school and your overprotective mother had nothing on the restrictions I grew up with. I was black, so I couldn't do this. I was a Chermant, so I couldn't do that. I was a prodigy, so I had to do whatever. And I was Baptist, so I couldn't do anything. It never stopped. You may not be aware of it, but being black in this society is to be constantly aware of rules about what you're supposed to do or not do. So the one overriding principle of my adult life is to be free," he said firmly. "Nobody is going to tell me what I have to do or can't do or should do. Nobody. No man or woman, white or black."

He paused to compose himself.

"One of the things that appeals to me is that you have dreams of your own, needs of your own, a life you want desperately to live. I know you're attracted to me. But, Eleanora, the last thing I want is to possess you or for you to possess me. I want to share music, art, dinners, lovemaking with you — within the context of freedom. So I'm not concerned if you can't do Paris with me, or LA, or New Orleans. There'll be plenty of other opportunities. And if you can't get away, it confirms for me that you are a separate individual with your own life. It's OK. When you pay attention to things in your own life, it's like giving me a gift of freedom."

Eleanora nodded. She did understand. She also realized that she'd unwittingly assumed Connie would be a replacement for Aaron. She hadn't consciously thought about it, but she'd entertained an expectation that she would still be a housewife — only with someone who would also be her lover. He'd court her, take her on dates, love her generously — and nurture her children. But she saw more clearly now that was not what Connie envisioned. He wanted a lover, a companion, a soul mate — but without the restrictive responsibilities of marriage. He didn't want a housewife. And, she began to realize, she didn't really want to be one anymore.

Connie resumed speaking. "Eleanora, I'm as new to this as you are. You won't believe this, but it's true. You're the first white woman I've ever dated."

She looked at him skeptically.

"It's true," he said. "I've had sex with white women, of course. But I've never gone out to dinner with a white woman, as we did the other night. I've never allowed myself to think about getting into a relationship, a real relationship, with anyone before — black or white, or red or yellow for that matter. So, I'm on new ground here myself. I don't know how this is going to work out for either of us. Maybe it won't work out at all. Maybe there'll be too many problems."

He paused to consider his own words.

"Maybe it's timing, or my pushing 51. I don't know. But for the first time, I feel ready to explore something I never explored before. So you and I, we're each doing something totally new. Whatever it is, let's let it play out. Let's just explore it day by day. All right?"

"I hope I'm not too much of a big baby for you."

"I hope not too," he admitted. "And maybe I'll be too demanding, or too selfish, or insensitive, or wild. We'll just have to see."

She studied his face. "I know I don't have to tell you," she said, "in fact, you might even prefer that I don't tell you, but I'm going to say it anyway: I've already fallen in love with you. I can't help it. It just happened. You've captured my heart."

"You're right," he said, smiling his amused, twinkly smile, "I knew that. What you don't understand is, you captured mine too. So we're both showing some courage here, risking a broken heart. I don't know if you've ever had your heart broken." He looked at her questioningly. "Anyway," he continued, "it's been a long, long time for me. But I guess we're up to it. Here we are, ready to do our high-wire act — a death-defying leap into the unknown."

Grinning, Eleanora sat back to have a more encompassing view of him. "It's interesting," she said, "knowing that you're just as vulnerable as I am makes me feel better."

"Hmm," he mused, "maybe a little streak of sadism there somewhere?"

"Just a tiny one," she said, pinching his biceps.

"Ow," he yelled.

"Now, I've really got to run."

"Will I see you tomorrow?"

She shook her head. "I'm playing in church tomorrow morning, then taking the kids out for lunch, then working at the Lounge. How about Monday evening?"

"If you come here, I will cook up something fancy, New Orleans style."

"How can I refuse? Do you want me to bring anything?"

"Just your hot body," he smirked.

"As long as you're ready for it. I don't want to tax you too much."

"I am at your disposal. Grind me into the ground, if that's what you need to do."

She gazed at him tenderly. "Fat chance," she said.

Chapter Twenty

Eleanora relished her new job at the Lounge. Many of the patrons were locals who came to hear the jazz. The clientele was loyal and some of the faces had already become familiar. As the evening wore on, other musicians drifted in, some of whose names she recognized. The Lounge had a warm atmosphere and she was proud to represent her father, welcoming friends and guests into his establishment. The scene was so homey that it didn't feel like a business at all, although she soon realized what good businessmen Buster and her dad were.

She swayed to the growling, sexy rhythms of the blues group that was performing. Their energy and high spirits were infectious. During breaks between sets, her father or Buster introduced her to the musicians or to special friends or guests. Remembering names and faces came easily to her, which helped make everyone comfortable. As the musicians prepared for their last set, her father suggested she go home. It was nearly 1:00 a.m.

"You've got a big day tomorrow and you'll be back here tomorrow night. Get some rest and say hi to the kids for me when you see them."

"I will," she said, giving him a hug. "I have to tell you, I love being here with you. It's tiring and my feet are killing me, but it doesn't really feel like work. It's more like you're giving a party and I'm just helping out."

"Having you here it makes my life complete." They glanced briefly into each other's eyes and then self-consciously looked away. "Go," he said, "get some sleep."

She kissed him on the cheek. "*A domani,*" she laughed, and went to collect her coat.

The next morning, Eleanora was almost late getting to the church for her first service at 8:00. With no time to make tea before she left home, she found herself dozing during one of Peter's sermons. By the end of the service, she was tired, but looked forward to seeing Julie and Zachary. It had started to drizzle and leaves were falling on the wet streets. She knew they could be slippery, so she took extra care on the roads.

Eleanora pulled into the driveway and honked the horn, but no one emerged from the house. Finally, she got out of the car and hurried to the front door. She hadn't anticipated rain and shivered slightly as she waited for Aaron to answer the door.

"Yes?" His tone was businesslike, as if she were a salesperson.

"Hi, Aaron. I'm here to take the kids to lunch." He stared blankly. "Well, are they ready? Should I wait in the car?"

"I'm sorry, but they can't go with you now. They're cleaning their rooms." It was clear he wasn't going to invite her in to wait.

"Aaron, I don't understand. I told them I'd pick them up after work. They can clean another time."

He shook his head. "No, I told them they have to do all their chores today. You saw them yesterday for breakfast and they didn't do their chores then, so they have to do them today."

Eleanora bit her lip. Rain dripped down her face and her feet were getting soaked.

"What else are you making them do today besides clean their rooms?"

Aaron lowered his eyes with a bored expression. "Well, seeing as how you don't live here anymore, I'm not sure that's any of your business." He stood in the doorway like a Swiss Guard, holding the newspaper in one hand like a lance.

"Can they take time off for lunch or are you making them work straight through until sunset like migrant farmers?"

"Don't get nasty with me," he warned.

"Will you answer the question?"

"They'll eat when they're done. When that will be is up to them."

"Aaron, cut the crap," she said, emboldened by the unfairness. "You're punishing me through them and that stinks. I'm asking for three visits a week. They have a right to see their mother, for God's sake. Now why don't you just let them come with me? I'll have them back in an hour if cleaning is suddenly so damned important to you."

"I'm sorry, but no. I told them to have everything done by today. If they chose to let their chores go, that's not my fault. Obviously, seeing you wasn't important to them."

Aaron turned to close the door.

"Wait a minute," she said. "I'm not done yet."

"Yes?" Again, that arrogant tone. She thought he was actually looking down his nose at her.

"What happened on Friday night? The kids tell me you and Julie had a pretty intense argument."

Aaron sneered. "Your daughter has picked up some of your snotty, disrespectful traits. As their father, discipline is not only my right, but my obligation. And what goes on between them and me is not any of your business. You don't live here anymore, remember?"

"Are you serious?" Flabbergasted, she was momentarily unable to make her mouth work. "Do you really believe what you just said? Do you hear yourself?"

"I'm perfectly serious."

"No, Aaron, I know you're not that stupid. My God!" Eleanora looked around, as if pleading for some sanity or assistance from a neighbor, a passerby, God in heaven. Somebody. Finally, struggling to retain some semblance of calm, she wiped wet hair from her forehead and spoke in quiet tones through clenched teeth.

"Aaron, I am still their mother. No matter where I live, I retain the same rights and responsibilities as you do. If I ever hear that you are hurting them, that you are causing them physical or emotional harm, then you are the one who will be deprived of parental prerogatives. You hear me? I'm warning you. Lay off those kids. Stop filling their heads with nonsensical accusations about me. Stop threatening them. And, as for today, when I tell my attorney what kind of a bastard you're being, she'll have you in court so fast you won't know what happened."

"Are you finished?"

Eleanora pulled out her cellphone and punched in Julie's number. After a few rings she realized the phone was in Aaron's pocket. She stared at him incredulously. How could he stoop to this?

Aaron nodded slightly. "Zach's too," he said with a snide smile.

Realizing her own impotence, rage flooded her. Nothing short of doing him bodily harm would satisfy. The thought flashed through her mind like a quick pulse of lightning: She would gladly spend the rest of her life in prison for smashing the life out of him.

Back in her car, Eleanora looked up at the windows for a sign of her kids, but saw no evidence of them. In a moment of panic, the bottom dropped out of her stomach. She dialed 911 and explained that she had been denied access to her children, and was concerned that her husband might become violent. A few minutes later a patrol car pulled up and an officer approached the front door. Aaron opened immediately. He must have been watching the whole time. The officer entered the house and emerged a few minutes later.

"Your kids are OK," he said when she rolled down her window.

"You're sure? You saw them?"

"Yeah. I spoke to them. He's got them cleaning the house, doing laundry, like that. They're not too happy, but, you know, they're kids."

"But they're all right?"

"Yeah," he said. "I'm sorry. There's nothing else we can do."

"I understand," she said. "Thank you. Really, I mean it. I was so worried …" She felt herself about to blubber, but squeezed out a sad smile of resignation. He nodded and returned to his car. Eleanora drove off, leaving her children behind.

She wanted desperately to telephone Connie, but chose not to. He was expecting an afternoon to himself and she refused to intrude on his freedom. She also didn't want to burden him with this absurdity — the kind of nonsense he had deliberately excluded from his life. She had to learn to deal with these frustrations on her own. After a moment's reflection, she thought: *What else is new? I've always coped with problems on my own. Who else has ever been there? Certainly not Aaron.* She decided to go home, get something to eat, and take a long nap. Hoping Aaron would soon relinquish their phones, she left voicemail messages for Julie and Zachary to call when they could.

Later that afternoon, Eleanora sat with a book in her lap and sipped a mug of tea, drinking in the view of the river. Her cellphone rang.

"We're sorry we couldn't call earlier," Julie told her. "Dad just let us stop cleaning now because I have to leave for work."

"Don't apologize, I know it wasn't your fault."

"Dad didn't tell us until about 11:00 this morning that we could only go if everything was finished. He hadn't said that before. He'd just told us we were responsible for getting it done — he never put a deadline on it until this morning."

"I believe you. I knew he'd pull something, I just never expected this."

"He had us in the laundry room when you came. We couldn't even come upstairs to say hello."

"When I didn't see you kids at the windows, I was afraid he had done something to you."

"I know. Dad was really pissed when the police came and demanded to see us."

"I'm sure he was, but at least I got to know that you were OK. Listen, I'm going to my attorney tomorrow morning. Is there anything else he's doing that I should know about?"

Julie thought for a moment. "Well, it's hard to say, but I think he's drinking a lot more than he used to."

"Have you seen him drunk?"

"Not falling down, staggering drunk, but definitely not normal."

"I understand," she said. "How's Zachary?"

"He keeps a lot in, but I know he's really, really furious. He hardly said a word all day. I half expect to see steam coming out of his ears."

"Julie, I want you to be there for him — for you guys to be there for each other, you understand?"

"I know, Mom. We are. Listen, I've got to go. My ride is here."

"OK, sweetheart. I love you."

Eleanora called Zachary, but he didn't answer. She left a message telling him she understood what happened, that she loved him, and would see him Thursday evening. Then she made notes for her meeting with Carmella. She was furious that Aaron was using the kids to get back at her. She hoped Carmella could stop him.

Eleanora arrived at work rested and energized. The rainy day served to keep people at home and business was slow. Buster had taken the day off and her father schmoozed leisurely with the regulars. Taking a cue from the weather, the musicians indulged themselves in slow, jazzy blues rather than the more rowdy beat of last night's performance. At one slow point, Eleanora had the opportunity to tell her father what had happened earlier that day.

"Ellie, if you want me to, I know some people …" He raised his eyebrows. "I'm just saying, if it comes to that, I can be helpful, you know?"

Eleanora was shocked. Her father *knew* people? People who could do what? Break Aaron's legs? Kill him? Make him disappear? Then she realized: Her father was willing to go to any extreme on her behalf. He cared that much. She put her hand on his cheek and kissed him.

"Thanks, Papa. It means a lot that you'd do that for me, for the kids. But I don't think I could live with it."

He nodded and sipped his drink. "Of course."

Chapter Twenty-One

When Eleanora awoke on Monday morning, she stretched luxuriously on Irene's queen-size bed and stared at the shimmering light dancing on the bedroom ceiling. She had an appointment that morning with Carmella, and plans to meet Connie later in the afternoon. Glancing at the clock, she decided it might be too early to phone him — she had no idea yet what his sleeping habits were like. The idea occurred that she might stay over at his condo that night, and she thought about what to bring with her.

Eleanora also realized she had not yet informed her mother of her separation. Impulsively, she reached for the phone and dialed. No answer, which was strange — her mother rarely left the apartment. She called her aunt's number. After a few rings, Velia answered.

"Zia, it's me, Eleanora."

"*Ciao, bambina.* How are you?"

"I'm fine, Zia. I just called Mama to see if it was OK to stop by later on, but there was no answer. Is everything all right?"

"Oh, Eleanora! Didn't you get my message? I called last night. I spoke with your husband. Such a cold fish, that man. I told him that your mama had a stroke. She's in the hospital."

"A stroke? When? How is she?"

"Yesterday morning. We were having breakfast downstairs in her apartment. All of a sudden she gets this look like she's terrified and puts her hands over her ears. Then the next thing, her eyes roll up into her head — I could see only the whites. Then she fell over onto the floor. I called 911 and they took her to the hospital. I was there all day with her. I called you as soon as I got home. Your husband said he would tell you."

"How is she?"

"She's not so good. She's in a coma. They said the stroke affected her brain. She's going to be unconscious for a few days, maybe longer. They don't know. She's in intensive care."

"Which hospital, Zia?"

"NYU Downtown. It's not too far from here. I take the bus."

Eleanora's mind raced. "Zia, I have an important appointment this morning, but I'll come over after I'm done. I can probably be there around noon."

"You'll come here? At noontime?"

"Yes. We can go visit Mama together. Would that be OK?"

"Sure. That would be good. You want something to eat when you get here? Some soup? Or pasta?"

"Some soup would be fine, Zia. I'll see you then."

"All right, dolly."

Eleanora shut her phone. It had been a long time since her aunt had called her by her pet name. It brought back a sweet feeling from childhood. But the news of her mother's stroke sat heavily in her stomach. She was surprised how sad she felt, given the hostile estrangement she usually felt toward her mother. And Aaron! How could he have not given her the news? How cruel!

Hoping to see Carmella a little sooner than scheduled, she arrived early for her appointment. Eleanora had barely been seated in the waiting area when the attorney came to escort her into the office. An elegant-looking woman in her early 50s with graying hair and glasses, Carmella Rotundo wore an expensive pants suit with a silk scarf at her neck. Her appearance inspired confidence.

Once seated, Eleanora told Carmella about Aaron's refusal to allow her access to her children and failure to relay the message about her mother's hospitalization.

As Carmella took notes, she explained to Eleanora that she had not yet heard from Aaron's attorney. Her plan was to get an immediate court date to establish some ground rules. In the meantime, in view of Aaron's behavior with the children, she urged Eleanora to consider staying in the house.

"We can make a pretty good case that it's not in the children's best interest for him to have custodial responsibility," she told Eleanora. "I think we should ask the court that he remove himself from the marital home, that you move back in, and that he pay you for support."

Eleanora acknowledged the wisdom of Carmella's advice. The idea of being reunited with her children felt good, but in some ways it felt like taking a step backward and giving up something — dreams perhaps. She imagined a colt relishing the freedom of being released from a corral, only to be reined back in.

On the other hand, it was clear Aaron was not being a responsible parent. He was destructive to the children, who did not deserve to be scapegoated. What they *did* deserve was a mother to protect and advocate for their well-being. Carmella said she'd rework the agreement to reflect this new demand.

Eleanora decided to use the Hoboken PATH station near Irene's condo. Once in the city, she took a cab to her aunt's apartment. Velia greeted her with a hug, and Eleanora was saddened to see her eyes red and puffy from crying. Waiting for the pot of lentil soup to warm, Eleanora was struck by the difference between her aunt's apartment and her mother's. Zia had a contemporary taste in furniture and decorations. A popular photograph by Ansel Adams hung on one wall as well as a colorful reproduction of a painting by Gaugin. A large-screen TV sat on a modern stand in the living room. Eleanora wished her mother had been more like Velia — participating in life instead of merely harping.

As they ate their soup, Eleanora brought her aunt up to date on what had been happening. She even mentioned Connie.

Eleanora saw her aunt's eyes widen with concern.

"He's Negro?"

Eleanora blanched at the outdated vocabulary.

"He's not Italian?"

"No, Zia. He's not Italian."

"And he's not Catholic?"

Eleanora shook her head.

Velia sighed. "There could be so many problems. Are you sure that's what you want?"

"I know, Zia, it may be hard. I don't know what will happen. The divorce may be too much. I don't think Connie wants to be tied down with family responsibilities. It might not work out." Saddened by the admission, she looked away to regain her composure.

"But for now, I'm glad to have him in my life," she continued hopefully. "It's wonderful to feel passion for someone and to feel cared about. He sees me. You know what I mean? I feel alive."

Velia gently laid her hand on Eleanora's. "I know. I remember what it was like. It's sad that you never had it with that husband of yours." Velia flicked her thumbnail against her teeth in a gesture of total contempt. "And your mama, too, she never knew what it was like to be in love, to be so consumed that nothing else mattered. My poor sister never knew what it was like to feel the blood in her veins."

"Zia, how did my mother and father end up together? I don't think they ever liked each other. Why did they get married?"

Velia tossed her head in disgust. "Ah, it was stupid, so stupid. Your mother never told you?"

125

"No, she never talked about anything."

"All of us — me, your mother, my sister Terezina, your Nonna and Nonno — were born in Sicilia, in a small village called Castelanna. Then it was maybe less than a 1,000 people, including the surrounding countryside; all small farms, vineyards, and olive orchards. It was very peaceful, but after the war life was difficult. We were very poor and everything was in short supply. Your Grandpa and Grandma Palotta decided we should come to America. That was in 1950 when I was 13. There were some relatives in New York, so that's where we came. Right here to this building, where we've always been."

Eleanora recalled hearing stories of how poor the people in Sicily were after the war, desperate for packages from their American relatives. "It must have been very strange for you when you arrived, a teenager in a foreign country."

"The whole neighborhood was Italian then, full of immigrants like us, from Sicilia and southern Italia. It was almost like being home." Velia paused for a moment, finishing her soup and reminiscing.

"The Albaneses lived only a few blocks away, so the two families knew of each other. Your Grandma Albanese was concerned about Giuseppi, your father, when he was a young man. He was out every night, playing the trumpet and meeting lots of American girls. Then she got cancer and her dying wish was he should marry a good Italian girl and make plenty of *bambini*. He told her, Mama, I don't know any nice Italian girls, and she said how about Eva Palotta?"

Eleanora sat back and let the story sink in. Velia carried their dishes to the sink. She returned and continued her story.

"Your father didn't want to marry anybody, but his mother was dying of cancer, so what could he do? And your mother was already 26 years old — a spinster. My father thought he'd have her on his hands forever. She didn't want to get married either, but my papa made her. He threatened to throw her out on the streets if she didn't marry Giuseppi."

Eleanora had no clear memories of her grandparents; they had all passed away when she was quite young. But she had heard stories of her grandfather's fiery temper and she remembered his loud, rough authoritarian voice.

"So they got married and, at first, my parents were very happy. After all, Giuseppi was not only Italian, he was Siciliano. That's what made him such a wonderful catch. But there was one problem: After the wedding my parents found out that Giuseppi's family was from a village called Anselmi, which was just a few miles from Castelanna, where we had lived. You could ride your bicycle, it was that close. But the people from Castelanna hated the people from Anselmi. I never understood why. It went back to before the war. Some blood feud between families or something." Velia shook her head at the absurdity of it all.

Eleanora got up to make some tea and leaned against the sink, arms folded, waiting for her aunt to go on.

"Once my parents discovered your father's family was from Anselmi, all hell broke loose — even though they had immigrated before the war and your father was born here. That didn't matter. Your father could do nothing right in their eyes. From then on, they wouldn't talk to him and he wouldn't talk to them and my poor sister was caught in the middle — an enemy, a traitor to both sides. Nothing made my parents happier than when Eva finally succeeded in driving Giuseppi away. To tell the truth, I don't know how he stood it for so long."

Eleanora felt confused. She had vivid recollections of her mother's stubbornness and unyielding character. "Zia, I don't understand why my mother gave in to that pressure. I always saw her as unmovable, not some wishy-washy push-over."

"The problem with your mother was that she never had a mind of her own when it came to our parents. She was always the 'good girl' of the three of us. Terezina, the middle of us three girls, was headstrong and rebellious; she always got into trouble. My father beat her, almost from the time she was a baby. Stubborn like a donkey. Your mother saw what trouble Terezina was always in and learned very early not to be like her. Like you, your mother almost went into the convent, but at the last minute my parents decided not to let her go. I think my mother just didn't want to give her up. At any rate, she was their favorite, their baby, and even after she married Giuseppi, she was more their daughter than his wife — or your mother."

"Zia, how come you never told me this before?"

Her aunt shrugged. "I thought you knew."

After a small lunch, they took the bus to the hospital. Eva was in a semi-private room; the bed near the window was also occupied by an old woman in a coma. Eleanora went to her mother's bedside, trying to ignore the ominous hum of the monitors. An IV tube was connected to a needle inserted into the back of Eva's hand, fastened by strips of tape. Although oxygen flowed through small tubes in her nostrils, her chest barely rose and fell. Her dry skin looked even whiter than usual. Uncombed hair created a halo around her face, and Eleanora unconsciously brushed a stray strand from her mother's pale forehead. There was nothing else to do. It was like looking at a dead person.

Gerard R. D'Alessio

Eleanora felt strangely calm: *She's been dead her whole life. This is how she's always looked.*

Eleanora thought about the story Zia Velia had told her. She vaguely remembered hearing about Aunt Terezina, who had run away as a teenager and spent her life traveling around Europe. The family received occasional postcards bragging about how Count So and So or some rich businessman was treating her to an exciting and lavish lifestyle. Her grandparents considered Terezina a whore and prohibited her name from being mentioned in the house.

"Zia, whatever happened to Zia Terezina?"

"She died of lung cancer. So young, only 45, but she smoked like a chimney. Don't you remember? She was too sick to come to your wedding."

Eleanora didn't remember hearing about Terezina's death. She doubted it had even been talked about in the family. Turning her attention back toward the bed, she studied her mother in repose. Free from the obligation to feign a relationship, she thought over Velia's comment that Eva never had a mind of her own. There was truth in the sentiment: Eva had always been an appendage of Nonna and Nonno, like some loyal, unthinking soldier in the war against the Albaneses. As soon as Giuseppi left, her mother moved Eleanora back into the apartment where Eva had been raised — and she never left it again.

Didn't she ever have any ambitions of her own? Eleanora realized she had never asked.

"Zia," she said, turning to her aunt, who was silently saying her rosary, "did my mother ever want to do anything, be anything? Didn't she have any dreams?"

Velia thought for a while. "Your mother was still a little girl when we left Sicily, maybe nine years old. At that time, we only thought about having enough food. There was no room for dreams. We wished only for food and good weather and for our father not to beat us too often. When we came to New York, it was assumed that one of us would be offered to the church. Being a nun was not for me. Already I was too interested in boys and dreamed about getting married and having a family of my own. Well, I got my Pio, but we never had any children." She smiled at Eleanora. "You were my *bambina*. You and my baby sister." Velia glanced at Eva with glistening eyes.

"I was just thinking last week how any confidence I have in myself came from the love I got from you. It just occurred to me that the same was probably true for her," Eleanora indicated the bed where her mother lay. "You were a good mother, Zia. You were always full of love."

Velia smiled and mouthed a thank you. "Eva was a good girl, but so timid. She was like clay in our parent's hands. The only thing she ever thought of was becoming a nun. I think she was disappointed when my mother wouldn't let her go. Maybe she never got over that. Maybe all she ever wanted was to marry God."

Eleanora turned to study her mother's face, as if it could reveal something profound, some secret of her life. She suddenly realized why her mother had been so intent on sending her to an all-girl parochial school — to keep her virtuous, fit for a life of prayer behind cloistered, convent walls. Eva had expected Eleanora to fill her breast not only with pride but also to satisfy her own unfulfilled dream. *How angry and disappointed she must have been when I got pregnant.*

In escaping the sentence her mother tried to impose on her, Eleanora realized she incurred a different one — equally smothering, equally deadening. Instead of vowing obedience to God, she ended up being ruled by Aaron; instead of being the good daughter, she became the dutiful wife. Instead of following her own dream, she was driven by Aaron's needs. She had only her music, the lifeline that kept her from disappearing altogether under the wake of someone else's life. And now, if she moved back into the house, how much of her new dream might she have to surrender?

As she drove north along winding Boulevard East to Connie's condo, the golden rays of the setting sun reflected back from the Manhattan skyscrapers across the river. Her heart raced as she pulled into the parking area. When the elevator door opened, Connie was waiting with open arms. *It feels so good to be home, to rest against this chest, to be held.* Eleanora turned her face upward and kissed him eagerly. She hadn't realized how much she hungered for his strong embrace.

Once behind the closed door, she dropped the small bag she'd been carrying and wrapped both arms around him, caressing the back of his neck as they kissed. She struggled out of her coat and let it fall to the floor.

"Let's go to the bedroom," she suggested. Giggling, she broke free and ran, kicking off her shoes as he lifted her onto the bed. She kissed him while he removed her clothes. Breathless, they collapsed, naked and happy, into each other's embrace. She couldn't wait to love him. Giddy and intoxicated, she relished expressing her intensity without inhibition — and was especially thrilled by his obvious, enthusiastic reaction to everything she did. But she also loved his tenderness and passion, the way he gently stimulated her nipples, his hot breath on her neck, the feathery touch of his fingers brushing her shoulders or the small of her back, his moist kisses in the crook of her elbow or under her ear, the tickling sensation of his wet mouth sliding across her belly.

She knew he enjoyed spontaneity. The image of them at the piano flashed briefly through her mind: They were playing off of each other, unrehearsed, surprising themselves. Matching the tempo, she followed the rhythm of their bodies unquestioningly, without doubt or judgment, lifting her pelvis to him while he thrust against her. Smiling at herself, she allowed squeals of pleasure to be pumped out of her. She squeezed her own breasts without inhibition as orgasmic convulsions rumbled within her and, at last, Connie stiffened.

He collapsed onto her, breathing heavily, sighing over and over again. She liked the comforting weight of his body on hers. She squeezed him with her arms and legs. *He's mine*, she thought joyously. *He's mine. I love him and he's mine.* She felt her vaginal muscles squeezing his penis, hugging it, not wanting to let it go, ever. After a few minutes, Connie regained his breath and rolled off her.

"My goodness gracious," he said, a tone of awe in his voice, "where in hell did a good Catholic girl like you ever learn to fuck like that?"

"See what you've let loose? There was a devil inside me."

"I don't know about a devil, but if we keep going like this you're going to turn me into an old man long before my time."

"No," she cooed, pulling his face closer, "I'm going to keep you young forever."

As they lay entwined, Eleanora shared the news of her mother's stroke and Aaron's failure to pass Velia's message on to her and the children.

Connie told her that he would be doing a concert the following weekend in Houston to raise money for the victims of hurricane Katrina. This would be his second benefit concert to benefit the cause.

"My family was lucky," he explained. "They're a good distance away from New Orleans, so weren't subjected to any of the flooding — only the wind and rain, which didn't do any serious damage to them. But I know a lot of people who were totally wiped out. I have to do what I can."

He was quiet for a few moments. "I thought about asking you to come along, but it'll just be down and back. I'll be making a quick stop to see my folks and my brother, but," he paused, "I'm not sure they're ready to meet you."

Eleanora looked at him quizzically. "Would they be upset that you're dating a white woman?"

Connie was genuinely amused. "Well, they would be surprised in view of my 'black is beautiful' history. But no, they wouldn't be upset. They might question if you're white enough."

"What does that mean? White enough?"

Connie couldn't help himself. He dissolved into a real fit of laughter, the likes of which Eleanora hadn't seen since she was among girlfriends in high school.

"What's so funny? Italian isn't white? What?"

Connie struggled to speak coherently. "No, what I mean, sweetheart, is that there's this whole package. To my parents, white means wealthy. And not just wealthy, but old southern money. Aristocratic. And Baptist. You're a northerner, a Catholic, divorced — or soon will be — and not from a wealthy old southern family."

"You're kidding," she said, her voice full of disbelief.

"I told you they were prejudiced and narrow-minded. They might be happy that their son finally wised up and realized he'd never get anywhere in this world chasing around with black women who were beneath his station. But they could be upset that I'm still not ready to join their world."

"So they'd think I'm not good enough for you."

"They might," Connie conceded. "Maybe they've changed. Maybe now that I'm older and they're older, maybe they would just be happy that I've found someone I might want to settle down with. Maybe," he gave her a sly grin, "give them a couple of nice light-skinned grandbabies."

"Ooh!" Eleanora looked at him questioningly. She wasn't sure whether to take him seriously or not. Was he considering having children with her? Did she want more children? She'd be 38 in a few months. Crying babies and dirty diapers and sleepless nights immediately came to mind — as did an image of Todd, still a baby after 14 years. And having children meant getting married, didn't it? Was Connie saying he wanted to marry her? Already?

"Babies?" she asked incredulously, half-rising up.

"It was just a thought, something I found myself thinking about, that's all."

Eleanora fell back on the bed and pulled the hair away from her face. "Babies," she repeated.

"I didn't mean to frighten you. I just wanted to let you know it was a thought I had, a picture that popped into my head: You, me, a baby or two, standing on the veranda of my parents' home. Everybody happy. Their being happy that we're in love. I just wanted to share it with you, that's all."

Eleanora caught her breath and turned to him. She saw the hopefulness in his eyes, his kind and gentle smile. She saw the love in his eyes and reached up to stroke his cheek.

"It's a beautiful picture, Connie. And who knows, maybe that's what will happen." She thought for a moment. "I would love to marry you. I love you and want to love you forever. And I want to make you happy — whatever you want, I want to give you because I love you. But babies — I don't know, Connie. I don't know if I'm ready for more babies. I really don't."

"It's OK, sweetheart. You don't have to. We don't have to. Listen," he said, leaning over her, "I don't need you to make me happy. That's my job, my business. You aren't responsible for how I feel. All I need is to know you love me. That's all. Just look at me the way you do." He smiled. "And fuck me the way you do. That's all I ask."

Eleanora smiled, again feeling an excited sense of pride in her newly discovered sexuality. "But loving you isn't just feeling passion for you, Connie. It's wanting to do for you, to treat you generously." She searched for a way to express the feeling bursting within her. "My doing what you would like is a way of showing you that I love you."

"I understand. I feel the same way. Wait till you see the dinner you're going to get."

Eleanora laughed and licked her lips in mock anticipation.

"I know we want to make each other happy. I'm just saying we can love each other without feeling obligated to do *everything* to please each other. If there's something you don't want to do, it doesn't mean I'm going to feel unloved."

"Yes. I really do know that. Up here," she said pointing to her head. Then she pointed to her heart. "In here, I need to be reminded."

They lay quietly for a while, watching the sky grow darker and the lights across the river become more numerous. Eleanora allowed herself to indulge in a fantasy of what it might be like to be married to Connie, to share music and even children with him. She imagined the kind of estrangement they might experience with his parents, although that wouldn't be so different from the practically nonexistent relationship she had with Aaron's parents. She wondered how Zachary and Julie might feel if she had more children — maybe especially biracial children. She imagined Zachary might feel some jealousy and resentment.

And what might marriage and children mean for her? Would she feel as confined and limited as she had with Aaron? And if she wasn't going to devote herself to raising his children and being there for him, why would Connie want to bother getting married? She decided it was too much to think about too soon. Just let it unfold. She realized she was giving Connie an involuntary hug, as if to remind herself he was there, that for the moment at least, they were together.

When Connie went into the bathroom, Eleanora stood at the full-length wall of glass overlooking the Hudson River. Even though she knew no one could see her in the darkened room, she felt a thrill standing naked in front of the wall of glass. It's like being invisible. *No one can see me. Only Connie can see me.*

Suddenly, he was behind her, his arms around her waist, one hand messaging a breast, one hand caressing her belly. He kissed her neck.

"You are so beautiful," he whispered. "I wish I were 10 years younger so I could give you what you deserve. I hate the idea of having wasted these years without you."

She turned to him, pushing his erection down between her legs. "Ten years ago, I wouldn't have been available for you. I wasn't awake. I wasn't born yet. I wasn't alive yet. Ten years ago I wasn't even a gleam in your eye or in mine. I didn't know I existed."

"You exist now."

Connie laid her gently down on the floor. With the soft plush carpet under her, they made love slowly and patiently with millions of lights and eyes watching disinterestedly.

Later, Connie was in the kitchen making blackened catfish filets and a New Orleans vegetable stew with black-eyed peas, sweet potatoes, tomatoes, and okra with lots of spices and magical ingredients. Eleanora took advantage of the time, sipping the mojito he'd made for her and playing the piano.

"I want you to know," she hollered, "that I don't love you just for your body."

Connie laughed easily as he faced her from across the island-based range where he was cooking. "I'm glad you're enjoying it."

"What? The piano or your body?"

"Please, sweetheart, for now just love the piano."

Eleanora decided to try some experimenting. She let herself play the way she felt. This was new for her — and wasn't easy. She changed notes, in a sense rewriting the song and breaking rules. She became absorbed in letting some essence within her flow through her fingers and into the keys until it emerged as music. The room vibrated with her own expression. When she looked up, Connie was standing there with a glass of chilled white wine in each hand.

"It sounds like you're really relaxing and loosening up," he said, extending a glass to her. "You're starting to flow. Just keep doing what you're doing, letting it emerge." He smiled. "Think of it as sex," he said, smiling mischievously. Eleanora smiled and wiggled her ears in response.

"Oh, wow!" he exclaimed. "How did you do that?"

"I'm full of surprises," she giggled, taking the glass from him.

The evening was surprisingly warm for early October and they ate dinner on the balcony, which looked almost directly down onto the river. The glittering lights from the city reflected off the slowly flowing water. A CD played in the background.

"Is that you on piano?" she asked, and he nodded.

"An old one," he acknowledged. "Sarah Vaughn was a wonderful singer to accompany. She had such a wide-ranging talent. She knew how to use her voice to get precisely the effect she was striving for."

They talked quietly about music, his career, and the dates he had lined up. Then she shared how much she enjoyed working at the restaurant. Being with her dad and Buster and the musicians was an obvious pleasure, but she had been surprised at her interest in the business itself. She even had some thoughts about improving the menu.

Eleanora thoroughly relished her introduction to New Orleans cuisine. An accomplished cook herself, she appreciated Connie's skill in this arena as well. They had wine with dinner, and later Connie served espresso with a small liquor glass of something delicious. When the night became cooler, Connie got a sweater for each of them and they watched the boats' slow movement on the river.

Eleanora suddenly felt self-conscious. "Oh! I almost forgot. I thought I might stay the night, but I never asked you ...."

Connie shook his head slowly from side to side.

"It's not all right?" she asked, a sudden look of alarm on her face.

"Eleanora, of course it's all right. I saw the bag you brought. Of course I want you to stay."

She sat back on her chair, relieved. "Good, because if it wasn't all right, I would have had to seduce you again."

Connie made a cross with his two index fingers and thrust it at her. "No you don't," he warned. "Keep away!"

"Don't worry," she laughed, "you're safe for now. You've gotten me too drunk to do anything."

"Are you really drunk?" he asked.

"Absolutely," she said, "not falling down drunk, but a little bit tipsy."

"You're a cheap date," he teased.

"That's because I'm not used to drinking this much. Give me some time to practice and I won't be so cheap."

"Oh, so you want to cost me dearly, is that it?"

"Yes. I want to be worth everything to you."

"That much?"

"Yes. I want you to think I'm worth that much."

Connie leaned over, forcing her to look him in the eye. "Would you like to know how much I think you're worth?"

She looked at him warily. "I don't know. Is it safe?"

He stood up and took her by the hand. "Come with me."

Connie led her into the living room and sat her down on one of the chairs facing the piano. He shuffled through some sheets of music, then began to play. The piece was not familiar, but Eleanora thought it was beautiful — melodic, with an intriguing theme that repeated throughout. It was spirited yet serious; slow and gentle, yet strong and passionate. When he was finished, she realized she'd been holding her breath.

"That was lovely," she said, "but I don't recognize it."

"I should hope not," he said seriously, "I just finished writing it. It's a portrait of you."

"Of me?" She felt herself sobering up quickly. "That's how you see me?"

She rose from the chair and went to him.

"Not only do I love it," she said softly, but with passion, "and not only do I admire your talent and ability, but I understand now that you really do see me and love me for who I am. Like you know my soul. I will never forget this moment. This is how it must have been at the beginning of the universe. There's way too much happiness to be contained inside just one person. I have to explode all over."

She kissed him tenderly on his lips.

"What a dear man you are," she whispered.

Chapter Twenty-Two

Rising behind the Manhattan skyscrapers, the sun brightened the edges of the opaque drapes and let in enough light for Eleanora to see her surroundings clearly. She was still holding onto Connie's arm, draped heavily across her waist. She extended her neck to see the clock — just after 7:00. Stretching, she let her eyes close again. *I'm so fortunate.* But then her thoughts expanded beyond the cocoon of Connie's apartment: her mother's stroke, the upcoming legal and financial battles with Aaron, her kids. Even her relationship with Connie, despite its wonders, was fraught with uncertainty. She was wise enough to know that the first weeks of a relationship were not a valid indicator of the long run. Still, she was grateful for the momentary happiness.

Unconsciously, she caressed Connie's hand and pulled it to her breast. He nuzzled her neck sleepily and mumbled that he was going upstairs to the building's gym for about a half-hour. He liked to work out a few times a week, but it depended on whether he had worked the night before or not. Eleanora teased him about needing to keep in shape for her and said she'd have breakfast ready when he was done. The truth was, she was aroused and ready for more lovemaking. *This is what it must be like for a new bride who's in love,* she thought.

While Connie was gone, she showered and dressed, then rummaged in the kitchen before deciding to make an omelet with leftover vegetables from last night's stew. Eleanora also found everything she needed to make fresh biscuits and while those were baking, she made coffee for Connie and tea for herself. By the time he had returned from the gym and emerged from the shower, breakfast was ready.

The morning sun shone directly onto the balcony and, despite a cool breeze, the warmth of the sun made it delightful to eat there. It glittered off the river like diamonds and Eleanora relished the contentment of the moment.

Her phone rang at 9:00 a.m. sharp. Carmella had arranged a court date for Wednesday morning at the Hackensack courthouse, and had received a phone call from Aaron's lawyer.

"I know this *caffone* by reputation — a real asshole, if you don't mind my using legalese. The guy is a first-class imbecile. His MO is to obstruct anything and everything you try to do. I'm only telling you this so you'll be prepared: Stay calm and let me handle it."

Eleanora tried to absorb the information. *Stay calm*!

"By the way, the lawyer's name is Carmine Putz. Can you believe — generations of this family and nobody's had the sense to change it? Anyway, I told Carmine that his client screwed up big time by not letting the kids see you on Sunday, so we'll see them in court Wednesday morning. When they see a copy of our separation, that's when the war starts. Be prepared, but don't worry about it. I love this shit."

As he cleared the breakfast table, Connie overheard the gist of the conversation.

"I wish I could help," he said, "but I know this is something you just have to get through. I'm here for emotional support, but I don't know if I can do anything other than that."

"You can't change Aaron, that's for sure," she sighed as she dried the dishes. "I don't want to burden you with my whining and complaining."

"I appreciate that. Part of me doesn't want to know too much, to get caught up in all the bullshit. But I want you to feel free to share what you're going through. I want to be here for you."

Eleanora remembered his words from last night — that she wasn't responsible for making him happy, that all she had to do was love him — and echoed the thoughts back to him.

"Promise you'll tell me if I'm dumping too much on you."

"I will," he said, reaching over to kiss her.

When the evening rush had passed at the Lounge, she had an opportunity to talk with her father. "Zia Velia told me about when you and Mama got married — how you did it to please your mother."

"Yeah. What a stupid thing to do. And yet, if my mother were here today and asked me to do something, I don't know if I could refuse her."

"Did you love her that much?"

"Yeah, I loved her, although I think it had more to do with the way I was raised. Your grandparents were real old-school. You did what they said — or else. From an early age, I did what was expected. I don't think, looking back, that I ever defied them. I may have tried to argue, persuade them, but when it came right down to it, if they wanted me to do something, I did it. And you know, they were usually right."

He laughed. "That's one of the most infuriating things about parents — they're usually right. And they were right to be concerned about me. If they only knew! Part of me thought it was time to grow up, so I wasn't totally opposed to the idea of getting married. It's just that, without their push, God knows when I would have gotten around to it — not with the women I was running into. And your mother, she wasn't bad looking. Not then. She had a nice set on her, you know?" He gave an embarrassed laugh. "So I figured, why not give it a try? Christ, if I had only known what I was getting into."

"Zia Velia told me about the feud between the two towns in Sicily."

"I never heard of such nonsense," her father shook his head. "My parents came here in the late 1920s, before the Depression. They were so young, I don't think they even knew about this stupid goddamned feud. So we were all shocked as hell. But I tell you, to the Palottas, we were the worst of the worst. Once Eva's parents found out we Albaneses were from Anselmi, that was the beginning of the end. Your mother withdrew from me and never came back. I tried to talk sense into her, but it was no use."

"I remember the night you left."

He grimaced. "Yeah, that was the hardest thing I ever did. I never forgave myself for walking out on you."

"I understood. I really did. Part of me was glad you had the chance to escape."

He pulled her close and kissed her forehead. "Now it's your turn," he said softly.

Later, Eleanora called her aunt. Velia's voice was empty. "Still no change. I don't think your mother is going to get better. There's no life, no spirit."

In her heart, Eleanora agreed with her aunt. Later, she shared this with her father.

"If there's a funeral or service, let me know. I want to be there for Velia's sake. She was always a good person. This will be tough on her."

Back at Connie's condo complex that evening, Eleanora used the parking pass he had given her to drive into the underground garage and the key he'd given her to enter his condo. The fact that he had given her access into his life meant a great deal to her. Hearing him at the piano, the weariness of the day evaporated and she felt a surge of excitement.

Seeing him hunched over the keys in concentration, the stars of the city glittering behind him, was like stepping into heaven. Eleanora stood silently, not wanting to disturb the vision, but he sensed her presence and glanced up. He gave a boyish smile and started playing, "When I Take My Sugar to Tea."

"I've kept some water hot for you — figured you might want a cup of tea," he nodded toward the kitchen. "How was work?"

"Good, fun. Not too busy. I got a chance to talk with my father. I really enjoy being there."

Connie had put out a small assortment of teas for her. His thoughtfulness registered and she smiled to herself.

"It's really neat that you have this opportunity to spend time with your dad. I'm sure he's grateful for it, too."

"Oh, he is, I can tell. Yes, I'm lucky to have this chance. These past 20 years, Aaron put such obstacles in the way, it wasn't worth the fighting and arguing every time I wanted to see him." She thought for a moment as she prepared her tea. Connie got a glass of ice water for himself. "Now I realize that I could have — should have put my foot down a lot sooner. I should have left a lot sooner."

"Why didn't you?"

Eleanora looked at him, her eyes wide with disbelief. "I didn't know I could. Can you believe it? It's as simple as that. It never occurred to me that I had a choice. It never dawned on me that it was possible."

"What made you realize?"

"I don't know. It sort of all came together — one thing after another, and then, there I was, telling him off."

In the living room, they sat on the leather sofa and talked about their day. Connie looked pensive. "I guess sometimes we get into a habit and never question it, never realize there's another way of thinking about something, another way of behaving."

"What are you referring to?" she asked, a note of concern in her voice. Eleanora was afraid he was going to tell her something she didn't want to hear. Stroking his arm, her hand wavered momentarily, as if to stop him from telling her some bad news.

"I was just thinking about you enjoying getting close to your father again, and I thought about my relationship with my father and with my mother, too. I've been so angry with them for so long, I guess I never questioned it. I just assumed I was right and justified and they were wrong. Now I'm thinking, maybe when I go by there this weekend … Who knows? Maybe I can think something different."

Eleanora reached out to him, partly in relief and partly to convey her support. "I think it would be good to try," she said. "Whatever happens, you'll be glad you tried."

In court, Eleanora was very impressed with Carmella's professional demeanor and skills. She was totally in control and persuaded the judge to her point of view on every matter that came up. Eleanora was surprised at how well Carmella kept her emotions in check. *Poor Carmine Putz, he doesn't have a chance.* He looked and sounded as ineffectual as she had been led to expect and she wondered why Aaron chose such a boob to represent him. *He must be very cheap. There can't be any other logical reason.*

Outside, as she walked toward the parking lot, Eleanora saw Aaron approaching.

"That's quite a shark you have there," he said, gesturing toward the retreating figure of her attorney.

Eleanora thought of a number of retorts, but decided to exercise some discipline. "She's just doing her job. Don't take it personally."

She thought he looked ill at ease. "So," he said slowly, "you'll be coming by tomorrow night to pick up the kids?"

"And Saturday morning and Sunday at noon."

Aaron slumped in resignation. She could see that he accepted his defeat on this issue and she knew he wouldn't cause any more trouble regarding visitations. As Carmella had instructed, she said nothing about the separation agreement that would be forwarded to Mr. Putz, containing her request that Aaron move out of the home. She simply told him that his attorney would receive a copy of the agreement in a couple of days.

"Anything you want to tell me about it?"

"No," she said, shaking her head, "it's better if you and Mr. Putz go over it yourselves." She had all she could do to keep from giggling whenever she said the lawyer's name.

Back at Irene's condo after work, Eleanora checked in with the kids, then called her aunt. Her mother's condition had not changed, and Zia Velia sounded depressed. When she got off of the phone, Eleanora felt sad, but she was more concerned for her aunt, who would be losing a significant portion of her life when Eva died. Eleanora realized with a sharp stab of sadness that when her mother died, she would lose any hope she'd harbored that someday her mother would really love her and be proud of her — the way Eleanora loved

Julie. Once Eva was gone, those hopes would turn to dust. She thought she should feel sadness and loss at her mother's impending death, but the emotions weren't there. The idea of her mother's death was just that — an idea, an abstract concept.

Alone with her thoughts, Eleanora found herself missing her children and Connie. Melancholy seeped in and filled her soul with a heavy lethargy. She reached out for the phone and called Irene.

The voice on the other end of the phone was a welcome relief. Irene was delighted to hear from her. She had been thinking of coming into Hoboken to pick up a few items from the condo, so Eleanora suggested they have an early supper, she'd be glad to prepare something.

When Irene arrived, Eleanora opened a bottle of wine and the two women sat in the living room watching the late afternoon sun paint New York a rich golden color. Irene quickly deflected questions about her own life and insisted on hearing about Eleanora.

"Irene, I don't know whether I'm coming or going. I feel like I'm in love for the first time in my life. I've never been so happy, never knew it was possible. Still, my head reminds me of so many potential problems: the kids, Aaron, Connie's family, even our ages. We've had two very different lifestyles. I don't know if we can mesh them."

"You're kind of rushing things a bit, aren't you, honey? How long have you known each other? A couple of weeks, maybe?"

"Ten days."

"Exactly. Listen, I know you two are generating a lot of heat. My goodness, how many wonderful, wonderful songs have been written about what you're experiencing? It's beautiful and magic — but it doesn't last. No two people can sustain that white heat forever. Believe me, it will die down, and then you'll see what's really there."

"I know," Eleanora said regretfully "I know what you're saying makes sense. I've tried to tell myself the same kinds of things."

"Listen to me. I know what I'm talking about here. The problems that you and Connie will have to face — race, your kids, his family, friends, age, everything — that's the stuff life is made of. And what will determine how your relationship progresses — or if it'll progress — is how you two go about working together to solve those problems. The goal isn't to find someone with whom you won't have problems; the goal is to find a partner who will work with you to solve them. You two will do what you naturally do —if the way you communicate with each other works, that's great; and if it doesn't, well then, it was just one of those things. You hear me?"

Eleanora hugged her. Both women had tears in their eyes. "You have so much love in you, Irene. I'm so happy you're in my father's life. And I'm so happy you're in mine. You have no idea how strange it is to have someone show faith in me, that I have enough sense to work something out, that I can trust my own feelings and instincts — instead of telling me what I should do."

"And you have no idea, Eleanora, how I've yearned my whole life for a daughter I could love."

Eleanora realized in that moment that not only did she not have to apologize for what she perceived as her own weakness, but that leaning on Irene was the equivalent of giving something to her. It allowed Eleanora to feel some confidence in her own nature. Things would work out, one way or another. Whatever happened would be right. She trusted that. She had faith.

After a dinner of broiled fish, linguini with oil and garlic, and a small spinach salad, Eleanora left for rehearsal. Although the session went well, she was unable to shake the perception that some of the women were standoffish toward her. She mentioned it to Peter.

"What did I tell you?" he shrugged his shoulders. "Don't let it get to you."

Eleanora asked about Bethann Winters.

"I haven't heard anything, Ellie. I'm not in any official loop. As far as I understand, nothing legal is going forward until she's declared mentally competent to stand trial, and I don't think that will be anytime soon." He changed the subject. "How are you doing? How does it feel to be single again?"

"Oh, Peter, I'm not exactly single. I still have two children and an estranged husband I've got to do battle with."

"I know. I'm talking about dating. Are you seeing anyone?"

Eleanora hesitated. She felt reluctant to acknowledge that she was seeing someone — and not just anyone, but a special someone. On the other hand, she didn't like to lie and was having trouble thinking up a story on the spur of the moment. It dawned on her that the delay was, in itself, an answer.

"There is someone," she acknowledged. "I guess I'm just not ready to talk about it yet." Ignoring a compulsion to explain, she said abruptly, "I hope you'll understand, Peter."

"Of course," he said. "It's just that I have a special interest in you. I want you to be happy. If there's anything I can do, if you need to talk — about anything — I hope you'll feel free to call on me."

"I will, Peter. You're a good friend. Thank you."

In the church parking lot, Eleanora was about to head to Connie's when a rapping on the passenger window startled her. It took a moment to realize it was Zachary.

"Zach, honey, what a nice surprise. What are you doing here?"

"Oh, Mom," he moaned, shaking his head, "big trouble."

"What?" she asked, grabbing his shoulder. "What happened? Are you all right? Tell me."

Zachary's face contorted. "It's Dad. We got into a major fight back at the house. Julie ran off. I don't know where she is. I've tried calling, but she doesn't answer. I'm not sure if she has her phone with her."

"What fight? Tell me what happened."

"Well, Julie's been having a problem with Roy, her asshole boyfriend."

"I know," Eleanora interjected, "I remember her saying something about that."

"Yeah, well, Dad heard about it somehow. I think he heard them arguing on the phone. When I came home Dad was yelling at Julie, calling her all kinds of names. I tried to get in between but Dad threw me out of the way. I banged my arm and my shoulder when I fell." He reached up with his left hand to indicate where he was hurt.

"Your father pushed you down?"

"Yeah. He knocked me across the coffee table. Julie ran upstairs and locked herself in her room, but Dad broke her door down."

"He what?"

"He was crazy, Mom. I didn't think he was that strong, but he just smashed it in. I ran upstairs and grabbed him from behind, and Julie ran out of the house. Dad broke free and went down the stairs after her — and I pushed him."

"What? You pushed …?"

Zachary shrugged his shoulders defensively, but his eyes were wide with fear. "I didn't want him to catch her," he said. "I didn't mean to hurt him."

"What happened to him, Zach? Where is he now?"

"I think he was knocked out for a few seconds. When I saw him starting to move, I figured I'd better get out of there or he'd kill me for sure. I didn't even grab my emergency bag. I just jumped over him where he was lying on the stairs and ran out."

Eleanora leaned over the steering wheel, her head in her hands. What the hell was happening? With one sweep, it felt as if everything had been knocked apart, their lives scattered about like broken pieces. She reached out to Zachary.

"It's OK. You were right to help your sister. I'm proud of you." She started the car. "We're going to tell the police what happened. Try to reach Julie again.

Leave a message for her to call us."

She peeled out of the parking lot and sped toward the Leonia police station. She identified herself to the desk sergeant and told him of the domestic violence.

"I don't know how hurt my husband may be, and I don't know where my daughter is. She's not answering her cellphone."

"I don't think she has it with her," Zach offered.

The sergeant called a squad car to assess the situation at the house. He asked Zachary for a description of what his sister was wearing when she left, and asked for the names of her friends, including her boyfriend.

"I don't think that's where she'd be," Zach said.

Eleanora looked at her son in puzzlement.

"Why don't you think she'd go to Roy's?"

Zach hesitated only a moment, "Because that's what they were fighting about. I think Julie was breaking up with Roy and Dad heard them. Anyway, he found out why she was angry at Roy and that's what set him off."

"Why would Dad be so angry at Julie for breaking up with Roy?"

Zachary grew more uncomfortable, but Eleanora persisted.

"I don't know all the details, but it was something about sex. There were rumors going around school."

"What rumors? Zach, tell me."

He shook his head. "I can't tell you. Don't make me. Ask Julie."

In a panic, Eleanora realized Zachary was being loyal to his sister, and she felt a momentary admiration.

"Try her cellphone again," she said. "It's OK. I understand your position." She turned to him again. "Is there anything else you can tell me?"

He shook his head glumly.

A call came in from one of the patrol cars. Nobody was at the Hoffman residence. Some lights were on, but the door was locked and nobody answered. Eleanora offered to go open the door to see if Aaron was unconscious or injured. The patrol car would wait there for her. She and Zach were about to leave when Peter rushed into the station.

"Eleanora. Thank God I've found you. Are you all right?"

"Peter, what are you doing here?"

"I saw you race out of the parking and I figured you had some kind of emergency. I went to your house and a squad car pulled up. They told me you'd be here. What do you need me to do?"

"I don't know, Peter. We're going back to my house now. Aaron might be hurt. And Julie's missing."

"I'll meet you there."

At the house, Eleanora fumbled with her keys but finally unlocked the front door. The lights were on, but Aaron was no longer lying on the stairs. Zachary ran upstairs to check all of the rooms. No one was home and Aaron's car was gone. She checked the answering machine — no messages. They gave all of this information to the patrolman, including a description of Aaron and his car. After a few minutes, he returned and told her that none of the names she had given the detective at the station had checked out. Nobody had seen Julie.

The patrolman discovered blood on the baseboard at the bottom of the stairs.

"That's where my dad fell and hit his head," said Zachary, looking at his mother for support. Eleanora put her arm around him. A few minutes later, Detective Park, an officer from the Juvenile Unit, arrived at the house and sat down with Eleanora and Zachary.

Eleanora had no idea where Aaron might be, but assumed he was looking for Julie. Detective Park, a Korean man who looked to be in his early 30s, asked where Aaron worked. She gave him the address of the accounting firm in Teaneck, and he called the Teaneck police to see if Aaron might be there. The desk sergeant had already called Roy's home, but Detective Park decided to go there and see if Aaron had showed up, or if Roy could help clarify the situation. Eleanora also suggested the fast food restaurant out on the highway where Julie worked. In the midst of their conversation with Park, Peter arrived at the house.

When Park left, Eleanora and Zachary sat silently in the kitchen. Stunned, they each felt emotionally drained, yet agitated. The patrolman remained outside in his car. Peter joined them at the kitchen table. Zachary looked across the kitchen table at his mother.

"Am I going to get in trouble for this?" he asked.

"I don't think so, honey. You tried to do a good thing — protect your sister. Nobody is going to blame you." She thought for a moment. "This is why I don't think it's a good thing to have guns in the house. God knows what any of you might have ended up doing if a gun had been available."

Eleanora tried to think — and spurred Zach to do the same — of where her daughter could possibly have gone. She assumed Julie had left the house with little or no money. If she didn't go to a friend's, then where? Eleanora got up suddenly and went upstairs to Julie's bedroom. A minute later she came back down with her daughter's backpack. In it were her cellphone, keys, and wallet. She went out to the patrol car to tell the policeman. While she was talking to him, Zach came to the front door.

"Mom, Grandpa is on telephone."

Eleanora rushed back inside. "Papa?"

"Ellie, what the hell are you doing there?"

"It's a long story, Papa. There's been — I don't know what to call it. The kids had a fight with their father and now both Aaron and Julie are missing."

"Julie's here."

"What? She's with you?"

Relief flooded her.

"That's why I'm calling. She showed up at the Lounge about 10 minutes ago in a cab. I figured I'd better call Aaron and let him know she's safe. I didn't expect you would be there. I was going to call you next."

"How the hell did she take a cab there?"

Her father laughed. "She had the good sense to tell the cabby her grandfather would pay."

"So she's all right?"

"She's fine. She's upset. She didn't really get a chance to tell me any of the details, only that she had a row with her father and ran out of the house. She was terrified that Aaron was going to hurt her."

"Papa, can you put her on, please?"

"Sure, baby, she's right here."

Eleanora let out a deep sigh as she waited for her daughter to get on the line. Julie was safe. That was all that mattered. She didn't know what she had feared, only that she had considered the possibility that Aaron might have found Julie and physically hurt her.

"Mom?"

"Oh, honey. We've all been so worried. Nobody knew where you were."

"I'm sorry you were worried. I thought I'd get here to Grandpa's before you even knew I was gone. Is Dad still acting crazy?"

"He's not here. We don't know where he is. We have the police out looking for both of you."

There was a slight pause. "My God, you think he's coming after me?"

"Julie, don't worry. He would never think to look for you in Newark. You know he wouldn't go near your grandfather's place. I assume he's driving around town trying to find you. Also, you should know, your brother pushed your father down the stairs to keep him from running after you. Apparently, he suffered a concussion and was unconscious for a while, but we really don't know how hurt he is."

"Zach did that? The kid has guts. You should have seen him, the way he grabbed Dad from behind and was hanging on like a bronco rider."

"I know. He told me." She glanced at Zach and gave him a wink. "Would you like to talk to him?"

Eleanora motioned for Zach to take the phone, then walked outside with

147

Peter to tell the policeman that her daughter was safe. She was reluctant to tell him where Julie was — in case they found Aaron, she didn't want anybody telling him. She stood outside in the cool October night air with Peter, allowing Zach some privacy with his sister.

Eventually, Zach called her back to the phone.

"Julie, listen, I think it's better if you stay at Grandpa's, at least for tonight."

"There's no way I'm going back into that house with Dad," her daughter reassured her.

"All right, then. I'll put some of your stuff together and bring it out tonight. God knows what's going to happen here. Put Grandpa on for a minute."

She heard Julie handing the telephone over.

"Papa, will it be all right if Julie stays there for a while?"

"Of course. I assumed she'd stay here, as long as she needs to."

"Good. Thanks, Papa. And how about Zachary? Do you have room for him there at your house?"

"Sure. You could stay here too, only somebody would have to use the sofa."

"I might end up doing that, Pa. Listen, things are still very confused here, but at some point I'll be coming out. I'll call you before I leave."

"That'll be good, sweetheart. I'm going to take Julie back to my place now. Buster can handle things here."

Eleanora returned to the kitchen, where Peter and Zachary were making coffee. She asked Zachary to put together anything he might need for the next couple of days, and he volunteered to pack a bag for Julie as well.

Eleanora realized she'd have to contact the school — and then she remembered Connie. Realizing she would have to forfeit waking up with him in the morning, she felt a surge of frustration, but the kids were her priority.

She excused herself from Peter and went onto the porch to call Connie. He didn't answer, so she left a message telling him there had been a crisis and that she was going to her father's with the kids.

When she returned to the kitchen, Peter had a cup of tea waiting for her. "How are you holding up?" he asked.

"I don't know. I'm less concerned about Aaron now that I know Julie is safe with my father. I guess I'm most concerned about what provoked this whole thing in the first place. Zachary said there were rumors at school about Julie, something sexual, but he wouldn't be more specific. I'll just have to wait until I can talk to Julie."

"Zach won't tell you?"

"He doesn't want to be forced into saying anything. He's trying to protect her, but I'm not sure from what." She sighed in frustration and picked up her mug.

Zach came downstairs with two stuffed duffel bags.

"I was wondering," he said as he sat down at the table, "whether Dad might have gone to the hospital." Peter and Eleanora looked at each other.

"That sounds like a good idea, Zach," she said. "Why don't you ask the officer if they've checked the hospitals. And while you're at it, see if he wants some coffee."

Zach jogged out to the front of the house and returned with Detective Park.

"Hello, Detective. Would you like some coffee?"

He accepted a mug from her.

"Please, Detective, sit down. Tell me, have you found out anything?"

Park rubbed his face with one hand before leaning forward. "Regarding your husband, still no sign of him. We've checked around his place of employment in Teaneck, and all of the hospitals in Bergen County. We're in the process of checking Passaic and Hudson counties. He hasn't been seen at the addresses of your daughter's friends or at her place of employment, and none of our own cars have seen him within the town limits. Anywhere else you can think of where he might be?"

Eleanora shook her head, but Peter spoke up. Looking at Eleanora, he asked, "Is it possible he might have assumed Julie would go to your place? Might he be wherever it is you're staying?"

She shrugged, indicating it could be a possibility.

Detective Park called the Hoboken police and gave them the description of Aaron and his car. A few minutes later, a call came back — no luck. "Well, it was a good idea and at least they're on the lookout in case he shows up."

"Did you find out anything when you went to Roy's house?" she asked.

"Not really. The boy was there with his parents. They denied hearing from either your daughter or your husband. When I confronted him with the fact that I knew they'd had an argument on the phone earlier this evening, he tried to downplay it. He denied that she was breaking up with him, or that she had any reason to. I didn't let on that you knew where she was," he added, looking at Eleanora. She was grateful for his sensitivity to her concerns and thanked him for that. "I don't know that I believed anything the boy said, but since your daughter is all right, I really didn't feel I had the right to intrude on the privacy of their relationship. It would have been different if he had been suspected of a crime."

"I understand," she said.

"With your husband, it's a different matter. It's clear he assaulted your daughter, or at least attempted to, and we'll question him more closely once we locate him."

"What about my son?" she asked. "He's not going to get into any trouble for what he did, is he?"

"No," he smiled, "your daughter is lucky he did what he did. Otherwise, who knows?" This is what Eleanora had thought, but it was comforting to hear the detective confirm that for her.

"Now what?" asked Peter.

"I suggest we leave a note for Mr. Hoffman, in case he returns. I see no reason for me to continue to have a patrol car here. We'll just wait to hear from him."

"Then my son and I are free to leave?"

"Just give me a number where I can reach you." He paused. "If it becomes necessary for me to get a statement from your daughter, I'll contact you directly."

Eleanora planned to leave a note for Aaron, letting him know that both children were safe — but she decided not to. *The hell with him. Let him worry.*

Eleanora and Zachary were on the way to her father's house when her phone rang. It was Connie.

"Right now, everything is OK," she reassured him. "I'm taking my son, Zachary, to his grandfather's. For a while, we had no idea where Julie was, but it turns out she took a taxi there earlier. It looks like I'll be staying there tonight, too. There are some things I have to talk to Julie about."

"Is there anything I can do?"

"I don't think so. Aaron tried to assault Julie and Zach tried to stop it. Aaron has disappeared and the police are looking for him now."

"How are your kids? Are they all right?"

"Yes. They're both fine — at least physically. But this means I have no choice, I have to seek custody. There's no way they can stay with him after this. They're both frightened to death of him."

"Yes, of course they would be." He paused. "I'm going to miss seeing you in the morning," he said softly.

"So am I...."

"Why don't I call you tomorrow?"

"Please do. I'll fill you in on everything then."

"I want you to call me right away if another emergency pops up, all right?"

"I will. Goodnight, Connie."

Eleanora put her phone away and Zachary looked at her curiously. "That was the man Dad was upset about? The one he said you were having an affair with?"

"Yes. That was Connie."

"You're dating him now?"

"Yes. I am." Zachary remained quiet. After a long pause, she glanced at her son. "What are you really asking me, Zach? What is it you really want to know?"

He shrugged his shoulders and turned to look out the window.

"I told you before, I just met him and I didn't go out with him until after I moved out — after your dad and I were separated. I never cheated on your father. It never even occurred to me." She saw him barely nod his head.

"Come on, Zach, look at me. Tell me what you're concerned about, what you really think about me seeing Mr. Chermant."

"I don't know, Mom. It's just weird. I know you and Dad don't really love each other. Julie and I have talked and I understand you have a right to be happy. It's just that it's kind of embarrassing, having a mother who's dating a black guy. Maybe if it happened later on, after you and Dad were separated for a while and we got a chance to get used to it, I might even think it's cool, the way Julie does. But everything happening together, it's all jumbled up — your moving out and working, Dad drinking and being a jerk, this trouble with Julie. It's like the whole family is a huge embarrassment. And it's messed up enough without adding the fact that my mother's dating a black musician. Christ, how much more weird can it get?"

Eleanora couldn't help but smile. "You're absolutely right, Zach. It is one big mess. I can't even imagine how I might have reacted if my mother had gone out to dinner with someone the day after my father left." She imagined such a scene and had to laugh at its impossibility: Eva in a house dress, her hair tied back in a bun, speaking only Italian and sitting in a neighborhood Italian restaurant with someone like Connie. Impossible! She glanced at her son and saw that he was smiling, gratified perhaps that she empathized with him.

"Still, I want to tell you, Zach, Mr. Chermant is a very nice gentleman. And I'm looking forward to you and Julie having the opportunity of meeting him."

Zach rolled his eyes and let out a little moan.

"I understand," she said quickly, "that meeting Connie is not high on your agenda right now, and I respect that. I'm not going to push anything on you. God knows there's enough on our plates as it is. I'm only saying it's something that I'd like to happen before too much more time goes by. I think he's going to be an important person in my life and you and your sister should meet him." She leaned toward him for emphasis. "Listen to me. Nobody is more important to me than you and Julie, and if he's going to be in my life, then he should meet the two of you. It's as simple as that."

Zach nodded. "Yeah. I guess."

After a few more minutes, Eleanora asked him, "I was just thinking, Zach, aside from Buster at Grandpa's club, do you know any other black people?"

Zach thought for a few moments and then shook his head.

"You don't have any African American kids in any of your classes?" she asked.

Again, he shook his head. "We have plenty of Asian kids — more than half the school is Korean or Chinese or Japanese. But we don't have any black kids at all. And none of our teachers are black. And there aren't any black storeowners in town, so how would I ever get to meet one?"

"You're right," she said, comprehending for the first time how white the town was. "Why does it make a difference to you that Mr. Chermant is black?"

"I don't know. I don't know him. I mean, if you like him and you say Grandpa likes him, then he's probably OK."

"You're right, Zach. But you answered my question. His being black is really beside the point. The real issue is what kind of a person is he. And I have to tell you, I'm really proud of you. I like the way you think."

Chapter Twenty-Three

The following day, Eleanora went to the Leonia police station to meet with Detective Park. He seemed eager to share the interview he'd had with her husband earlier that morning.

"He called me about 1:00 this morning and said he just got home and saw my note. He became incensed when he learned that you had let me into his house. I suggested he come to the station this morning and I'd explain everything to him, but he said he had to go to work. I mentioned that we had gone to his place of employment in our effort to locate him, because we were investigating a complaint of domestic violence at his home. When I mentioned that, he reluctantly agreed to come to the station at 8:00 a.m.

"When he arrived, I asked him about the bump on his head," the detective continued. "He said he didn't think it was any of my business and I told him that in an investigation of domestic violence, evidence of a blow to the head could prove relevant; perhaps a felony had been committed. The word *felony* apparently got his attention, and he agreed to tell me what happened.

"When he got home after work, he heard his daughter on the telephone arguing with her boyfriend. She mentioned something about sex and he got concerned. When he asked her what the argument was about, she refused to tell him and left for work. That was it, no domestic violence other than some raised voices and certainly no reason for his estranged wife to be in his house, making outrageous accusations against him. He said you were being either hysterical or outright malicious in order to buttress claims for more alimony or a larger divorce settlement. He even asked if he could bring charges against you for trespassing or illegal entry.

"I told him that his daughter hadn't gone to work after their argument because when I'd been in the house, I'd seen a detailed schedule of the children's chores and activities — that he had made up — and his daughter was not scheduled to work last night. I pointed out that he'd just claimed he was very concerned at hearing Julie arguing with her boyfriend, and now he's saying he let her off, without any explanation, and claiming she's going to work? I confronted him — if she'd said that, he'd have known she was lying."

Eleanora appreciated the detective's powers of observation and took delight in Aaron being done in by his own obsessive need for control. "Hoisted on his own petard," she chuckled. "And you were absolutely right, Detective, Aaron would never let Julie get away with being that disrespectful."

"Furthermore," Park resumed, "I pointed out that after your daughter *supposedly* walked out, he never saw her — or heard from her — again. Not a word. And this morning, she's still not home — and he *still* doesn't know where she is. She's been out all night and he didn't even ask me — not one single question — about her. Not one. I asked him, how did he think that looked? Well, he admitted that it didn't look too good."

Until that moment, Eleanora hadn't realized that Aaron hadn't questioned Julie's absence, even though he had no idea where she was or what had happened to her. Eleanora was newly outraged.

Obviously Detective Park was deriving satisfaction from relating his interview with Aaron, and continued with his account "No, not good at all. I told him, to be perfectly frank, it looked like he was either a totally indifferent father or lying. Either way it didn't look good. That's when he admitted he had gone after her. He described how he'd grabbed her and shook her, trying to get her to tell him what her argument with her boyfriend was about. But she broke away and ran upstairs, then left the house. That's when I asked him how your son figured into his story."

Again, Eleanora had been so caught up in the recounting of events that she didn't realize Zach hadn't even been mentioned up to now.

"Well, Mrs. Hoffman, at that point he just let out this big sigh. He realized then that he had to tell me everything. He said your son came home and heard your husband and daughter arguing. He tried to get his father off his sister but Mr. Hoffman pushed him out of the way and he fell across a table or something. That's when Julie ran upstairs. Your husband ran after her and kicked in her door. He said he just wanted her to tell him what happened. He felt strongly that as her father, he had a right to know and was furious at her for refusing to talk to him, for defying him.

"That's when your son entered the room and grabbed your husband from behind, allowing Julie to run out of the room. Your husband said he went after her and must have tripped and fallen down the stairs and banged his head. I don't know if he has no memory or knowledge of having been pushed by your son, or if he's protecting him.

"When he came to, the house was empty. He went to a sports bar and had a couple of beers. When he got home, he saw my note. He assumed the kids were staying out for a night until he cooled off. He argued that he didn't think what happened constituted domestic violence, and that a father has a right to try to get his kids to answer a simple question."

The report about how Aaron had spent the evening sounded to Eleanora like the self-centered thing he might do.

Detective Park continued. "I told Mr. Hoffman that I agreed he had every right to question his daughter if he believed she was in trouble, and that he had an obligation to assess the situation in order to help her. But, Mrs. Hoffman," the detective said, wagging a scolding finger, "I told him he totally failed to comprehend the damage he'd done in going about it the way he did. At that point, your husband challenged me and became belligerent. He asked how I could accuse him of hurting his kids. Just because I had a badge, did I think it made me an expert on his family? What could I possibly know about an American family?"

Eleanora had a perfectly clear image of Aaron's arrogant tone.

"I asked him," Park went on, "if he was saying that as a Korean I can't comment on his behavior? He kind of hedged and questioned how I could understand a his family when I wasn't even an American myself."

The detective paused here, looking down at the papers on his desk. He shook his head. "I have to admit, Mrs. Hoffman, your husband really rubbed me the wrong way. I take pride in being professional, but he really got under my skin."

"I understand completely, Detective. Aaron has that effect on people."

He took a breath before continuing. "Anyway, I asked him if I'd be an American if I'd been born here, and he tried to weasel out of what he'd been implying. He said that he only meant that Korean culture is different from Western culture — that there are different values, and therefore there's no way I could understand him or his family.

"So I told him that if I were newly arrived in this country, I might agree with him, but my parents have been here for over 50 years. My sisters and I were born here, raised right here in this town. I went to school here and watched TV as a kid here. I probably had a couple of the same teachers his children had. We lived just a few blocks from where he lives now. My parents still live here and so do I, with my wife and children — all three generations. So I told him, I understand this culture very well.

"Mrs. Hoffman, I've been a detective in the Juvenile Division for over 10 years. I've dealt with dozens and dozens of kids who've been assaulted and battered and abused by their parents; sexually and physically and emotionally abused — in this very town. I told him that. And I said I understood him very well — and that what he did last night constitutes assault and battery — a very serious charge. I spelled it out for him: He could be arrested. He had terrorized his daughter and his son — and now they're scared to death of him."

Eleanora grasped the gravity of the situation and felt a sense of relief. This would have put the fear of God into Aaron. She felt reassured that he would have learned a lesson and she knew the children would be safe with him after this.

Park continued with his report. "I told him that I wasn't accusing him of having bad intentions. I couldn't comment on what's in his heart. Maybe he did love his kids. Anyway, I thanked him for his cooperation and informed him that the children were safe with you. I indicated that a detailed report of the incident would be available to both your attorneys. And I told him the county prosecutor would review the matter and it was possible he might be charged."

Eleanora sat back on her chair, across the desk from Detective Park. She pictured Aaron just as the detective had described him: arrogant, controlling, defensive — and finally — embarrassed and ashamed. He was in danger of losing everything and she pitied him.

She thanked the detective and teasingly said she hoped she wouldn't have occasion to see him again in his official capacity. Outside in her car, she made an appointment with Carmella to report the incident and revise the custody demands she would be making.

From the police station, she drove to the high school and asked to meet with the principal. Eleanora intended to move both children to a new school. The principal was puzzled, but when she explained the circumstances, he called in the superintendent of schools and one of the guidance counselors. Everyone was extremely cooperative and assured her that the paperwork necessary for transferring Zachary and Julie to a new school would be completed by that afternoon. All she had to do was provide the name of the person to send the transcripts to.

Emotionally exhausted, Eleanora called Connie. When he answered, she growled into the phone, "Get ready for me. I'm coming to get you."

"I'm ready now. Where are you?"

"Maybe 10 minutes away."

"I can't wait," he said. "I've missed you. How long has it been?"

"Two whole days. Much too long. I'll see you very soon. I love you."

"Yes," he said. "I love how you love me. Get here soon."

When Eleanora emerged from the elevator, Connie was standing at the open door to his condo wearing only a silk robe. At the sight of him she thought of leaping into his arms and wrapping her legs around his waist, but she imagined she might succeed only in knocking him down.

Later, resting in each other's arms, Eleanora told him what had happened when she'd arrived at her father's house the previous night. Her father and Irene had already talked with Julie and Irene had the good sense to take pictures of the spot on Julie's cheek where Aaron had slapped her and the bruises on her arms where he'd grabbed her. She took pictures of a big black-and-blue mark Zach had under his arm, from when Aaron pushed him. She put the pictures on a flash drive to give to Carmella.

"Eventually, everyone else went to bed and Julie and I stayed up. I made some tea and we talked. At first, Julie had been reluctant to tell me what happened. She felt so ashamed, she didn't know if she could tell me."

But with encouragement, she told her mother about her sexual involvement with Roy. She didn't think Roy had been with anyone else and wasn't concerned about getting a disease from him. She had been to Planned Parenthood and had a prescription for birth control pills. Eleanora wasn't surprised to hear of Julie's sexual activity, but admitted she hadn't really allowed herself to think about it either. Julie told her mother that in addition to having intercourse, Roy liked receiving oral sex.

"Can you imagine my own daughter, 17 years old, doing that before I did? That was a shock to me and I guess she saw it in my face. I told her it was all right, that I was just surprised — my baby doing that with that stupid boy. On the other hand, I was a little envious that she's so liberated at her age."

Eleanora continued to recount what Julie had told her. Roy had been pressing her to go down on him in front of his friends. He wanted to show off. She had said no — that what they did together was private. But he persisted, telling her that it was important for him to show his closest friends what a real girlfriend was like. He said it hurt him that she wouldn't do this to make him happy. Julie told her mother she didn't know why she agreed.

Eleanora recalled the pain in Julie's voice when she asked her mother, "Why did I think I was supposed to do everything he wanted me to do? What made me think it was my job to make him happy — no matter how unhappy it made me, as if I had no right to say no?" So Julie finally gave in and said she'd give Roy a blowjob while his three friends watched — even though she was livid with Roy for pushing her and furious with herself for giving in.

"Oh, Connie, I felt like crumbling on the spot. My heart just broke for her. The look in her eyes, pleading with me not to judge her. She felt so ashamed, so naked and vulnerable in front of me. I don't know how she kept from breaking down, but you could see all her grief and shame right there on the surface. She was filled to bursting with it. I don't know how I kept from sobbing. Me, I cry at dog food commercials. I just pulled her to me. What could I say? There were no words to express what she needed to get and what I needed to give.

157

I just held her until she began to sob and let it all out. I just held her and absorbed her tears and her rage until she pulled herself together."

Eleanora was close to blubbering at that point and Connie pulled her closer to him. "There's more," she said. "I looked at her, my baby. She was so guilt-ridden and ashamed. I told her she didn't have to tell me anymore, but she insisted. She said she needed to get it out."

With difficulty, Eleanora continued her description of what Julie had so tearfully shared with her. She recounted Julie's description of how Roy made her get on her knees in front of him and suck his dick while his three asshole friends watched.

"Listen to this, Connie: She said that usually, when she does that to Roy, she covers his penis with her hand when he's ready to come, so it doesn't get all over. 'You know,' she said, looking at me, 'you probably do something like that with Daddy.' Can you imagine? If she only knew."

Eleanora could not help but visualize what came next: Roy putting his hand on the back of Julie's head when he came, making her take it in her mouth and swallow it. She didn't want to, but she didn't have any choice. Eleanora heard Julie's strained voice telling her: "Can you believe it, Mom, even then I didn't want to do anything that would embarrass him in front of his friends."

Then, after he came, he laughed and asked his friends if they wouldn't like some of that? And they all said yeah. Julie had been incredulous. What she had just allowed herself to do was horrible enough — now Roy wanted her to blow his friends? He told her to do it for him. Then Julie said one of the boys, Lee, opened his pants. Roy held her by her hair and the next thing she knew, Lee's erection was in her mouth and almost immediately he came all over her face. And then it was Frank and Ken. All the while, the boys were egging each other on. Eleanora was sobbing at this point. The sadness she felt for Julie was so immense, so overwhelming — but so was her rage.

"Oh, Connie, it was horrible. They kept saying terrible things to her, laughing at her, and she had their cum all over her face, in her eyes and hair and on her clothes. It's so disgusting. I took her into my arms and held her. The next day in school, some of the kids looked at her strangely and smirked. Some of the boys asked her if she wanted to blow them. There was graffiti in the girls' room saying Julie Hoffman gives lessons in cock-sucking and stuff like that. By the end of the day someone had written on a blackboard in one of her classes: *For the best bj in town*, and then her phone number. She said that she was never so humiliated and ashamed. She just wanted to disappear. None of her friends stood by her. Nobody did anything to support her. Even in class, when someone made a crack, none of the teachers did anything."

Eleanora paused to get a tissue to wipe her eyes. She glanced at Connie and thought he looked grim. His jaw was set and his lips pressed together.

"Go on," he said, "tell me what happened next."

"So, yesterday she was on the phone with Roy telling him that she never wanted to see him again, that he was a cruel, stupid bastard and she wanted to kill him. Connie, she told me she even thought if she were dead, she wouldn't have to deal with it. That's when her father came home. He must have overheard her tell Roy that he'd made her feel like a whore. Aaron wanted to know what it was all about, but there was no way she was going to tell him anything."

Connie held her tightly. He kissed her hair and her forehead. Then she told him about how Aaron had gone after Julie, how he smacked her when she wouldn't talk to him, how Zachary tried to protect his sister, and finally, what Detective Park had told her. When she was finished, she lay quietly against him.

"You realize," he said quietly, "those boys raped your daughter."

"I know."

"Are you going to do anything about it?"

She shook her head against his chest. "I can't, Connie. I can't put her through a legal process. It would be like getting raped all over again. She's been through enough humiliation and degradation. I can't subject her to some ruthless defense attorney attacking her, accusing her, raping her again. I won't do it."

She felt him nod and knew he understood. She knew she was being a coward, but she was unwilling to sacrifice her daughter on some altar of idealism. She'd rather endure the guilt of not charging these hoodlums with rape than subject her daughter to additional public ridicule and harassment.

Gradually, Eleanora became aware of Connie's body tensing. She heard the muscles of his jaw clenching. She raised her head and looked at him questioningly.

"I have to tell you something," he said after a long silence. "When I was young, not even as young as these boys, but a young man, I behaved like them. Not the exact same thing. I never raped anybody. I never pressured anyone to do anything she didn't want to do, but I treated women with the same callous attitude. I thought I was cool, that it was manly to use women sexually. I'm not proud of having been that way, immature and selfish and cruel. Maybe most young men go through that phase when all they want is to get laid, when the way to measure your manliness is by how many girls you fuck, how many you get to suck your dick. I'm just so ashamed that it took me as long as it did to get through that phase, to grow up and to realize what I was doing to people."

Eleanora sat up and looked at him, half-propped up against the headboard. He looked so forlorn. She'd never experienced him like this. At first, he avoided her eyes, but she reached out to touch his face. He pressed her palm against his cheek and glanced up at her.

"Eleanora, I hate those bastards for what they did to your daughter and what they've done to you. But I understand them too. I see myself at their age. If I had been one of Roy's friends, I might have done what they did. I hope I wouldn't have, but I don't know. And, we're lying here , the two of us cradling your grief because of what happened to your daughter — and I feel like I don't have a right to be here with you."

Connie confessed this in a barely audible whisper. She looked into his eyes and saw them full to the brim.

"You're not that young man anymore, Connie. You said you hate those boys because you hate that part of you. I hate them for a totally different reason. I hate Roy because of how he manipulated Julie's desire to please him. I see myself in her and I realize that Aaron — or any boy — could have manipulated me and taken advantage of me the same way Roy took advantage of her. I hate him as I hate that part of me. And I know that I still — even though I know better — I still could fall into the same trap of thinking that I should give myself away, that I could betray my own instincts in favor of someone else's wishes. It's the part of me that allowed myself to stay with Aaron for so long. And I hate myself for that."

Eleanora made Connie look at her. "Part of what I love about you is that you struggle against letting me do that. I know you haven't said it yet, maybe it's a man thing, but I know you love me. I know you value who I am. You respect my feelings, my needs. You truly want what's best for me, even if it might not be what's best for you. You don't have to tell me. I see it. I feel it."

Connie kissed her gently on the mouth. "You're right, of course."

"About what?"

"That I love you."

Eleanora smiled. "Now, that wasn't so hard, was it?"

Connie shook his head. "No, you're mistaken. It was very hard. I really fought against saying it. I was afraid I'd say it too easily and end up using you. I didn't want to do that. I was also afraid that I might be only a novelty for you and that after an initial attraction, you'd decide I was too much trouble — you know, the age thing, the race thing, religion, your kids. The truth is, I was afraid you would dump me."

"What?" It came out as a squeal. "You were afraid that *I'd dump you*?"

"Yes, I was."

"My God. Oh, Connie, Connie."

Their hands began to trace the contours of each other's bodies and soon she was straddling him. She rode him slowly while he caressed her body and they looked into each other's face, mouthing words of love.

Chapter Twenty-Four

That afternoon, Eleanora brought Carmella up to date regarding the events of the previous evening. She gave her attorney the pictures of her children's bruises and reported what Detective Park had told her. They discussed her wish to transfer Julie and Zachary to a Catholic high school, as well as her decision to quit her job playing for the church in favor of working at her father's Lounge and studying piano.

"After last night, Carmella, I'm determined to have custody of both Julie and Zach. Aaron can have visiting rights — if they're willing to see him. If I'm the primary parent, he'll have to pay me child support. Also, if the children are living with me, the house should be sold and the assets split. If he wants to keep it, then he's got to buy me out. I don't care which he chooses, but I need my share so I can buy my own place for the kids and myself. If he gives any push-back, threaten him with a civil suit for the mental anguish he's caused the children and me by assaulting his own daughter."

"Oh, Mama Bear, I love it when you're angry," Carmella smiled. "Yes! And don't forget, since we're letting him believe this move is necessitated solely because of his assault on Julie, he's also going to be responsible for the private schooling. And, since there is such inequity in your earning power — because he kept you at home all these years — it's only reasonable that he pay you a generous alimony, not to mention the lion's share of the children's college tuitions when they begin."

Eleanora agreed. She had been quite prepared, only a week or two ago, to ask for as little as necessary. Now, buoyed by fury and resolve, empowered by the recent events, she was demanding her rightful share. She liked feeling her strength. For a change, she wasn't frightened at all. After ironing out the details, including a discussion of medical coverage and life insurance, Carmella assured her she would easily shove the whole package down Putz's throat.

"Or up his butt, whichever way he wants it."

Full of self-justification, Eleanora headed to St. Mary's Catholic high school in Rutherford and made arrangements for Julie and Zachary's transfer. She did not go into any of the details of Julie's traumatic experience with Roy. Instead, she attributed the transfer to being the result of her estranged husband's violent assault on his daughter necessitating an emergency move on their part. The school administrators were sympathetic, and glad to be getting two excellent — and paying — students. Eleanora made the call right there for the mailing of the transcripts, then left to return to her father's, tired but exhilarated by the full day's work behind her.

After picking up the kids from her father's, Eleanora drove to her temporary condo in Hoboken. On the way, she reassured them that they would go back to the house in Leonia to get their belongings, but would remain at Grandpa's. For now, she wanted to show them where she was staying. When they discussed where she would consider buying a place, both kids had lots of opinions.

They rode the ornate, old-fashioned elevator together. When Julie and Zachary saw Irene's layout, with the high-ceilinged, wood-paneled walls and view of lower Manhattan across a boat-filled Hudson River, they asked if they could live in a place like this.

"Isn't it great?" she smiled. "I love it too, although there's not enough room for all of us. But this is something you can aspire to someday — there are a lot more exciting places to live than a house in the suburbs."

After a quick walk around the neighborhood to show them the variety of ethnic grocery stores and services, all within walking distance, they boarded a PATH train to lower Manhattan. It had been a long time since either of the kids had been into this part of New York, and they gazed at everything like tourists. Eleanora piled them into a taxi and they headed for the hospital, where her mother lay silently. Velia was sitting by the bed.

Eva looked like a cadaver. Her pale white skin stretched tautly over her now frail, bony body, and the sweet smell of death hung heavily in the room. Velia embraced the children to her hungrily. She couldn't stop commenting on how much they had grown since she had last seen them, and — despite their discomfort — Eleanora saw that they basked in this exuberant display of familial love.

Both children were disturbed by the sad, lifeless state to which their grandmother had descended. Velia reported that the doctor had said there were signs that she was growing weaker. Eleanora embraced her aunt and felt the older woman's tears soaking into her shoulder.

Eleanora seized the moment to make an announcement. "As you know, I've been spending time with Mr. Chermant. I've told him about what we've been through, including Grandma being in a coma. He wants to be as supportive of us as he can. He asked if he could come here today to meet you, but I thought it would be better if we had this time alone. It's been a long time since you guys got to see Zia Velia, or Grandma for that matter." She thought she noticed some sense of relief on their faces.

"But I did suggest that he might want to meet us for dinner later. He wants very much to get to know you all." She quickly added that Connie already knew her father and Irene quite well.

Velia was the first to speak. "Good, dolly. I'm looking forward to meeting this man of yours. Maybe he'll have a friend for me!" Everyone laughed.

Julie added her two cents. "That's fine, Mom. I'd like to meet him, too."

Eleanora looked over to Zach, who shrugged his shoulders. "Why not?" He seemed more interested in where they would go for dinner.

"Connie said he likes a restaurant on Thompson Street in the Village. He'll meet us there about 6:00, so we have another hour or so to visit with Grandma. Dinner is his treat."

Velia made a face of approval and Eleanora glowed inside. She wanted them to like and accept him — but even if they didn't, she was prepared to continue seeing him. She was swiftly learning that her life, after all, belonged to *her.*

They continued to catch up on what had been happening in each other's lives, and the plans for a new life that was just beginning to take shape. Both children were eager to move to a new school. Zach expressed some regret over separating from his friends, but minimized it by saying they could email and play games online anyway, so this really wouldn't be much different.

"Aren't there any girls who are going to miss you? You're not leaving any broken hearts behind?" Zia Velia inquired.

"Afraid not, Zia. I guess I'm not what girls are looking for."

Julie attempted to reassure him. "Give them time, Zach. They'll wise up about what's really important in a guy. I just hope I meet someone who's got what you've got."

"Same back at you." Both could sense the sincerity and depth of the compliment.

Connie was already at the table when the waiter showed them into a back room. He rose to greet them.

Velia smiled and said quietly in Italian to Eleanora, "He's dark enough to be Sicilian."

Connie laughed. "Si, Senora, southern Sicily." Velia's hand flew to her mouth and she stared wide-eyed in embarrassment. But Connie leaned over and put his hand on her shoulder.

"It's all right, Senora, I take it as a compliment."

Everyone laughed, and the ice was broken.

Connie ordered a bottle of wine for the table and poured glasses for Eleanora and Velia. The children had staked out places on either side of their mother, and Eleanora found herself gazing across the round table at her handsome lover, seated between her aunt and her son. Connie offered his sympathies to Velia on the sad news of her sister's grave illness. He took her hand in both of his and offered soothing words that brought a smile to the older woman's face, as well as a swell of tears. Zachary had his face buried in the menu, but Julie was observing Connie closely and Eleanora was proud of what her daughter saw.

Connie turned his attention to Zachary and offered to help him with the menu, which was in Italian. After everyone ordered their main course, Connie suggested they also enjoy *Il Grand Antipasto* while they were waiting for their entrée, and asked if anyone wanted to try the highly recommended *tortellini en brodo*. He had looked directly at the three women and they all acquiesced.

The dinner was leisurely and companionable, with delicious food, unobtrusive yet attentive service, and a finale of scrumptious desserts and coffee. Connie had not asked Julie about her ordeal, instead saying only that he understood she'd recently suffered a difficult experience and that he was sorry to hear about it. Julie appeared to appreciate his sensitivity and Eleanora was pleasantly surprised by the well-informed, adult-level conversation her daughter maintained with Connie throughout the meal.

Afterward, outside the restaurant, they thanked Connie for the wonderful dinner. He shook hands with Zia Velia — calling her Zia — but she pulled him to her and kissed him on the cheek. This apparently set the stage for Julie, who embraced him and kissed his cheek as well. Zachary settled for a hearty handshake. Eleanora put both arms around his neck and planted a big kiss on his lips.

"I've been wanting to do that for the past two hours," she laughed. "Thank you, Connie. It couldn't have been better."

"Will I see you tomorrow?" he asked.

"I hope so," she said. "There's loads to do and tomorrow night I'll be at the Lounge, but hopefully I'll see you in the afternoon. I'll call you."

He reminded her that he would be leaving the next night for New Orleans

"Hopefully, we'll have a few hours before I leave for the airport."

They dropped Zia Velia her off at her apartment house and took the train ride back to New Jersey. Julie and Zachary were in good spirits, teasing each other and talking about what their new living arrangements might be like. Finally, Eleanora came right out and asked what they had thought of Connie.

"I liked him," said Julie. "I think he's classy. He's intelligent and sensitive and he dresses nice."

Eleanora looked questioningly at Zach, who just smiled at her. "Well?" she asked.

"I thought he was cool," he said. "Like Julie said — intelligent and thoughtful. He didn't talk down to me and he had a good sense of humor. I liked him."

Eleanora was delighted, but her primary reaction was one of astonishment that it had gone so easily. She was still feeling disoriented by all of the topsy-turvy changes in their lives — and yet, her family appeared to accept her dating another man, an older man, a black man, without any qualm at all.

Julie and Zach returned to talking about their new living arrangements as if further discussion of her relationship with Connie held no more significance. Either that, or they're afraid to ask what's really on their minds: *Am I sleeping with him? Am I going to live with him? Am I going to marry him*? And then, re-membering her conversation with Connie: *Am I planning to have children with him? Well, if they have these questions, they'll ask sooner or later.* She could al-ready see that her children were more resourceful and better able to handle themselves than she had given them credit for. That observation gave her a feeling of pride, but then she thought of how Julie had allowed herself to be emotionally manipulated by Roy.

She recalled the conversation she'd had with Zia Velia about how Eva had never been able to assert herself with her own mother. Eva had lived her life as an appendage, never breaking free and establishing an identity of her own, never free to have her own thoughts, goals, dreams. Now Eva was waiting to be carried over death's threshold and all of her possibilities, all of her might-have-beens, would be gone forever.

Eleanora had managed to rebel against Eva's expectations that she, too, would be passive and submissive and obedient. Still, her rebellion had been only partially successful. Even though she had managed to escape the cage her mother built for her, she had brought a compliant mindset into her marriage. She had more gumption than her mother — she had insisted on her music, for example — but still felt obliged to do everything to make Aaron happy, no mat-ter what. Being a good person meant being a good wife who made her hus-band happy.

Eleanora had aimed to be successful where her mother had failed utterly.

She had believed that her inability to make Aaron happy was evidence of her inadequacy — which confirmed her mother's critical view of her. And she feared she might have conveyed this principle to her own daughter. Hopefully, the experience Julie had suffered had taught her a valuable lesson. *God knows, I said everything to her that I could think of to drive that home.*

From Hoboken, Eleanora drove her children back to their grandfather's and decided to stay the night rather than drive back to Irene's condo. She wanted to be there for them in the morning and make their breakfast. She was eager have her own place with the kids, and intended to start looking as soon as possible.

Chapter Twenty-Five

Eleanora and Irene made pancakes for breakfast, weaving around each other in the kitchen easily, like old friends. Joey and Irene were so authentic and accepting that Julie and Zach felt right at home. Eleanora enjoyed this sense of family regained and extended, and the kids were glad she was there to feed them, just as she had always done. It made her feel more solid.

Eleanora told her father about their visit to the hospital and about her mother's deteriorated condition. He brought up some memories — of times when Eleanora was still quite young, of family gatherings and big holiday dinners before the Palottas discovered the old Sicilian feud of their villages. Julie and Zach asked their grandpa what their mother had been like as a young girl, and Eleanora was both embarrassed and pleased at his overt bragging — what a good student she was, how pretty, what a good person.

After breakfast, Eleanora and her father sat on the back porch with their mugs while Julie and Zachary helped Irene clean up. It was then that she confided in him and told him how Julie had been raped. He was shocked and outraged, but kept his emotions under control. They continued to talk quietly until the kids came out to join them.

Later, Eleanora took Julie and Zachary to their father's house and waited in the driveway while they gathered up some belongings. Relieved that Aaron was at work, she took the time to reflect on the events of the past two weeks. It felt like a lifetime! She was already a different person — suddenly grown up and in charge of her life. Her kids — and even Aaron — had changed as well.

Now she looked at her old house through different eyes. The wide driveway, the azaleas and rhododendron and manicured lawn, now felt somewhat artificial. Rather than missing the homey comfort, she felt alienated and detached from it. The feelings of stifled suffocation circled around the house — but she was no longer confined. Now her wings were strong, and she was ready to use them.

Julie and Zachary exited the house, dragging big plastic garbage bags filled with their stuff. When it had been packed into her car, Eleanora brought the kids to the Lounge for lunch. She was determined to show them where she worked, to dispel the derogatory image Aaron had created. She was also looking forward to showing them off. They hung out in the kitchen while Emilio made lunch for them, and Buster joined them at the table for the meal.

"I hear you're all camping out with Joe and Irene," he joked, "pitching tents on the living room floor, catching poison ivy."

"It's not that bad, Mr. Jones," said Julie. "Actually, we're having a lot of fun there. We haven't seen our grandfather in a long time and Miss Duffy is a really neat lady."

"So she is," Buster agreed, "Well, if you like it enough, maybe we can get you to stay. Maybe even put the two of you to work here." They responded enthusiastically, thinking of money to be made in a summer job, and turned to Eleanora in hopeful anticipation.

"Let's take it one step at a time, guys," she suggested. But the possibility of a family business appealed to her, and she enjoyed the warmth of the relaxed atmosphere.

After she dropped the kids off at her father's house, she stopped at a realtor's to start the process of looking for new accommodations for herself and the children. Back at Irene's condo, she changed her clothes then headed for Connie's.

She couldn't wait to see him. Hungry for his touch, she marveled at the discovery that she was still capable of this kind of passion after 20 years of a monotone marriage to Aaron. Now she felt alive. She soared. Music coursed through her. Her senses were alive, sharply defined. *Life is so amazing*!

Finally in his arms, she wanted to consume him with her kisses. It felt so right to be with him again, to run her fingers through his wiry hair, to see herself reflected lovingly in his laughing eyes, to feel the little bristles of his moustache against her lips. In bed, she enjoyed stroking his long, lean body, and seeing the contrast of her olive whiteness against his smooth dark skin.

It was also obvious that Connie experienced great pleasure exploring her body. She delighted in how aroused he was by her, amazed that she could ignite that kind of intensity in anyone, never mind someone as seasoned as he was.

After their lovemaking, Connie brought a tall glass of iced tea back to bed for each of them. In each other's arms, they lounged in a pool of contentment. Eleanora shared her plans to buy a small house that would be convenient to him, the Lounge, her father's house in Nutley, and the children's new school in Rutherford.

"I also want to be near New York," she added. "I'm determined to study piano seriously, so being close to the city is essential."

Connie said he knew a number of excellent teachers in the city.

"Maybe next week, when you're back from New Orleans, you can give me their names and tell me something about them," she said eagerly. "Of course, everything depends on Aaron going along with my requests. Right now I have nothing, *nienta*. Hopefully, he won't delay things too long, but the truth is, he could string things out for quite a while."

"If he does, I think that assassin lawyer of yours will make him pay a helluva price for it," Connie told her. They laughed at his image of Carmella arriving at Aaron's front door with Putz's head under her arm in a hammerlock, threatening to castrate them both if he didn't agree to everything on the spot.

Eleanora drove to choir rehearsal with a heavy heart. Although the practice went well, she again felt a cool estrangement from some of the women with whom she had previously been close. When she inquired if something was bothering them, they greeted her with wide eyes and fixed smiles, denying that anything was different and making excuses about the busy holiday season ahead. After practice, Eleanora sought Peter out. She found him in his study, looking somewhat harried.

"You look like you've had a long day," she said from his doorway.

Peter looked up, startled. "Oh, hi, Ellie. Yeah, it's been hectic around here. We've been busy getting up collections for the victims of Hurricane Katrina. It's just a lot of work on top of everything else."

"Well," she said, easing herself into one of the chairs across from his desk, "I hate to bring tidings of more bad news."

A wary look came over his face and he slouched back on his chair, waiting.

"I've decided to stop playing piano here. I'll stay for two more weeks, until the end of the month, but that'll be it."

"Good God, Ellie. Whatever made you decide to leave us?"

"A few things, actually. Julie had a bad experience with her boyfriend and then Aaron got physical with both of my kids, so I've pulled them out of school. For the time being, they'll stay with my father. I'll be getting a place for me and the kids and spending more time working at my father's and studying piano."

"My God...." After a few moments, he looked up at her. "To be honest with you, I did hear something about your daughter. I understand it was ..." — he struggled for a delicate enough word — "*crude* is the only word I can come up with."

She wasn't surprised. If it was going around the school, as Julie had said, of course parents would hear the news and, like water running downhill, it would end up in the gutter.

"Just to set the record straight, Peter, those rumors were spread by a group of boys, including her so-called boyfriend, Roy Kattman, who raped her and forced her to do things she didn't want to do. The whole bunch of them are lucky we're not pressing charges against them, those bastards." She was surprised how much venom she had expressed. Apparently, her uncharacteristic outburst surprised Peter as well.

"Well, I'm not surprised to hear that she was a victim," he said quickly. "Knowing you as well as I do, I couldn't believe what I was hearing."

"Well, don't believe those dirty rumors," she said emphatically, "though I know many will. It's just too hard to combat. I feel it here with the choir. Some of them are looking down their noses at me because of the filth they're hearing. And Aaron's behavior the other night just adds to it. I'm sorry, Peter, all of this crap is just too unpleasant and totally unnecessary. I don't want to deal with it. I don't have to. So, two weeks. I can give you some names of other pianists, if you're interested, who might be willing to take my place here."

"OK," he said quietly, yielding to the determination in her voice, "that would be helpful. What reason should I give, if people ask why you're leaving?"

The question sounded funny to her, and she laughed. "I don't care, Peter. Tell them whatever you're comfortable with. Tell them I'm fed up with their pettiness, if you want to. It no longer matters what anyone thinks. Tell them I've flown the coop."

Peter gave her a wry smile, not sure of what to make of her attitude, so unlike the conventional church pianist he'd thought he'd known. Eleanora picked up her things and turned to leave.

"See you in church," she said, the words trailing behind her as she made her exit.

Instead of returning to Irene's condo, she drove to her father's club. Too revved up to go home to bed, she didn't want to be alone. The club was relaxing, and she looked forward to listening to some live music, or even helping out for a couple of hours. Her father and Buster were delighted to see her and they appreciated her help. Even some of the regular patrons were beginning to know her, and she felt welcomed by a crowd of familiar faces.

Irene stopped in around 10:30. Huddled together like old friends, Eleanora realized she was laughing and having fun — and the unfamiliar feeling struck her as almost new. *My God, have I had so few adult women friends in my life?* A ghost-like image of the haggard, red-eyed Bethann flashed like heat lightning.

Arriving back at Irene's condo after midnight, she felt tired but calm. She had planned to plop right into bed, but the New York skyline beckoned and she sat in a window seat, intoxicated by the twinkly lights, like stars — an infinite universe — waiting to be explored. Her cellphone interrupted her reverie.

It was Connie. After they caught up on the day's events, Eleanora fell contentedly into bed. It was soft and comforting and she sank into it, not feeling alone at all.

Chapter Twenty-Six

Saturday morning, Eleanora woke to lightning and thunder. She was surprised by the power — wind blew the rain hard against the windows, making it sound like hail. Stretching out in a warm, dry bed and listening to the storm made her feel secure.

She called her father's house and asked the kids if they still wanted to go out for breakfast, and they eagerly said yes. Zach had something to tell her, but he'd wait until they were together. Eleanora was barely out of her shower when the phone rang again. It was Carmella Rotundo.

"I have good news and I have bad news, Ellie. Let me give you the bad news first." Eleanora held her breath, prepared for gloomy disappointment. "We asked your husband for half of his pension plan," Carmella went on, "because in New Jersey the wife is entitled to one-half of all of the family assets — and that includes the husband's pension plan. Well, Putz," Carmella couldn't completely suppress a sarcastic snicker, "decided to stake his manhood on that issue, vowing a fight unto death or something, saying he would not let his client be so unscrupulously taken advantage of.

"I told him that I understood his position, but that he had to give me something I could bring back to my client. I said you were as mad as hell about what Mr. Hoffman did to your daughter, and that you gave me pictures that show the bruises he inflicted on both children. I offered to send him copies if he wanted and said I was sure the judge would appreciate seeing them. I told him you had your heart set on receiving half of Mr. Hoffman's pension plan. Then I suggested there was a small possibility that you might consider taking the house in exchange. I complained that Mr. Hoffman was sure to still come out ahead, but I thought I could sell my client on that.

"Putz thought for a moment, if you can call it thinking, and then he agreed it was a deal. So, Mama Bear, you get the whole house and — you get it now instead of having to wait until hubby retires for you to get your share, which he could have made you do with his pension plan."

Eleanora was flabbergasted. She had been hoping for maybe $150,000 or $200,000 from the sale of the house. Now she would have twice that, maybe more.

"Carmella, you are wonderful," she said with relief.

"You can thank your husband for hiring such a putz," she howled. "I tell you, Ellie, I have loved working this case. It'll never be more fun than this. I feel like a young lioness again. Essentially, you got everything you wanted: the house, alimony, child support, the works. Aaron will start looking immediately for a place to live, and the agreement will go to court next week to be finalized. Then all you have to do is wait for 18 months before the divorce is granted. Meanwhile, you have no restrictions or limits on how you live your life. I'll keep you posted as we move along from one step to the next."

Eleanora thanked her. She was thrilled to have this advocate in her life and knew she could trust her judgment on any legal matter that might come up in the future. She dressed, put on her raincoat, and dashed through the downpour to her car.

At her father's, the kids ran to the car, Zach carrying a plastic bag. "Mom, wait till you see," he said as he extended the bag toward her. "You won't believe this. You have to look." Both kids watched her eagerly.

"OK," she said, intrigued by their excitement. She couldn't help getting caught up in it, like waiting to unwrap a present.

"Look at these," Zach said, his face filled with anticipation. Eleanora opened the bag and saw it contained photographs. She reached in and pulled one out.

"What on earth?" She looked at her children in disbelief.

"That's Ken and Roy!" Julie yelled. "Look at the rest. Wait till you see."

Eleanora slowly removed the rest of the photographs. Even without the running commentary from her son and daughter, she recognized what they were: pictures of Roy and three of his friends, their pants around their ankles, holding each other's penises. It looked like they were masturbating each other.

"Julie, are these the boys?"

"Yes, those are the dumb bastards. Can you believe this? And they had the nerve to spread those rumors about me."

"But how? Where?" Eleanora couldn't form a sentence.

Zach couldn't wait to tell her. "Last night my friend emailed them to me. He got them from another kid. By now everybody in the whole school has them. This morning, Roy and the others are saying that some big guys forced them to do it, but nobody believes them. Somebody said the pictures were taken with Roy's own cellphone. I think it's perfect justice for those assholes.

They're a total laughing stock. It's so awesome."

Eleanora was embarrassed by the pictures in front of her. She shoved them back into the plastic bag and stared, amazed, at her children. Thinking of the humiliation that each of the boys would suffer, she felt a little guilty taking pleasure in someone else's misfortune — but a smile of satisfaction spread onto her face just the same.

Julie broke the awkward silence. "I was praying for some kind of justice, only this is more perfect than I could have dreamed. I guess God does work in mysterious ways," she speculated.

"I'm not sure God had anything to do with it," said Eleanora, half to herself. She wondered if somehow her father was behind this, and even considered the possibility that Connie might have had a hand in it. Who else could have arranged this? She didn't accept for one minute that these sadists would voluntarily jerk each other off and then advertise it on the Internet. "Still, if anybody is going to get credit for it," she mused, "it might as well be Her. At any rate, I think this calls for a celebration. Pancakes or waffles?"

As she drove, Eleanora snuck glances at her daughter. It was heartening to see Julie this calm after what had happened to her. *Revenge is sweet.*

During breakfast, Eleanora admitted that the photos had embarrassed her, but that she was proud they felt comfortable enough to share them with her. She described the repressed and uncommunicative atmosphere in which she had been reared.

"If your grandmother had ever seen a picture like any of these, she would have erupted like Mount Vesuvius, crossed herself three or four times, and dropped dead on the spot." Then she asked if their grandfather had seen the pictures.

Zach answered. "At first I only showed them to Julie because I knew she'd be thrilled to see these guys totally embarrassing themselves and have it broadcast all over the school and the Internet. She told me she'd heard you telling Grandpa what happened, so I thought maybe I should show the pictures to him. It was kinda weird, but Julie said these assholes should be embarrassed, not me — and the more people who saw them, the better. So I did."

"And what was his reaction?"

"He asked if these were the same guys who had hurt Julie and how I had gotten the pictures. And then he said it served the fuckers right."

During breakfast, the realtor called to say a house in Nutley had just come on the market that she wanted Eleanora to see. They made arrangements to drive over after their meal.

The house was just what she was looking for: large enough for her and the kids but small enough to be low maintenance. A charming stained-glass window on the landing, chair railings, and ceiling molding created an inviting atmosphere. Outside, simple landscaping surrounded the small Tudor-style home. The neighborhood was established and family-oriented, and the kids especially loved the proximity to their grandfather's house. Eleanora thought it would sell quickly and was tempted to make an offer on the spot, but thought it wise to get some input from Joey and Irene.

Back at her father's, she was describing the house when her cellphone rang again. It was Zia Velia: Her mother had passed away that morning. Eleanora was surprised at how calmly she took the news. She had long ago mourned the lack of her mother's love. Maybe grief would slowly seep in at some point in the future, but now her only emotional reaction was concern for her aunt. She offered to help with arrangements, but Velia said she had talked to the funeral director earlier in the week and everything was taken care of. The viewing was set for Sunday and the funeral Monday afternoon. Eleanora asked Velia if she would like her to come into the city and stay with her, but her aunt said she preferred to be alone. Eleanora understood. Velia suggested that after the funeral she and the children should look around Eva's apartment to see if there was anything she'd like to have.

The heavy rain made Saturday night business at the Lounge slower than usual. After the dinner crowd had ebbed, Eleanora had a chance to speak with her father.

"Irene and I walked past that house the other day," he said, "and it looks like it's been well maintained. I'd go for it if I were you."

It confirmed her thoughts, and she planned to call the realtor in the morning and put in a bid.

She turned to her father. "I was thinking about those pictures that Zach's friend sent him." Giuseppi looked at her, eyebrows raised. "I was just wondering, Papa, if you knew anything about how that happened."

"How Zach's friend emailed him the pictures?"

"Don't be coy, Papa. It's a strange coincidence that a couple of days after those boys did those awful things to Julie, they end up having this done to them."

"Is that what happened? I thought they were just a bunch of gay kids getting off on each other."

She fixed her gaze on him. "You don't think there's anything odd about the story that some 'older big guys' made them do that?"

"How should I know?" he said shrugging his shoulders, a hint of a smile visible under his moustache.

"That's what I'm asking. Do you know anything about it?"

"Look," he said, lowering his voice, "when we were talking yesterday in my back yard, didn't you say you wish those bastards would have to endure the same shame and humiliation that Julie did?"

Eleanora recalled the conversation.

Giuseppi pulled her to him and kissed her on the brow. "So you got your wish. Just accept that it happened. Divine retribution. Let Julie have some satisfaction and put all of this behind her."

He glanced over her shoulder and then back into her face. "You know how much I love you and those kids? Now excuse me for a minute, I've got to say hello to someone."

Eleanora watched him lovingly as he greeted a guest. Her father. She felt more his daughter now than ever before, but she also regarded him with objective eyes and saw a complex man: a gentleman, a musician, an artist, a friend — but also one capable of defending his brood. She admired his strength and his resolve.

Back in Irene's condo, she lay in bed wondering how Connie's concert had gone. She missed the sweet look in his eyes, his amused smile, his masculine scent. Noticing the stirrings of her own arousal, she scolded herself for indulging in romantic fantasies; they would only keep her awake. Her phone rang and she eagerly anticipated his low, musical southern voice.

"Ellie, it's Aaron."

She froze with the sudden shock of fear and disappointment.

"Aaron? Why are you calling at this hour?"

"I just thought you should know, that's all. I thought, it's only right that Ellie knows."

"Know what? What are you talking about?"

"The graffiti that was spray-painted on our garage door tonight. I thought you'd want to know, considering it will soon be your house."

"Aaron, it's 2:30 in the morning. Either tell me what this is about or leave me alone."

"Well, it's about your sweet slut of a daughter. Don't you want to know?"

"Aaron, I'm hanging up ..."

"Don't you dare hang up on me, goddamnit. It's painted on the garage door like an advertisement: 'Julie Hoffman — cocksucker supreme.' Are you proud of your daughter? Following in your footsteps. Like mother, like daughter?"

Grateful that Julie was safely at her father's, Eleanora felt badly that Aaron had to deal with the humiliation and the mess. She knew how he regarded oral sex — in his mind, nothing was more dirty and depraved. For his daughter to be regarded this way was worse for him than if she'd become pregnant.

At the same time, she was incensed by his dismissal of Julie. Was he drunk? Crazed with anger?

"I'm appalled to hear that, Aaron. I hope you'll call the police and do what's necessary to have it removed. I suspect Roy Kattman had something to do with it."

She hung up, her heart racing. *That bastard — calling just to upset me, as if it's my fault or Julie's fault.* She recalled so many little instances that reflected his inability to care for anyone else. For 20 years she'd put up with his lack of consideration for her and the kids. She had made excuses for him, chalking it up to his preoccupation with work. But with the clarity of distance, she realized she had been denying her own anger and loneliness.

The phone rang again and she answered with trepidation.

"Hey, sugar." It took only an instant for Connie's sultry voice to register in her brain. "The concert was a big success. They raised lots of money. We had quite a number of major stars, and a great group of musicians, but I wish you could have been here."

"Oh, I missed you too, but I have to tell you something — my mother died this morning."

"I'm sorry to hear that."

"They're having the funeral on Monday afternoon. Do you think you can make it?"

"Of course. I'll get an earlier flight on Sunday night after I visit my family."

"Are you sure that's all right? I hate to interrupt anything."

"No, it's fine. I want to be there for you."

Connie asked how Julie was doing and Eleanora told him about the pictures of Roy and his buddies. From the surprise in his voice, she realized he hadn't had anything to do with it. She told him she had wondered if he might have played some role in it.

"I'm flattered you think I'm capable of doing something like that, but I wouldn't have the faintest idea of how to go about it. When I was a kid, even though I was big for my age, other boys used to try to provoke me into a fight. But I wasn't allowed to do anything that might hurt my hands. That whole physical part of growing up, testing yourself against others, was something I missed out on. So the fact that you see me as getting payback on a bunch of hoodlums, that just makes my day."

Chapter Twenty-Seven

On Sunday morning the sky was a deep blue and the air crisp and cool — a complete reversal from the drenching storm of the day before. As Eleanora drove along Boulevard East to church, she relished the glittering skyline and brilliantly colored leaves against the solid blue sky. At church, Peter announced to the congregation that she would be leaving in another two weeks, and she was overwhelmed by the number of people who wished her well and thanked her for making each service an enjoyable one. Wondering if their kindness merely reflected a relief to be rid of her and her scandal-ridden family, she ultimately chose not to question their sincerity.

When the last service was over, Peter waited until the members of the choir had finished talking with Eleanora before he wandered over. "We're going to miss you, Ellie. It won't be the same without you."

"I'm not gone yet, Peter. I'll be here for two more weeks."

"I know. I just wanted to express what's in my heart. It's been special having you here, knowing you as a person, aside from what you've given to us musically."

"Thank you, Peter. It's important to hear you say it. Lately I haven't felt quite as welcome by some of the women as I used to. So it's nice to hear you say that I'll be missed."

"Oh, definitely," he blurted out. And then, with more restraint, "But I know what you're referring to. It's a shame some people are like that. By the way, have you heard the rumors about your daughter's ex-boyfriend?"

Eleanora played dumb. "No. What are you referring to?"

"From what I hear, he and three of his pals got drunk the other night and ended up — how shall I say this — in a compromising position together. Apparently, they were foolish enough to post pictures of themselves on the Internet. Everyone in town knows about it and the boys are having quite a tough time of it. People are saying they got what they deserved after what they did to your daughter. I guess, on reflection, people realized your daughter wasn't capable of the things these boys said about her."

Eleanora tried to keep a look of surprise on her face, but she was relieved to hear that people were thinking twice about Julie. She looked forward to passing that information on to her.

Peter shrugged. "I guess sometimes God works in mysterious ways."

"Yes, Peter, sometimes She does."

Eleanora drove across the George Washington Bridge, but this time decided to drive downtown along the West Side Highway to enjoy the foliage on the Jersey side of the river. For a moment she forgot that she was on her way to her mother's viewing.

At the funeral parlor, Eleanora rushed to embrace her aunt. Zia Velia was dressed completely in black, and Eleanora guessed it was the same outfit she had worn to bury her husband many years ago. Eleanora was surprised by the number of people from the neighborhood, many of whom she hadn't seen in at least 20 years. Reconnecting with them was heartwarming — she had forgotten this aspect of her earlier life at home, tending to focus only on her mother's bitterness. But outside their apartment, there had been a sense of community. Eleanora remembered bringing food to neighbors who were ill, or shopping for them in the local butcher, fish store, produce market, and bakery. She remembered that the neighborhood was filled with people whose histories and families she knew.

Her father arrived with Irene, Zach, and Julie. Giuseppi also looked surprised to see so many familiar faces, although he didn't always remember the names. He embraced Velia warmly and introduced her to Irene. Julie was surprised that her grandmother had known so many people, since she rarely left the house. Eleanora explained that they came primarily for Velia's sake — she was the one they had a relationship with. She didn't bother to add that she felt the same way.

Fighting a twinge of guilt that she couldn't generate more feelings for her mother, she suddenly had an upwelling of sorrow mixed with regret and anger. She had always missed having a mother — often desperately. After her father had left — she stole a quick glance at him — the loneliness was even worse, but she had felt shut out of her mother's life long before that. Depression, silence, perpetual indifference, and irritability had kept her mother at a distance, as if she existed on the other side of a castle wall, cold and impenetrable.

Eleanora wiped her eyes and took a deep breath. Out of nowhere her father's arm came around her shoulder.

"You all right?" he asked.

She shook her head slightly and attempted a smile. "I'm just remembering stuff. You know, seeing all these people, old faces, old memories. It wasn't all bad, but Jesus, I sure wish she had been different. I wish she could have loved me. I wish I could have felt that from her. Just once."

Her father nodded silently. Eleanora didn't need him to say anything. For the 24 years since their separation, he had never spoken badly of Eva, but Eleanora knew it was her mother's inability to show love that had driven him away.

Startled by a laugh, she glanced up to see Irene and Julie engaged in conversation. So full of life, Irene had a wonderful capacity to love. Eleanora was grateful to have her energy as part of their lives. She thought of the house she was hoping to buy, just a short walk from her father's. A picture of family meals popped into her mind, and she smiled.

When the viewing hours were over, Velia suggested they go to a restaurant that had been in the neighborhood for over 50 years. Zach wondered out loud if they were still using the original tablecloths. The owners' granddaughter, now a young woman and herself a mother, was their waitress.

Giuseppi told them about places in the neighborhood where he had played his horn when he was a younger man. "Don't forget," he reminded them, "I didn't leave New York until I was 46. So I played down here and in the Village and uptown, in Harlem, for a long time."

Irene teased him. "I'm surprised we didn't run into a flock of your old girl-friends." Momentarily flustered, Giuseppi glanced briefly at his daughter before answering, "Well, it's a small funeral home. If they all knew I was coming, they would have had to sell tickets."

Eleanora flashed him a smile. "It's all right, Papa. I hope you had lots of girl-friends then. Really. You needed them then. But you don't need them now," she winked at Irene. "Besides, I think you've got more woman than you can handle now."

Everyone laughed, and Zach especially took it all in. Eleanora noticed how he looked at his grandfather, as if assessing him for the first time. *This is what it's like to be a man. I could be a man like this.* Eleanora felt something pop in her chest, like a bubble of tension, and suddenly she was totally relaxed. Life was what it was. Things worked out. If her father had stayed, this day never would have happened.

"Papa," she said, raising her wine glass, "I know it's Mama's death that brings us together today, but I just want to say that I'm so grateful everything worked out the way it did. I'm glad you and Irene are together, that I've got these two great kids, that I'm working with you at the Lounge, and I've got a beautiful new friend as well. So here's to life."

"Ellie, it's me, Aaron."

Alone in Irene's condo, Eleanora was awakened by her phone. Would this man haunt her for the rest of her life?

"Aaron? Why are you calling?"

There was a moment of silence. "I know it's late, but I wonder if it would be OK with you if I go to your mother's funeral tomorrow."

"You want to go to my mother's funeral?"

"I didn't want to just show up. I thought it would be better to ask you first."

"Aaron, you disliked my mother even more than I did. Why on earth would you want to go to her funeral?"

"I've known the woman for 20 years. You'd go to my mother's funeral, wouldn't you?"

"I don't hate your mother," she blurted. Still, the point he was making had some validity.

"Besides," he added, "I'm assuming the kids will be there and it'll be an opportunity to see them."

"Aaron, after what happened, the kids are not looking forward to seeing you. And a family funeral is not exactly the right time for a reconciliation."

"They're still my kids, Ellie."

"You say that like they're your possessions. They're not. They're people, Aaron. They don't belong to anybody. You own cars and houses and maybe dogs, but not people."

"I didn't mean it that way. I'm only saying it would be an opportunity to see them. I miss them."

"If you want to interact with your children, call them. As far as tomorrow is concerned, it's a private family gathering."

Again, silence.

"You know, Ellie, you always do this to me, shut me out. You know that? Do you have any idea how infuriating it is when you to constantly ignore me? You walk away from me. You hang up on me. In every way you make me feel like I'm invisible, like I don't exist. You're a real bitch, El, a real fucking bitch."

Eleanor heard in the click of the receiver the sound of a sudden ending. She hung up her phone, surprised by the irony: His anger at having been made to feel like a nonperson was so similar to what she had experienced with both him and her mother.

Almost immediately, the phone rang again. She was relieved to see it was Connie.

"Hi," she said, "where are you?"

"We just touched down. I wanted to let you know I'm back."

"Do you want me to come get you?"

"No," he chuckled, "but thanks. My car is in the parking lot."

"You must be very tired."

"Well, it's been a long day."

"Too tired to stop off here? You could stay the night."

"Eleanora, please don't get me excited while I'm still on the plane."

"I can't wait to get you excited. I want to get you very excited."

"You've got to stop," he whispered hoarsely into the phone. "You know how narrow these aisles are. I won't be able to walk out of here."

She laughed delightedly. "So I'll see you?"

"Yes, you'll see me, probably in about an hour."

"I'll be waiting."

"Don't start without me," he said. "I love you."

"You'll love me more later," she laughed.

A little over an hour later, her bell rang. She kissed him desperately and awkwardly. Without letting go of each other, they maneuvered themselves inside the condo and managed to close the door behind them.

"It's so good to feel your body again," he murmured. "I missed you. I missed kissing you." Eleanora pressed herself into him, feeling his erection against her thighs.

"Come," she said, leading him into the bedroom, where she had lit candles around the bed. Kneeling on the bed, she slowly undressed him, and he lifted her thin nightgown over her head. He knelt above her. The way he looked at her made her feel beautiful. She pulled him down so she could feel his body pressing against her breasts. She tasted the remnants of coffee on his tongue and smelled the lingering aroma of aftershave. Every nerve in her body was exposed and straining toward him.

Finally satisfied, they lay in each other's arms, content and calm. She was enjoying the naturalness of her lovemaking with Connie so much — in contrast to the moralistic, mechanical automatism she'd experienced with Aaron.

"You make me so happy," she said.

"I could tell — I lost count of how many orgasms you seemed to have."

"Like ocean waves, they just keep coming."

Eleanora told him about Aaron's phone calls and about the house in Nutley, and Connie described the concert and visit to his parents.

"I got to my parents' house late this morning — they had planned a big

183

lunch. My brother, Ben, and his wife, Cecelia, were there. They had been to the concert too."

Although his parents were proud of his success, he explained that they would have preferred him to be in the classical field rather than jazz.

"Ceci asked if I was seeing anyone, and I told them all about you," he went on. "My brother and my parents let her ask all of the questions. They just sat back and listened. Ben's mouth was open," Connie chuckled at the image, pressing his own jaw into his chest in imitation, "and I think he forgot how to close it. None of them could believe that I was dating — had fallen in love with — a white woman after all these years of short-term relationships with black women. They wanted to know all about you, your family, your kids, your husband, what religion you are, what kind of house you live in, what kind of car you drive, where your kids go to school. And, of course, they wanted to know what had attracted me to you."

Eleanora was fascinated by their curiosity and how much of it focused on status. Connie had prepared her for this, but she was surprised that material possessions could matter that much.

"What was their reaction?"

"Interesting," he said, "Ben and Ceci were concerned for me, about the kinds of problems I'd encounter dating a white woman. They're worried your children might have problems accepting me as your lover. Ceci also wondered what kinds of hostility you might run into being with a black man. My parents were more focused on my financial welfare, and needed assurance that you aren't more interested in my success and my status." He grinned as he shook his head in wonder. "They were concerned you might be what they called a gold digger or social climber, using me to satisfy your own ambitions."

Eleanora was incensed. How could they accuse her of such motivations without knowing her? She took such pride in her own integrity. Then she realized that this was a logical concern. Connie had told her about how important their social and economic status was to them.

Connie continued. "My mother brought up the age issue. She wondered if that would become more of a problem as I got older. I told them that we're very much in love right now, but we're just starting our relationship. It's way too early to start figuring out how we might feel about our age difference in 10 or 20 years. Anyway, they all want to meet you. They'd like me to bring you down some weekend."

"To check me out?"

"Um hmm," he nodded. "You think you might be up for it?"

"It feels a little like giving a recital."

Connie laughed. "Yes, well, there is that aspect — wondering if you're going to fuck it up, if they're going to like you or think you stink."

Eleanora thought about it. "Actually, I'm looking forward to meeting them. I'd like to meet your sister and her family, too, let them get to know me. But the truth is, I don't think it'll make any difference. Do you?" she asked suddenly.

"You mean, could their reactions change how I feel about you?"

She nodded, searching his face for a clue.

"No," he said softly, "I can't imagine anything they might say or do that would change how I feel about you." Then he laughed, and she looked at him curiously.

"I was just thinking," he said, "theoretically it would be possible for you to do something really outrageous that might make me think, oh boy, I didn't realize she could be like that. Then I remembered a time when I was going to Juilliard. I went out to dinner with a couple of friends. One of them had his own business and was showing off how successful he was. I was really impressed — not with the money, but the fact that he had made it all on his own at such a young age. I remember we went to a very classy restaurant in Manhattan, Barbetta's, and at one point this guy actually blew his nose in the tablecloth."

Eleanora gasped.

"Then later, he was smoking a cigar and instead of putting it out in the ashtray, he squashed it down into the remains of his dessert." Eleanora shook her head.

"The guy was a real pig and I never wanted to have anything to do with him after that. I heard that years later, he was cheating on his wife and she marched into his office and killed him."

"She what?"

"Yep. Stabbed him in the chest. It was in the papers."

"My God." Eleanora was shocked that Connie could have known a man like that.

"At any rate, I don't think there's much chance of your blowing your nose on my mother's tablecloth." He laughed at the absurdity.

"My God," she said, "I hope I don't fart at the table."

Connie whooped. "Eleanora," he said, "don't you know? White people don't fart."

"Well, I will be on my very best behavior."

Finally, Connie caught his breath. "Sweetie, you don't have to worry. You just be your own natural self. They may not love you like I love you, but it'll be OK. You're fine just the way you are."

Chapter Twenty-Eight

On Monday morning, Eleanora showered and dressed while Connie went home to change his clothes. She thought he looked very handsome and dapper as he stepped from the elevator wearing a long leather coat and sunglasses. When her father arrived, there was some discussion of who would ride with whom. They finally decided that Zachary would go with Connie in his car while she and Julie went with her dad and Irene. Eleanora knew her son was excited about riding in Connie's car and she thought it funny how Zachary insisted on calling him Duke, as did her father. *I guess it's a man thing,* she said to herself.

Velia was waiting for them at the funeral home. Even with a touch of makeup, she looked gray and haggard. Irene fussed over Velia and Eleanora was impressed by her genuine caring. *She would have made a wonderful mother. It's a shame she and my father never had the opportunity to have kids.*

She glanced at her father, who was talking with Connie and Zachary. *My God, Zachary is taller than his grandfather.* She noticed how her son had sought out the company of his grandfather and Connie, and it was evident to her how much he missed having a father figure he could relate to. She had always thought Aaron was a decent father because he was a good provider and decent role model, but now she saw that her children had missed feeling loved by him just as she had. Aaron simply lacked the capacity to make others feel genuinely loved and valued. It seemed like such an ordinary thing to make someone feel cared about. Irene and Velia had that capacity in spades. But in her mother's eyes, she had felt unworthy of any positive feeling. Suddenly Eleanora felt a twinge of guilt for not having been able to make Aaron feel valued.

Scanning the room, she saw that Julie had joined Zia Velia and Irene. Julie's eyes met hers and her daughter smiled. What a lovely smile she has. *She looks happy. Maybe she'll be all right after all.* Eleanora walked over and joined the women in her life.

Velia was discussing how Eva's opinions and values had been solely determined by their mother and father. "Eva never had a thought that hadn't been fed to her by our parents. After they passed, she clung like a tiger to all their old ideas. No matter what I said, I could never change her mind about anything. Our parents died in 1981 and 1982 — before you were born, Julie — and Eva never had a new idea after that. It's like that old TV program, what was it? *The Twilight Zone.* Time stopped still in 1982 for Eva."

"At least you didn't go along with it," Eleanora said. "You allowed yourself to progress, to live."

Velia turned to her niece. "Yes, and you don't know how hard I tried to get her to join me, to go shopping or to eat, to play cards. But no, she stayed in her apartment, listened to the Italian radio station, read the Italian paper, and cooked. Is that a life? She might just as well have gone into the convent. She would have been exposed to more, believe me."

The church service was brief. Despite having seen Eva every week for who knows how long, the priest had no idea who she really was. His words sounded hollow and artificial.

Eva Palotta Albanese was gone, and with her went any chance of Eleanora ever experiencing a mother's love. She had tried to make her mother feel loved, but it was always deflected. She never let anything in — least of all love. She was a stone.

From the church, the trail of cars wound through Little Italy, giving the corpse a final look at the neighborhood. At the cemetery in Brooklyn, Eleanora stood between Connie and her children. She noticed her father standing back a little, as if he didn't have a right to be there.

Eleanora watched the men lower her mother's casket into the ground. When her turn came to throw a rose onto the coffin and say a last goodbye, she was surprised to find her eyes filling. *Well Mama, I hope you're in heaven where you always wanted to be, with God and the angels. I hope you'll be with your mother and father and find peace.*

A tear slid down her cheek and she quickly wiped it away, embarrassed, as if her mother were there to criticize her for crying. *How silly — I can cry if I want to.* With Connie's grip on her shoulder, she felt safe. *With Aaron I felt provided for. Maybe that's why I thought he was an OK dad. Now I feel protected. Connie actually cares about me and will put himself on the line for me, make a sacrifice for me. With Aaron, it was all about him; I was supposed to sacrifice for him, not the other way around.*

And then she made the connection: It was the same with her mother. *I was there to take care of her, not the other way around.*

Looking up into Connie's big brown eyes, she saw his concern — but also the smile lurking behind, like a mischievous boy. With a glance back at the grave where her mother now lay, she thought: *You probably wouldn't have liked him, Mama, just as you didn't approve of anything else in life. But he sees me, he knows who I truly am inside, and he loves me. It's too bad, Mama, you never knew how that feels.*

Leaving the somber cemetery behind, they decided to go to a local Italian restaurant to relax over food and drinks. Although the restaurant wouldn't serve alcohol to Julie and Zachary, the carafes of wine found their way around the table and everyone drank a toast to Eva.

Eleanora turned to her aunt. "Zia," she began, "the kids and I are buying a new house in Nutley, New Jersey. We'll be just a 10-minute walk from Papa. Why don't you come live with us?"

Velia was startled. She didn't understand. "You want me to live with you — with you and the children?"

"Why not? We'll have enough room. We'd love to have you. I'm sure there's a senior center nearby where you can play cards and bingo."

Eleanora saw her aunt's mind working as her eyes flicked this way and that, considering all of the possible reasons why she couldn't leave Broome Street. Finally, she said she'd think about it. Eleanora knew the kids would be in favor of the invitation.

Everyone was eager to hear about Connie's trip to New Orleans and the devastation from the flooding that he'd seen. He became emotional as he described the layers of corruption and incompetence that had conspired to destroy a major city, a unique culture, and the lives of so many thousands of people.

"Many of my friends — artists and musicians, fine people, talented people — they're just wiped out. Their homes, studios, collections gone, all gone. It's criminal."

Eleanora wanted to take him in her arms and rock him like a baby. Both Julie and Zachary asked him many questions, and again she was proud of the mature discourse between them. *That's my doing, not Aaron's. I taught them that.* And her chest swelled.

As they were getting ready to leave the restaurant, Eleanora heard Julie and Zach reminding Zia Velia that they'd love to have her live with them.

"It'll be like having another mother in the house," said Julie. Zach rolled his eyes and gave out a theatrical groan as he looked at his mother. "But in a good way," Julie hurried to clarify

"Let's do this," suggested Eleanora, "when we're all settled, you'll come stay a few days, a week, and see how it is. Then you'll decide."

"Yes," she said, "I'd like that."

Outside, Zach asked if he could ride back to New Jersey in Duke's car, but his grandfather reminded him that school started tomorrow, so he and Julie had to go with him and Irene.

Zach looked at Connie and his mother for help, but Connie shrugged his shoulders.

"Grandpa is right," Eleanora confirmed, "but there will be other opportunities," and she looked inquisitively at Connie for the reassurance she didn't really need. When they had said goodbye, she watched her father walk toward his car, Irene on his arm and Julie and Zach trailing behind. She turned to Connie, "Zia Velia wants me to look around my mother's apartment to see if there's anything I might want. Do you mind waiting for me?"

"Actually, I'd love to see where you grew up."

"You sure? It's a dingy old place that smells like garlic and stale cigarettes."

"It would be like looking into your past, if you don't mind?"

"No, I don't mind at all. I just didn't want you to feel obligated."

Velia had been watching this exchange between them. "I like how the two of you pay attention to each other. You remind me of how my Pio and I used to be, each one taking care of the other. It makes me feel good to see that kind of love again. Your father and Irene are like that, too. It's good to see him so happy — he and Eva never had that, not even when they were first married."

Eleanora unlocked the door to her mother's apartment and reached for the light switch. An unadorned ceiling fixture bathed them with dim light. There were only three rooms: the living room with an old, stuffed chair and sofa and two old-fashioned end tables, each with a tarnished brass lamp and faded shade; the kitchen, with its chipped sink, small refrigerator and stove, and oval Formica table with chrome chairs and faded plastic seat covers; and her mother's bedroom.

"It's smaller than I thought it would be," Connie said.

"It felt bigger when I was a teenager. We moved here when I was 14, right after my father left. My grandparents lived next door and Zia Velia and Zio Pio lived upstairs — my aunt still lives there. We had two bedrooms where I lived before we moved here, now there's only the one bedroom. I slept out here," she indicated the living room, "on the sofa. Can you believe, it's still the same sofa?"

In the kitchen, a ceiling light illuminated the dinginess. A layer of grease made the surfaces sticky, and Eleanora doubted that the walls had been painted since she had left in shame 20 years ago. The linoleum flooring was cracked and marred. A grocery list, written in Italian, hung on the refrigerator door by a magnet in the shape of a faded watermelon slice, and Eleanora remembered how it had once looked so colorful. She slid open a drawer and surveyed her mother's stock of cutlery, looking in particular for an old Mickey Mouse fork and spoon she had treasured as a child, but was no longer there. A colander and a cheese grater hung from a hook over the sink, along with a pronged spaghetti spoon, whisk, soup ladle, and assorted old utensils.

In the cabinet, Eleanora saw the stack of familiar white dinner plates and soup bowls and an odd assortment of glasses, including some wine goblets and old jelly jars. She could almost see herself — a skinny, awkward 14-year-old sitting at the table with her mother, forever old in her cotton housedress over a full-length slip, tight-lipped, frowning, and sharp-tongued. Focused on the plates in front of them, they hardly exchanged a word.

We never saw each other, never acknowledged each other.

In her mother's bedroom, she flipped the light switch and a bedside lamp went on. Eleanora doubted that her mother ever read in bed. The room was bare of personal effects, the only picture was of the Sacred Heart. On the dresser lay a discolored lace runner, a string of rosary beads and a cross, a simple plastic comb, and a brush. *It's a nun's cell.* As she switched off the lamp, she noticed the light from outside shining through the bedroom window.

Peering out the window of the unlit room she saw the dark, empty street below and a moonless triangle of black sky above. She shivered slightly and her eyes teared up. Then a chair scraped on the kitchen floor, startling her, and she heard a man's low voice. Her heart fluttered. She felt a weakness in her legs and she reached for the dresser for support. Hurriedly, she covered the distance to the bedroom doorway.

"Connie!" she exclaimed when she saw him sitting at the kitchen table.

"What?" he asked, putting away his phone.

"I thought — I thought you were my father getting ready to leave." She gave a self-embarrassed laugh.

"I'm not going anywhere," he reassured her. "Are you ready to go home?"

Her eyes sparkled as she took his hand in hers, relief flooding her.

"Yes," she said, "I'm finished here."

A Killer Romance

Theresa

"Theresa!" She heard someone calling her name.

"Theresa!" There it was again.

Ma. Time to get up.

Every morning was the same. Ma's grating, complaining voice and Theresa's internal struggle: to get up, or to remain comfortable and peaceful under her quilt.

And every morning she got up. She had no choice — she was too conscientious, too responsible to skip work. For a fleeting second or two she entertained her resentment toward her mother, but then it was gone and her bare feet hit the cold linoleum. Stretching her toes toward her slippers, she sighed in resignation and pushed herself away from heaven to stand firmly in reality.

The rush was on: pushing through her morning routine, hurrying to finish before her younger brother and sister started their accusatory pounding on the bathroom door. Back in her bedroom, which she shared with her sister, she finished dressing, brushed her hair, and applied a touch of makeup — not that it helped.

She assessed her reflection in the mirror: plain. Average to the point of invisibility. Colorless.

Back toward the kitchen, on tiptoe, she pressed herself against the hallway wall to avoid a collision with her sister, Tina, who was just now exiting the bathroom, and made way for her brother, Anthony. Cigarette in hand, Ma sat at the cluttered kitchen table in her nightgown and robe, gazing absently at the small TV and drinking her coffee. Juice and coffee gulped down, Theresa grabbed her jacket from the hook on the wall, waved absently to her mother, and was out the door.

A typical morning.

Theresa hurried to the trolley for the slow ride to the subway into Philadelphia's Center City. Arriving breathless after the brisk walk from the station, she stopped in the ladies room, got coffee from the small office kitchen, then collapsed in her desk chair. At 7:40 she was ready to begin work. Harold Kwan, her boss, would enter the office in five minutes. She knew he was always pleased she was there before him, a full quarter-hour ahead of the official start of the day.

A typical morning.

Harold gave Theresa a cheery smile. He made a point of letting her know that he not only felt fortunate to have a conscientious secretary, but that he took pride in it, as if he was responsible for instilling such dedication and enthusiasm into her. Harold bragged that his employees were a reflection of his superior management skills. This proof of his capabilities, Theresa reasoned, was evidence of his inevitable future — taking over his father's company and expanding its operations — so her diligence made him happy.

Harold did not suffer fools. He often said so — usually followed by firing someone with little or no notice. Theresa liked to see him smile at her — it meant he was unlikely to fire her.

Gladys and Pansy arrived, wordlessly dropping their purses on their desks before filling their mugs with fresh coffee. Gladys and Pansy, who had worked for Harold and his father forever, only morphed into sentient beings after their morning coffee.

From her desk, Theresa could see almost everything that went on at Jonas Computer Services, Inc. People in billing, tech services, human resources, and the mailroom all passed in front of her. She knew almost all 75 employees by sight, and most of them by name. Gladys and Pansy knew their families as well, and Theresa wondered how they learned so much about everyone's lives. Her desk sat in front of theirs, and yet they always reeled in information that was news to her.

"Oh, we have our sources," they laughed.

Struggling to keep her mind on work, Theresa found herself reliving the visit with her aunt the night before last. Dinner with Aunt Dorinda was always a highlight — an acceptable excuse for not having dinner at home with Ma and Tina. At 15, Tony ran with a gang and was rarely home. Ma didn't even try to control him, and Theresa had long since given up trying to be a positive influence. The last time she made an attempt to talk to him about it, he threatened to hurt her if she didn't mind her own business. Ma never even raised an eyebrow.

Aunt Dorinda said she wasn't surprised, given the home he'd grown up in.

"You are the only good thing to come out of that family," she said, "and your mother can't take any credit for that. You did it all on your own. Anthony is going to end up in jail before the year is out. Just watch. And that sister of yours, I'm surprised she's hasn't gotten pregnant by now."

Theresa knew it was true. The 17-year-old had a terrible reputation and Theresa secretly wondered if Tina was prostituting herself and using the money for drugs.

"I just hope she can stay in school and graduate. She only has one more year," Theresa said hopefully.

"She'll never make it. I'm surprised she didn't quit when she turned 16," Dorinda said.

"She only stayed in school because, if she quit, Ma would make her go out and get a full-time job to support her," Theresa remembered.

Dorinda laughed and turned the hamburgers on the grill.

"Trish would take to pimping for her, if she could. One way or another, she's counting on Tina to kick in her share, just like you do."

Right again. Dorinda had Tina figured out to a tee. Trish had never done an honest day's work in her life — and when she did have a job, as a cashier or barista or waitress, she got fired for cheating the customers or being short in the register. Even now, Trish used men as a tool for money, collecting boyfriends and expecting them to help out with her bills. Theresa wasn't sure if you could actually call it prostitution.

"What's happening with you, Terry? Any action in your love life yet, or are you still thinking of becoming a nun?"

Theresa laughed. Dorinda always teased her, saying Theresa was not just the only virgin she knew, but probably the only 20-year-old virgin in Philadelphia.

"How could anything happen? I'm at work all day. Where would I meet anyone? Besides, look at me: Plain Jane. Who'd be interested?"

"How about that boy you mentioned?"

Theresa frowned. "Who?"

"The one at work, the tall one with the blonde hair."

"George? No, nothing. Every once in a while, he passes in front of my desk and I try to catch his eye, but he quickly looks away. I think he's very shy."

"Maybe he's not into girls."

"I don't know. Pansy said he's been there about a year and she's never heard anything about him. He keeps to himself."

"Then you're going to have to be more aggressive. You can't always leave it up to the guys, you know. Why don't you call him?"

Theresa thought about it while she set the table. Dorinda put the burgers on a plate, and brought pasta salad, sliced tomatoes, and soda to the table.

"Well?" her aunt nudged her.

"I can't just call him out of the blue! What would I say? *I think you're cute, do you want to go out?*"

"You're a very bright girl, Theresa. Invite him to something. Ask him to do you a favor. I don't think it really matters what you say — either he'll be open to talking to you, or he won't."

Theresa had made the decision to take her aunt's advice: Be more proactive! But 8:00 a.m. came and went and there was no sign of George at the office. She wondered if he was really sick. Theresa had followed her aunt's advice and left a voicemail message yesterday, but he hadn't returned her call. And no wonder! She'd been so nervous, stumbling over her words and babbling. How embarrassing!

Well, nothing to be lost by calling again. So she dialed the phone, this time leaving a more sensible message asking when he'd be returning to work.

He called about an hour later. They didn't talk long. He was getting over the flu and would be back to work within a few days. He hadn't sounded angry that she had called twice, and she considered that a good sign.

Theresa thought about him the rest of the day. Tall and slim with light blonde hair, he dressed well and carried himself proudly. His reserved manner gave him an air of maturity.

There weren't many men she found attractive. Most were immature and made too much of an effort to appear macho, like her brother. Even the men in her mother's life were childish and irresponsible or brutish and bossy. Her own father had left when she was two and she hadn't seen him since. Ma told her he had died of an overdose — and maybe he had. Trish was not known for her veracity.

Tina and Anthony's father, Duane Harris, had spent most of the past 10 years incarcerated for dealing drugs. When Theresa thought of the disreputable men in her mother's life, she wondered how she had survived without succumbing to the immoral environment. As Dorinda had said, Theresa was the only one in the family with brains and ambition and a moral code. Why her? Tina and Anthony had been to the same Catholic schools, so why had she emerged with different attitudes and values?

Some would say it was because her siblings were half black, but Theresa knew race had nothing to do with it. As far back as she could remember, she had made the decision to be her own person, chart her own course, and survive in spite of her mother's influence.

On Monday morning, Theresa was surprised to see George approaching her desk. She felt the hot flush creeping up her face. He stood in front of her wordlessly.

"Back to work, I see," she blurted obviously. *Oh, God! How lame.*

"Yeah," he said, "I just wanted to thank you for calling to see how I was."

"Oh, that's all right. No trouble." *I sound like I'm six years old!*

"Well, it was thoughtful, you know, nice. I just wanted to thank you."

"No worries. I'm glad you're feeling better. The flu can be such a downer."

"Yeah, well, I guess I'd better get to work."

As he walked away, Theresa heard Gladys and Pansy humming the wedding march. She felt herself blushing again.

"What am I going to do with you two? You're making something out of nothing."

They all laughed, but inwardly Theresa was pleased. They noticed every-thing. Maybe they had seen something, some indication of interest that she had missed. A tiny ray of hope took hold. She'd give him some time to make a move, but if he didn't, she would make another attempt. Aunt Dorinda would be proud. One thing Theresa knew about herself: She could be persistent. She could make things happen, like graduating in the top 10 percent of her class while working 40 hours a week at two jobs. *I'll give him two days, and then I'll follow up.*

At her desk later that day, she remembered her one abortive romance in high school. Bert had been a top student and active in student council. Most of the girls thought he was kind of geeky, but Theresa was attracted to his serious qualities — his ambition to go to MIT for engineering and his sense of respon-sibility. He had asked her to a school dance and then to a party, but then he'd lost interest. She thought maybe it was because she hadn't been responsive to his clumsy sexual groping. Dorinda said it was impossible to tell — men seem to lose interest and disappear for no reason at all.

"Maybe someone else caught his eye," her aunt had mused, "or maybe you had spinach in your teeth. You'll never know. But you're plenty attractive, Terry. You're bright, you've got a good figure and dynamite eyes. And if all he's inter-ested in is getting his rocks off, then good riddance. You want more than that."

Still, Theresa wondered. She had never really felt love from anyone other than her aunt — certainly not from any guy, or even from her own mother and father. Aunt Dorinda was the only one who had ever told her she was attractive or had a good personality. She wondered what was wrong — was she inherently unlovable? Is that why her father had left? Did that make her a failure from the get-go? Was there no sense in trying to be anything, because she was just a worthless piece of shit anyway? If only someone could love her, she reasoned, her life would not be futile. She would not just be taking up space on this earth.

The next day, she emailed George that she had a favor to ask him and would he be willing to meet her for coffee after work. Finally, late in the afternoon, he responded that he was busy but available after work on Friday. Theresa was nervous at the prospect, but also very pleased with herself. Her determination was paying off.

The atmosphere at home was stifling. As Theresa stepped into the apartment, she heard Tina and her mother in a shouting match over money. Ma called her a greedy, selfish bitch. In the doorway of the kitchen, Theresa saw her mother dressed as usual in a light robe. The only time she bothered to dress was in the evening, when she went out with friends to a local bar.

"Terry, did you cash your paycheck?" her mother asked.

"No. I didn't have time."

Trish looked at her younger daughter, a half smile on her face.

"That was your last hope, honeybunch. You'll just have to do without, like the rest of us."

Tina looked at her sister, her eyes big with desperation.

"Can you lend me $20?"

Theresa knew better. Lend? What Tina meant was *give*. Her sister was adept at manipulating others — especially her boyfriends — to cater to her many demands. This was just another scene in the unending competition between Ma and Tina as to who would have bragging rights about who had more. Besides, she would probably only use the money for drugs.

"No," Theresa said, "you know that whatever I have left after I pay Ma is barely enough to get me through the week."

Tina was persistent. "We can go right now to the grocery store. Buy some food and you can give me $20 from the change. Come on, you know I'm good for it."

Tina looked at her mother for approval. Trish rolled her eyes as she blew out a long stream of smoke.

"Sorry, Tina, I won't do that," Theresa said.

"What's the matter with you?" Tina cried. "Why are you siding with Ma? Why do you give all your money to her? You know she's just using you."

Ignoring her, Theresa went to her room and plopped down on the bed. That battle had nothing to do with her. Every two weeks she brought home $541, and $300 went to her mother for rent. The rest was used for transportation, lunches, clothing, and entertainment. That left less than $500 a month, and from that she was secretly saving for tuition to the community college. Theresa desperately wanted to be a nurse, but no one would help her with the expenses. Maybe she could get a Pell Grant for the tuition or a college loan, but Trish would still expect her to pay for her room and board. Her goal was to save $100 a month, but wasn't always able to do it. During the past two years she had saved almost $2,000, but knew it would disappear in a second if anyone in her family found out about it. It was hers only as long as it remained secret, so she kept her savings book in a locked drawer in her desk at work.

She heard the door slam and knew Tina had left. Good riddance.

Tina had everything Theresa lacked — captivating looks and personality — and yet she squandered it on local trash. She spent all her time partying — or recovering from it — instead of applying herself to her schoolwork. Theresa hoped her sister would not get pregnant or die from an overdose. Anything else would be a gift from God. She forced herself to get up and wash her hands and face, then returned to the kitchen where her mother had put two frozen dinners into the microwave.

"Looks like it's just us old women tonight. You want chicken parm or crab cake and rice?"

"Whatever," Theresa said dully. "The chicken, I guess."

Trish nodded and lit a cigarette. After setting the table, Theresa got a can of diet soda for herself and a can of beer for her mother.

"How's work?" her mother asked. "You should be up for another raise soon, don't ya think? You been there almost two years now."

"It was two years at the beginning of July. Mr. Kwan said they're waiting until September to do their reviews, so nobody will hear anything until after that."

"That stingy Chink bastard doesn't know what a good deal he's got in you. Well, you let me know if you get a raise. You know how tight things are here. The damned food keeps going up and I expect our rent will go up this fall, too. And the electric bill is going to be a bitch, especially the way our young princess keeps the air conditioning going full blast."

"You should say something to her about it."

"Ha! You think she'd listen to me? Tina thinks she's full grown and has the world on a string. She'll find out soon enough ..."

"She should be working. It's not fair that I'm the only one in the family with a job. It shouldn't all be on me."

"She says she can't find one."

"When has she looked? She's hardly ever here. What does she do all day, anyway?"

"It's none of my business, toots. As long as she and your brother stay out of my hair."

"They're both headed for trouble, Ma. I hear things."

"Yeah. Well don't bother your butt over them. They can take care of themselves."

"Ma, Anthony is only 15. You want him to spend his life in prison like his father?"

"He'll be all right. You just make sure you don't get yourself knocked up and lose your job."

"Christ, Ma. How the hell is that gonna happen? The Angel Gabriel going to come in through the bedroom window? And if he did, he'd sure as hell pick Tina."

The two women ate their suppers in silence. With each bite, Theresa became more aware of her anger. She glanced at her mother and felt disgust at everything she saw — the abject slovenliness, the self-centered obsession with manipulating everyone to cater to her needs. Trish received disability payments for some alleged injury, but there was nothing wrong with her. She'd done waitressing and bartending in the past — she could do it again.

It had been years since her mother had hit her, but Theresa still remembered the violent temper — and that memory kept her from pushing the issue. *But why was she so violent with me and Tina and never with Anthony?* Theresa didn't have any reasonable answers. In some ways she envied Tina, who had endured Trish's beatings by defiance and rebelliousness, whereas Theresa had been cowed. *Someday, when I've saved enough, I'm out of here! Then let her see where she is without me. Let them all see.*

Friday, after work, she waited outside the coffee shop where she and George planned to meet. The weather had cooled and she felt relaxed and empowered by the breeze that brushed her bare arms. It felt good to be away from the stifling office and out in real air. She took a deep breath and smiled to herself.

George loped toward her in long strides.

"Hi," she said, "thanks for coming."

He nodded, and a hint of a smile flickered across his face. He followed her inside. Theresa ordered a latte and paid for it herself. George got a coffee and joined her at a small table.

"You said you had a favor to ask," he began.

"Yeah. I feel like such a jerk, but I didn't know what else to do. I mean, I hardly know you, so I really don't have any right to ask you to help me."

He looked at her over the rim of his cup and waited for her to continue.

"Well," she said, forcing herself to maintain eye contact, "I'm thinking of buying a laptop computer."

"Uh huh."

"We don't have any computers at home," she stumbled on, "and my only experience is with the PC at work. Anyway, I thought it's about time I joined the 21st century and got one, but I'm not sure how to go about it."

Theresa observed George as he sipped his coffee. This was the first time she had really seen him up close. He was handsome in an unconventional way: a very strong chin and fine features, but something was off, not quite symmetrical. It made him more interesting. She knew his nature was quiet and reserved, even shy, so she wasn't surprised at his lack of response. His calm, confidence made him even more compelling.

"So you want to pick my brains about a laptop?"

"I was hoping you wouldn't mind. Since you work in the tech department, I assumed you'd know way more than I do. I have no idea where to start or what to ask."

"Did you ask anyone else to help you?"

"I don't really have anyone to ask. I guess I'm something of a loner. I've got a couple of girlfriends from high school, but I hardly ever see them since they went off to college."

"You didn't go?"

"Well, actually, I did get accepted to a nursing program. But my mother is on disability and she decided the family needed an income, so I started working for Mr. Kwan right after I graduated. That was two years ago."

"Bummer."

"I'll say. But I'm saving some money and if I get a Pell Grant or something, I'll be able to do it."

"Where would you go?"

"The Community College has a good program and it's the least expensive."

George cracked a thin smile. "I'm taking a course there in computer science. I'm only doing data entry now at work. It's a dumb job, brainless. In fact, you're not supposed to think. That would get in the way. What I want to do is programming or tech support. I'm into both the software and the hardware side."

"You should have gone to college for that."

"Yeah, well, we couldn't afford for me to go away to school and I'd be damned if I was going to live at home and commute. I figured I'd do it on my own and if it took a few years longer, so what. I've got all the time in the world."

Theresa thought George was enjoying himself. He asked how she spent her time and she pointed out that she had knitted the short-sleeved sweater she was wearing. Later she realized she'd been so nervous that she had failed to ask him questions about himself.

The entire meeting went so much better than she had ever dared hope. George agreed to go shopping for a laptop with her on the following Saturday, but he also suggested that they go out for pizza on Wednesday. A date! Her first in almost two years. She couldn't wait to tell Aunt Dorinda.

But nobody at home would be pleased. Tina, in spite of all her boyfriends, would be jealous, although Theresa couldn't imagine why. Tina would find George much too reserved for her tastes. And Ma would be threatened that someone else might have some influence on Theresa. The next morning, she called her aunt and they made plans to meet for brunch. She told Dorinda all about her coffee date with George.

"I really like him," she said.

"I can tell," Dorinda joked. "I'm trying to remember when I've seen you so excited."

"Did I tell you he asked me out to dinner this Wednesday?"

"Yes. Is that when he's hoping to get you in the sack?"

Theresa blushed.

Dorinda laughed. "My God, look at you — red as a beet."

"I can't say I'm not thinking about it" Theresa confessed. "I mean, he is very attractive in a different kind of way. But I'm planning to go slow with that. I mean, I've waited this long, I can wait a little longer."

"Nervous?"

"Of course I am. I know he's experienced. He told me about his girlfriend in high school. Apparently, she was the prettiest and most popular girl in the school. They were voted the best couple or something for the yearbook. Did I tell you he was captain of the swim team?"

"Captain? Impressive. He must have a wonderful body — long and slim and muscular."

"Dorrie!"

"Only kidding, sugar. I've got my hands full as it is. Last thing I'd need is a boy-toy to be a mother to. I'm really happy for you, Terry. And you're perfectly right to take it slow."

"I know I'm attracted to him physically. And from the little time we spent together, I think I like who he is. But how can you tell if there's potential for love?"

"Right now it's attraction, maybe lust. Love comes after you've gotten to know each other. Don't rush it, just keep exploring as long as it seems worthwhile. When you've done that long enough and you still feel interested and excited and happy, then you'll discover that you're in love. Be patient."

"You're always so reasonable. I'm so lucky to have you in my life. I can't even trust my own mother to tell her what's going on."

"I know."

"Do you think things might work out with me and George?"

"How the hell could I know? I'll tell you this: If he falls in love with you, he's got good taste. If he doesn't fall in love with you, he's a jerk. God knows, there's enough of them around. Sometimes I think that's all there is."

"Sometimes I think it's hopeless."

"Look, sugar, you are who you are. You've got to accept yourself, the good and the not so good. None of us is perfect. But you can't keep depending on someone else's opinion to define your worth. You've got to believe in yourself. You're a great person. I wish you were mine. I couldn't be prouder. But it doesn't make any difference what I think or what George thinks or anybody else. You have to know you're OK."

"I hear you. But that's so hard to do when nobody else tells you that. You're the only one who makes me feel good about myself — you and sometimes Mr. Kwan."

"Sometimes it's hard for me too. Some guy will sweet-talk me and it feels good. But I don't count on it. When it comes right down to it, I've got to believe in myself, otherwise it's all bullshit."

Throughout August, Theresa and George tentatively explored their relationship together. Theresa sometimes emailed him at work and asked him to lunch. About once a week, George suggested going to a small local restaurant for dinner — usually pizza or hamburgers. Theresa tried recommending a Chinese or Vietnamese or Indonesian place to eat, but George preferred the more commonplace and Theresa was happy to accommodate. Despite his attempt at cool assurance, Theresa gradually became aware of a little-boy quality that appealed to her. Part of her felt like nurturing and protecting him. Catering to his wishes made her feel good.

In early September Theresa noticed a change in George's behavior. When she stopped to think about it, she realized he had been acting differently for the previous week or two. Just after Labor Day it came to a head. They were out for a hamburger and fries and she thought he was acting nervously — looking around at people, fidgeting, picking at his food, not really paying attention to her. Finally she asked what was wrong.

He leaned forward, scrutinizing her. "What do you mean?" For a moment she became unnerved. She hadn't expected him to react so aggressively.

"You seem nervous lately, that's all. You're jumpy. You can't sit still."

"I'm fine."

"George, you've been mumbling to yourself and biting your nails. You've hardly eaten."

"I said nothing's wrong."

Theresa sat back in the booth. "Don't treat me this way, George. I thought we were becoming close friends. Please don't dismiss me. I'm not stupid. I'm concerned about you, that's all. If you don't want to tell, me, then fine. We might as well call it quits if you can't tell me what's bothering you."

She turned her eyes away and chomped down on her burger. She realized that she was furious with his dismissiveness.

After a tense silence, he spoke. "OK, I'll tell you." He paused and lowered his voice. "All I can think about is us. I think about us all the time. I mean all the time. I can't fall asleep at night because all I think about is us — doing it, I mean. You know, sex. I keep imagining what it will be like. It's like my mind is on fire, night and day. Just talking about it makes me hard. I think I'm going crazy from it, Terry. I'm having trouble concentrating at work. I've stopped going to class. I'm not eating. I can't control it any more."

Theresa was stunned. Of course she'd assumed he'd been thinking about sex, just as she had, but for him to be so overwhelmed with lust for her that he couldn't eat or sleep? That he couldn't work? Had to quit school? Her first reaction was to be appalled by his lack of control.

But that quickly morphed into self-doubt. How could anyone be so consumed by passion for her? Maybe Tina drove men crazy, but not her. She was incredulous. Maybe he was lying. Complimenting her in this over-the-top way in the hopes that she'd be swept off her feet, right into bed? But she could see how exposed and vulnerable he felt. She feared he was hurt by her silence. She had to say something.

"Wow. I don't know what to say. I had no idea. I'm really flattered — nobody has ever felt like that about me before. I'm sorry, if I'm tongue-tied ..."

George made a gesture as if to wave it all away. "It doesn't matter. I shouldn't have said anything. I can see you didn't want to hear it. You kept pushing me, so I told you."

"I did, and I appreciate your honesty. It's just that you completely surprised me. And I'm not ready for that yet. I've never done it before. I have to take it slowly. I hope you understand, George. I don't want to hurt your feelings, but I can't rush it. It has to come naturally for me. I want it to feel right."

"Sure. No big problem. Like I said, I didn't want to say anything about it. I know we have to take it slow. I understand. Honest."

Afterward, thinking about what he'd said, she decided that if she was going to lose her virginity, it might as well be with George. If what he was saying were true, he really was head over heels about her. And she was pretty sure she could control the situation and go at her own pace. The more she thought about it, the more determined she became. Besides, given his plea, it would be an act of mercy on her part. She smiled at the idea.

But over the weekend, Theresa didn't hear from George. She left a message, but he didn't return her call. On Monday, she sent an email, but he never responded. Maybe she'd totally blown it. She was surprised at how upset she was at the prospect of losing the relationship. She was afraid that he was dumping her, that she wasn't good enough. Maybe she just didn't know how to be a girlfriend. What was wrong with her?

Finally, on Tuesday morning he stopped by her desk and asked her to meet him in the cafeteria. She told Gladys and Pansy she'd be back in a few minutes and saw them smile at each other.

Theresa told George she was glad to see him. "I was worried. You didn't answer my phone call or my email."

"I've been busy," he said. "Preoccupied. By the way, you haven't seen that guy from the mailroom around, have you?"

"Which guy?"

"You know, that Eddie guy."

Theresa shook her head. "I don't think so. Why?"

He shook his head. "No reason. It's nothing."

"I was hoping we could get together," she blurted out.

George gazed at her thoughtfully, then turned away. When he looked at her again, he gave her a brief smile. "Can we go to your apartment?"

Theresa hadn't told him anything about her family. She had managed to avoid the topic all together, and allow him to believe that she lived alone.

"No," she said, "that wouldn't be a good idea. I was hoping we could go to your place." She saw him bite his lip. "Is there a problem with that?"

"No, I guess not." They were silent for a moment and she started to get antsy about returning to her desk. "Why don't we go out for dinner on Friday and then back to my place afterward?" he suggested.

"I'd like that," she said.

Before they parted, Theresa made George promise they would stop short of intercourse and, whatever they did, he'd agree to wear a condom. She explained that she was probably being overly cautious, but she'd heard too many horror stories from her mother and the nuns while growing up. "It's going to take me some time to get over these fears, so just give me time, OK?"

George agreed. He may have been disappointed, but she thought he seemed pleased by the prospect. She went back to her desk, reassured that he wasn't dumping her.

After work on Friday, to her surprise George suggested going to China-town for dinner. He'd even brought a bottle of wine. Theresa was nervous, and by the time they got to his apartment, she was still a little lightheaded from the wine. The small studio apartment consisted of a kitchen partially separated from a larger area that served as a bedroom-living room. The space was neat, orderly, and sparse — a bed, small table with two chairs, second-hand dresser, laptop computer, radio, and some books.

Theresa placed her jacket over the back of one of the chairs. George sat beside her on the bed. Seeing that he was unsure of what to do, she smiled and leaned toward him.

Saturday afternoon, Aunt Dorinda took Theresa out for lunch. As they sat in the crowded diner, Theresa shared her thoughts about the previous night.

"It didn't go at all like I thought it would. I knew I was going to be tense and nervous, but I didn't expect George to be that way too."

"Maybe he was holding back," her aunt interjected, "and letting you take the lead because he was unsure of how comfortable you were going to be. Maybe he was just being considerate."

Theresa shook her head. "I wondered about that, but I don't think so. It was more like he didn't know what to do. He didn't act at all like I thought he would. I mean, first of all, he's not a great kisser. For a guy who went steady in high school with one of the most popular girls, I thought he'd be more sure of himself. I was the one who started the French kissing. I opened my mouth and he pressed his lips against my teeth like he didn't know what to do."

Dorinda waited for her niece to continue. She was curious, but didn't want to press Theresa with too many questions.

"Then he started to feel my breasts," Theresa sounded incredulous. "I mean, Jesus Christ, Dorrie, guys have been trying to feel my breasts since sixth grade. You'd think he'd know what to do. He was like a blind man examining something new and unfamiliar. It felt like a medical exam! Nothing he did had any real sensitivity or passion. And, he didn't even touch me, you know, down there. Even after I touched him. It was like he wasn't interested."

"It sounds to me like he's very inexperienced and afraid of making a complete fool of himself. Personally, I think he's been feeding you a line of bullshit about his high school experiences."

"I think you might be right. Now that you mention it, he said he'd been a swimmer so I expected his body to be more athletic. I asked if he still swam and he said no, he hadn't been able to find a pool that was convenient. But if he's been going to Community College, I'm sure they have a pool. It doesn't add up."

"Sounds like you're not sure what to believe," Dorinda said thoughtfully.

"Well, I'm glad I went to his apartment. I think I got over some of my anxieties. It was the first time I've ever been completely naked with a guy and had a chance to see a hard-on and all."

"Did he come?"

Theresa blushed. "Twice. That was a first for me too. But all in all, you're right — I was disappointed and now I'm not so sure I trust him. He doesn't seem to be who he said he was. Maybe he's just shy and was trying to impress me, so he exaggerated what he did in high school. That doesn't mean he's a bad person. Maybe I should cut him some slack."

Dorinda looked straight at her niece. "Jesus, honey, that's your shtick, isn't it? Taking care of other people, taking responsibility for them."

"No I don't."

"Yes you do. You've been taking in lost puppies and wounded birds since you were in kindergarten. You're still taking care of your own mother, for Christ's sake."

Theresa felt as if she'd been slapped. "What am I supposed to do? Abandon them? Go out on my own and let Tina and Anthony fend for themselves? Ma isn't going to take care of them."

Her aunt softened. "Seems to me they're fending for themselves and there ain't much you can do about it. Are you going to keep Tina from getting pregnant? And Anthony — you're keeping him on the straight and narrow?"

Theresa slumped back in defeat. "Still," she said, "somebody has to try. If I didn't at least try, then I'd feel like shit if something happened to them."

Dorinda finished her coffee. "So that's what you're going to do with Georgie-Porgy? Rescue him from his own ineptitude?" She suddenly started to laugh. "I can just picture the two of you — the blind leading the blind."

Theresa smiled. "Yeah, it is kind of funny, the prospect of me teaching him the finer points of making love."

"Just be careful, OK? Don't put all your eggs in one basket. You've got too much to offer, don't settle. You want someone who's capable of being a full partner. You don't need another lost little boy to rescue."

Theresa wasn't surprised that she didn't hear from George over the weekend. He usually restricted his communications to working hours. If she called him on weekends or evenings, he rarely called back until later and gave some excuse, like visiting his sick mother in New Jersey. On Monday, he barely acknowledged her wave and attempt at eye contact. The next day, she learned from Pansy that George's supervisor had called him on the carpet and really "chewed him out." *So that's why he's in such a bad mood.* She decided to give him the time and space to lick his wounds. *He's probably upset and embarrassed. I'll wait until the end of the week before I contact him.*

On Friday, he passed in front of her desk without acknowledging her, but Theresa was taken aback by his unkempt appearance. Unshaven and rumpled, he looked like he had spent the morning helping to unload one of the trucks. She called him at his workstation and invited him to dinner. He seemed distracted.

"I have to go up to my mother's," he told her. "She's moving into a place for seniors and I have to clean out the house."

After an awkward silence, he suggested that she come to his apartment that night. Relieved that he wasn't dumping her, she was surprised to feel herself recoiling.

"Tonight's not too good for that," she lied. "I'm just about to start my period, and I'm usually crampy and out of sorts."

He sounded disappointed, but it was often difficult to tell precisely what he was feeling. Later, she realized that part of her reluctance to see him was because of his disheveled appearance. Something wasn't right.

He agreed to meet for lunch on Tuesday, but arrived still looking disheveled. Theresa tried to make conversation, but he was distracted and vague. Finally, she asked if he was all right.

He smiled at her. "Don't worry, Terry. I'm fine. Everything's under control, believe me. There's no need for you to be concerned."

"You're sure?" she asked. "Because you look like you're not taking care of yourself. Is it your mother? Are you worried about her?"

He chuckled. "No problem. Everything is cool."

Theresa didn't believe him, but she had conveyed her concern and there was no sense pushing him.

After dinner on Friday night, they went back to his apartment, this time without the benefit of having finished a bottle of wine. It had been two weeks since she'd been to his apartment and she was surprised to find it in such a state of disorder — the bed unmade, clothes strewn about, dirty dishes piled in the sink.

George kept shaking his head, as if he had water in his ear. Theresa tried not to pay attention — she had been having more sexual fantasies since their last encounter and had been masturbating to them. She was hoping they might go a bit further this time. Waiting on the bed in anticipation, she noticed that he seemed to be poking around the apartment looking for something.

"Come sit down with me, George," she said invitingly.

No response.

"Are you looking for something?" *Had he purchased something? For her? For them? A token of affection? A sex toy?*

"I'll be right there," he said irritably. Mumbling to himself, he finally sat down stiffly.

I'll be damned if I'm going to take the lead again. She lay back onto the bed, the peculiar smell of dirty sheets filling her nostrils. George lay down and kissed her with closed lips. She put her arms around him and turned her hips to his, but his response was lackluster. There was no strength in his embrace, no throbbing erection against her body. He interrupted his kissing to look about.

"What's the matter?" she asked softly. "You seem distracted."

"Nothing's wrong."

"You don't seem excited to be here with me. Did I do something wrong the last time?"

"Jesus, Terry, what's with all the goddamned questions? I said nothing is wrong. Are you calling me a liar?"

What's wrong with him? He's as jittery as a bedbug.

"I'm just wondering, George. You don't seem interested. Are you thinking of somebody else?"

"Jesus, Terry, just shut up and stop with the goddamned questions, will you? Let's just lie here together, OK? Don't talk."

Theresa let him put his arms around her, but she felt how tense he was. There was nothing romantic or caring in it — more like he was keeping her quiet, holding her there because it was safer than letting go. She was surprised to find herself crying. Frustration? Confusion? A realization that this relationship was coming to an end? She squirmed against his hold on her. He let go and rolled over onto his back.

"Maybe you better just go home," he announced to the ceiling, as if he had read her mind. She sighed. Of relief? Resignation? Defeat? She wiped her face

and started to say something.
    He must have sensed it. "Just go."

Andy and Tawanda

Saturday

Andy's hand was on the phone in the middle of the first ring. "Romano," he answered. After a few moments, he closed the cellphone and leaned over to kiss his wife.

"Again?" she murmured.

"Go back to sleep."

"It seems like you just got home."

"I know. There's been a shooting."

"When will I see you?"

"I don't know. I'll call you later. Go back to sleep."

"Be careful," she said. He kissed her again and left the bedroom. He had gotten in the habit of putting his clothes for the next day on a chair in the hall — everything except his gun and his badge — so he could dress quickly without disturbing her. In 20 minutes, he was on the 2000 block of Fernon Street in Point Breeze. The crime scene guys had just arrived, along with three squad cars and a reporter from the *Inquirer* named Willy Escobar.

"You might as well be working a night shift," Escobar said. "I see you out here at night all the time anyway."

"You mean the morning." He turned to the approaching officer in charge. "What've we got?"

"Somebody heard shots and phoned it in. We found this: young white male in the van, shot three times in the head, through the windshield. The van kept going, bounced off a couple of cars, there," he said, pointing back down the street, "and then smashed into the telephone pole."

"Anything else?"

"We're combing the area for the shells. We'll wait till it gets light before we start ringing doorbells to see if there're any witnesses."

"ID?"

We didn't find any on him. Maybe the CSI guys will find something. We're checking the plates and the VIN now."

Andy nodded. Johnson should be here by now. He kept looking up the street for a sign of her car.

"This one's a head-scratcher, detective," the officer added.

"You mean more than usual?"

"Yeah. Come and take a look at the vic."

Andy ducked under the tape and followed the officer to the van. The crime scene crew was still setting up floodlights, so the only light was from a lone streetlamp halfway down the block. The door was open and the uniform shined his flashlight onto the dead driver.

"What the fuck is this?" Andy said.

The body of a white male slumped over the steering wheel. A mask, maybe a balaclava Andy thought, covered the bottom half of his face. The top half was pretty much shot away.

"It's only the first of October, for Christ's sake. What's he doing with that on?"

"That's not all," the cop said. He shined his flashlight into the back of the van. "There's some weird shit back there: handcuffs, a machete, a couple of locked tool chests."

"OK, thanks." He saw headlights pulling up to their little jamboree. That's Johnson, he thought. About time. He watched his partner park her car and walk briskly toward him. Davis, CS crew chief, approached him at the same time. Davis filled them in.

"He was dead instantly. All three shots hit him full in the face. They're looking for shell casings now."

"What do you make of the mask?" Andy asked. Johnson hadn't said a word yet.

"Who knows?" Davis said. "The vic was a young white male. No ID yet. We didn't find anything on the body or in the glove compartment, but we'll take the van in and go over it, see what we find."

"Drugs?" asked Johnson.

Davis shrugged his shoulders.

"What else?" Andy said. "Out here, at 2:00 in the morning. A white kid? With that mask on? He was up to no good, that's for sure."

"We'll do a screening on him. We'll let you know what we find."

"When do you think that'll be?" Andy asked.

"Shit, Andy, it's Saturday morning. We won't have a full staff until Monday. Call me Tuesday."

Andy looked at his partner. "I guess in the meantime we try to find out who this kid is and why he's here."

"And who shot his face off." Tawanda Johnson felt strange opening her mouth and speaking — her first words since she was awakened a half-hour ago. "Christ, are Friday nights always like this? Young gang bangers knocking themselves off?" New to their district, she was still getting adjusted.

They watched the crime scene guys take the body away. A tow truck came to haul the van back to where they could investigate for clues about the kid's identity. Escobar assessed the information he already had: unidentified young white male shot three times on Fernon Street in the Point Breeze section of Philadelphia. No witnesses yet. No apparent motive. He might as well go back to the station and write it up.

A few minutes later, a uniform approached Romano and Johnson.

"We ran a trace on the plate — it belongs to a 2002 Hyundai reported stolen last year in Jersey."

"What about the VIN?" Andy asked the cop.

"A 1999 Ford van, registered to a George Hladic. Here's his address." Andy copied it down.

"It's over on Powelton," Andy said to his partner. "You want to leave your car here and we'll go over in my car?"

"Shit, no, I'm not leaving my car out here. Be nothing left when we come back."

"OK," he said, "let's swing by the 17th and you can leave it there."

As Andy went to his own vehicle, he saw the cops up and down the street with their flashlights and metal detectors looking for shell casings. Maybe they'd get lucky. Maybe the citizen who phoned in the shooting saw something. Wouldn't that be nice for a change?

Driving to the district headquarters, Andy let his imagination go to work. A young white male, in Point Breeze at 2:00 a.m. Shot three times in the face. Accurate shooting, not all that common. The vic is wearing a mask or balaclava. What for? Handcuffs? Machete? Locked tool chests? Stolen plate a year old, from Jersey? Shot while he was driving? The shooter would have been right in front of a moving vehicle. He shook his head. This was a strange one.

Wanda parked her car at 20th and Federal and they headed to Powelton. Maybe George Hladic was the vic. But maybe Hladic was still alive and some other bastard was driving the van, which would raise a host of other questions.

Andy hoped for simplicity. He prayed for simplicity. "Let's hope this doesn't get too complicated," he said out loud.

"You might as well pray for a raise," Wanda said.

It was a little after 3:30 a.m. when they pulled onto the 3600 block of Powelton Avenue. They climbed the front stoop and examined the row of bells with their flashlights. None had a name attached.

"I don't want to wake up the whole freakin' house," Wanda whispered. "Who knows if Hladic even still lives here? Lets go back to headquarters, get some coffee, and look up the landlord."

Andy agreed. "We'll pick up your jalopy on the way," he suggested.

"Jalopy? My car is newer than yours," Wanda said indignantly.

"Even so, it can't compare to this creampuff."

"Maybe one of these days, somebody in my family will spring for one of these for me."

"I hope so," he said. "Then you can do the chauffeuring and I'll sit back and relax."

At district headquarters, they sipped coffee while looking up the landlord for the house on Powelton. At 6:00 they called the owner, found out which apartment belonged to Hladic, and made an appointment to meet the landlord there at 8:00. They had also pulled up Hladic's driver's license and now had a picture to go with the name. Because the vic's face had been obliterated by the shooting, it was impossible to make a definite ID, but the license described him as 19 years old, six feet two, blond hair, brown eyes, 170 pounds. Could be him.

In the meantime, the uniforms had brought back half a dozen shell casings and dropped them off at ballistics. They decided to go home, get an hour's sleep, and meet at the Powelton Avenue address about 7:50. Andy said he'd write it up for the captain after checking out Hladic's apartment. Meanwhile, uniforms would canvass the Fernon Street area to see if anyone admitted to witnessing anything.

Tawanda returned to the apartment she shared with her sister and mother. When she'd left a few hours earlier, no one had been home. Mom worked nights at her cleaning job and wouldn't be home until close to 8:00. Shirley was probably at her boyfriend's. Tawanda figured that pretty soon, Shirley would move in with Kevin and then it would be just her and Mom against the world.

But when she unlocked the door, she heard the radio playing, then noticed her mother's jacket on the back of a chair in the living room.

"Mom? How come you're home so early?" she called out.

Wanda flopped onto the sofa, pushed off her shoes, and closed her eyes. She had almost fallen asleep when she heard her mother coming down the hall.

"We finished early and my knees were acting up, so Mr. Atkins said why don't I leave a little early. I wasn't going to argue." She sat down heavily on one end of the sofa as Wanda pulled her knees up to make room. "Were you out working already?"

"We got a call, a shooting in Point Breeze. Some white boy got his face shot off. I have to go back out in a while and meet Romano over in the Mantua section of University City."

"What's a white boy doing in Point Breeze? Looking to score some drugs?"

"Maybe," her daughter answered. "Might be something more than that."

When Andy let himself into his three-story home on South 13th Street, he expected everyone to still be asleep. He was surprised to hear his wife in the kitchen before 6:00 a.m. on a Saturday. He went through the hall that led to the back of their house and found Anita sitting at the table, drinking coffee and reading the morning paper.

"Hey," he said.

"I thought you might be getting back. You want something to eat, or is it back to bed?"

He kissed her and took a sip from her mug.

"Hey," she said, "that's mine. I'll get you a cup if you want."

"No, I just wanted a sip, it smelled so good. I think I'll lie down for an hour."

"OK," she said, "when do you want me to wake you?"

"I've got to meet Wanda about 7:50, so 7:00 is good."

"All right. I'll fix you something then."

He headed upstairs to their bedroom. Nick and Jenn would probably still be asleep when he left. Hopefully, he'd see them at dinner, although on a Saturday night they'd probably be heading out with their friends. He took off his shoes and dropped back onto the bed he had abandoned over four hours ago.

At 7:50, Andy parked his car on Powelton and walked toward the house they had visited earlier that morning. It was an interesting neighborhood — fine old houses, impressive architecture. Once upon a time, people with money had built these three- and four-story homes in what had then been the country, a couple of miles outside Center City. Now, they were all rentals, chopped up into tiny apartments for students from Penn or Drexel. Maybe Hladic was a student with a mother and father somewhere wondering why he wasn't answering

the phone.

Wanda was already in front of the building, talking with a short, round, Asian man. *She carries herself like a professional,* he thought. She also had a smile a mile wide, filled with more white teeth than a person could count. But usually, she was all business, conveying a mixture of respect for others and personal authority. He was happy to have her as his partner.

"Detective Romano," she said as he approached, "this is Mr. Han, the owner of the building."

Andy held out his hand, which Mr. Han grasped and shook with a surprisingly firm grip.

"Good morning, Detective," Mr. Han said without any trace of an accent. "Detective Johnson tells me you are interested in looking at the apartment of George Hladic."

"That's correct. We have a picture of him from his driver's license." He took out his iPhone and showed Mr. Han the picture of the deceased. "Is that him?"

"I think so, but to be honest, I see so many young people — there's a lot of turnover in these apartments, you know. I'm not 100 percent sure. But he does look familiar. I think that's him."

"We'll check it out. Lead the way, Mr. Han."

They followed the landlord up the steps of the old three-story brownstone. Mr. Han unlocked the front door and they followed him up three flights to an apartment at the rear of the building. Mr. Han knocked perfunctorily on the door, then inserted his key into the lock and pushed the door open. Andy entered first, announcing loudly that they were Philadelphia police, but the small studio was empty.

"OK, Mr. Han, thank you for your help. If you could leave a key with me for the time being? When we get Mr. Hladic's, then I'll return this to you."

"Of course, Detective," he said, removing the key from where it nested with numerous others on a large key ring. "If there is anything else I can do ..."

"Actually," Andy said, "here's my card. If you could send me a copy of the rental records you have for Mr. Hladic, if you've done a background check, any forms he may have filled out ..."

"No trouble at all, Detective."

Mr. Han left, putting Andy's card in his pocket, and the two detectives started their examination of the apartment. Aside from a bed, there was a table with two chairs and an old three-drawer dresser. A small goose-neck lamp positioned near a corner of the table and a cheap ceiling fixture in the kitchen made up the lighting. Sunlight peeked around the edges of an opaque shade on the lone south-facing window. Andy raised the shade and studied the backs of the surrounding buildings. Each one had a small yard that seemed to be unused except for storing unwanted debris.

He turned and surveyed the room: a laptop computer on the dresser along with a couple of books, a notebook, and a small radio. The sink and drain board contained a few dirty dishes and a pot soaking in water. A teakettle squatted on the stove. The bed was unmade and dirty socks and underwear lay discarded on the floor.

Wanda opened the closet. Andy went through the dresser drawers.

"This kid doesn't own shit," Andy said. "Have you found a wallet? Receipts, pay stubs?"

"Not yet. There are some shoe boxes on the floor of the closet …"

"There's got to be some letters, a phone book …" Andy looked around again and saw a wall phone in the kitchen and an answering machine on the counter. He lifted the receiver and got a dial tone. He made a note to request records from the phone company. Then he hit the play button on the answering machine. An older woman's voice: "Hi, honey. Guess you know who this is. It's Thursday morning. Please call me. There are some things I need at the store this weekend, if it's at all possible for you to take me."

The caller ID said Mrs. Sonia Hladic and listed a northern New Jersey number. The mother? Andy wrote down the number. That was the only message. He rummaged through the kitchen cabinets and drawers and found a wallet and a bunch of receipts.

"Bingo!" He glanced over at Wanda, who was fiddling with the laptop. "Anything there?"

"Not yet. He's got it password protected. We'll give it to the lab." She joined him at the kitchen counter.

"Why don't you check out the bathroom?" Andy emptied the drawer's contents into a plastic evidence bag and then got the computer. He was about to take a look in the closet himself when Wanda came out of the bathroom.

"No drugs, not even ibuprofen. Toothpaste and toilet paper, soap and two towels. That's it."

Andy went through the closet, checking jacket and pant pockets and the shoeboxes on the floor. Wanda went back to the kitchen and searched the fridge, freezer, and cabinets again.

"Let's interview the other residents," Andy suggested, "see what we can find out about this kid."

Wanda started on the third floor and worked her way down. They knocked on every door, but not everyone was home. An hour later, they returned to district headquarters. As soon as they walked into the squad room, their lieutenant called them into his office.

"While you two were out gallivanting, these reports came in for you on that

Fernon Street shooting last night."

Andy glanced at the papers and handed them to Wanda.

"Looks like we're off to a decent start, Lieutenant. We have an ID on the victim, a kid living on Powelton Ave. We collected a bag full of papers to go through, and there was a message on his answering machine from his mother. I'll give her a call."

"Anything else?"

"Yes, sir," said Wanda. "We got his laptop. I'll bring it down to the lab. The kid's got it password protected."

"OK," said the lieutenant. He pointed to the papers she held in her hand. "The ballistics from the shell casings should point you toward the perp. Wrap it up soon, OK?" The two detectives nodded and left the office.

"You heard the man," Wanda said, laughter in her voice. "Wrap it up soon."

"What else? That's his mantra, probably says it to his wife when she's making breakfast."

"Or whatever," she said, chuckling. "I'll bring the computer down."

"Yeah. Maybe he's got an enemies list on it and we'll wrap it up soon."

Andy went through the papers: pay stubs from Jonas Computer Services in Northern Liberties, receipts from a hardware store, groceries, pizza. He called Jonas Computer Services and got a recorded message that they were closed until Monday morning at 9:00. Inside the wallet: driver's license, car registration, Social Security card, Visa card, $43.00. The books from the top of the dresser: *Beginning Computer Science* and *The Principles of Programming*; a notebook on computer stuff, with class times and name of the instructor. The kid was taking a course at Community College. So far he looked clean and straight, with no sign of drugs. The database didn't turn up anything on him: no record — not even a traffic stop. So what the hell was he doing in Point Breeze at 2:00 in the morning?

Tawanda brought two mugs of black coffee.

"We have his place of employment," he told her, "but they're closed until Monday."

"You want me to call the mother?"

"No," Andy said, "I'll do it. I just wanted to wait. You know, to be sure."

"We had, what, four people from the rooming house identify him?"

He dialed the Jersey number and left a message. "Mrs. Hladic, my name is Detective Andrew Romano. I'm with the Philadelphia Police Department. I need to speak with you as soon as possible. It concerns your son, George." He left his cellphone number.

"This is always the shit part," Wanda said.

"Tell me about it. You know, even when these kids are obvious slime balls, their mothers, their fathers, they don't see them that way. They're still their little babies. And this kid, it ain't just because he's white, but he seems pretty straight, you know? He's working, he's going to college, he's making it on his own."

"I know."

"Every time, Wanda, every freakin' time we go through this with some kid, I think of my own. It doesn't matter who they are, how fucked up they are, what shit they've done, I think: There but for the grace of God go I. It could've been my son or my daughter and somebody calling me. You know?"

"I know, Andy."

"Shit." He took a deep sigh. "So what's the story on the ballistics and the witness canvassing? We might as well zero in on the perp now. You know, *wrap it up soon.*"

"Nine millimeter. They're checking the casings for fingerprints. They found six casings, so looks like three missed their mark. But we'll check the slugs we get from the coroner's office with open cases. Maybe we'll get lucky."

"And the canvassing?"

"One woman on Fernon Street. She heard squealing tires and looked out just as a shot was fired. She saw a black male running east on Fernon. She said it looked like the van was trying to run him down. The man turned and fired a bunch of shots, then jumped out of the way as the van crashed into a couple of cars, then continued toward 20th Street and banged into a pole. The shooter ran back west toward 21st."

"Any description?"

"The usual," she said, "black, dark clothes, a hoody, medium height and build. She didn't see his face, but she said he ran like a gang-banger."

"Let's take a look at what else was going on in that neighborhood last night. Maybe the shooter tried to rob Hladic and he took off after him. See if there were any muggings or other disturbances."

"You got it."

Just then, Andy's cellphone rang. It was Mrs. Hladic. Wanda decided to look at last night's sheets to see if there was any related action in Point Breeze near the site of the shooting. When she came back, Andy was rocking back in his chair twirling a pencil between his fingers. She raised her eyebrows questioningly.

"She's getting somebody to drive her down and ID the body."

"When?" she asked.

"Tonight."

"You want me to go with you?"

He let out a sigh. "Yeah, I think it'd help to have a female there."

"Right." She looked at the notes in her hand. "Just about the time of the shooting, 911 got a call of a mugging in progress on 21st Street, just around the corner. Looks like your hunch may have been right."

"Maybe," he said. "So we're waiting on Mr. Han's information on Hladic, the phone company records, fingerprints from the shell casings — anything else?"

"Hladic's employer on Monday morning, maybe re-interview the witness on Fernon Street."

"Oh, the computer and the van, and the vic's body itself," he added.

"Right, the lab guys said we should call them Tuesday, but we can check in with the medical examiner Monday morning. They might have something by then. And ballistics for the slugs they pulled out of the vic."

Andy pushed himself away from his desk. "OK then. Not much more we can do today. What say we grab lunch and see if we can close out some of the other shit we have open?"

Andy called his wife to say he'd be home for dinner, so she wouldn't keel over when he walked in the door. He usually arrived an hour after everybody else had finished eating and had disappeared into their own private lives.

He was greeted by Anita with a drink in hand. "Saturday night and you're home for supper. The kids are still here. We're a regular, normal family."

Andy sipped the drink. "Umm, Old Fashioned?"

"How is it?"

"Like heaven. It's good to be loved."

"It's good to have you home at a decent hour. Consider this a reward."

"What about some lovin'?"

"Don't get greedy. Drink now. We'll see about that later."

He hung up his jacket and joined her on the sofa.

"So?" she said.

He knew she was asking about the case that had pulled him out of bed that morning. God, it seemed so long ago.

"A 19-year-old white kid, originally from Jersey. His mother is coming down tonight. Wanda and I have to meet her at the morgue later."

Anita rolled her eyes. "I might have known."

"She's in some assisted living up there."

Anita nodded as he sipped his drink.

"So this kid, he's going to Community College, taking computer courses, has a job, living on his own. Something of a loner, doesn't have much of a social life, judging from what his neighbors have to say. And last night he's in Point Breeze. Who knows, maybe he's just driving through?" He paused and stared into space.

"What?"

Andy shook his head. "No, he wasn't just driving through. He was up to something, this kid. He was driving a van with a stolen plate on it. So maybe it is all about drugs. Maybe he's supplementing his pay by dealing. He wouldn't be the first." He put down his drink. "Anyway, there was a report of an attempted mugging right before the shooting. Maybe it's related. A witness says the kid was trying to run down some black guy who turned and shot him. Three times in the face. Nothing left." He took another sip. "It's sad, what these kids do to each other. So much waste. It could just as easily be Nick out there, you know?"

"You think I don't worry?" she asked. "It's freaking scary out there, Andy. All those guns. And drugs."

"The kids staying home tonight?

"You think they ask me? They'll let us know when they come down for dinner."

"What'd you make?"

"Chicken cacciatore, your grandmother's recipe, with pasta and salad."

"That's what I love about you."

"Yeah, I know. You married me so you wouldn't starve to death."

"That wasn't the only thing."

"I know. You and your appetites. Which reminds me, don't forget, we're going to your Uncle Dom's for dinner tomorrow."

"I won't forget. I'm looking forward to seeing my brother and everybody. The only thing that would keep me is if I get called."

"Right. OK, call the kids. Dinner's ready."

When Tawanda arrived home, Shirley was in the kitchen preparing supper. Their mother was still getting ready for work. Wanda greeted her younger sister. "What are you making?"

"Mama put a meatloaf together. I'm just making potatoes and some greens."

"Want me to help with anything?"

"You can set the table. Otherwise I'm good."

"How's Kevin?"

"He's fine. We're going out later. A friend of his is having a little party."

"You staying over again?"

"You're so nosy," Shirley said with a huge grin on her face. She had the same toothsome smile as her sister. "You'd think I was one of your perps under investigation."

"I'm only doing my big-sister job. Keeping track of what's going on. You two getting serious?"

Shirley shrugged. "He wants me to move in with him."

"And ..."

"And nothing."

"Well, what are you thinking, baby?"

"Well, I am thinking. I didn't say yes and I didn't say no."

"You tell Mama?"

"She says to think long and hard about it. Too many young women not taking themselves seriously enough. She says why not wait until Kevin finishes school, passes his bar exam, has a job. Otherwise I might end up supporting him with my nurse's pay."

"Uh huh. And what do you think?"

"Well, Kevin says it's because of his school and my rotating shifts that we don't get to see each other as much as we'd like. If we were living together, it would be easier."

"I asked you what you thought."

"I think they each have a point. I'd like to see more of Kevin, but he's barely scraping by with what his family gives him and his loans and scholarship. If I were there, it would be a big help to him. And it would be a way for me to get out on my own."

"You think he wants to get married eventually?"

Shirley nodded. "We've been talking. He wants to wait until he's working and I agree. But that doesn't mean we can't be living together in the meantime."

"Sounds like you're getting ready to pack your bags."

"You think so? I thought I was more undecided."

"Well I'm glad to hear you haven't made up your mind yet. But I won't be surprised if I find I have a bedroom all to myself one of these days."

Annabelle Johnson entered the kitchen. "I see my girls have everything ready. Table all set and everything."

"Jeez, when was the last time we all sat down to dinner together?" Tawanda asked.

"It sure has been a long time," Annabelle agreed. "Between your jobs and your love lives, I hardly ever get to see you together."

"You can add your own schedule to that, Mama," said Shirley. "We're usually gone in the morning before you get home."

"Well, there is that," their mother agreed.

"Well, at least my love life is no longer a problem," Wanda said with a chuckle, as if it were some meaningless thing to be taken lightly.

"That reminds me," Annabelle said, "Reggie must have left another three or four messages for you today. When I heard it was him, I didn't even pick up. Lord, that man does want to talk to you."

"He's been calling my cell, too. I'm not talking to him, it'll only encourage him."

"No more chances, huh?" Shirley's eyebrows arched, her fork suspended halfway to her mouth.

"No. No more chances. I've given that Casanova too many chances as it is. He thinks he's so damned good looking he can get away with anything. Well, no more. I deserve better."

"Why don't you try working up some passion about it? A body might think you were wishy-washy." Annabelle held a sly grin on her face and Tawanda laughed.

"Daddy never would have pulled this stuff with you."

"Your daddy was an exceptional man, sweetheart. I hope you each find somebody like him."

"I think Kevin is like Daddy was," said Shirley.

"I hope so, child. I dearly do hope so."

Tawanda met Andy at the medical examiner's office. As she entered the door to the lab, she spotted a middle-aged white woman and an older man sitting on a bench in the hallway.

"Mrs. Hladic?"

The woman looked up with a face weary from a lifetime of suffering. She nodded wordlessly.

"I'm Detective Johnson. I work with Detective Romano."

"This is Mr. Novak. I don't drive, but Mr. Novak said he'd bring me down. Mr. Novak lives at St. Anne's with me." She turned to the man. "Thank you, Franklin. I don't know what I would have done if you hadn't been right there."

"Nice to meet you, Mr. Novak. Let me go in and see if Detective Romano is here yet."

Andy was talking with the ME. "Dr. Grear said they put the face together as well as they could, but it's going to be rough on her," he told Wanda. "He was just telling me about their preliminary report. All the screens aren't back yet, but so far no sign of drugs."

"The lab results should be in by Tuesday," Dr. Grear said. "I was telling Andy that we sent the three slugs to ballistics this morning. That should also be ready by Tuesday."

Wanda thanked him. "I just spoke with Mrs. Hladic out in the hall. She's here with a friend."

The two detectives walked back into the hall and Andy introduced himself. "Mrs. Hladic, if you'll come with us, please." She got up with some difficulty and the three of them walked back into the ME's office complex and down the hall to the viewing station. Holding the woman's arm, Wanda thought how frail and beaten down she appeared, even though she couldn't be that old.

A lab tech rolled a stretcher up to the window and pulled back the sheet. The head and naked upper torso of her son appeared, pale white, bluish with three small craters in his face: on his forehead, his left cheek, and where the rest of the nose had been. *A nice tight cluster,* Wanda thought appreciatively. *This perp knows how to shoot.* She felt Mrs. Hladic's body sag.

"We're sorry for your loss, Mrs. Hladic. It's a terrible thing for any parent to have to see one of their children like that," Wanda said, her hand on the mother's shoulder.

"He was my only child."

"Do you have any idea why this might have happened?"

"No, my son was a very private person. He didn't confide in me at all. I'm not even sure I know the name of the company where he worked. I call him and all I get is the answering machine. Sometimes I call just to hear his voice, but he usually doesn't return my calls. Only if it's something special, like a little while ago when I moved into St. Anne's and sold the house and he came up to help me empty it out. I'm not strong like I used to be, especially since my husband died. Now all my family is gone. I have nobody."

Wanda spoke gently. "Mrs. Hladic, we have to keep your son's body here for a few more days, but then we'll release it to you. Perhaps you can give me the name of a funeral home we should contact ..."

The mother looked at her, uncomprehending. "I'll give you my card," Wanda said, reaching into her pocket, "and when you've selected a funeral parlor, have them call me. Can you do that?" Mrs. Hladic nodded.

The two detectives looked at each other. There was no need to prolong this. She wasn't interested in any information at this point and didn't appear to have any to share with them. They escorted her back to her companion and watched as they slowly made their way toward the exit.

"Dr. Grear did have some information for us," Andy told his partner. "Remember last night ..."

"You mean this morning."

"Right, this morning at the crime scene, the kid was wearing some kind of mask?"

"Yeah, a balaclava, you said."

"Right. Well, we couldn't see it, because of all the blood, but he had smeared his face with burnt cork."

"What? Like kids do on Halloween?"

"Yeah. Plus, he was wearing camouflage pants and had a knife strapped to his right leg."

"What kind of knife?"

"Like you get in the Army & Navy store, a military knife."

"Sounds like he was out on some kind of mission."

"Exactly. This kid didn't just happen to be in Point Breeze because he made a wrong turn. He was there for a reason."

Sunday

As Andy drove his family to his uncle's restaurant, he was aware of the pleasure he took in driving the Lincoln Town Car his father had "sold" him for one dollar. It had been only three years old with less than 20,000 miles — one of the perks of being the son of a successful businessman. The fact that the business was maybe not 100 percent legitimate — well, that was another story. But Paolo Romano had raised two fine sons: Andrew, a detective, and Emelio, a federal prosecutor. Funny how they both went into law enforcement. Actually, Paolo had enthusiastically encouraged it. A proud father, he had never asked either of them to participate in his business. Anita and the kids enjoyed his family, so celebrating Emelio's birthday together was an event everyone looked forward to.

Wanda often busted Andy about the car and his having a rich father, but nobody ever hinted at the fact that Paolo was involved with organized crime. Whether they didn't know or had too much respect for the family, Andy didn't question. But he was grateful he'd never had to defend his father's business dealings — or the creampuff of a car.

At the restaurant, a valet parked the car and inside they greeted Uncle Dom, who still hung around the restaurant even though his son, Nicky, managed it. Andy gave his older brother a bear hug. After dinner, the two brothers sat at the bar with their father, sipping coffee and liquors,.

"So, Andy," Emelio said, "what are you doing with yourself these days? I heard Anita telling Mom that you were called out at 2:00 a.m. yesterday."

"It's like being a doctor on call. You never know when. I'm just thankful that the phone didn't ring this afternoon. It was a great dinner."

"Tell us. What was it?"

"A shooting in Point Breeze. A 19-year-old white kid." Andy gave them some of the bizarre details of the case.

"So what do you think?" his father asked. "Drugs?"

"That's what I assumed at first. But there's something odd about this kid. He's a real loner. No friends. Has a decent job, goes to college for computer science. And, so far, no indication that he's been using — although when the screens come back, that could tell a different story."

"What about the shooter?" asked Emelio.

"We may have a line on him. We got partial prints from the casings and we have the slugs from the kid's head, so we may get a match. Chances are the guy is from the neighborhood, a gang-banger. At least he runs fast."

"And he's a good shot," said his brother.

"Extremely — and that's unusual. This is somebody who practices. We'll probably hit the gun clubs once we have something more to go on."

"Well," Paolo said, "I doubt I'll hear anything about it, but if I do I'll pass it on."

"Hey, how's your partner doing — what's her name, Tawanda?" his brother asked.

"She's good, Mel. Going through a rough patch right now, broke up with her boyfriend, a real Don Juan. She found out he was screwing around on her."

"He's not the first guy. Besides, you cops have a helluva reputation for that."

"And lawyers don't?"

Andy felt that familiar tension creeping in. His brother always found some way to put him down, to insinuate that attorneys were better than cops. He was annoyed with himself for rising to the bait. If Mel had to engage in put-downs to make himself feel better, that was his problem.

"It's just that she's very straight," he said, trying to put the dig behind him, "and she thought he was playing straight with her — and then she caught him cheating. Apparently it happened more than once, so she gave him the heave-ho. But she's feeling a little down about it." He didn't exactly feel comfortable talking about Wanda's private life, even to his brother and father. He changed the subject.

"How are you doing, Dad? You and Mom OK?"

"Oh, we're fine. Did I tell you we're going to Italy next month?"

Andy was glad his parents were able to enjoy life. "Where to this time?"

"We rented a little place outside of Florence for two weeks."

"Sounds nice," said Emelio, "but won't it be a little chilly?"

"No, it's the perfect time to go. Not too hot, no crowds. We'll have some of our family from over there come and visit. It should be beautiful."

Later, as everyone was getting ready to leave, Emelio put his arm around his brother's shoulders. "Hey," he said, "I didn't mean anything before, you know, about cops having a reputation for cheating. I was just busting my kid brother."

"Don't worry about it," Andy said. He wondered if his father had told Mel to apologize. He knew Emelio loved him, and thought it was his job to be the big brother: older, wiser, superior in every way. That's the way big brothers were. But it got to be a pain in the ass sometimes.

On the way home, he told Anita about his parents' upcoming trip to Italy.

"We should go sometime," she said. "If we wait too long, the kids won't want to go with us."

Andy eyed his 15-year-old son and 12-year-old daughter in the rearview mirror for a reaction.

Jennifer rolled her eyes almost imperceptibly, and Nick kept his face buried in his cellphone.

"That might be a good thing," Andy told his wife.

Monday

Tawanda and Andy decided to split the investigation. She would cover Hladic while Andy followed up leads on the shooter. She decided to speak to the employer first, then check out the landlord's information and phone company records. On Monday morning, she arrived at Jonas Computer Services.

A long hallway ended in a T. Directly in front of her was a glass-walled office with the word *Administration* on the door. A pleasant-looking young woman looked up from her desk and smiled at Tawanda. The nameplate on her desk read Ms. T. Rodriguez.

"May I help you?"

Tawanda showed her badge and gave her card to the receptionist. "Good morning. I'm Detective Johnson from the Philadelphia Police. May I speak to whoever is in charge?"

"Mr. Jonas Kwan is the owner and CEO, but he's not in. Mr. Harold Kwan is our vice president in charge of operations. May I tell him what this is in reference to?"

"We're conducting an investigation involving one of your employees."

Theresa's eyebrows registered mild curiosity, but she maintained her fixed smile while she buzzed her boss.

Mr. Kwan emerged from his office.

"Detective ...?"

"Johnson."

"Harold Kwan. Won't you please come into my office?"

Seated across the expanse of Mr. Kwan's desk, Tawanda spoke first.

"One of your employees was shot and killed early Saturday morning. Anything you can tell us about him may help find the person responsible."

Mr. Kwan blanched visibly. "What is the employee's name?"

"George Hladic." She produced a printout of his driver's license photo. "Do you recognize him?"

Mr. Kwan nodded. "Yes, I recognized the name. He works in our data processing department. Let me get his supervisor. I'm sure he will know much more about the young man than I do."

He picked up his phone and dialed directly. "Timothy? Harold here. Can you come to my office? Yes, right now. Oh, and please bring George Hladic's employee file." He turned back to Tawanda. "Mr. Kim is in charge of our data processing department."

"How long has Mr. Hladic worked here, Mr. Kwan?"

"Let me see. Offhand, I'd say a little over a year. Mr. Kim will have that information." He paused, as the situation sank in. "How could something like this happen?"

"I know it must come as something of a shock, Mr. Kwan, to hear that one of your employees has been killed. We're investigating the circumstances. That's really all I can tell you at this point."

At that moment, Mr. Kim came in carrying a thin manila folder. The tall, thin man sat next to Tawanda.

"Mr. Kim, Detective Johnson is investigating the death of Mr. Hladic, who was shot and killed over the weekend. She's here to gather any information you can tell her about him."

Mr. Kim fiddled with his glasses. "Mr. Hladic, George, has worked in my department since last July," he began. And then he looked directly at Wanda. "Did you say he was shot? Murdered?"

"We're not sure of the circumstances, Mr. Kim. We're just beginning our investigation. That's why it's important that you tell us anything you know about Mr. Hladic."

"Yes, of course. Well, as far as I know this was his first job out of high school. He was hired in July 2009 to do data entry, and he performed very well for the first few months."

"And then?"

"It's hard to say. My first impression was that he is a bright young man, although he kept to himself. He appeared studious, serious. I presumed he would improve and advance within our department, that he might have a future in programming or some other aspect of our work."

"But that didn't happen?"

"The quality of his work leveled off fairly quickly. I know he was attending Community College, taking courses in computer science. Maybe he wasn't as bright or as conscientious as I'd thought, because he stopped showing the advancement that I'd hoped for. And then, perhaps in the past month or two, there was a noticeable decline."

Tawanda waited for him to gather his thoughts and continue.

"He started arriving late to work, or occasionally even missing a day without notice. When he didn't come in this morning, I assumed it was another indication of his lack of dependability. He'd started coming in unshaven, dressed inappropriately, not showing the proper respect for the workplace. About two weeks ago, I gave him a formal warning. It's right here in his file."

"And how did he respond to that?'

"He improved in some ways, but his affect was strange. He'd look at me oddly. I didn't know what to make of it."

"What do you mean, look at you oddly?"

"Difficult to explain. He would stare at me, with a strange smile. To tell the truth, it made me feel uneasy."

When Tawanda asked how Hladic had fit into the workplace culture, Mr. Kim indicated that he rarely talked with any of his co-workers. Most days he ate at his cubicle. Sometimes he went out for lunch, but Mr. Kim had no knowledge of what he might have done during that time.

Tawanda thanked Mr. Kim and Mr. Kwan for their cooperation. She handed one of her cards to each of them and asked them to call her if they thought of anything else.

Walking to her car, she reviewed what she knew so far: All descriptions of Hladic were consistent — an introverted, socially isolated loner with little if any social life. Not the kind of person who would provoke someone into murdering him. All the evidence suggested the shooting wasn't a result of a personal grievance.

After the detective left, Mr. Kwan met with the head of Human Resources and then called Pansy into his office. When she came out, she signaled to Gladys to meet in the kitchen. A few minutes later, Pansy approached Theresa's desk.

"Honey, come into the coffee area with me for a minute, OK?" Theresa looked at her questioningly, but Pansy gently took her by the arm and steered her toward the break room.

"Theresa, did you notice all the commotion this morning, with the detective and Mrs. Hastings from HR, in and out of Mr. Kwan's office?"

"Yes?"

"Here, sit down." Theresa sat down.

"It had to do with that young man," Pansy said cautiously.

"Which man?"

"The one you've been interested in, George Hladic."

"What about him?"

"Terry, I hate to tell you this." She paused grimly. "Somebody shot him. He's dead."

"What?" *Dead? Shot?* "When? How?"

"Saturday." Pansy waited a moment. "The detective couldn't say anything more about it."

"My God." *George shot?* She looked imploringly at Pansy. "Was it an accident? Why would somebody shoot him?"

"I don't know, honey. I told you all I know. Maybe later the detective will be able to tell you more."

How could such a thing happen?

Pansy placed a hand on Theresa's shoulder. "Can I get you something?"

Theresa shook her head. "I don't believe it. You're sure there's no mistake?"

"I don't think so."

Theresa stared blankly out the window.

"Do you need anything?"

Theresa attempted a smile. "I'll be OK, Pansy. Just give me a few minutes to digest this. It's just so unbelievable."

Pansy left her sitting at the small table. The words echoed in her head: *George is dead.* George, dead — shot! Shouldn't she be sad? But all she felt was shock and disbelief. Numbness. She did feel *some* sadness — after all, he was so young. But she was surprised that she didn't feel anything more profound — grief maybe. After all, they had been sexually involved. *But we'd broken up and I didn't expect to see him again. I didn't want to. He'd been just too immature and too freaking weird.*

The images swirled: of him unshaven, his clothes rumpled, his apartment in disarray, the sour smell of his unclean sheets, his distracted behavior. No, if she were honest with herself, she'd become repulsed by him. Friday night had broken the spell and she was free. She didn't feel as though she'd lost part of herself, and there was no reason to!

Then the thought occurred to Theresa that perhaps George had committed suicide — over her. Well, that would be too sad for words, but it would only prove how messed up he was. It was sad that they'd broken up, but it was the right thing to do. She didn't want to be with someone so unstable and immature.

Still, he was dead. Dead! That seemed so unreal. *No one so young should be shot dead. No one.*

Later, she called her Aunt Dorinda and told her what had happened. Dorrie insisted that Theresa come over that evening for dinner. She wouldn't take no for an answer.

Back at her desk, Tawanda looked over the material from Hladic's landlord. There was nothing they didn't already know. His application for the apartment gave his former address in northern New Jersey, where he'd lived with his parents. He'd paid his rent on time. The phone records contained only a few outgoing calls to his mother's phone; the incoming calls were from his mother, his place of work, and — just a handful over the past couple of months — from a Theresa Rodriguez. Tawanda looked up and frowned. The name sounded familiar. Then she had it: the nameplate on the receptionist's desk at Jonas Computer Services. She made a note to follow up on that. Then she sought out Andy. She found him in Lieutenant Mackey's office.

She took a seat next to Andy, across from the lieutenant's desk.

"How'd it go?" Andy asked.

"Not much new. Everybody agrees Hladic was a loner. He'd been there a little over a year, since he graduated from high school in Jersey. His boss said that at first it looked like he had a lot of potential, but then he petered out. In the last month the boss had to reprimand him for slacking off in his work habits and his appearance. Then I just noticed in the phone records that he'd received a couple of phone calls from the secretary to one of the big honchos there. It's probably work related, but I'll follow up with her. How 'bout you?"

"Not much. I was just telling the lieutenant that we won't have anything on ballistics or fingerprints until tomorrow. Ditto on the ME's final report, including the drug screens. Oh, the computer lab sent up a transcript of a file they found on the laptop."

"Did you read it?"

"Not yet. Why don't you take it, since you're doing the vic part of this for now?" He handed her a manila folder.

Lieutenant Mackey leaned forward. "What about the CSI report, Andy? Did they find anything on the van?"

"They said to go down after lunch and they'd have a preliminary report."

"OK," said the lieutenant. "Do what you can to close out some of your open cases, Andy, while you're waiting on these reports. Johnson, you finish up on Hladic. Tie up all the loose ends. Let's wrap this up soon, all right?"

"Yes, sir," they said and returned to their desks.

Sitting back on her desk chair, Tawanda was about to read the document retrieved from Hladic's laptop when Andy interrupted her. It was 6:00 p.m. before she realized she hadn't followed up with Ms. Rodriguez or read the Hladic transcript. She resigned herself to read the report at home that night, and follow up on the Rodriguez phone calls tomorrow.

Too chilly to be outdoors, they stayed in Dorinda's kitchen, savoring the heat from the oven where the tuna casserole was baking. Dorinda had bought an inexpensive bottle of wine.

"Helluva way to lose a boyfriend," she said. "Isn't having him rubbed out a little over the top?" It succeeded in evoking a smile from her niece.

"The funny thing is we had already broken up," Theresa confessed. "He was such a jerk Friday night. When I asked him what was wrong, he told me to shut up and go home. I thought: *Screw you. I don't need this.* I've seen enough macho assholes in my life bossing my mother around. I don't need that crap." She caught her aunt's eye. "So I had already decided it was over."

"So what happened then? Did he own a gun? You think he did it to himself?"

"It's possible, I guess. He seemed distracted about something. He was all jagged and edgy. But if he did kill himself, it wasn't because of me. I mean, he was already coming apart. I didn't make him that way."

"Oh, honey, I know. Of course you didn't have anything to do with it. Is there any way to find out how it happened?"

Theresa glanced quickly toward the living room, where she'd left her purse.

"The detective who came to the office this morning left her card. I thought I might call her tomorrow and see if she'll tell me anything."

Dorinda brought the casserole to the table and spooned out servings for each of them.

"I should feel more sad," Theresa said, "but I don't. It's so confusing — like I'm still a little pissed at him for being such a jerk Friday night. You'll laugh at this Dorrie, but the thought flashed through my mind today that it would have been real romantic, in a tragic Romeo and Juliet way, to have a lover killed under mysterious circumstances. But in my mind, we had already broken up — so it's like he cheated me out of that tragic romance. Isn't that crazy?"

"We all see too many grade B movies," Dorinda reassured her. "At one time or another, we all want to be tragic heroines. But, yeah, I know what you mean.

You wanted it to be all about love, didn't you?"

Theresa thought for a moment. "I didn't love him. I was attracted to him and thought he was good looking, and gentle. I think I felt a little protective of him, like he was vulnerable, like he was just emerging from his shell and not completely formed. I think I felt tenderness toward him. But mostly, I think I wanted him to love me. I wanted to be able to say that somebody loved me. That's why, when he told me how desperate he was to make love to me, it was so tempting. It was my chance to feel loved and desired."

"That's very seductive — needing to feel needed. But it ends up being a trap. The more dependent they are on you, the more you feel obligated to take care them. You end up being enslaved."

Theresa thought about that. "It's so sad though, isn't it? Just 19 years old and shot dead. And for what?"

George

—◦/◦/◦—

That night, alone in her apartment, Wanda curled up on the couch and began to read the transcript of George Hladic's journal:

June 2010: I'm not sure what it will mean if you are reading this. As of now, I do not intend to let anyone read what I write. Therefore, there is a likelihood that I am dead or have been captured and this manuscript has been discovered. The truth is that I do want you (whoever you are) to understand what I'm doing. But I don't want you to find out before I'm ready. I don't want to be stopped. I don't want to be caught and punished. I don't want to be subjected to ridicule. I couldn't stand that — I'd rather be dead than subjected to humiliation and harassment. I want to keep my freedom in all things and that includes the freedom to indulge my compulsion.

I kill people.

I think of them as mercy killings, but I know that you, everyone, would call it murder. I understand that in the eyes of society, I am a serial killer. I can't risk being discovered, because I know what would be in store for me — which, by definition, means I am not insane. Still, when it's all over, for one reason or another, I do want to be understood and that's the reason for this journal.

I probably should start at the beginning.

The only name I'll give you is Chip. It's a nickname and I'll tell you how I got it, but not yet. First, I want to tell you about my parents. You will not find two more fearful, more passive, submissive, amorphous blobs. Each is incapable of making the simplest, most basic decision. How they ever got together, decided to get married, to have sex, etc., is beyond me. Each is an utter slave to conformity. Routine keeps them content, secure, and safe. Talk about religion being the opiate of the masses! Routine is their heroin. They crave it and would die of withdrawal symptoms if they were deprived of it. Change of any kind is so disruptive that it causes them to have panic attacks. On the other hand, being given direction by someone perceived to be in authority — which is almost everyone — makes them feel secure.

Mom and Dad were no spring chickens when I was born. They were well into their 30s when they met. I hesitate to say they fell in love. I can't imagine either of them feeling intense emotion other than fear and anxiety. And to allow themselves to lose emotional control (orgasm!) is beyond my ability to imagine. I wouldn't be surprised if I was conceived on their first successful attempt at sex — and that they haven't repeated it since. The experience of my father ejaculating must have frightened each of them. I may be wrong, but that's how I see them: not retarded, but socially isolated and inept.

Neither of them had friends when I was growing up. Their involvement with the neighbors was polite and superficial. I could say that, like water bugs, they live only on the surface of life. But they could never achieve the level of energy that water bugs have. They are more like pond scum, lying passively, waiting to be eaten.

I have very few memories of anyone other than the three of us being in our house. Dad was a clerk in a bookkeeping department of a large and stable corporation. Mom never held a job of any kind. She lived with her parents until she married my father and then they moved into the house where I was raised.

Perhaps I'm making them out to be more incompetent than they were. They're not retarded. They are simply afraid to think on their own and reluctant to let in any new knowledge. Their goal is to insulate themselves. It's nearly impossible for them to take any initiative — they eat the same boring meals on a weekly schedule, are addicted to watching the same infantile TV shows week after week, and adhere to the same programmed bedtimes and mealtimes. Nothing ever varies. They are enslaved — no, enraptured — by the calendar and the clock. Automated boredom.

Is it any wonder I am the way I am?

Needless to say, I was a fearful, timid, socially isolated child. It was difficult for my mother to let me go to school. She never got over her separation anxiety, and of course that affected me. Like the flu, I contracted my fear of abandonment from my mother (as if I'd inhaled it from her). But even more frightening than my fear of being separated from her was my fear of being consumed by her — although that developed later.

Of course she doted on me. She'd have liked to swallow me up. What else did she have? I was her little baby doll. And, like a doll, she moved my limbs and put words into my mouth because, to her, I was inanimate. I had no brain, no mind, no emotions of my own. All of our interactions were permeated by her fear of losing me — losing herself. Terror was the sea in which we floated, desperately clutching each other for some hoped-for support.

The more I passively submitted to her routines, the "better" I was ("Such a good boy"). Resisting her expectations was "bad." Developing a mind of my own, ideas of my own, thoughts or feelings of my own, was very bad. Eventually, I learned that giving voice to them was the real danger. But neither of them was capable of enforcing any discipline. They simply got flustered. As a young child, I needed them to be in charge, to afford me some sort of protection. If they became flustered, my life quickly deteriorated into chaos — and that felt quite dangerous to me. Therefore, I learned to keep them in their comfort zone while I kept my own developing thoughts and feelings to myself. And so I grew — in secret.

As an infant, I may have relished being enveloped in my mother's attentiveness. As a young child, I accepted it as normal and felt lucky being able to hide behind her skirts and protect myself from the dangerous world out there. But by the time I was an adolescent, still crippled by her constant clinging, I began my struggle to break away. I needed to breathe on my own, to govern my own mind, to think my own thoughts. At the time, I couldn't imagine actually feeling any degree of control over my own life.

I have to interrupt my history to bring you important news. Last night was number 13. I noticed her on the subway, her big, pouting lips hanging loosely apart, like she was too weary to close her mouth. She had heavy-lidded eyes and was bordering on fat. I could tell how depressed she was, how fed up with her miserable life she was. I felt like I read her mind. I knew exactly how despondent she felt, how tired she was of living one futile day after another, her self-loathing for being just one more anonymous, fat, stupid, ugly woman. I understood the helplessness. Nothing she could do to change her life, no one to help. Her ugly misery cried out to me. It didn't occur to me until later that it is almost one year to the day since I did my first. Maybe the anniversary was subconsciously in my mind and helped me to make the decision.

I stayed on the train and followed her out the door at her stop. Up on the sidewalk, I watched her walk slowly down a poorly lit residential street. No one was around. I quickened my pace and within a block I was right behind her. In one smooth motion I threw the wire over her head, crossed my hands behind her neck, leaned into her back, and yanked upward on the handles of my garrote. She didn't make a sound.

It was so easy to put her out of her misery — and yet no one else had thought of doing that for her. It fell on me to rescue her from her despair. It always falls on me. And what thanks do I get? Well, I don't really expect any. Who would be sensitive and gracious enough to recognize my good deed and express any gratitude? Certainly not her parents who, in all likelihood, professed to have loved her. Just like mine did.

I left her lying in the shadow of the stoop, walked back to the subway station, and resumed my journey. I felt exhilarated. I masturbated when I got home, reliving the whole scene. Isn't that what we're here for — to experience pleasure? Putting that fat, ugly woman out of her misery made me feel important. I exulted in it! I take pride in it! I take immense pleasure in it!

It was only when I got home that I realized I'd forgotten to take a souvenir. I have quite a collection. I don't take pictures or save newspaper clippings or obituaries. The little mementoes I collect aren't distinctive or easily identifiable as belonging to the victim. I don't like using that word — I think of them simply as the departed: poor souls who have been relieved of their earthly torments.

I know that you are thinking: *bullshit*. They're victims and I'm a murderer. That I'm either some psychopathic bastard incapable of feeling for another person, or a psychotic lunatic. I'm neither. You'll see. Just read on. As you get to know me, you won't be so quick to judge. But even if you don't change your mind, I don't care because I know I'm right. And if you can't sympathize with my point of view, it will only show me how brainwashed you are, how incapable of thinking for yourself. Like my mother and father and all the other brainless robots like them. Automatons!

Back to my history. By the time I reached middle school, I was an emotional wreck — but because my grades were acceptable, nobody paid much attention to me. I was so withdrawn that the other kids mostly ignored me, except for the taunting. Therein lies the tale of my nickname, Chip.

In addition to the psychological obstacles, I also had a physical handicap, which, of course, nobody did anything about. I had a receding chin, the result of my jawbone not growing. To say that I had an overbite is to say that King Kong was not your average monkey. My upper teeth protruded so far I could hardly close my mouth. Everybody called me *Chipmunk* — which was eventually shortened to *Chip*. Even the teachers! No one saw the derision, the ridicule that it inherently implied — further proof that my feelings didn't matter to anyone. I was a nonentity. My parents never noticed that their only child was a freak. They also called me Chip! Can you believe it? Their total lack of awareness is mind-boggling. To them I had a teensy little overbite. They thought I was cute!

Thank God that in my freshman year of high school, a guidance counselor noticed my depression and referred me to the child-study team. But my parents didn't want to rock the boat. They feared that being the subject of scrutiny by the school psychologist would mark me with some kind of stigma. Can you imagine such obtuseness? They couldn't face the fact that I'd been living with a stigma — my misshapen face — since birth. They couldn't deal with anything that might upset their routine.

I might as well be totally honest here — it wasn't only my parents who were afraid to accept a referral to the school child-study team. I was also reluctant. It was my default mode to resist change. I was, after all, my parents' child. If it weren't for my resistance, they might very well have given in to the request for the child-study team to get involved. The truth is, despite my torment, my resistance to change was a force to be reckoned with. My parents were incapable of moving me if I didn't want to be moved. But being as passive and submissive to authority as they were, they did acquiesce and agree to send me to a private psychologist who wasn't associated with the school — but only because I agreed. That's how I came to meet Doc.

Although part of me was terrified at the prospect of therapy — and in truth, I remained clammed up for months — part of me recognized that this was a possible road to some sort of salvation. No, that's not right. *Salvation* smacks of some kind of religious intervention. *Salvage* is probably more like it — salvaging something from this disastrous wreck of a person.

I began to see Doc when I was 14 and continued through high school until the summer following my graduation a year ago. By then, I was ready to leave my comfortable nest and begin to fly on my own. Those four years saved my life. I'd been headed for suicide prior to entering therapy. I'd been totally unaware of the rage pent up inside of me. Prior to therapy, I'd been aware only of terror — of humiliation and ridicule and taunting. I longed hopelessly for some miraculous relief from the inevitable misery of each day.

Gradually, I came to understand that much of my fear resulted from projecting my murderous rage onto others. I was afraid everyone wanted to hurt me — verbally, emotionally, or physically. Of course, that fit right in with my parents' view of the world. I had already been conditioned to embrace routine like a life preserver and to fear anything and everyone new. Doc helped me acknowledge and accept my anger, although he couldn't make it go away. It had been accumulating for years; I had a supply of rage to last a lifetime. Even now, I can feel it swelling within me, ready to explode. Sometimes the roar of rage is so deafening I can hardly think. I can only say that it's far better to experience that expanding pressure from within than to endure it from without. Far better for someone else to be on the receiving end than me. Don't be holier than thou about this — you'd feel the same way. That pressure is only relieved when I've successfully rescued some other miserable soul. Nothing like doing a good deed to perk up the spirits.

There are times when I feel the pressure mounting and I consciously decide to join with it, like a surfer uniting with the momentum of a wave as it builds and crests. These are the times when I feel the exhilarating power of my rage. I can't control it, but I can ride it as its master. I am most euphoric in that moment of culmination, when I've released someone from a life of further misery. It is a wonder that I don't always ejaculate right there at the murderous scene.

My fear of anything new carried over to foods. I ate only white bread, Corn Flakes, or pancakes, and drank only milk or apple juice. I didn't like meat, mostly because it was hard for me to chew with my severe overbite. Forget vegetables or fruits (other than bananas) or spices and condiments of any kind. By the time I met Doc, my menu had expanded to include French fries and mashed potatoes, and he helped me gradually increase the range of food I would eat. Sometimes he'd bring food from home or a restaurant into the office for us to try together. Sometimes he'd take me out to a fast-food place and we'd experiment with something new.

During this process, which spanned our four years together, he not only got me to try new foods and thereby improve my nutrition (hamburgers, cheeseburgers, and pasta were some of his early victories), but in the process my self-image shifted. He had encouraged me to break out of my comfort zone and risk trying something new. In other words, I began to develop a tiny tolerance for anxiety. By the time my therapy ended, I could walk into most fast-food restaurants and eat like a normal person. You can only imagine what a luxury it still is for me to go into a restaurant, order something, and relax comfortably while I eat, knowing that no one is paying the slightest attention to me. I don't stand out at all. I am invisible. I am safe.

That leads me to one of the most important things Doc did for me: the surgery. Soon after beginning our work together, Doc confronted the issue of my nonexistent chin. At first, I denied having any feelings about it, but he persisted. Finally, he suggested that my parents arrange a consultation with a reconstructive dental surgeon. Of course, I was initially against it. But as my confidence grew and I began to take pride in my courageous exploration of exotic new foods, I became more open to the idea.

My parents, of course, did not want to go down that path. But Doc was an authority, and they were incapable of sustaining their resistance to both him and me. He even volunteered to go with us for the initial consultation, but by then I could manage them on my own.

When the surgeon explained that mine was a common condition with established procedures for correcting it — and showed before-and-after pictures of previous patients — I was astounded. I'd been certain I was the only person on the planet who looked like a chipmunk.

By then I was already entertaining fantasies of what it would be like to have a normal appearance. I would not be denied. I didn't care if they'd have to mortgage the house. Now that I knew it existed, I had to have it. It was life and death. Finally, my parents shrugged helplessly and nodded their assent.

I relate this as if it happened quickly. In reality, it wasn't until I was 17 that the surgery was performed, in June, after my junior year in high school. When I returned in the fall to begin my senior year, physically I was a different person. I had grown taller (over six feet), put on some weight, and had a normal-looking chin. I was good looking! I began to care about my appearance. I no longer let my straight hair hang down to cover a deformed face. I replaced the big, ugly owl-like eyeglasses I'd always worn. I took an interest in fashionable clothes.

I was still painfully shy and introverted, but I took pride in my new appearance. Up to that point, I had never participated in sports. My parents, giving in to my demands, had always managed to secure a physician's excuse for me to be exempted from physical education. But now — after hearing that I had a swimmer's body — I took lessons to improve my form. I lifted weights and took up running to develop muscular strength and speed. My whole life changed. Whereas I had previously looked at myself with disdain, now I took pride in my body and began to nourish it.

I must add, though, that despite my growing confidence, I remain as shy and introverted as I've always been, and the deep mistrust I'd learned to feel toward others remains a central part of my outlook. For me, the world is still a dangerous place.

Before my transformative surgery, I had looked upon my fellow unfortunates with the same loathing that I felt for myself. We were all in this cesspool of a life together: We looked like shit, felt like shit, ate shit, and were treated like shit. But post-surgery, I escaped to dry land, so to speak. And as my confidence grew, my disgust for the sad sacks I'd left behind also grew.

I have come to believe strongly that not only would the world be better off without those losers, but that they would be better off without the disdain of this world. It is how I had always felt about myself. Even now that I look like one of the chosen, the self-loathing is elicited every time I see a pathetic soul who reminds me of who I was — and I hate them for it! I hate them for their worthlessness, for the utter futility of their lives, for their weakness and self-pity.

And yet, I pity them too. I continue to empathize with my former fellow-shit-heads. I know how they despair. And this mixture of contempt and pity is overwhelming and intense. It consumes me. I often find myself singing along to that old Beatles song (although I substitute a more appropriate word): "All those *loathsome* people, where do they all come from?" Those poor bastards don't deserve the lives they have. No one deserves to be consumed with self-hatred. I have no choice but to do something about it.

When I was 17, before my surgery, a young girl was murdered, strangled, and left in the weeds beside a country road not far from where I lived. She had been missing for only an afternoon and evening before her body was found. The day after the story appeared in the news, I was scheduled to see Doc.

He noticed that I was more agitated than usual, and I finally blurted out that I was the one who had murdered the girl. I could see he was surprised, shocked even, and that he wasn't taking me seriously. Although I don't think I ever convinced him I had actually murdered the girl, he understood that part of me wanted to commit such a crime, that my dark, inner rage had reached such enormous proportions. He finally succeeded in convincing me that I *probably* had not done it — that for me to have abducted the girl, strangled her, and dumped the body would have necessitated overcoming so many logistical problems that it would have been virtually impossible.

Still, within myself, I knew I could have done it — and might have if I'd had the chance (and maybe, just maybe, I really did do it!). After that, I was fixated on the idea of abducting someone, committing murder, and getting away with it. Such power! It grew from a daydream, a fantasy, into an obsession. I began to fantasize about people I saw: fellow classmates, people on the street — everywhere I went, I saw potential subjects. I spent hours planning the perfect killing and obsessed about every aspect of it: the victim, the weapon, the time and place, the escape, the clothes I'd wear, the alibi I'd prepare.

Suddenly, my life had meaning. I had a purpose. My entire being became organized around this goal: to find and remove from this world as many lonely, miserable, homely people as possible — the deformed, the defective, the worthless. What a worthwhile purpose I could dedicate myself to. I call it *waste management*.

Once I'd made the decision to pursue this important work, I felt free, confidant, and powerful. Of course, I knew I would have to keep my secret from everyone, even Doc. All he knew was that I was no longer depressed, no longer a scared little rabbit. This epiphany took place about the same time as my surgery, so the timing was plausible: I blossomed into a normal-looking 18-year-old, intent on fulfilling my family's and Doc's hopes for me. They were filled with self-satisfaction at what a good job they had done in "fixing" me. Chip looked good. Chip looked normal. Inwardly, I laughed. They had no fucking idea of who I was, of the powerful being I had become. It wasn't any of them — certainly not my parents, not even Doc or the school counselors or teachers — who had found the solution. I had done it. I had transformed the chipmunk into a new being, awesome and powerful.

When I was maybe 15 or 16, I was fascinated by the monster in the movie *Alien*. I loved its awesome dominance, its shrewd, clever intelligence, and the frightening suddenness with which it displayed its breathtaking power. Its external appearance was terrifying enough, but then out of its savage mouth would emerge a second deadly, hidden head to strike unexpectedly and kill with fearsome force. God, I loved it. I wanted to be that monster. For a while, I imagined getting a job in the special effects department of a movie studio, but I never followed up on that. When I had the epiphany about my calling, my life's work, I felt the same sense of power that I had attributed to the Alien — as if I had become it. I had that same secret and terrible capacity for dominance. This made me so happy! I couldn't wait to implement my plan. I am so fortunate to know what I want to do, and to have the skills to do it.

You are probably wondering about my first kill. Actually, I admit I'm embarrassed about my first one. It was done largely on impulse — which is not bad in and of itself, but I took no precautions. I'm lucky it worked out. As I've mentioned, it was almost exactly a year ago, soon after I graduated from high school. I had borrowed my parents' car to drive to Philadelphia for a job interview, but I told them I was going to the shore to spend the day at the beach. They were happy for me, thinking I was no longer the reclusive mole I'd been until then.

They were hoping to live their lives vicariously through me. Ha! They had no idea I was planning my escape from them, that I would soon be out of their house, free to pursue my exciting new life (trash removal? recalling defective models?), but one they might find a bit too thrilling for their tastes. Ha-ha!

The interview went well and I got the job. I spent the rest of the afternoon exploring the city, thinking about where I might find an apartment. Eventually, I stopped at a small pizza place. By the time I'd finished eating, it was getting dark. As I started driving home, I saw a decrepit homeless man pushing a shopping cart across the street about a block ahead of me. I don't remember if I thought to look if there were any cars behind me. That's how impulsive I was. Without thinking, I turned off my headlights and stepped on the gas. I must have been going close to 60 when I hit him. I was careful to miss the shopping cart, but I hit him squarely. I can still hear the thump. He went flying into the air, I don't know, maybe 15 or 20 feet high. It was beautiful, like slow-motion ballet. I had to swerve slightly to avoid hitting him again. I took the next right, turned my headlights back on, and slowed to a normal speed.

I was exhilarated! I had actually done it — actually killed someone after a full year of fantasizing about it. What a rush! I almost came in my pants. How astounding that I'd given it so little thought, that I hadn't considered the risks involved. I was lucky there hadn't been any witnesses, but I couldn't take credit for that. I'd been stupid.

Back in New Jersey, I found a place to evaluate the damage to my father's car. The front grill was cracked and some shreds of clothing were stuck in crevices. I removed those, then stopped at a car wash to remove any evidence that might place me at the scene. The next day I told my father that someone had backed into the car while I was on the beach. He had the car fixed, as I knew he would. Perfect crime numero uno.

But later, I grew more and more dissatisfied with myself. I had been stupid and impulsive, and the kill had been completely anonymous. Using a vehicle felt too removed. I wanted a hands-on encounter, to physically experience the elimination, to feel the cessation of life.

It is not my intention to bore or impress you with a catalogue of my kills over this past year. As exciting as it's been, it involves meticulous planning. If not for my cautious nature, I would have a list of hundreds — because God knows there's no shortage of candidates: people who have given up on their lives, misfits who have abandoned hope, unfortunates who experience nothing but futility and hopelessness, leftovers who are an affront to the senses and a pollutant in the general gene pool. But I can't very well accommodate all of these poor souls, can I? I mean, who do you think I am, Jesus Christ, Superstar?

No, I have had to be selective in order to avoid a premature termination of my calling. If I don't look out for number one, who will? You? And, I ask you: Doesn't this caution and social awareness prove, in and of itself, my sanity? Admit it: I am very well organized and realistic. I am not some disorganized and fractured schizophrenic. I am not delusional — and just in case you were wondering (Listen up, Doc), I am not schizoid!

I have tried to choose a variety of subjects: age, gender, body type, race, occupation, location, method — all of these have been deliberately varied. I'm an equal-opportunity savior and I have done my best not to show favoritism to any particular type or class of person. Of course, this makes it that much more difficult for me to be apprehended; actually impossible, I'd say. I intend to continue my work for years and years. It's good to have a purpose in life, but another virtue is that the slow pace of killing keeps it interesting for me. If I were removing one a day or even one a week, I'd be more likely to grow bored and sloppy. I don't want my life to become a boring routine. This is meaningful work. Every aspect of the planning and the execution is deserving of patience and respect and, yes, even reverence. It's like what they say about vacations: Planning is half the fun.

The fact that I leave no evidence of either sex or robbery as a motive has, I am sure, kept the authorities scratching their heads. Very little, if anything, ties the cases together. I must clarify one aspect here: I have not tortured anyone. I wouldn't do that. All of them died very quickly. Yes, some have so repulsed me that I have given in to the urge to beat their faces to a pulp. I can't really explain the rage that overcomes me at those times. It is not the norm. But even in those cases, the person is already dead when I have given vent to my fury.

There is nothing at all, nada, to lead anyone to me. All of which gives me a kick. It's all right there in front of them: They're all losers. CAN'T YOU SEE? THEY'RE ALL MISERABLE LOSERS!

But then, sometimes I wonder if the authorities aren't more clever than I give them credit for. What if they do see the connection — that all of the victims are depressed, ugly losers? What if they don't care? What if they secretly condone the service I'm doing? The idea that the police are secretly behind me, cheering me on *sotto voce*, intrigues me.

July 2010: The other day, on my way to work, I saw a license plate that contained, in anagram form, the four letters of my nickname. Curious. Is someone trying to send me a message? Of course, it might just be a coincidence. But I don't think so. This bears watching.

My mother is very ill. She left a message on the answering machine she bought me. That's the only way she can get in touch with me. She has not been well since my father died three months ago. They were both such poor lost souls, but at least he held a job and went to work every day. He had some responsibility. What did she ever do? She's incapable of making a decision on her own. Since he died, she calls me constantly. That's why I don't answer the phone anymore. I let the answering machine take all the calls. Who calls me anyway? Once in a while I'll get a call from work, but other than that, I have no friends. That's the way I like it. Once my mother dies, I'll get rid of the damn thing. Who needs it?

Mommy dearest says she's having trouble breathing. I shake my head in disbelief. I don't even want to call her back. If she weren't my mother, I'd kill her. She'd be my next one. But I'd be an immediate suspect. What's a poor boy to do?

I visited my mother this weekend. I think she might have pneumonia. I didn't take her temperature, but it felt like she was burning up. She should probably be in the hospital — but then she'd probably get better and I'd have to visit, take off work, be her good little boy. So I told her she looked OK, probably just had a cold, get some rest. I told her I'd come up again next weekend. Maybe I'll be an orphan by then.

No such luck. She's much better. Turns out she called the doctor on her own (she doesn't trust her own son!) and he had the pharmacy deliver antibiotics. Suddenly she knows how to think for herself? Some nosy neighbor must have poked her head in and told her what to do. Oh well. I'll have to visit again — another weekend shot to hell.

Coming home from Mom's, it started to rain and some jerk lost control of his car and plowed into my van. More inconvenience. Or is it? The driver seemed sincere enough, but he may have been an undercover cop assigned to put me out of commission. The van is an integral part of my plan, so now everything has to be postponed. But it raises the larger question: Are they onto me? I must be more alert. So far, I haven't spotted anyone following me. But it occurred to me that they might have planted cookies in my computer and may be reading this as I type. I know it's possible. If they have, what are they waiting for? Maybe they don't want to stop me.

Last week I had a stomach flu. It may have been food poisoning. I am suspicious. Then I received a phone call from one of the secretaries at work. Theresa. She'd heard I'd reported sick and wondered if she could do anything to help. She's plain-looking but not ugly, self-effacing and shy. I imagine it's unlike her to reach out to anyone, especially someone she hardly knows. We don't work in the same department and I've rarely had occasion to talk to her. I didn't speak with her, of course. I let her leave a message. But she called again the next day, asking when I'd be returning to work. It sounded like it might be official, so I called her back. She said she wondered if I might need some food or something. She had looked up my address and said it wouldn't be a bother to drop off some soup.

The thought of someone coming to my apartment put me into a panic. I immediately worried something would give me away. Of course, I told her I had everything

I needed and was sure I'd be back to work in another day or two. I wonder what her motive was. Is she working for the authorities? Should I avoid her — or let her in a little closer and see what I can find out? It may be my only chance to discover how much they know and what their plans are.

When I returned to work, I made a point of thanking her. It was difficult for me. I don't often talk to people, especially women. Theresa is almost as shy as I am, so it was pretty awkward. Our exchange was brief. Later, she sent me a message on my work computer saying there was something she wanted to talk to me about and wondered if I was free after work. That made my palms sweat. What was she after? I had to protect myself against this intrusion, this invasion. My first reaction was to not respond at all. But if she has some ulterior purpose, if she is working for them, this is my chance to find out. I suggested we meet after work on the coming Friday, July 30. We planned to meet at a coffee shop near our office.

Theresa was waiting outside when I arrived. We went in and ordered coffee. She explained that she was thinking of buying a laptop and since I worked in the technical area, she was sure I would be able to offer some helpful opinions. She asked if I would go with her to look at some models.

Why me? As Theresa spoke, I studied her more closely than I had before. Plain. Skin too white, no makeup. Nose too large, lips too thin, teeth uneven. But there was something appealing as well. It might have been precisely because of these defects that I felt a strange, perhaps sympathetic attraction.

If I were to pick someone to spy on me, to recruit as a police informer, this is not the kind of person I'd choose. Theresa is too introverted, too lacking in confidence to undertake a dangerous mission that requires initiative and duplicity. When I learned that she began working for the company right out of high school (like me) and had been there for a whole year before I started, I realized she could not have been a police plant.

As I relaxed my guard, it struck me that this was the first conversation with a female I'd had outside the office. Doc would be proud that I had the courage to try something new, to take a risk. I smiled at the thought, and Theresa smiled back at me. That may seem like a small thing to you, but it was a new experience for me. I think I even blushed. It was exciting. Feeling expansive and daring, I impulsively suggested we go for pizza. Theresa seemed truly happy, and that made me feel good. I felt in control.

I found out more about Theresa's rather restricted life. Apparently this was the first time in quite a while that she had been out with a guy. And she doesn't have many friends. She does most things alone. I detected no appeal for pity.

The fact that Theresa seems content with her life makes me wonder why she sought me out. Why would she be interested in me? I can't help but wonder if she's trying to find out more about my secret work. At the very least, I should keep my guard up. I have to be prepared.

I saw another license plate today that contained the letter C plus all the numbers of my birthday. Someone is trying to get my attention, but why? Is it a threat? I am keeping my eyes and ears open. I lay traps around my apartment to tip me off if anyone has entered when I'm out. So far I haven't detected anything. But if they are monitoring my computer, they would have no need to break in, would they? I'm on high alert all the time, because I'm ready to do number 14 later this week.

Wednesday, August 4: Terry and I had dinner tonight. We were both nervous. I'm not sure of her motives. Could she really just need help buying a computer? Or is there some other reason? She seemed on edge too — and that would be natural if she's undercover, wouldn't it? Although now that I'm home again, I feel more certain that she is not spying on me. She hardly asked any questions about me. I let it slip that I've been taking courses at the Community College and she wanted to know if I had any problems keeping up with the homework and working full time.

She did mention that she had a boyfriend in high school, but that he went away to college after graduation and they drifted apart. I was waiting for her to ask if I'd had a girlfriend, but she never did. I believe she really respects other people's privacy. She doesn't pry. Anyway, I lied and told her I'd had a few girlfriends and had gone steady with one. I said her name was Marcia. Marcia was actually one of the prettiest girls in my class. I also told Theresa that I'd been on the swim team. Imagine that — me a high school jock dating the prettiest and most popular girl in school. I couldn't stop laughing. Terry thought it was because I was having such a good time. The amazing thing was that she believed every word I said.

It's Friday night. Everything went like clockwork. After work, I came home, got the van, and drove it to my destination. I changed the license plate to one I had stolen. At 10:00, I drove to the parking lot of the strip mall to pick up my subject. Her name was Donna and she worked as a clerk in a convenience store. The first time I saw her sullen, morose demeanor, I knew I would put her out of her misery. I parked in the shadows near the garbage bins behind the buildings. A few minutes later, she shuffled out of the rear door of the store and started toward her car. This was her nightly routine. The owner sent her home a little after 10:00. No one ever met her. As she neared her car, I pulled up alongside of her.

"Excuse me, Donna," I said. She stopped as I got out. In one swift move I put a knife to her throat, slid open the side door of the van, and forced her in. Once inside, I handcuffed her to the paneling on the walls of the van and put duct tape over her mouth. I drove away. Nobody had seen a thing.

Gerard R. D'Alessio

I never torture my victims, nor have I ever sexually abused anyone. But now I had a different motive. If I continue to see Terry, at some point she will expect us to become sexually involved. I've never had any sexual experience with another person. I've seen porn, of course, and I know what to do, but I've never done it. Donna would provide an opportunity to practice — kill two birds with one stone. Besides, she was so ugly that it would be doing her a favor to give her this experience before putting her out of her misery.

I found a deserted area to park the van and then I spread-eagled her on the sheet of plastic covering the floor of the van, tying her ankles to the side panels. Then I cut her clothes from her body. I was surprised that her body was not as ugly as her face. Her unblemished skin felt surprisingly smooth. Her breasts weren't as large as I would have liked, but they were softer than I thought they would be. I stroked her nipples with my fingers. I thought they would feel more erotic, but they didn't. They just felt rubbery. I licked them and found them tasteless. I'm not sure what all the fuss is about. Even so, I got hard. I took off my pants and underwear in front of her and let her see my big erection, but she turned her head away and kept her eyes squeezed shut. I wasn't sure why. Well, it doesn't matter.

It was the first time I had ever been naked in front of anyone and I found it exciting, even though Donna seemed to recoil. It was cool in the van with the motor off and the night air circulating around my naked body was arousing. I rubbed my hard-on against her nipples, between her breasts, and along the side of her face. She kept making whimpering sounds as if I was hurting her. I wasn't hurting her. I thought she would have enjoyed what I was doing.

Then I knelt down and examined her pussy. It was different from what I'd expected, but I can't say how. I didn't really have any clear expectations of what the inside of a vagina would feel like. I inserted the head of my boner into her, but only part way.

But now that I knew what a woman looked like, felt like, and smelled like, I had to restrain myself. I couldn't risk leaving a DNA sample inside her. I let myself enjoy the feeling of staying inside her, unmoving, and then I withdrew and got dressed again. I tied her two socks together and strangled her with them, then dumped her naked body into the vacant lot and threw her clothes on top of her. Then I rolled up the plastic sheet that had covered the floor and secured it with duct tape. On the way home, I dropped the plastic into a dumpster. I didn't masturbate until I got home.

I think Terry is interested in me. She keeps seeking me out, writing emails, suggesting we go for lunch. I can also tell from the way she looks at me. She smiles a lot and looks happy. It would feel good to have a woman interested in me for who I am, but part of me still doesn't trust her. How do I know she is who she says she is? Still, I enjoy our time together, even if part of me feels like I'm playing a game of wits with her. I suppose if we have sex, that would prove she's not an agent of the authorities. But we have not progressed to that point.

I'm not sure where it would even happen. I will not have her over to my apartment. She could plant a listening device, a camera, who knows what. And she hasn't invited me to her apartment. So far, we've only gone to small local places to eat. Maybe she wants me to take her out on some kind of formal date and spend a lot of money. But she knows how much I make. Maybe that's why she's holding back: I don't make enough money for her. But then why does she seem so interested? I guess I'm not the first man to be confused by women.

Meanwhile, I've decided on my next target for my Savior Project. He is a clerk in our shipping department. Eddie — a morose, irritable, obnoxious asshole. No one can stand him. I don't have anything to do with him, but Terry has to work with him sometimes and he gives her a hard time. I'd be doing him a favor as well as everyone else who has to deal with him.

No one knows I'm even aware of him. Whenever Terry mentions him to me, I feign indifference and change the subject. As far as she'd remember, we've never discussed him. Now I need to do some research and get #15 started. This one is even more of a challenge. It's the closest a target has been to my own life space; being an employee of the same company could put me on some sort of list of potential suspects, so I have to be careful. But the challenge is part of the excitement.

It's been almost two weeks and I've only come across one newspaper article about Donna, my #14. Another "brutal murder" — that's how they always refer to it, if they mention it at all. You'd be surprised how many of my rescues have gone unmentioned. I didn't see anything in the paper about #13, the subway girl. I guess there are just too many dead bodies for the media to pay attention to. But the lack of information is, in itself, an indictment of the deceased's life, the meaningless of it. No one misses them. Good riddance. Not even worth mentioning. It's proof that I'm disposing of worthless trash. The one article about Donna mentioned that she had "apparently been strangled." They always do that — withhold or change a few minor details so when some poor psychotic bastard steps forward to confess, they'll know if he really did it or not.

I've decided to get rid of the souvenirs I was keeping, in case Terry comes over unexpectedly. Only now I have no proof that I've done any of it, and I'm surprised to find that my memory isn't as clear as I thought it would be. They're all jumbled together. Did I strangle or stab that one? Sometimes I wonder whether I've done any of them at all. Maybe I'm dreaming the whole thing. Maybe none of this is real. How would I know?

I'm getting overloaded, all charged up and full of electricity. I've been waking up

251

at four in the morning too revved up to get back to sleep. Even at work, I'm having trouble focusing on my (mindless) job. My mind wanders to more important details: How I will eliminate Mr. Asshole? When will I have sex with Terry? I keep remembering Donna, how smooth and warm her body felt, how Terry's body will feel, what it will look like. I have to stop what I'm doing and masturbate to relieve the tension. My supervisor looks at me funny because I'm making so many trips to the men's room. I have to control myself, but it's difficult. I have to bring both of these plans to fruition soon or I'm going to lose it. But I can't spy on Mr. Asshole's private life if I'm with Terry — and I can't be with Terry if I'm staking out #15. I'm going crazy.

I stopped going to class at the Community College. I can't focus on it. No big deal. It's not as important as my life's work. That, and thoughts of Terry. There's no room in my brain for anything else. Everything is buzzing, electric buzzing. I wonder if I glow in the dark.

September: Last night, Terry and I were having a burger at a local pub. She asked me what was wrong! What did she mean?

She said I was all antsy and fidgety.

At first I denied it, but she persisted until I blurted out that I can't stop thinking about her, about being with her (she knew what I meant).

I can't believe I've lost so much control.

She seemed flustered by my outburst. She knew what I was saying, what I wanted, but she didn't say she felt the same way. Maybe she felt threatened. Maybe she isn't attracted to me after all. Maybe she really is some plant from the authorities and can't have sex with me. I felt stupid.

Is she really Saint Theresa? Is she in my life to change me? Or is she in my life to confirm that I'm doing good things? If she's a saint, she's not going to have sex with me, and if she does have sex with me, she's not Saint Theresa.

She tried to smooth it over, saying no one had ever said anything like that to her before, she was flattered but not ready for that yet. I tried to make her think I was all right with that, but she knew I was hurt and angry. So for now, my attention is directed at Mr. Asshole. He's going to get my full and undivided attention.

I followed him home and know where he lives in South Philly. I know when and how he travels to and from work. As I suspected, he's a loner. He eats most of his evening meals in a local restaurant about a half mile from where he lives. Waylaying him on his way home from there will be easy. I have a machete I bought at a flea market this past spring (I've used it once before). I'll be waiting near the van, wearing a disposable poncho in case of blood splatter. The side door of the van will be open. As he passes, I'll swing around with the machete and, if I'm accurate, decapitate him in one blow. But even if his head isn't totally severed, he'll bleed to death in seconds. I'll strip off the poncho and drop the weapon, hop in the van (motor running), and away I go. Of course, I'll have to make sure no one else is around. If there is, I'll postpone it to another night. Right now I'm set for Monday night, the day after tomorrow.

I completely ransacked my apartment, but can't find the hidden speaker. Someone has been calling my name — not calling, more like whispering. And they are using my given name. The voice is familiar, like I should know who it is. It's impossible to ignore. It's driving me crazy. I have to leave the apartment to be free of it. Obviously, someone is trying to warn me about something.

My mother has been calling again. She hasn't been feeling well, could I please come up and visit? I'M BUSY, MOM! I HAVE THINGS TO DO, PLACES TO GO, PEOPLE TO KILL!

And Terry has been calling me. Of course, I haven't answered the phone. Let her stew. She sounds apologetic. She says she wants to see me — and she knows what I want, so does that mean she's ready? Maybe I should wait until she begs for it.

I bought a lightweight balaclava for tomorrow night. It'll obscure my hair and the bottom half of my face. I stole some license plates from cars in parking lots, so the van can't be traced to me. I can't leave anything to chance. The Savior thinks of everything.

What? Who is that? Identify yourself, goddamn it, or stop taunting me.

I did it. It went exactly as I'd planned. God, it was so great. He never knew what hit him. With one swing I cut through his spinal cord and down into his left shoulder so the head hung by just a few strands of muscle on that side. The blood! It shot out like it came from a hose. Good thing I was wearing the poncho. Some got on my shoes. I hadn't thought to cover them. No one was around and the van shielded me from the other side of the street. When his body hit the ground there wasn't a sound, and the blood started spurting and gushing. I dropped the machete and stripped off the poncho and was back inside the van, door closed, in less than 15 seconds. This one will make the papers, I'm sure. I can't wait until Terry reads about it and tells me somebody offed Mr. Asshole. I wonder if she'll be pleased at what I've done for her, even though she'll never know it was me. I'm almost tempted to tell her. No, I shouldn't do that.

What? I said stop calling me!

I can't believe it — just one small story in this morning's papers. You'd never notice it if you weren't looking for it. An unidentified Asian man was brutally attacked and murdered. Unidentified? So nobody at work knows yet? No one is saying anything about Eddie's absence, but people are looking at me strangely. Could they possibly know? It proves that I'm being watched. They must have cameras on me.

I took a chance and asked Theresa where the mailroom clerk is today — the guy who is such a jerk. But she changed the subject and said she'd been thinking a lot about our last conversation. She hadn't meant to suggest that she wasn't feeling the same way. She said she does. It was only that she was frightened because she's never had sex and she's been told so many horror stories by her mother and the nuns while she was growing up that she has always been filled with fear — of getting pregnant, of not knowing what to do, of disease, of being betrayed. She said she's afraid of sounding childish or neurotic, and that her lack of experience would turn me off.

She's also scared to death that sex is going to be very painful for her the first time, so we agreed that we would not go all the way yet. That made her feel more comfortable. In reality, I have my own anxieties and so I'm willing to take it one step at a time.

God, I get hard just thinking about it. This woman actually wants me to fuck her. She said she was hoping we could use my apartment, because she's afraid of anyone finding out.

Bad news. Today's paper reported a witness who saw a white van in the vicinity of the murder. The story went on to say that a white van may have been implicated in some other unsolved murders. Of course, there are thousands of white vans and nothing to single me out, except Eddie and I both work for the same company. I'm not worried, but I'll have to be careful.

The article didn't actually say that, not literally. But it was there, in between the lines, a special message to warn me. No one else would have recognized it, but I knew. I know they know and now they know that I know that they know.

What? That damned voice again. Who is it? Stop it!!

Last night Theresa and I went out for Chinese food and then came back to my apartment. I bought an inexpensive bottle of wine, so we were both a little buzzed. My apartment is clean and orderly, not a mess like you might expect from a single guy. I made sure there wasn't anything that might arouse her suspicions, but I worried that she might hear the voice if it called me. (Thank goodness she didn't. Apparently, it doesn't want anyone else to hear it.)

We lay down on the bed and started to kiss. I think knowing we were not going to go all the way allowed us both to relax, but I have to admit I've never been into kissing that much. I'm sure it has to do with my earlier life as a chipmunk, just being sensitive about my mouth in general. But kissing Theresa was surprisingly enjoyable. The idea of somebody sticking her tongue in my mouth had always disgusted me, and it will take some getting used to, but the actual experience wasn't as disagreeable as I'd expected. Having my arms around Terry, feeling her body up against mine was really exciting. At first I was embarrassed about my hard-on pressing against her, but then I realized she was pressing herself into it.

Her skin was silky smooth and, although her breasts were smaller than Donna's, they were firmer. Her nipples were smaller but she seemed to like when I touched them. Not like Donna. I don't think she came, but I did. It's the first time I've ever worn a condom, but after fiddling with the first one, Terry saw how I did it and then she helped put the second one on. Yes, she made me come twice. Even if it takes a while for us to actually work up to real intercourse, I'm satisfied with what we're doing now. We might even get into oral sex, although I'll admit that the idea of it disgusts me (it makes me think of Jeffrey Dahmer and cannibalism — eating someone's genitals. Ugh!). But it's supposed to be a big deal and I want to try it at some point. After all, I do have the courage to take risks. I'm not even worried about having her in my apartment again.

My supervisor called me into his office earlier this week and bawled me out. He said my production has fallen way off, and he asked why I've been coming to work unshaven and looking like I've slept in my clothes. He said I used to be a reliable worker, but now I'm off in lala land. I mumbled something about my mother being ill and I had to travel back and forth to New Jersey. I said she's getting better and I'll be back to my old self soon. He said he was sorry to hear about my mother but that I'd better shape up or he'd have to let me go. When I left his office, I wondered how he'd like to be #16.

Actually, I can't stop thinking about it.

And wouldn't you know, I got a call from my mother. I thought it might be Terry, so I picked up the phone. She said she was selling the house and moving into an assisted-living complex. Good — now I'll really be free of her. But she needs my help cleaning out the house. So I'll have to go up this weekend and work my butt off, instead of being with Terry and making plans for Mr. Supervisor!

She kept at me the whole weekend. What's wrong? I look terrible. Aren't I eating? I look like I've lost weight. Why am I so quiet? When was the last time I had a haircut? Am I deliberately growing a beard? I told her there's nothing wrong. I'm just busy. I've got a lot on my mind.

The house is stripped bare. A naked house. My goodness, what will the neighbors think? A scandal. Lots of stuff thrown out, including me and Mom. Only bare bones left for the realtor to show. I could show her some bare bones. I could show her a boner. Ha ha. I took a couple of things that used to be in my old bedroom, in Chip's room. Chip doesn't live there anymore. No more Chip. Goodbye Mr. Chips. So long, it's been good to know ya. Hahaha. What? Shut up. Leave me alone. I don't want you calling me anymore.

Aha! Now I know you! I finally recognize your voice: Chip. Good old Chip, risen from the dead. Calling me from the great beyond. Fuck off, Chip. I have nothing to say to you, you chipmunk piece of shit. Chipshit. I'm not you anymore. Go away!

Today at work, Mr. Supervisor-know-it-all saw me give him the evil eye. He knows he'd better watch out. People are looking at me. They pretend they're not, but I see them. I ignore them but I register it in my brain, my computer-like brain where I keep all my information. They think they're so smart, but I know they're watching and talking, scheming. It won't do them any good.

Terry seems worried too. I see the look in her eyes. I asked her what she's worried about and she lied. She said it was nothing, but I know — I read her mind — she knows what I'm planning. I smiled and told her everything is under control. I can't wait for us to get together again at my apartment, but she said she's getting her period, so we have to wait. I said OK, but I know. I'm not stupid.

Terry has been avoiding me. I know it's because she doesn't want to be implicated in what I'm doing. She thinks she's protecting me, but she's really protecting herself. She doesn't know what I can do to her if I want to. I'm being patient with her like I promised I would, but I hear Chip's voice in my ear: *Do it. Do it.* Over and over like a broken record. Like a mantra. It's a constant humming in my brain: *Doitdoitdoitdoitdoit.* I don't even pay attention to him anymore. Chip no longer exists. Only I exist, and he has no right to tell me what to do. He's not even here anymore, is he? Are you? You stupid shit. Where's that stupid little chipmunk chin? It's nowhere, stupid. It's gone. See this chin? This is my chin. So fuck off!

Terry and I went out to eat last night, but Chip kept buzzing in my ear and it was difficult to pay attention to what Terry was saying. She can't understand what's happening. We came back to my place, but Chip kept up his nonsense and I couldn't get into the mood. Terry is starting to think I'm no longer excited by her. She asked a ton of questions: Don't I like her anymore? Do I think her body is ugly? Am I angry because we hadn't done it yet? Is she doing something wrong? Questions, questions, questions, questions. Shut up! I told her to just be quiet. But I heard her crying. I wanted to yell at her to stop the goddamned crying. Just shut up!

I don't know if she'll want to see me again. Well, who cares? Who needs her? Who needs anybody? The hell with them. Everybody looking at me. Just wait until I get my plan together. Then they'll see. I know what I have to do. I need to steal a gun. Then I can kill Mr. Shithead Supervisor and whoever else is around. They all deserve it anyway. I know what they think. They're glad I'm not there, upsetting them with my superior skills and, yes, my superior looks.

Tonight I'll drive into a high-crime area, a black area. Then when I see a mugger I'll run him down. I'll take his gun and bullets and be on my way. Easy as pie.

I waited for an hour on a darkened street and hardly anyone passed by. I didn't see any muggers so I moved to another location. Nothing. I drove all over rundown black neighborhoods and didn't see anyone carrying a gun. Did they know I was coming? Are they afraid of me? Now what do I do? I can't take out the whole office with a machete and I don't know how to make a bomb.

It's getting hard to think straight, with Chip talking in my head all the time. I think and think but I can't come up with a solution. I can't remember when I've slept last, or eaten. Chip is telling me to pack it in. He wants me to be #16. Is that what it's come down to? Me or Mr. Supervisor? Maybe I should just take him down one on one, mano a mano, like #15. I could do it exactly the same way — just him alone on the street at night, not at work with everybody around. That would be suicidal. That's what Chip wants.

I'm not alone in my apartment. There's noise in my head, like static. Somebody's trying to get through on my wavelength, and now Chip's voice is being joined by others I don't recognize at all. They're all telling me to do things. I play music pretty loud, to try to drown them out. A neighbor complained. He'd better watch out. I've tried putting cotton in my ears, but that doesn't help. At work, I've tried to Google it, to see if I can find a solution, but I get back weird messages, so I've decided to stay off the Internet all together. I think the computer is reading my mind and sending my thoughts out to everyone. I've decided to only leave my apartment at night. It's too dangerous otherwise.

I think Theresa might be behind all of this. It all started with her. I think she and Mr. Supervisor have conspired with each other. How foolish I've been not to have seen it all from the beginning, although I had my suspicions. Didn't I? Well, tonight will put an end to all of that. I'm going out again to find a gun. Hopefully, after tonight I'll have everything I need and then, Monday morning at work, it's time for retribution.

Tawanda put the report down with a sigh. It was after 9:00. She telephoned Andy.

"Romano," he answered.

"It's me, Wanda."

"What's up?"

"I just finished reading the transcript of the file the computer lab found on Hladic's laptop."

"Yeah?"

"He's a serial killer."

"What?"

"He claims to have killed 15 people over the past 15 months, including that decapitation down near Seventh and Snyder last month."

"You're serious?"

"To coin a phrase, Andy, I'm dead serious. He was prowling Point Breeze looking for a mugger he could run down with his van so he could obtain a weapon in order to take out people at work."

"Jesus."

"Andy, you've got to see this. This is big. We could possibly close out 15 open homicides."

"I'm on my way over ..."

She went into the kitchen and put on some coffee. There would be work to do. It looked like Eddie, the decapitated Asian man, was also an employee of Jonas Computer Services. And what about young Theresa Rodriguez? What a narrow escape she had! Talk about being unlucky at love. But then again — she'd been very lucky, considering what Hladic had planned.

When Andy arrived, she handed him a mug of coffee and the transcript of the journal. When he finished, he looked up.

"Holy shit," he said, as he picked up the phone to call Mackey.

In the lieutenant's office the next morning, Mackey told them: "Look, this is bigger than huge. I don't want anyone getting wind of this until we've got it wrapped up. Otherwise, we'll be inundated with media and the mayor's office. Politicians will come out of the woodwork. So keep a lid on. If we're lucky and close a dozen cases or more, there'll be promotions all around. If we're unlucky, this wacko has just dreamed up the whole shit-load. If that's the case, no one else needs to know. Wanda, follow up at that computer place. Andy, get on the outstanding lab and ballistics reports. Let's see what we can find out from that van. I'll get the files on all the outstanding homicides since last July. Any questions?"

Theresa

Tuesday

Theresa's phone rang before Mr. Kwan had arrived at the office. A female voice spoke to her. "Miss Rodriguez? This is Detective Johnson. I was in your office yesterday morning."

"Yes, of course. Actually, I was going to call you this morning."

"You were?"

"After you left yesterday, I found out that the employee who had been killed was George Hladic. We were friends. I was wondering if you could tell me anything about what happened." She paused. "Was it suicide?"

"No, Miss Rodriguez, he didn't shoot himself." Wanda waited for that to sink in. "I'd like to ask you a few questions about your relationship with George. Is there someplace at the office we can talk privately?"

"Yes, I'm sure there is." Theresa thought of the break room.

"Fine then. I'll be there in about a half hour."

Theresa led the way into the empty room and closed the door. "Coffee?"

"Police officers never say no to coffee. Thanks."

The two women sat down at the table.

"Please tell me how George was killed," Theresa began nervously.

"George was found shot in his van in South Philly about 2:00 a.m. on Saturday morning. As far as we can tell," the detective explained, "he was trying to run down someone who then turned and shot him."

"That doesn't make any sense," Theresa shook her head. "That's not like him at all. Why would he do that?"

"Theresa, there's a lot about George you aren't aware of."

"I'm not sure what you're saying."

"George kept a journal on his computer …" Tawanda said slowly.

Theresa recalled seeing a laptop on his dresser. "Like a diary, you mean?"

"Sort of. In it he described what he referred to as his *life's work.* He also mentioned his relationship with you. That's why I wanted to talk with you."

"He wrote about me in his journal? What did he say?"

"He mentioned that the two of you met for dinner or lunch a few times, and that you were becoming physically involved."

"You read that? God, I'm so embarrassed."

"There's no need to be. But I need to ask you: Did George ever refer to his *life's work* or anything like that? Something that was really important to him?"

Theresa struggled to remember. "The only thing that comes to mind was that he said he'd like to become a programmer or learn more about computers. He said he liked both the software and the hardware side."

"Nothing else?"

"Not that I can think of. He was taking computer classes at the Community College."

"Did he mention any other people to you?"

"His mother. She was sick and he'd have to visit her. He seemed to resent that."

"Anyone else?"

"I don't think so."

"Did he ever mention Donna?"

"Donna?" *Another girl. I knew it. He was seeing somebody else.* Wanda waited for a reply. "No, he never mentioned her. I'm sure I would have remembered. The only other girl he mentioned was Marcia, an old high school girlfriend in New Jersey."

Wanda nodded. *The fake girlfriend.* "What did he have to say about his supervisor here at work? Do you remember?"

Theresa thought. "I know Mr. Kim bawled him out recently, but I don't remember if he told me or if I heard it from Pansy and Gladys." Wanda raised her eyebrows. "The other two women in my office," Theresa clarified, pointing with her face back toward her office.

"Did George have any reaction to that?"

"He seemed upset that week, but no, I don't think he said anything about it to me."

"How about Eddie Nguyen. I understand he worked in the mail room."

"Oh, yes, Eddie. He used to work here. But I haven't seen him in a while, now that I think of it."

"Did George ever speak about him?"

Theresa shook her head and then stopped. "There was once, I think, he asked if I'd seen Eddie, but we were talking about something else. I don't remember. I think that was the only time he brought up his name, but I'm not sure."

Wanda seemed to have run out of names, so Theresa took the chance to ask the question that was nagging at her. "Detective, what do these people have to do with George or me? This Donna you mentioned, was he seeing her? Were they dating?"

An image of her recently banished boyfriend flashed through Wanda's mind: Reggie's beautiful, handsome face and physique, his twinkly eyes, his mellifluous voice, the sexy smell of him — and a feeling of rage swelled within her. *The bastard, dirty rotten cheating no-good philandering narcissistic bastard.*

"No, Theresa, we don't have evidence that George was seeing anyone else. If it's any reassurance, you were the only girl in his life."

Theresa suddenly felt anxious: If he hadn't been cheating on her with someone else, then why was the detective questioning her?

Tawanda considered what she could risk telling this young woman. Lieutenant Mackey didn't want any information to get out, with the other murder cases still open. On the other hand, she empathized with Theresa and realized the girl needed to understand who she had been involved with.

"Theresa, I am certain that you would soon have discovered for yourself — if you already hadn't — how mentally unstable George was."

Theresa nodded.

"What you couldn't have known was how dangerous he was."

"Dangerous?"

"Well, for example, the night he was killed. He was trying to run someone down."

"But why would he do that?"

"The simple answer is that George wanted to kill the man."

"Kill him? I don't understand."

"What I'm saying, Theresa, is that George was attempting to murder someone — and that person shot George in self-defense, and killed him."

"I don't believe it."

"We have a witness. And George wrote about his intentions in his journal."

Theresa couldn't speak. *George? A murderer?*

"All I can tell you," the detective went on, "is that George had a mental illness. I'm not an expert. I'm not a psychologist or psychiatrist, but George was seriously mentally ill — and dangerous. George was suspicious of everyone and everything. He hallucinated voices that told him to do things," she hesitated, "and he thought you were part of a conspiracy against him. Your life was in danger."

Theresa's eyes widened. The implications gradually became illuminated. Was George planning to kill her?

"Holy shit," Theresa muttered. *Ohmygod, I knew he was weird, but this?*

Tawanda took out her iPhone and showed Theresa a picture of Eddie Nguyen's head.

"Is this Eddie from the mail room?"

Theresa looked and nodded and then examined the picture more closely. "Is that head …"

Tawanda sighed. "Yes, decapitated."

Theresa looked up. "George?"

Tawanda nodded.

"My God. He did that?"

"Yes. With a machete, a couple of weeks ago."

"Jesus."

"Theresa, you can't blame yourself for anything. George was seriously unstable long before you became involved with him. He was very good at covering up his illness, partly because he was so suspicious of everyone, so paranoid. But you suspected he wasn't completely normal, right?"

Theresa nodded. "Actually, Friday night when I saw him, he was behaving so erratically that I decided it was over. I didn't need anyone in my life who was going to mistreat me or be so insensitive, so self-absorbed. But I had no idea it was this serious."

Tawanda's cellphone rang. It was Andy.

"Wanda, we've got the shooter. Partial fingerprints from the casings match Douglas Williams of the 2300 block of Tasker, practically around the corner. Medium height and build, black, 21 years old. Arrested once before on suspicion of mugging, but he got off. Dishonorable from the army for drug abuse. But he learned to shoot straight. Got a sharpshooter's medal in basic training."

"That's great news, Andy. Congratulations."

"That's not all. Looks like CSI is coming up with a shitload of stuff from the van. Hopefully, it'll help us ID some of those victims."

"OK good. I'll be back there within the hour."

"You interviewing the girlfriend?"

"Yeah, just about finished."

"OK, then. See you back here."

Tawanda hung up. "Theresa, we're just beginning the investigation into other crimes George may have been involved with. Please don't discuss these details with anyone else. Hopefully, within a couple of weeks, we'll have gotten down to the bottom of things. At that point, I expect there will be major media coverage. Do you understand?"

"I think so."

"When the story breaks, the press will want to interview anybody and everybody who ever had anything to do with George Hladic. Reporters will be swarming all over this place. It will come out that you were his girlfriend. I can't keep your name out of this, but I can promise you that George's journal and what he wrote will remain private." As she said this, she wondered if the journal might be subpoenaed in a future civil suit or court hearing. "So don't worry about your privacy being violated in that respect."

It dawned on Theresa that everyone would know she had dated George. They would assume she'd slept with him, a murderer. She shook her head. "No, I couldn't handle that." *I don't know if I want to continue working here where everyone will know; with everyone talking behind my back, girlfriend of a murderer.*

"Theresa, listen to me. You haven't done anything wrong. You have nothing to be ashamed of. The best way to deal with the media, when they come swarming down, is to not give them what they want. No comment. Period. Say it often enough and they'll leave you alone. Just remember, you have nothing to say. You know nothing. OK?"

Theresa nodded. *Yeah, but what if that doesn't work.*

That evening, Theresa went to see her aunt. When she arrived, she asked Dorinda if she had any wine. With a puzzled look, Dorinda brought out a bottle and two glasses.

"You are not going to fucking believe this," Theresa began. When she finished recounting the story — including her intention to quit her job at Jonas Computer Services — Dorinda sat back on her chair, mouth agape.

"Maybe," her aunt looked her directly in the eye, "this is a good time to start taking care of number one. I mean you."

"Yes," Theresa nodded, "I've been thinking about that. I could have been killed by some paranoid lunatic. And what would I have amounted to? You've said it many times, Dorrie — I've put my life on a back burner while I took pride in sacrificing myself for a family full of selfish bitches who never appreciated anything I did for them. It's time I start living. My life, not theirs. I've wanted to be a nurse for as long as I can remember. I can't stay in that job anymore. And I don't want to live at home anymore. It's time I started paying attention to my own needs. I matter too."

Dorinda went to her niece and embraced her.

"I could have been killed, damnit. And for what? Dorrie, will you help me? I need to start fresh."

"Sugar, you know I will. I'll do everything I can. And you'll do it. No one is more determined than you. If you got through this, you can get through anything. Trust me."

Together Again

One

Noreen reached across the kitchen table for the bottle of vodka, but it slipped from her hand and tottered at the edge of the table beyond her reach. Lunging for it, she lost her balance and fell face down on the floor. The hollow sound of the bottle rolling away from her echoed as the precious fluid poured out. Instinctively, she tried to scramble after it, but the room swam in a blurry haze. Angry tears of frustration sprang to her eyes. *I'll just lie here for a minute and catch my breath. There'll still be enough left for one good drink. Maybe the pain in my belly will subside if I can get just one more drink.*

Noreen put one arm under her face and closed her eyes, fully intending to rest only briefly. When she awoke, it was dark. At first, she was unsure of where she was or what time it was. Night? Early morning? She pushed herself onto her hands and knees, but her body felt painfully stiff and cramps sharply stabbed her gut. She felt dizzy and nauseous as the darkened room swirled around her.

With just enough light to recognize the kitchen table, she oriented herself to her surroundings. Crawling slowly across the floor, her hand slipped in the stream of spilled vodka and she fell face forward again, banging her jaw on the tile. She licked the liquor from the palm of her hand, then resumed her efforts. Reaching her destination, she leaned back against the stove, picked up the mostly empty bottle, and raised it to her lips. After a good long swallow, she sank back, grateful for the familiar burn.

What time is it? Will Walter be coming home? Is he already home? Will he find me like this? She'd have to stand to see the clock, and she wasn't sure she could make it onto her feet.

267

Walter pulled into the driveway at his usual time and noticed immediately that the house was dark. *Damn.* Chances were Noreen was asleep in their bedroom, even though it was dinnertime. Her inner clock was all screwed up. She was just as likely to sleep during the day and roam the house at night. Maybe she'd gone to an AA meeting. Maybe she'd gone to pick up something for dinner. He thought of just backing up and driving to Gloria's, but decided he'd better go inside and check if Noreen was blacked out again.

Entering the front door, he turned on the hall light and closed the door. He called out for Noreen, but heard only an empty echo in response. In the kitchen, he found his wife slumped against the stove, her legs spread lazily on the floor, an empty bottle cradled in her arms.

Shit. Not again. He squatted down beside her. Her mouth hung slack and he smelled the sour vomit that was streaked down her blouse and pooled on the floor.

"Nor!" he called to her. "Noreen. Wake up. It's me. Come on, wake up."

No response, even after shaking her by the shoulder. Her body was limp, dead weight. Walter pushed himself up from his squatting position, breathing heavily.

Noreen had started attending AA meetings a couple of years earlier, but she relapsed frequently. *To hell with her, let her suffer the consequences. If she chose to get herself tanked — again — then fuck her.* He was tempted to walk out, forget he had ever been there, and go to Gloria's. But what he wanted more than anything was for her to stop drinking. He dialed 911.

Seven weeks later, Noreen sat on the edge of the hospital bed, dressed and waiting for Walter to pick her up. She made a striking figure, even elegant. At 45, she carried herself — when sober — with confidence and grace. She still had a good figure and, thanks to Walter, dressed in flattering clothes and jewelry. Today she looked radiant. Almost two months without drinking — admittedly, with the help of medication — made her feel stronger than at any time she could remember. When Walt came huffing into the room, she was genuinely glad to see him.

"Hi, sweetheart," she gave him a big smile as she rose from her chair, "I've been waiting for you."

"I got here as soon as I could," he apologized as he approached to a kiss her. "You all ready?"

She nodded, glancing at the few bags that contained her belongings.

"I'll get these," he said. "Anything else? Robe, slippers? You have all your medicine?"

"It's all there. Everything."

"Anything we have to do? Sign out or anything?"

"We're all set. Everything's done."

"OK," he took her arm, "let's get out of this place."

When the elevator doors opened to the busy lobby, she felt like she was beginning her life all over again. *This time I'm going to do it right. This is the last time I'll be in a place like this.* She couldn't wait to get home, back in her kitchen.

In the car, she turned to her husband as he squeezed himself into the driver's seat.

"Walt," she said. "I want to thank you again for all you've done. I would have died that night if you hadn't found me. I want you to know I realize that. I'm truly sorry for everything I've put you through. You don't deserve it. I know I've made promises before, but this time it's different. I won't ever put you through this again."

He leaned over and kissed her. "You don't have to thank me, Noreen. I'm your husband." He looked at her seriously. "I hope you understand how sick you were, how close you came to dying." He looked at her questioningly.

"I know. If it weren't for you, I'd have died there on the kitchen floor, in my own urine and vomit. I owe you my life."

"You don't owe me anything, Nor. It's what you owe yourself — a chance. If you ever drink again, you're going to kill yourself. You remember what the doctor said? Your liver, your pancreas, your kidneys, they can't be put through this kind of ordeal again. This is it. Your body won't give you anymore chances."

She knew she'd be in for a lecture. Part of her was even grateful for it. Not that she needed reminding, but she was determined to take advantage of all the help she could get, including Walter playing the role of parent to her naughty little girl. *Well, I was. Naughty. To say the least!*

She stared out the window as Walter drove through the busy Philadelphia streets. It was good to smell the cold air, to see traces of snow on the ground. She had spent Christmas in intensive care and New Years in the hospital's alcohol and drug abuse inpatient program. It was good to be out.

"You want to stop for lunch?" Walter asked.

"Not today. I'm eager to get home." Then she sat up suddenly. "Is there anything in the fridge? We probably have to do some food shopping."

"I got stuff yesterday. I think we have everything we need," he reassured her.

Noreen sank back in her seat and smiled.

"You think of everything," she said. "I'll make you a nice lunch when we get home. It'll be good to be back in my own kitchen again."

"It's good to have you home."

—————

Noreen sorted the mail, put her clothes away, checked the laundry (Walter had done only the absolute necessities), and opened the refrigerator (too much bread, not enough vegetables or fruit). In the living room, she quietly enjoyed the view out the front picture window. Walter joined her.

"Have you heard from Frances at all?" she asked.

"I left a message when you went into the hospital and she called back and left a message saying she hoped you'd be OK. Other than that, we haven't been in touch."

Noreen detected a tone of forbearance in his voice. What more could she expect? She received the news with sad resignation. Frances, or Fancy, as she now preferred to be called, had moved out when Noreen moved in with Walt, two years ago. Frances and her boyfriend, Lou, had shown up when Noreen and Walter got married a year later, but their relationship remained distant and strained. She wanted her daughter back in her life.

Noreen sighed and felt the slight stirrings of desire for a drink.

"You want some coffee or something?" she asked.

"No thanks," he answered, picking up the newspaper, "I'll wait until we have lunch."

"I'm going to give Linda a call. I have to get back into the program."

"After lunch, I should go in to work for a couple of hours," he said absently.

Noreen called her sponsor from the phone in the kitchen, and the two women made plans to attend a meeting later in the afternoon. She felt some relief after taking that step and was able to enjoy making lunch for her and Walter. As she constructed his sandwich the way he liked, stacked solidly with meat, cheese, lettuce, and tomato, she felt a welling up of affection for him. With a keen sense of appreciation for what a good, kind man he was, she realized again, with some guilt, what she had put him through these past years.

They made plans for dinner at home — rather than tempting fate at a restaurant with a bar — and Walter kissed her goodbye on his way to the office. A bit afraid to be alone in the house, she left early to meet her sponsor at a diner where they had often gone after AA meetings.

"So how are you doing?" Linda asked. "You look fabulous."

Noreen flipped her hand back and forth. "A little shaky — scared I'll slip again, but I'm determined."

"And physically?"

"Physically I feel better than I have in a long time. I can tell you, Lin, I don't ever want to go through that again. The cramps, the stabbing pains. The doctors said they were surprised I pulled through — my kidneys and pancreas and liver were all shutting down. Thank God it was Walter who found me. Can you imagine if it had been Frankie?"

"Your ex? He would have kicked the shit out of you."

Noreen heaved a sigh of relief. "Thank God he's out of the picture."

Linda raised her glass of ice water in salute: "To your ex and mine. May they rot in hell."

The two women spent the next hour talking about Noreen's hospitalization and how determined she was to remain in the program.

"In the beginning, at least a meeting a day, maybe two. And I'm going to start individual therapy at the hospital outpatient program. That's once a week. I'm really determined this time, Linda. I'm really scared. And the dreams I had while I was in there! I mean, I've been in rehab before — what? — half a dozen times? But this time it scared the crap out of me." She shuddered. "Alcohol and Frank, two evils I don't ever want in my life again."

"It's good you're scared, Nory. You should be. It'll help keep you straight. Don't ever forget what you're telling me now. If you do, you can bet your boots that I'll be the first to remind you."

Noreen laughed. "I'm counting on it."

Later that afternoon, Noreen went to an AA meeting. She knew some of the people there, but some newcomers had joined while she was hospitalized. She introduced herself and shared what she'd been through the past two months. Afterward, during coffee, a number of her old friends approached and welcomed her back.

"It's good to be home," she said, warmly embracing them. "I can't think of anyplace I'd rather be than here." She was grateful that this support was available for her — and she was determined to make use of it.

Noreen stopped at the supermarket on the way home to buy some fish, as well as the produce that Walt failed to include in his concept of food. When the groceries were unpacked, she called her daughter, and was surprised to catch her at home.

"Fancy? It's me, Mom. How are you?"

Her daughter sounded groggy.

"I'm working nights, Ma. I don't get to sleep until the morning."

Noreen didn't want another fight. Frances could be so touchy.

"I was hoping we could get together sometime," Noreen said. "It's been a long time since I've seen you. I miss you."

Frances declined her mother's invitation to dinner — in order to avoid sharing a meal with Walter — but eventually agreed to meet Noreen for lunch the next day.

Too agitated to fall back asleep, Fancy smoked a joint to relax. What a pain in the ass this was going to be, having lunch with her mother tomorrow. Why did she ever agree to that? She inhaled deeply and allowed herself to mellow out. It was only 4:00. She still had another five hours before she had to show up for work. Fancy padded into the small kitchen in her bare feet and opened the fridge. Lou had brought home chicken breasts and roasted potatoes from work last night. As assistant manager of food service at the hotel, he always brought home leftovers. Good thing. Cooking was not her strong suit.

Another perk was that he was hardly ever home. Poor Lou. He worked 12-hour days six days a week, with only Thursday off. That meant they hardly saw each other, which was fine with her. It was bad enough putting up with the creeps at work without having to satisfy Lou and his bizarro demands. She could handle one day a week together. She took out some chicken and opened a beer while she finished her joint. After one last inhale, she dropped the dish into the sink and extinguished the roach in the empty beer can, then aimed herself back toward bed.

At 6:30, Noreen heard the car in the driveway. When she'd been drinking, she had always served beer or wine with meals. Now, feeling a lack of confidence in herself, she had no alcohol in the house at all — only water or diet soda or iced tea, at least for a while. Maybe forever. Walt trudged into the house from the garage clad in a heavy overcoat. The forecast was for much colder weather tonight, maybe even snow.

"Hi," he said, kissing her on the cheek. His lips, still cool, felt refreshing. "How was your first day home?"

She told him about meeting Linda for coffee and attending an afternoon meeting.

"I also called Frances. I'm meeting her for lunch tomorrow."

"That's nice," he said, sitting down at the kitchen table. "You two should see each other. It's a shame the way she's shut you out of her life."

Noreen brought a platter of broiled fish, bordered by bright yellow lemon

everything.

Noreen interrupted his calculations and asked if he'd like some dessert and coffee. He watched her walk into the kitchen, appreciating the way her rear end filled out her jeans. *Either way, it could work out.*

———

At 7:00, Fancy's cellphone rang and she roused herself to answer it. She knew who it was even before she heard his rough, gravelly voice.

"Hey, cupcake, time to wake up."

"I'm up, Lou."

"Bullshit you are. You'd sleep forever if I didn't call."

Fancy rolled her eyes. "Now I'm up."

"Don't get testy with me. Remember, you asked me to call you. Right?"

She sighed wearily. "Right, thanks. I'll see you in the morning when I get home."

"Try getting home a little early. Maybe we can do our thing before I have to leave for work. OK?"

She nodded into the phone.

"OK?" he repeated.

"Yeah," she said, "I'll try."

"It's been a while."

"I said I'd try, didn't I?"

There were a few moments of silence. "OK, then. See you in the morning. Love you."

"Yeah," she murmured, "me too."

Fancy forced herself out of bed. Stripping off her panties, she padded into the bathroom to take a shower. After finishing off the supper Lou had brought home, she chugged a can of beer, checked that her make-up was just right, and shoved her costume into her purse. She started for the door but quickly spun around and returned to their bedroom. Examining the bowl of pills on Lou's nightstand, she pocketed some red and some black, uppers and downers.

This week, she was working a private club in south Jersey. The agency didn't want their dancers staying at any one place too long, so they made a point of rotating them around the circuit every week or two at most. Some-

…'d work two or three different clubs in the same week.

…n by her dancing, but there'd be hell to pay if her mother

…Mom was concerned, Fancy worked the night shift in an

…ing together small appliances. She stole the idea from a

…to do that kind of work. Of course Walter knew, but Fancy

Two

The hospital routine had reacquainted Noreen with waking up at a relatively early hour. No more lying in bed till noon, lazy with booze, writing herself out of the daily script of life. This morning, her first at home, she awoke when Walter's alarm sounded and rose full of energy and determination to make this a productive day. She looked forward to making a special breakfast for Walter — it had been so long since she had been a real wife to him. She slipped on a fleece sweat suit, woolen socks, and slippers and charged into the kitchen like a woman on a mission.

When Walter came downstairs 20 minutes later, he could hardly believe the scene. The smell of coffee and bacon drew him seductively into the kitchen. A tall glass of orange juice awaited, and even his vitamins and blood pressure pills had been set out for him.

As she poured coffee, Noreen greeted him. "Good morning, hon. I wasn't sure how you might want your eggs this morning, so I made them easy over. Is that all right?"

Walter gave her a good morning kiss before sitting down.

"Easy over is perfect. You really are determined to make a new start, aren't you?"

"Absolutely," she said. "If there's anything special you want to eat, please tell me. Otherwise, I'll just follow my instincts."

"You've got great instincts," he said, surprise still in his voice.

Noreen enjoyed the look of delight on her husband's face as he consumed his eggs and toast. Walt enjoyed his food and she knew that the old adage about the way to a man's heart was certainly true of him. She wasn't sure if there was anything as important — maybe his job as bank manager, certainly not sex. When he finished his coffee, Walter pushed himself back from the table with a satisfied smile.

After a perfunctory kiss, she heard the garage door open and close — and suddenly found herself facing the day totally alone.

Part of her recovery program was assessing options for how to spend her time. What would give her life purpose? What was the motivation to stay sober, to stay alive? In addition to making sobriety the priority, she had decided to make a major effort to be as good a mother to Frances as she could at this late stage. At 20, Fancy had been on her own — not counting Lou — for over three years. Noreen realized that her daughter wouldn't exactly welcome the idea of being mothered at this point in her life. Noreen was a day late and a dollar short, but she intended to do what she could to be a resource for her daughter.

But in addition to making amends to Frances and Walter, she had to find a purpose for her own life. She considered going back to school next summer or fall semester for certification as an English teacher. Alone at the kitchen table with another cup of coffee, she made a schedule for herself: attending AA meetings, continuing the hospital outpatient program, researching schools. With a tentative schedule in place, she felt grounded. It was a supporting framework around which she could construct her week. The anxiety of uncertainty alleviated, Noreen took a shower and prepared for her lunch with Frances.

Driving home after work, Fancy glanced at her watch: 4:30 a.m. She had been dancing for six hours, then had to go off with that Russian asshole after closing. She didn't mind the sex so much — she was resigned to it being part of the job and she counted on the extra money. But the staff expected freebies and it was her turn. He actually hadn't been that bad, but she was pissed to miss out on the money.

The effects of the pills were wearing off. Ordinarily, she'd take something when she got home to help her sleep, but Lou would be waiting for her this morning. Fancy shook her head in disbelief that a grown man could be as fucked up as Lou. Depressed to the point of being suicidal, he worried constantly. He had to count and recount everything. He had pills for depression, pills for anxiety, pills for blood pressure, pills for diabetes — not to mention his vast collection of uppers and downers.

But his sexual fetishes were by far the craziest: women's lingerie, spanking with a hairbrush, enemas. She had a quick flash to the first time she found him lying on the bed, squeezed into a pair of panties and an oversized bra. He had begged her to beat him, and she had collapsed in tears beside him because she couldn't bring herself to hurt him.

Later, she had surprised herself. Hitting him and shoving things into his ass actually gave her some pleasure — although she felt way too embarrassed to ever to tell anyone. Sometimes she was left feeling like she had demeaned them both. Well, when she got home, she'd whack his ass good while he jerked off and then she'd take a pill and go zonko for a few hours until she had to have lunch with her mother. *God, why did I ever agree to do that?*

Noreen pulled into the parking lot of Gabe's Diner and sighed at its grungy appearance. In general she liked diners — you could get anything you wanted at any hour of the day, or linger comfortably with just a cup of coffee and talk with a friend for hours without feeling guilty for not ordering more. She liked the casual neighborhood feel and lack of pretension. But this run-down place looked like the last refuge for lost souls. She imagined the end of a lonely road at night — but here it sat on a main street in a big city like a homeless beggar surrounded by civilization.

She knew Frances lived nearby. Looking at the neighborhood, Noreen figured her daughter and Lou rented a small and neglected dump, not unlike the diner itself.

Waiting out front, she spotted Frances loping down the street toward her. Even though she was too far away for Noreen to see her face, she could tell from the tall, thin body, the hunched shoulders, the stiff-legged stride that it was her girl. The long orange scarf wound around her neck, flapping after her like the tail of a kite, and matching woolen cap made her look like a waif, and Noreen felt a surge of affection. She murmured a silent prayer, then smiled and waved. Frances leaned forward awkwardly and offered her cheek to be kissed without taking her hands from her coat pockets.

"You look cute in that outfit," said Noreen. "Adorable."

Frances allowed a brief lipless grin and proceeded up the steps to the entrance. They found a booth inside.

"Did you get any sleep?" Noreen asked.

"A couple of hours."

"What time do you get off from your shift?"

"Around 7:00," she said.

Noreen nodded and retreated behind the menu. Frances ordered a beer with her burger. Noreen winced but said nothing, and ordered coffee and soup for herself. They remained silent until the waitress brought their beverages.

"So," Noreen began, "you're making it quite clear that you're doing me a big favor by being here today."

Frances took a long drink from her beer without looking up.

"And it is a huge favor. I understand that. And I appreciate it. Really." Noreen paused briefly, hoping to elicit some kind of acknowledgment. "I just wanted you to know that when I was in the hospital, I think I hit my bottom. At least I hope I hit my bottom."

Frances glanced over the rim of her glass, but remained silent.

Noreen continued. "I'm telling you the same thing I told Walt. I know I've made promises before and haven't been able to keep them, but I want you to know that I feel more determined and stronger than I have since I met your father, and I'm going to do everything I can — anything I have to — to stay sober. And one of my main goals is to try to make up for everything I owe you."

"You don't owe me shit."

The waitress brought their food. Fancy ordered another beer.

"Look, Ma, you have your life and I've got mine. I don't expect anything from you, so you don't owe me anything. There's nothing you can do for me now, unless you've got a million bucks you want to give away. Otherwise forget it. I don't need anything from you."

Noreen was prepared for the hostility and resentment. She absorbed it willingly, believing she deserved every bit of venom her daughter could muster. Maybe it would be good for Frances to spit it out.

"I know I can't make up for all those years of not being there for you. I'm deeply, deeply sorry for having failed you so utterly. I'm here to apologize, although I know that doesn't change anything. I was never an adequate mother to you. I'm sorry I was a drunk. I didn't protect you from your father. I'm sorry for all of it. And I know none of that can ever be undone and that breaks my heart."

Fancy sat motionless.

"However, I do intend to start over," Noreen went on. "I need to reclaim my self-respect. And I want to be here for you. I know you're not a little girl anymore. You're an independent and beautiful young woman and I want you in my life. I want to have a relationship with you. I want to be a resource for you. Do you understand what I'm trying to say?"

Frances glared hard at her mother, then sat back and took a sip from her beer before answering. When she did, Noreen saw that her daughter's eyes were glistening.

"Those are great words, Ma. Great fucking words. And you're right — they don't change a fucking thing. You want to be here for me?" She shook her head in disbelief. "Where the hell have you been all my life?"

Noreen saw Fancy's lips begin to tremble. She wanted to reach over, take hold of her daughter's hands, console her, but Frances turned her head and looked out the window.

"All those years with Daddy. All the shit we all went through. Where were you then?" she spat. "Why weren't you there for me then? That's when I needed you."

"I know," Noreen whispered.

"You left us alone with him."

"I never left you," Noreen quickly protested. "How can you say that?"

"Ma," she said, drawing it out, "you left us alone with him for days, weeks maybe. At least it seemed like it."

Noreen puzzled over that for a minute. "Are you talking about when he put me in the hospital? I didn't leave you — he fractured my skull. Don't you remember? He broke my ribs, my arm, my wrist. Jesus Christ, Frances, I was in the hospital!"

Frances refused to meet her mother's gaze.

"Dad said you brought it on yourself."

"My God, Frances, think about it. Do you honestly think I wanted to be beaten like that?"

Silence.

"Do you really believe I chose to leave you alone with him? If I wasn't physically there it's because I couldn't be. The fact that I didn't do more while I was there, I'll take responsibility for that. But I was a prisoner too. Not only of your father, but also of my own fear. It wasn't until we were free of him, after he disappeared, that I was able to even begin thinking rationally about it. How frightened I was all the time. I can only imagine what it was like for you kids."

"No you can't," Fancy whispered. "There's no fucking way you can even begin to imagine what I went through."

"Maybe not. Don't misunderstand me on this, Frances ..."

"Fancy. I can't stand the name Frances."

Now it made sense. Noreen had thought her daughter had just been searching for an identity of her own. But of course she wouldn't want to share a name with her father.

"I'm sorry," she said, "I didn't realize." She hesitated for a moment and then pushed on. "I'm not excusing my behavior for one moment. I was a coward. I was a drunk. I was neglectful. And I was also a victim, Fancy. I should have done more. I know that. Maybe I even knew it then. But I didn't know how ..."

Noreen felt herself beginning to lose it. Her chest constricted and started to heave. She licked her lips and surveyed the table for a drink. Her eyes fixed on her daughter's bottle of beer. She pushed herself back from the table and breathed deeply. She was aware Frances was watching her.

"I was saying that I didn't know how to do more. Your father ..."

"That bastard."

Gerard R. D'Alessio

"Yes. He kept us all in line, didn't he? I have two recurring nightmares: that I'll start drinking again and that Frank will show up in our lives again." The two women sat silently for a while. Fancy finished her beer.

"Honey, would it be all right if I call you every so often?" Noreen asked cautiously. "Maybe we can have lunch or go to a movie or something." She looked at her daughter expectantly.

"I guess."

Noreen had not dared to hope for more. Inwardly, she relaxed and a smile crept onto her face. "Thank you."

Outside, the two shared another brief sanitary hug. In her car, Noreen watched as Fancy walked away, shoulders hunched against her cold bitterness.

She drove straight to an AA meeting. By the time she left, she felt bolstered and returned home with a renewed sense of confidence and purpose. That night at dinner, she told Walter about her lunch with Frances.

"I didn't understand before, but she finally made me realize that she just can't tolerate being called by her father's name," Noreen explained, "so from now on, let's make a real effort to call her Fancy."

"You're much too tolerant of that kid. Fancy, my ass. The only thing fancy about her is her taste in drugs."

"You don't know that," Noreen defended her daughter.

Walter put his fork down and wiped his mouth with a napkin. "Come on, she's been doing everything under the sun since she was 13 or 14. Maybe before that. You know she was getting into your booze when she was 12."

"I know what she's done. But we don't know what her life is like now. She's got a steady job in that assembly plant. She can't be getting that high if she's going to work every night."

Walt resumed eating.

"Right?" she persisted.

"What do I know?" he said. "Maybe you're right. But I'd be goddamned surprised if that kid turned over a new leaf. Not living with that twisted nutcase."

There was no sense in arguing with Walter. He didn't like her daughter and there was nothing she could do about it. Well, Walter and Fancy didn't have to live with each other. As long as he was a good husband — and he was incomparably better than Frank — then she was grateful. He didn't have to love her daughter too. As long as he loved her, she was OK.

Three

The following morning the telephone rang while Noreen was cleaning up after breakfast.

"Hello?" she answered, wiping her hands on a towel.

"Ma?"

There was a moment of blank disbelief. For an instant, Noreen refused to believe what she'd heard.

"Frankie?" She already knew it was her son.

"Yeah."

"Where are you?"

"I just got into town. I'm at the bus terminal."

"You're here? In Philadelphia?"

"Yeah, I just got in a few minutes ago."

"How did you get my number?"

"An old friend up in Jersey told me you got married again and moved to Philly. You're the only listing for Walter Beckmeyer."

"My God, it's been forever. Why are you here?"

"It's a long story, Ma. I want to see you. You know, sit down someplace."

Noreen hesitated for just a moment. "You're just around the corner from the Reading Terminal. There's a diner inside, part of the market. I'll meet you there in about 45 minutes."

Noreen collapsed onto the kitchen chair, her heart pounding. Her mouth was dry and she wanted something to drink. Taking a can of diet soda from the fridge, she said a brief prayer of gratitude that there was no alcohol in the house. The first thing she had to do was to tell Walter and Fancy. She took deep, calming breaths as she finished her soda. Eventually, she was ready to make her calls.

Noreen had to look up her husband's work number because it was such a rare occurrence for her to call him there. She'd done that early in her marriage and he had been really angry.

"For goodness sake, Nor," he had scolded, "I'm the manager. What kind of example would I set if I'm taking personal calls all day? Please don't contact me at work unless it's an emergency."

Well if this wasn't an emergency, she didn't know what was. She punched in the number and got his voicemail. She hung up and dialed the main number. When a receptionist answered, she identified herself and asked to speak to her husband.

"I'm sorry," she was told, "Mr. Beckmeyer is not in today."

"That's impossible," Noreen protested, "I know he went in this morning. Please try again."

After a few minutes on hold, a man's voice spoke to her. "Hello Mrs. Beckmeyer. This is Harvey Drackett, the assistant manager. There must be some mistake. Your husband took a personal day today. We're not expecting him in until tomorrow."

"He's not there?"

"No ma'am. He won't be in until tomorrow. Is there something I might help you with?"

"No, thank you," she stammered. Bewildered, she reviewed the morning: they had breakfast together, he dressed for work …. If he wasn't in the office, where was he? It didn't make any sense. Why would he try to deceive her? Walter never lied. She must have misunderstood, or maybe didn't hear when he told her he had an appointment outside the office.

Shaking off the confusion, she dialed her daughter. No answer, no voicemail. Damn. She wished she knew where Fancy lived.

Finally she gave up and called Linda.

"Linda, it's me, Noreen. I just got a call from Frankie Jr."

"No."

"Out of the blue. He called from the bus terminal near Reading Market. He's here, in Philly."

"Christ, after six years without even a postcard? What does he want?"

"I haven't the faintest idea. Money, I would think. It's certainly not out of love for his mother."

"What are you going to do?"

"I said I'd meet him at the diner in the Reading Terminal."

There was a momentary pause before Linda asked her if she thought that was wise.

"I don't know. I couldn't think. Part of me felt like I should have invited him here, but there's no way I'd feel comfortable with that. I thought this was a good compromise."

"You want me to go with you?"

"No, I don't think that's necessary. It's a pretty public place. I should be all right."

"You want me to call you on your cell while you're with him?" Linda suggested.

"That sounds good. I'm supposed to meet him in about 40 minutes. Why don't you call me an hour from now?"

"OK, Nory. I'll talk to you then. Be careful."

Noreen tried to keep herself calm as she showered and dressed. By the time she arrived at the diner, she appeared relaxed and self-possessed. Scanning the customers, she spotted a young man in a rear booth. He was remarkably different from when she had last seen him, but the face was the same despite a moustache and goatee. He had his father's handsome looks, but the expression was forlorn behind long black hair. As she approached, she saw the tattoos on his upper arms. He was nursing a cup of black coffee. For a moment, she felt a surge of pity, but as she got closer, anger and fear welled up within her. He looked up.

"Ma?" He started to rise, but she quickly slid onto the seat across the booth.

"Look at you. All grown up."

He smiled sheepishly and tossed his head. "Yeah, I'm taller than Dad."

"Are you?" she said absently.

"So what's up with you?" he asked.

"I'm alive. I'm sober."

Frankie's head bobbed up and down as if agreeing with something profound. "That's good," he said.

"What brings you to Philly?" she asked, trying to sound casual.

A waitress appeared and Noreen ordered a cup of coffee. When she left, Frankie looked up.

"I thought it was time to come home." He paused. "Dad's dead."

"That should make you considerably taller."

Frankie let out a chuckle, then resumed his somber mood.

"Yeah, I guess so. Anyway, with his, you know ..."

"Being dead?"

"Yeah. I thought it would be a good time to come home, see you again, see my sister."

"Why?"

"You mean why would I want to see you and Frances?"

"Frankie, you've been gone for six years. Six years," she repeated, letting the sound of it sink in, like the telling of the hour by distant steeple bells. "Six years," she said again.

"I know."

"Six years, Frankie, without any acknowledgment that you even had a mother or a sister. No note, no phone call, not even a postcard, a Christmas card, nothing."

"I know."

"That's what we were to you, Frankie, nothing."

"I wanted to call. I wanted to write, but Frank wouldn't let me."

"He wouldn't let you?"

"You know how he was."

"Frankie!" Noreen shook her head in disbelief. "Do I look stupid to you?" She made an effort to keep her voice down.

He waited for her to continue.

"Do I? Answer me."

"No, you don't look stupid."

Noreen leaned across the table. "Then don't treat me as if I were. Your father wouldn't *let* you. What a crock."

"You know how he was, Ma. If he suspected you did something you weren't supposed to, he didn't let up. He'd be at you and at you, slapping you, hounding you, threatening. Don't you remember?"

"Of course I remember. But look at you. You're six feet tall, taller than he was. You're a man now. You expect me to believe that he had you cowed the way he — and you — had us cowed? The way you bastards beat us into submission?"

Tears welled and her vision blurred. She took a tissue from her purse.

Frankie gave a little laugh that sounded like a snort.

"If you only knew, Ma. He was just as tough on me, maybe in some ways even tougher. He'd handcuff me to a radiator or a pipe, whatever, and then beat me."

"I don't want to trade war stories with you, Frankie. We both know your father was a monster and I believe you had it tough with him. But you knew who he was and you chose to go with him. Now you're a man. You're bigger than he ever was and just as mean. Don't expect me to believe he could have kept you from making a phone call or dropping a postcard. Not for six years, Frankie. Not for all of that time."

"You're probably right. I probably could have managed to do that if I really wanted to badly enough. I thought of it from time to time. I'd wonder how you and Frances were doing. But you're right — Frank had me so brainwashed, I guess I'd written you off. He …" his voice trailed off.

"He what?"

"You know. He really didn't like women all that much."

Noreen watched her son squirm. "And you?" she asked.

She saw Frank's boyish smile emerge on her son's face, a sly bashfulness.

"I like women fine."

"But you don't respect us. We're just good for filling your needs."

Frankie looked her in the eye. "I'm not sure I'm all that familiar with respect. It's not exactly something I learned."

Noreen sighed in resignation. How could he have learned to respect anyone? Frank had only contempt for everyone and everything. People were simply objects to be used. How could his son be any different?

Her cellphone rang.

"How are you?" Linda asked.

"I'm OK. Everything is fine."

"You're sure? Do you want me to call you back in 10 minutes?"

Noreen thought for a moment and looked across the table at her big, handsome hunk of a son.

"Make it a half hour."

Linda said OK and hung up.

"Tell me about your father. How did he die?"

The waitress brought her coffee and refilled Frankie's cup.

"Lung cancer."

"When?"

"A week ago. I buried him then got my stuff together and made my way here."

"Where were you all this time? Where did he die?"

"We've been all over," he said, "mostly the southwest, Colorado, New Mexico. But lately we were in Idaho. That's where he died."

"So why come back here?"

"I really did want to see you and Frances. And I don't have anywhere else to go. I was hoping I could stay with you for a while until I figure some stuff out for myself."

"For six years you throw us away, and then show up out of the blue expecting to be taken in? To be welcomed back like you were a little kid who was lost and we'd be grateful you were found? You really expected that?"

"I didn't expect anything. I just hoped I could get to see you both and maybe it would work out. Maybe I could get something going and stay here, make it my home, again."

Noreen withdrew into her coffee. Finally she said, "Do you remember how you used to treat your sister and me when you were here?"

Frankie gave a blank stare.

"You don't remember?"

"I'm not sure what you're referring to."

"Think about it, Frankie. Take a wild guess."

"I don't know what you're talking about."

"Don't you remember punching me? And your sister?"

"Hit you and Frances? What are you talking about?"

Noreen stared at him, confused by his boyish innocence in the body of a grown man. She remembered how Frank could insist that black was white until she doubted her own sanity, questioned her own senses and experience, and was ready to accept his version of the world — even though she knew it was distorted and wrong. And now Frankie was doing the same thing.

"I'm sorry. I must have been dreaming," she said in a steely voice.

"I'm just saying that I don't remember," he began. "If you say it happened then I guess it did. I don't remember doing that. I can't picture it. I only remember being on the receiving end with Frank. The truth is, I don't have a lot of memories other than that. Like all I have of those first 16 years are memories of being beaten by him and a few snapshots in my mind of you and Frances. It's like my life started when I was 16 and living in a trailer out in the desert somewhere."

Noreen finished her coffee and wiped her mouth.

"Let me tell you something, Frankie. My mother was a drunk — like me. Only she never even attempted to get sober. She died when I was 15. I went from foster home to foster home over those next three years and at 18, I was on my own. I know what a person has to do to survive."

She looked him straight in the eye.

"When you were living at home, you turned into the enemy. It was you and him against your sister and me."

"No."

"And we grew to hate you. Do you understand?"

He shook his head as if to negate what she was saying.

"Maybe it is somehow conceivable that our relationship could change. I'm not saying it can't. But it would take a lot of time, Frankie. It's not going to happen overnight. I don't even know if I want to try. But for now? There's no way in hell I'll just accept you back into our lives. Do you understand? Both of us are fighting for survival right now. I almost died because of my drinking. I can't expose myself to that kind of stress again. I won't."

Frankie looked at her without saying anything.

"You stay in town if you want to. Get a job, get settled, keep in touch. If it goes well, maybe I'll be more trusting and feel less vulnerable. We'll see. But for now, don't expect me to open my life to you. I can't allow myself to do that."

Her son fidgeted in the booth.

"I hope you understand," she said, somewhat more softly.

He shook his head.

"Truthfully, I don't. It doesn't make any sense to me. I mean, I knew you'd be pissed at me for never calling or writing, but this other stuff, this crap about me being the enemy, I just don't get it. It's like you've got me mixed up with Frank. You think I'm going to beat you, the way Frank did? I can't believe what you're saying."

"Well," Noreen said, taking a five-dollar bill from her wallet and laying it on the table, "that doesn't bode well for the future then." She started to get up.

"Wait. Can't you at least give me my sister's phone number?"

Noreen thought for a moment. "No, but I'll do this. When you get a phone number where you can be reached, let me know. Then I'll tell her you're here. If she wants to talk to you, it's up to her."

Noreen got up.

"Ma?"

She turned.

"Thanks for coming down."

"Tell me. What happened?"

Noreen pulled out a chair at Linda's kitchen table. "It's strange. I was ready to kick him over the moon for all the pain and heartache he's caused me, not to mention Frances. And yet, there was a part of me that wanted to bring him home, give him a room, buy him new clothes. You know, become his mom."

Linda smiled. "At least you had the good sense not to act on those old instincts. I think you did the right thing. If he's really changed, let him demonstrate it over a period of time. Then you can take a chance and open up to him. But I'm with you — no way would I have just erased everything as if it never happened."

"It feels so weird having him in my life again. It's like I'm getting another chance, you know? I'm sober and he reappears out of the blue. The world's turned upside down. It's like a dream and I just woke up. It doesn't feel real."

"Don't get your hopes up, hon. Take it one day at a time."

Noreen studied her mug of coffee for a few moments. "Part of me would love for it to work out — Frankie, Frances, everything. But part of me has been so hurt that I don't know if I'm ready for any of this. I'm not sure I can do it. I know I'm not ready to relive the past."

"What do you think Walter will say about all of this?"

"Oh, that reminds me — before I left to meet Frankie, I tried calling Walter, and the assistant manager told me he had taken a personal day. He wasn't at the office. They don't even know where he is. But when he left this morning, I was sure he was going to work. I don't understand."

"Where do you think he went?"

"I don't know. I can't imagine."

"If you had to guess?"

"I don't know. Maybe he went … shopping?"

"Noreen, women go shopping. Teenagers go shopping. Men don't take a day off from work to go shopping."

"You're right," she said dejectedly, "especially Walt. Nothing is as important to him as his job."

The two women looked at each other in silence. Linda raised her eyebrows as she lifted her cup of coffee to her lips.

"I know what you're thinking," Noreen said.

"Well?"

"It's not possible."

Linda cocked her head questioningly.

"It's not," Noreen insisted. "Walt isn't even that interested in sex."

"He has a dick, doesn't he?"

"Of course he does, but he doesn't have a strong sex drive. It's not that important to him."

"Don't the two of you ever have sex?"

Noreen tried to turn away from the question. "Of course we do. Sometimes. Actually, not all that often."

Linda tilted her head and gave her a one-eyed stare.

"Well, I wish it were more often," Noreen confessed, "but Walt's just not that interested. It's silly, but sometimes I've even wondered if he could be gay."

"Well, maybe he's seeing a guy. Maybe he's got his own little boy toy."

"Linda! Stop it. That's crazy. Walt's not gay. No way."

"Maybe not. But he's not at work and it seems he gave you the wrong impression — if he didn't actually lie to you — so something's not right here. Did you try his cellphone?" Linda asked.

"He doesn't have one," Noreen said. "He's either at work or home and didn't want to be more available to the world than that."

"How are you holding up?"

"I'm shaky," she admitted.

"What about a meeting?" Linda suggested.

"Yes," Noreen agreed, "good idea."

After the meeting, Noreen shopped for supper and made sure she had a sufficient supply of non-alcoholic drinks in the house. At 6:30, she heard Walter's car pull into the driveway. A minute later he walked through the front door. She heard his usual cheery greeting.

"In the kitchen." Her tone mirrored his, although she wondered if his good mood was as false as hers.

"Cold as hell out there," he exclaimed, rubbing his hands together. "Smells good. Peppers and onions? Is that what I smell?"

Noreen made an effort to smile graciously as she offered her cheek for him to kiss.

"Yes, meatloaf, peppers and onions, and mashed potatoes."

"That sounds great. Boy am I glad you're back home."

As Noreen finished puttering in the kitchen, she found herself hoping her husband would volunteer information about his whereabouts during the day. And everything would be all right between them. She knew she would have to tell him about her meeting with Frankie, and that she had called the bank and discovered he was out for the day. She didn't want to catch him in a lie, and hoped he would surprise her with some benign explanation, something simple and natural. Something honest.

Walt sat down and spread his napkin on his lap. His cheeks seemed flushed, maybe from the cold weather. He looked good. Solid and prosperous and engaging. An All-American success.

"So how was your day?" he asked as Noreen seated herself across from him.

Unsure how to proceed, she reached for the salt, filled her glass with water, served her husband mashed potatoes. Afraid to meet his gaze, she searched for a way to elicit the innocuous explanation that would make her stomach stop quivering.

"Why don't you tell me about your day first," she said, smiling broadly. "Anything interesting?" Her eyes were wide with hopefulness.

Walt cocked his head slightly as he began loading his fork with meatloaf and mashed potatoes. "Nothing much," he said. "The usual."

She waited for him to elaborate.

"You know the bank business," he said offhandedly. "It's only exciting when something is wrong. It's good when it's routine." He took another mouthful. "So how about you? Did you go to a meeting today?"

She ignored his question. "So you didn't do anything special today?"

"No, why?"

"I had to call you at work today," she said softly.

He looked at her briefly and returned to his eating. "Oh yeah? How come?"

Noreen put down her fork. She could no longer make any pretense of being calm enough to eat. "I got a call this morning from Frankie Jr."

Walt's eyes opened wide and he rested his fork on the table.

"Wow, that's been, what? Five or six years he's been gone?"

"Six," she said.

"What'd he want? Touch you up for a loan?"

"Something like that."

"He's starving out in Colorado and needs you to send him a couple hundred?"

"Frank died."

Pause.

"What, did he get shot robbing a gas station?"

"He died of lung cancer. Last week. In Idaho. That's when Frankie decided to come east. He said he wanted to see me and Frances — and maybe settle down here."

Walter kept eating, occasionally looking up to gauge Noreen's expression.

"Did he want you to take him in?"

"He didn't come right out and ask, but I let him know that wouldn't be possible. Not yet."

"Good," he said. "I know he's your kid, but I don't want him here. I don't trust him."

"Me either," she said. "I've been through too much with him. I know what he's capable of. But it is possible that without the influence of his father, he might change." Noreen explained the parameters she had given to her son.

"Did he say what the two of them have been doing these past six years?" Walter asked.

"No. I didn't ask. Apparently they spent most of their time in the southwest."

"Whatever the two of them have been doing, dollars to doughnuts it was crooked."

Noreen had to acknowledge that was probably true. She doubted there was anything trustworthy about him. But maybe if he had half a chance …

"That ex of yours had to leave the state because of an armed robbery, didn't he?"

"Yes. That's when he left. A couple of weeks later Frankie was gone too."

They ate in silence for a few minutes. "So where were you when I called this morning?" Noreen asked.

"I don't know. Probably in a meeting. Why didn't you leave a message? I checked my voicemail."

"I wanted to talk to you, so I called the main number and asked them to find you — but they said you were out for the day."

"Who told you that?" He staring at her directly, challenging her, although his tone remained calm.

"Mr. Drackett. He said you took a personal day and wouldn't be in until to-morrow."

Walt took another forkful of meatloaf. When he looked up, he was smiling.

"It was supposed to be a surprise," he said. "I wanted to surprise you." Noreen stared at him. "I went to see a travel agent about a vacation for us. I thought maybe we could get away, someplace warm. You know, to celebrate your getting home from the hospital."

Oh! I was right and Linda was wrong. Everything is all right.

"Really?"

"I didn't want to tell you. I haven't finalized anything yet, but hopefully be-fore the end of the month, February for sure, we'll be someplace warm, relax-ing, stress free."

"Oh, Walt," her hands clasped across her breasts, "you don't have any idea how relieved I am to hear that. Oh, you're such a love." She went around the table to embrace him.

"What did you think? That I was out gallivanting, holed up in some Motel 6 with Miss Bimbo, having a matinee?"

Noreen didn't want to put it all on Linda. Walt was all too ready to criticize any of her friends.

"Well the thought did cross my mind. There's not much that can take you away from work. You always say your job comes first."

Walt was sopping up gravy with the Italian bread Noreen had put on the table in a little basket.

"It does, it does. But you run a very close second. I wanted to do something special for you, to show you how proud I am of what you're doing for yourself. For us."

Noreen relaxed and basked in her good fortune. Linda was a good friend and a very good sponsor, but her instincts weren't always right. She let out a comfortable sigh and picked up her fork. As she finished her supper, she glanced across the table at her husband. There were times when Noreen found herself comparing Walter with Frank. Physically, Frank won in a walk. He had a swimmer's body — not exceptionally tall, but lean and muscular. His good looks were what had attracted her in the first place — that and his charm and self-confidence.

Just after she graduated from college, Frank, 10 years older, was the first man she had been with. At least that's how she thought of him at the time. Compared to the boys she dated in high school and college, Frank was mature and knowledgeable. He could converse intelligently about almost any topic. She admired his masculine, decisive manner. Only later did she learn that he was a compulsive liar, a con man, a cheat, and a thief. What she had considered masterful became dominating and controlling, self-centered and selfish. It wasn't until after Frankie Jr. was born that she fully experienced his brutal anger toward women.

The first time they had sex, she had been excited by his forcefulness. There was none of the awkward tentativeness and shy fumbling that had characterized her sexual experiences with previous boyfriends. Frank took her. He ravished her. He threw her into a convertible and roared away. They fucked on beaches, in back yards, in motels, in stairways, in pools. Only after they were married did she discover that this belied a dark, angry, amoral disregard for anyone or anything that stood in the way of his own desires. Frank grabbed life by the hair and made it suck him off.

Walter, on the other hand, wasn't physical at all. Neither athletic not particularly sexual, Walter didn't demand that everything be done his way. He was considerate and thoughtful. Unlike Frank, Walt was incapable of lying and deceit — well, maybe little white lies, like today. Where Frank had been quicksand, Walter was her rock.

Cleaning up after dinner, Noreen felt exhilarated and depleted at the same time, as if she had just gotten off a roller coaster. Her first thought was to celebrate with a gin and tonic. She could almost taste the gin and quinine and lime. She shook her head to dispel the image.

"I'm going to get a soda," she announced. "Do you want anything?"

Walt seemed distracted. "Uh, yeah. Soda would be nice. Thanks."

Noreen disappeared into the kitchen, where she filled two glasses with ice and soda. She made a mental note to buy some limes tomorrow. When she returned to the living room, Walter was deep into the TV.

Four

At the time of her discharge from the inpatient rehabilitation program, Noreen had been given an appointment to begin individual therapy. As she sat in the waiting room of the outpatient clinic, she was approached by a buxom, light-skinned African-American woman.

"Mrs. Beckmeyer? I'm Tomasina Brown."

Seated in a chair across a low, round table from the therapist, Noreen studied the face of the woman opposite her. Tomasina Brown looked to be in her 50s. Her hair was strawberry blonde and freckles were noticeable on her nose. A twinkle of energy enlivened her eyes and she wore an expression of sincere interest on her face. Her tone was warm and unhurried.

"It would be helpful if I can get an overview of who you are. Perhaps we can start with where you were born and what it was like for you when you were growing up?"

Noreen took some moments to detach herself from the present and cast her thoughts backward through time. It was like looking at an old home movie of her life, or a photo album she hadn't seen in years and had all but forgotten.

"I was born in Jersey City," she began, "in 1961. It was a crowded, blue-collar industrial neighborhood. My mother and I were on welfare. I never knew my father. My mother was an alcoholic too — I mean, like me. I don't know if my father was. Probably. Seems like almost everyone my mother knew was a drunk. I didn't have any siblings. I don't know if my mother had any other pregnancies; none that I'm aware of. Sometimes, when I was younger, my mother worked as a waitress or a barmaid. As I got older, she became more physically disabled. I know she had diabetes. She got to be quite overweight. I think she had arthritis, too."

She paused while Dr. Brown took notes.

"When I was 15, my mother died of kidney failure as a result of her alcoholism. She wasn't even 40. Her body literally blew up on her. I remember visiting her in the hospital. The smell was disgusting. Everything, her arms and legs, her face, everything was swollen and huge, like cooked sausages that are ready to explode with their own juices, splitting their skins open. She was in terrible pain when she was awake, but mostly she was sedated."

Noreen shook her head recalling the scene. There was no way to convey the horror — she had actually feared that her mother's body would literally explode and spray blood and organs all over the room. She shuddered.

Tomasina looked up and indicated that Noreen should continue.

"I went to public school and was a decent student. When my mother died, I went into foster care. There were a couple of aunts, my mother's sisters, but apparently they had too many problems of their own. At any rate, they didn't want me. I guess I was still in sixth grade when I started stealing booze from my mother. Anyway, my foster parents found out that I was drinking and asked that I be removed. I had to change schools and homes a few times, but I'd always find a way to get high, even if it was only on pills or pot. But I really liked drinking. I still do. That's my problem. I think about it all the time."

Noreen smiled wanly. She knew people who didn't like the taste of alcohol but were determined to pickle themselves anyway. With her, the craving was at every level, starting with the sensation in her mouth, the yearning for the taste, that initial jolt to her nerves. Well, that's the way it was. Maybe, someday, that would change.

"What happened when you turned 18? Did you graduate from high school?"

"Yes. I graduated from high school in Paterson, New Jersey. Then I got a Pell Grant from welfare and received my associate's degree from the local community college. I went to William Patterson College for my bachelor's degree. I managed to get good grades, even though I was drunk much of the time. It was after I graduated and had a job as a sales rep for a cosmetic company that I met my first husband, Frank Petrillo."

"Tell me about him. How did you meet? What was it about him that attracted you to him?"

"It was in June 1983. I had my own apartment and was making decent money. This one night, I was at a bar flirting with everyone, when this man, older than me, handsome, comes up and slides himself right between me and some guy who was buying me drinks. I couldn't believe his nerve, busting in like that. The guy I had been talking to tried to stop him, but Frank said something and the guy shut up and turned away.

"Then Frank looked me up and down and said I was wasting myself in Paterson, that I should go with him to Manhattan, we could be there in 20 minutes drinking vodka martinis. He made me feel like I deserved more glamour and excitement than some local dive in Jersey could provide. He had a take-charge attitude and knew what he wanted.

"He was good-looking and expensively dressed — definitely not just jeans and sneakers. I thought *this is a man*. I went with him in his car, a convertible, and we zoomed across the Hudson River to New York, to some club downtown. Frank pulled me along like some little kid, calling the bouncer by his first name. And we went whooshing in ahead of everybody in line."

Tomasina looked up from her note-taking and encouraged Noreen to continue.

"Strobe lights flashed everywhere, music so loud you couldn't hear yourself think, everyone stoned or drunk. It was wild. One girl was stripping on the dance floor. Another was actually giving a guy a blowjob right there on the dance floor. I had no idea that kind of life existed. It was like Frank introduced me to another world. Afterward, he took me to the Jersey Palisades and we watched the sun come up over the New York skyline. Then he took me back to my place and we had sex like I'd never had it before."

"It sounds like you were drawn to his take-charge style," Tomasina reflected.

"Definitely. From then on, we were inseparable. After about six months, we got married. Frank told me he was a liquor salesman. Maybe he was, but now I know he robbed apartments, mugged people, held up stores. I had no idea at the time."

"Did his controlling behavior change after you were married?"

Noreen smiled wryly. "It definitely became less appealing."

Tomasina indicated that she understood. "Tell me about your marriage," she said.

Noreen described the simple ceremony in a local Catholic church. She had a girlfriend as maid of honor and Frank had a best man. That's all there was. Looking back, she saw the poverty of the wedding, but between them they'd had few friends or relatives.

"Frank found fault with everyone and convinced me that all we needed was each other. He told me both of his parents were dead and he no longer had any siblings."

Noreen told Tomasina about an incident that Frank had recounted to her after they were married. He was six, and his mother had a small birthday party for his sister who was turning four. Noreen pictured the little white Cape Cod bungalow he had described, set off from other houses at the edge of town, near a river that flooded every spring. She visualized it as run-down, with concrete steps leading up to the front door and perhaps a tricycle or other toys lying on the dried-up lawn.

Frank told her how his mother had brought out the homemade birthday cake with five burning candles, one for each year plus one for good luck. Neighborhood kids and their mothers were gathered around. Cameras must have been poised to record the moment when his sister would bend over the cake and blow out the candles. His sister wore her best party dress, and her blond curls hung down over her shoulders from under the big tissue-paper hat. As she leaned over to blow, Frank gave her a little nudge from behind, pushing her headlong into the cake.

Her hair seemed to breathe in the flames. In a flash, the paper hat was on fire. Panic. Bedlam. Screaming. The paper tablecloth and overhead decorations flared up and burst into yellow flames. His sister ran around the living room, her dress more quickly consumed by fire in the process. Smoke filled the adjacent rooms in an instant.

"She died. His sister died — and Frank told me he had stood calmly aside as if he was watching a movie and thinking how unbelievably helpless all the adults were. He knew then that he would always have to take care of himself. Adults, people, were stupid and useless, especially women. They — we — deserved what we got

"Apparently, his mother sank into a deep depression and, within a year, committed suicide. His father never remarried and finally died when he smashed his car into a telephone pole while driving drunk. I remember being amazed that when Frank told me the story, he'd expected me to feel sympathy for him. He had no feelings of remorse for what he had caused. When I said something about the tragedy of his sister dying so painfully and so young and his parents having to endure such a loss, he couldn't understand my concern for them. He said they deserved to die because they had placed so much value on a useless daughter who shouldn't have even been born. They already had an older child, him, and they forgot all about him."

Tomasina maintained an impassive face as she continued scribbling notes, but Noreen realized she was actively processing all of the information.

"Of course," Noreen continued, "I was already pregnant when we got married. I had been using birth control pills, but I was so drunk most of the time that I'd forget to take them. I had Frankie Jr. in July 1984. Frank insisted on the name."

"How did Frank respond to your pregnancy and to your giving birth to a son?" Tomasina asked.

"On one hand he seemed pleased to have a son. I'd hear him brag to other men about it. But he became more demanding. It was after Frankie was born that he told me he wanted us to meet other couples and have sex with them. I was supposed to be some kind of lure. I told him I didn't want to have sex with anyone else, and he said he wasn't asking, he was telling me what he wanted. When I protested, without warning he punched me right under my ribs. I thought I was going to die. I could hardly breathe. That's when the beatings started."

Noreen paused to catch her breath, as if she had just been hit. She shook her head. She felt so stupid and ashamed. She wanted to apologize to the sympathetic-looking woman across from her, but knew it wasn't necessary.

"I had been drinking for over 10 years by then. I hadn't matured — I still had the judgment of an adolescent. So I tried going along with Frank's wishes and even fantasized that he would be jealous if he knew someone else was having sex with me." Noreen laughed at herself derisively. "I felt like such a whore. Of course, I started drinking even more. The next year, I got pregnant with Frances. By then, Frank was slapping me around a lot. Whenever the kids cried, he beat me. If I threatened to leave, he beat me harder. If I tried to stop drinking, he'd force me to drink and then use me as a punching bag."

Pausing to let Tomasina catch up, she pictured Frank, that handsome boyish face, that easy smile. She saw it so clearly she could almost reach out her hand to caress it. Those eyes could be so seductive — and when he beat her they were hard, cold, calculating.

"He never beat me out of rage. He did it to teach me a lesson, to punish me, to control me."

Tomasina stopped writing and looked up.

"As the kids got older, he started in on them. First, it was just verbal, calling them names, putting them down. I was so used to it I'd barely notice. If I tried to make him stop, he'd take it out on me. Once I tried to leave and he broke my jaw. Another time he found out I'd called the Division of Youth and Family Services and threw me down the stairs and threatened to kill me. I'm glad he's dead."

"He's dead?" asked Tomasina.

"Yes, he died a week or so ago of lung cancer. I hope he suffered."

The therapist nodded. "I can see why you still feel that angry. But please continue. You were telling me about when the kids were older."

"When Frankie Jr. was about 12, Frank became very possessive of him. I was no longer allowed to say anything about Frankie's life, his school, his clothes, his meals, nothing. It was the males against the females. Frankie Jr. treated his sister just like his father treated me, and if I tried to stop him, Frank would beat me. Pretty soon, Frankie Jr. was beating me, too. I just retreated more into the bottle — which Frank made sure was always available. Frank could drink as much as I did without it hurting him. It was like his body was a boat that floated on a sea of alcohol and helped him reach his destination. My boat leaked and I'd sink every time."

"You felt powerless?" Tomasina asked.

"Anything I tried only made things worse. Eventually, I stopped even thinking about doing anything. I stopped thinking altogether. Then, six years ago, he didn't come home one night. I thought he was with another woman. Actually, I was grateful. But the next day, the police showed up and told me he was wanted for armed robbery. I felt relieved, like we'd been rescued. Then I found out that his record went back to when he was a juvenile. He and Frankie disappeared that day, I never saw him again. Frankie was 16. I hadn't heard from him until he turned up yesterday out of the blue, and told me that Frank is dead."

Tomasina looked up from her notes. "And what has your life been like these past six years, since Frank Petrillo has been out of your life?"

"I got a divorce six years ago, in 2000. I tried rehab a few times, but I always relapsed. Then I met Walter. We started dating in 2001 and in 2002 I moved to Philadelphia to live with him. Frances moved out. She was only 16 and I was against it, but she was staying with friends and, actually, I thought she might be better off. Walter wasn't sorry to be rid of her. Anyway, we got married in 2003. It's been rocky because of my drinking, but he's always been there for me, and this last go-round, I'd have been dead if not for him."

Dr. Brown asked about her drinking.

"This time I'm determined to do everything I can to stay straight. I'm doing a meeting a day and will do more if I need to, plus my therapy with you. But this phone call from Frankie has me scared to death. I feel like I'm a little iron filing being pulled by a giant magnet, like I'm being sucked into a giant vortex. Don't let me fail at this. I can't let myself go back to the life I had before. That would be worse than death."

They spent the remainder of the session discussing her conversation with Frankie. What was Noreen really afraid of? What did she think she might do — or not do? What alternative ways of coping could she think of? What was different between now and when Frank and Frankie Jr. were both at home six years before?

When Noreen left Dr. Brown's office, she felt calmer and less alone. She had a few minutes to kill before her AA meeting, so she decided to call Fancy. This time she was successful.

"Mom? Why are you calling me again?"

"I'm sorry to bother you. I really am, but I tried to get you yesterday and you didn't pick up."

"I must have forgotten to turn the phone off or you wouldn't have reached me now."

"Listen, I need to tell you something. Yesterday I got a call from your brother."

"What?"

"I met him in the Down Home Diner in the Reading Terminal Market."

"Why is he here?"

"Fancy, your father is dead. He died of lung cancer about a week ago. That's why Frankie came back. He has no where else to go."

"Dad's dead?"

"Yes. Fancy, Frankie wants to see you. I told him it'd be up to you if you wanted to see him."

"Of course I want to see him. He's my brother."

"Fancy, don't you remember how the two of them used to beat us? Both of us? Don't you remember?"

"How could I forget?"

"Then you may also remember that your father was a career criminal. Whatever they've been doing out west these last six years, you know it wasn't legal. Your brother has probably been living the life of an outlaw. I don't trust him. I don't want to be hurt again and I don't want you to be hurt."

"Frankie wouldn't hurt me, Mom."

"He did before."

"Yeah, well, that was because Dad made him do it. It'll be different now."

"Fancy, be realistic. Your father created your brother in his own image. If you choose to see him, I want you to promise to be careful."

"OK, I hear you. I'll be careful. When he calls, give him my number."

"No, I'll give you his number. I want you to be in control of this, not him."

"Whatever."

"I'm concerned about you, honey. I don't want anything to happen to you and I'm scared to death."

Five

At dinner, Noreen asked Walter if he'd made any progress on their vacation. "It's funny," she said, placing baked potatoes, string beans, and steak on the table, "I hadn't thought about a trip until you mentioned it, and now I can't stop thinking about it."

"Well," Walter said, cutting his steak, "I should hear something from the travel agent tomorrow. I have to see how much time I can take off, but we'll work it out."

After dinner, Noreen got ready to attend a women's AA meeting. This was her favorite group because it was small and intimate. She was nervous, but looked forward to talking about her relationships with her children in more depth than she could in the larger, more anonymous meetings. Walt was planning to run some errands while she was out. They agreed they'd have dessert and coffee when they were back home.

Walt kissed her goodbye, then watched her drive off. In his car, he called Gloria and told her he'd be there in 15 minutes.

Frankie assessed himself in the bathroom mirror of his hotel room and chose to leave his goatee and moustache untrimmed. He put on deodorant and aftershave lotion before he got dressed.

Looking down from the window at the nighttime view of central Philadelphia, he decided to go out on the town rather than call an escort service. Why pay for it if you can get it free? He slipped on his leather jacket and left his lair, a jaunty bounce to his walk down the plush, carpeted hallway toward the elevators.

While dancing, Fancy found herself wondering about her brother. She could only conjure up a fuzzy image of the skinny adolescent he'd been six years ago, when he'd left to join their father. She was relieved to hear that the bastard was dead. She hoped his death would free her from her nightmares about him. The new feeling of safety allowed her to relax, but she was also pleased for Frankie, knowing he'd now be free to be his own person. The possibilities were so liberating! Energized by her dancing, she made more eye contact with the customers, allowing her mind to explore the erotic fantasies that arose from their enthusiastic response.

Noreen arrived home from her women's group emotionally exhausted. The entire day had been consumed with re-experiencing old and painful memories — recollections she had successfully avoided by submerging them in alcohol. *I guess I didn't drown them, I only succeeded in preserving them.* More weary than anything else, she looked forward to plopping down on the sofa with Walt, having dessert and coffee, and numbing her mind with TV. Pulling into the driveway, she noticed he wasn't home yet.

Inside, she cut two slices of cake, put on a pot of coffee, and settled in front of the TV. An hour later she was beginning to worry when Walt barged in with a bag from Home Depot, complaining about long lines and slow cashiers.

Noreen commiserated with him as she got their snack. "I could have gone for you," she consoled. "During the morning, the lines aren't nearly so long."

Soon after Walt left for work the next morning, the phone rang.

"Ma, it's me, Frankie. I got a phone. I wanted to give you my number."

Noreen wrote down his number.

"Will you call Frances and give it to her?" he asked. "I'd really like to talk to her."

Noreen felt less fearful after her therapy session and women's meeting the day before. She realized intellectually that her apprehension was based on events that had taken place a long time ago. Neither she nor her children were the same people they were six years ago. Besides, now she was sober and had the support of a loving husband and a network of friends who cared about her.

It was her task to soothe herself rather than let old fears run wild and dominate her life.

"I will, Frankie. Did you find a place to stay last night?"

"Yeah," he sounded like he was chuckling, "I stayed at a hostel in Center City. Not exactly the Ritz, but it was warm and cheap. It's like a dormitory setup. But it was OK. I'm going out today to see if I can find a job. I've got enough money to tide me over for a little while."

"Good, I'm glad to hear it. I'd like to see you make it."

"Thanks, Ma. It means a lot, hearing you say that."

"Well, we'll take it a day at a time. Let me know how you make out."

"I will. And don't forget to give my number to Frances."

When she hung up, Noreen poured herself another cup of coffee and copied the number into her address book. She debated the pros and cons and then decided to call her daughter.

Even Fancy was in a better mood this morning.

"I just talked with your brother. He got himself a cellphone and wanted me to give you his number."

Noreen heard the scratchy sounds of her daughter scurrying to find something to write with.

"Honey, if you see him, please be careful."

"Relax, Mom. I'm not 14. I know how to handle myself with men. Frankie's not going to do anything to hurt me."

"Maybe you're right. I hope so. Just take it slowly, all right?" She knew better than to press further. "How's your job? You're OK?"

"My job is fine, Mom." There was a pause. "I might even be in line for a promotion. The supervisor said I'm doing really well and a position might open up as an assistant supervisor. It could mean a raise, although probably not all that much."

"I'm proud of you, Fancy. I really am. I hope you feel proud, too."

Noreen spent the next hour online researching teaching certifications. When she was done, she was confident that she had all the information she'd need to make a decision about where and how to start. She felt excited and strong. It was possible to finish the course work in two or three years, then after some supervised time in the classroom she could be a teacher. By the time she turned 50, she would be an experienced teacher. She could still have a rewarding and productive life. She made a date to meet Linda to share the news.

"I feel like I'm getting my life back," Noreen told her friend later that day. "I'd forgotten who I was when I was younger. I feel like I'm rediscovering myself, almost like meeting up with an old friend. When I was in college, I liked who I was. But not these last 20 some odd years. I haven't liked myself at all." She shuddered at the recollection.

"What are your plans?" Linda asked.

"I'm going to register for a class this summer and get my feet wet. I'm a little scared. I don't know if my brain will still work after all those years of boozing. Of course, it depends on what plans Walt wants to make for a summer vacation."

"I'm sure you'll do just fine," Linda assured her. "I'm excited for you. But why don't you plan your trip around your course? I'm sure Walt has some leeway in when he takes a vacation. There have to be some perks in being a branch manager. I don't see why you can't do both."

"You're right. I guess I'm in the habit of being at his beck and call. I never thought of it. The summer courses are only six or eight weeks, and we could do a vacation afterward." She took a sip of coffee. "Oh, by the way, guess where Walt was on Wednesday."

"I already did, but something tells me I was wrong."

"He was at a travel agent's making plans for us to go away this winter, probably to the Caribbean."

"No kidding."

"Yes. Maybe by the end of the month, or maybe in February. Isn't that great?"

"Yes it is, and you deserve it. And I guess you deserve my apologies. I'm always ready to think the worst of men."

"Yes you are."

"Well, they keep proving me right. Even this man I'm seeing now …" Linda glanced around and lowered her voice. "I haven't told you about him yet. I met him at one of the meetings about a month ago. I know, there's a rule against dating people from the meetings, but — well, he has even more years of sobriety than I do. He's pretty level headed — but he's married."

Noreen cocked an eyebrow.

"I don't know," Linda went on, "maybe that's part of the appeal. I don't think I really want to get serious with anyone again. I don't know if I'll ever be ready for that."

Noreen took another sip of her coffee and sighed.

"Linda, I have total confidence in your judgment. Having an affair with a married man usually leads to heartache, but I know you don't do anything without thinking about it first."

"Thanks. I just wanted to make the point: Here's this awfully sweet guy who seems to have his act together in so many ways, and even he's out looking for a little nooky on the side. The point is, he fits right into my concept of men."

Noreen wondered if Linda was also fitting into his stereotype of women.

"Well," Noreen assured her friend, "Walt doesn't fit into that picture. We enjoy sex when we have it, but it just isn't the most important thing in the world to him." She smiled, "It's easier to imagine Walt having an affair with a pot roast and mashed potatoes." They both laughed.

"The thing I'm really up in the air about is Frankie showing up," she told Linda. "I know Frances is going to see him." She shook her head in confusion. "I don't know, Lin, I suspect Frankie is even more like his father now than he was before he left six years ago. It's hard for me to believe they haven't been involved in all sorts of crimes. I'm scared that Frankie spells trouble and I'm worried for Frances — Fancy. But who am I to say that someone can't change?" She shrugged. "Look at you — you've been sober for over 10 years."

"And you ..."

"Well, I only have 52 days sober, but look at the changes I'm talking about. So maybe Frankie has changed. Anyway, like the people in my women's group pointed out, at least I'm different and Fancy is different and neither one of us is going to let him hurt us the way he used to."

"You're stronger now. You won't let it happen."

"I don't think Fancy will, either. I can warn her and try to point things out to her, but I don't have any control over what she does."

"Your head's in a good place, hon. You've got your eyes open and you've seen some shit. But you're prepared for it. You've got your resources lined up. I think if it becomes obvious that Frankie is reverting to form, you'll be able to do whatever you have to."

"Thanks," said Noreen, "I think so too. I only hope that Fancy will be able to." She shook her head. "I don't think she wants to see anything bad in her brother. I think she's in denial about him."

"Like you said, you can't control what she does."

"No," Noreen murmured thoughtfully, "no, I can't."

Fancy called her brother immediately after talking to her mother.

"Oh my God! " she squealed, "it's you. Where are you?"

They made arrangements to meet at Gabe's Diner, where she'd met her mother. Fancy raced through the little apartment getting ready. She scooped up a couple of Louie's uppers, then burst into the cold January air, half running the five blocks to the diner. She had considered inviting him to her apartment, but she was surprised to discover that her mother's warnings had restrained her. *No harm done in meeting him first at the diner.* After six years, she had no idea what to expect. How had he changed? How had she changed?

At the diner, she poked her head in and scanned the crowd for someone who might be Frankie. *Maybe he won't even show up.* Then she heard the hissing of a bus and saw a tall, dark-haired young man get off. She ran back outside and threw her arms around his neck.

"It's so good to see you."

"Hey, Fran. Goddamn, you look fantastic."

"So do you. You got taller."

"So did you, but you still don't have any tits."

She punched him in the arm and he laughed.

Inside, they took a booth toward the back.

"Wow, look at you," Fancy declared. "What have you been up to?"

Frankie smiled and shrugged. "This and that."

"That's all? Just this and that? In six years?"

"You know …"

"No. I don't know. I suppose I might if you'd called and told me. Then I might know."

"I know. I should have been in touch."

"You said you would, Frankie. That's what you promised me and I never forgot. I hung on to those words."

Frankie nodded.

"Then why didn't you? Six goddamned years, Frankie."

"I thought about you, Fran, I really did. It just wasn't that easy. Frank didn't want anybody knowing where we were."

"Mom said he was dead."

The waitress brought their food. Frankie put cream and sugar into his coffee.

"Yeah. He died a little over a week ago. Lung cancer." ·

"I'm glad."

"Me too."

"The bastard." Fancy looked at her brother. "How did you spend six years with him? How could you do it?"

"He was my father."

"He was mine too, but I couldn't have stayed with him. I'd have killed him — or myself."

Frankie laughed.

"What's so funny?"

"I'm just picturing that. A pipsqueak like you trying to kill Frank. It'd be like a baby going up against a grizzly."

"I'd have found a way."

Frankie leaned across the table. "Don't you think I tried?"

Fancy blinked.

"More than once," he said. "One night when he was sleeping I tried to slit his throat, but he woke up and cut me pretty bad." He pulled his shirt up and revealed a pink scar that trailed across his chest and belly. "Another time I tried to shoot him, but I missed. I hid in the woods for three days and didn't come out until I'd got bitten by a snake and was half starved and frozen. He sucked the venom out and nursed me back to health and then beat the living shit out of me."

"How did you live? What did you do for money?"

"Whatever we had to," he said slowly.

Fancy knew her mother was right. Whatever they'd been doing, it hadn't been legal.

He changed the subject. "How about you? What have you been up to?"

"I left when Mom moved in with Walter. At first I stayed at a girlfriend's, but then I met this guy, Louis. I dropped out of school and moved in with him."

"You working?" he asked.

"Of course," she said, swallowing coffee.

"Doing what?"

Fancy studied him for a moment.

"This is between us, OK? You don't tell Mom." He crossed his heart and held up his right hand.

"I'm a dancer," she told him.

"A dancer or a stripper?"

"A little of both."

"That's decent money."

"I do all right."

"And Louis, he works too? Or are you supporting him?"

"You nuts? I'm not supporting anybody. Louis has a good job with a hotel." She finished her coffee.

"How'd you like to come live with me?" he asked.

"What? Live with you? Where? How? On my money?"

"Don't be silly. Why do you think I came back?"

"What are you talking about? Mom said you came back because you had no place else to go."

"I know, that's what I told her. But what I didn't tell her is that Frank and I had a small horse farm, in Idaho. I own it now. It's beautiful. Mountains, woods, horses ...."

"The bugs, the grizzlies, the snakes ...."

"I'm serious," he said, looking her straight in the eyes.

"So am I, Frankie. No fucking way I'm going to live in the woods, sur- rounded by nothing — no music, no clubs, no shopping. What do I look like — a freaking cowgirl? Some hick?"

Frankie was laughing.

"It's not funny!"

"I'm sorry, Fran, I didn't mean to laugh at you. It's just that it's not like that at all. Besides," he leaned across the table and looked into her face. "I came back for you. I've missed you."

"You have a damn funny way of showing it," she pouted.

"I told you, there was nothing I could do. After a while, it felt like a lost cause. I stopped hoping I'd ever see you again. But inside, I kept thinking about you, kept remembering."

Fancy watched him, his loss for words, and remembered the special rela- tionship they had. "You know, I wanted to marry you," she said.

"I know. I did too." He paused, "I still do."

"Come on, Frankie."

"Seriously. That's why I'm here. I've got my own ranch. I want you to come out there with me. Fran, I need you."

"You don't need me, Frankie."

"Nobody else will ever know me the way you do."

Fancy studied him, not quite sure what he meant.

"And nobody will ever know you the way I do."

She knew that was true. "Frankie, we're brother and sister," she said softly.

"That didn't stop us before. You just said you wanted to marry me."

"That was then. I was only 12 years old."

"I thought it was more than just fucking."

"It was," she admitted, recalling the romantic visions she'd had. "But we were just kids then. And we wouldn't even have been doing it if it he hadn't forced us."

The waitress came to clear their plates and they each ordered a beer. When she left, Frankie leaned across the table.

"Then that's one thing I thank him for. If he hadn't introduced us to sex, we wouldn't have had what we had."

"I don't look at it that way. I can never forgive that fucker for what he did. He raped me. He forced me to suck him off, take him up my ass. That bastard."

Frankie looked out the window again. They were silent when the waitress brought their beers.

"I can only imagine how it was for you, him butt-fucking you like that. I re- member how you cried when you told me about it. I could kill him for that."

Frankie seemed at a loss for words. He stared into his cup.

"Did he continue doing that to you?" she asked softly.

"He never stopped, but it was different for me than it was for you. Frank had this way about him — he could make you think the way he thought, brainwash you. Eventually he made me feel like it was a good thing. Real men didn't need women, even for sex. It used to tear me up inside. On one hand, I felt used and degraded, like a freak, letting him fuck me up the ass. But I actually felt closer to him then, like I really mattered to him. And then I'd feel ashamed and then I'd feel guilty for feeling ashamed. It was fucking crazy, Fran. I didn't know what to think or feel or who I was or nothing."

"I know what you mean. I used to feel guilty too, for feeling any pleasure at all."

"How 'bout with me? Did you feel guilty for feeling good with me?"

"No. I was a kid. I thought we were in love. That's why it hurt so much when you left — and then I never heard from you. I thought I'd die from heartbreak."

"I'm sorry."

"I still love you, but it's different now. We're brother and sister. It wasn't right."

"It sure as hell felt right."

"Stop it, Frankie. We didn't realize what incest meant. It's wrong."

He hesitated. "I didn't really want to tell you this ..."

"What?"

Frankie took a deep breath and averted his eyes. "I'm not your brother." It came out as a whisper.

"What? What are you talking about?"

"Not your full brother anyway, only your half-brother."

Fancy screwed up her face trying to decipher what he was saying.

"Frank wasn't your real father, your biological father."

"Shit he wasn't."

"No. I'm serious."

"Frank Petrillo wasn't my father?"

"No."

"Then who the hell was?"

"I don't know. Frank told me that, after I was born, he and Ma used to do a lot of swinging."

She stared at him, wide-eyed.

"Yeah. He said during that whole year or two, they didn't have sex with each other at all. Every week, they'd be out banging other people. There's no way of knowing who got her pregnant with you. But it wasn't Frank."

Fancy couldn't imagine her mother having sex with anyone, let alone strangers. Yeah, she was a lush, but a straight-laced lush.

"I can't believe it," she said. "It's so unlike her."

"She's just a whore," he said, "like Frank said all along. All women are whores."

Fancy glared up at him. "Thanks for that," she snapped.

"Hey," he said, "don't blame me."

She steamed. "Then who should I blame? I was 12 fucking years old."

"I never made you do anything you didn't want to do."

"Maybe not, but that freak of a father certainly did."

They sat in silence.

"Fran, you see what I'm saying? It's not like we're real brother and sister. It's not like it's really this incest thing. All I ever dreamed about was having you out there in Idaho with me. It's like heaven out there."

Fancy shook her head and fingered her empty bottle of beer, looking around until she spotted the waitress. She yelled out and held up her bottle, indicating a refill.

"So what do you think?" he asked.

"This is crazy, Frankie. It's too much to think about. What about Louis? What am I supposed to do, just dump him?"

Frankie didn't answer.

"I can't do that," she continued. "I can't just walk out on him."

"You love him?"

"I don't know. I care about him. We take care of each other. He's a good person, Frankie. He's fucked up, but who isn't? He treats me OK. He's not like other men."

"Neither am I," he said.

Fancy pondered that for a moment. "No, Frankie, you are. You're exactly like other men, only maybe more so. All you think about is your cock."

"What else is there to think about?"

"I'm serious, Frankie. This isn't a joke to me. I deal with this shit everyday."

"That's exactly my point, little sister. That's all there is. The only difference is how good you are at it. From what you say, Louis ain't worth shit. He's not even a man. He's a pussy. If you were with a real man, if you were with me, you wouldn't have to be out there every night whoring yourself out to every Tom, Dick, and Harry." He paused and leaned forward, "Fran, if you were with me, you wouldn't have to do this shit anymore," he said more gently. "I'd take care of you. You can escape from all of this." He spread his arms wide to take in the diner, the noisy street, the dirty city, the pollution and crime and drugs and derelicts. All of it.

"Come with me, Fran. Neither one of us will ever get fucked up the ass again. Come with me. We'll be free."

Fancy stared at him. She felt the pull of his words. Was it possible to be free? Was this what she had secretly hoped for? She could give up the long hours of dancing, sucking the endless parade of anonymous cocks and faking orgasms to get a few extra bucks. Was it possible that heaven was in Idaho?

"You make it sound nice," she conceded.

"Do it, Fran. You won't be sorry."

Six

Fancy slept fitfully — dreaming, fantasizing, remembering, a kaleidoscope of stolen moments with her brother while their parents were out or unconscious. She remembered the times in junior high school when girlfriends giggled and talked self-consciously about their blooming puberty: menstruation, budding breasts, sprouting pubic hair, uninformed stupidities about intercourse and blowjobs.

All the while she felt like an experienced woman — not only knowledgeable in anatomy and the joys of sex, but in love, romantically and sexually in love with the handsomest boy alive. Her brother. But now he was no longer her brother, not really, only a half-brother. Did that make it only half wrong? Half right?

Those same memories recalled reels of images of her father — forcing himself on her, threatening her, insulting her, mocking her while he physically hurt her. But he wasn't her father. Is that why he hated her? She was somebody else's bastard. A mistake. Did that make it all right for him to use that big cock of his to beat her down, to grind her into nothingness? So many times she had longed to tell her mother, but was afraid he would kill her as he'd threatened to do. And her mother was oblivious. Or was she? Maybe she feared his retribution as much as Fancy did.

And yet it was true: Noreen hadn't protected her children. That sorry bitch. And now to find out that she was a whore too. Like mother, like daughter. Maybe that was why Fancy was a whore — because she was born that way, the result of her mother's whorishness. Just like she drank too much and used too many drugs — because her mother was a drunk.

Maybe her real father was someone her mother had loved. Maybe she was a love child, born of something positive, of some valuable impulse. Maybe

313

something would come of loving Frankie. Maybe she should let that happen. It could be the beginning of something beautiful for each of them, something good, something new, untarnished or spoiled by anything that had gone before. Starting over, a clean slate, everything brand new. Her and Frankie, mountains, blue skies, trees, horses, maybe a baby. Maybe he was right. She allowed herself to think of the two of them in her old bedroom, naked, fondling, fucking.

The alarm startled her awake. Stuffing her wispy costume into her purse, she grabbed a handful of Lou's pills and left.

When Noreen got home, there was a message on the answering machine from Walt. An emergency manager's meeting had been called — he wouldn't be home until very late. She shouldn't wait up. Disappointed, she decided to attend another meeting and grab something to eat with some of the others. It could be a fun evening after all. She thought of Linda and her new married lover — she was happy for her friend, but also worried. She didn't want Linda to get hurt.

Sometime after midnight, Fancy saw him walk into the club. She was on the pole and as soon as she saw his silhouette against the light, she knew. He stayed in the back of the room, watching her. She ran her fingers over her crotch and smiled at him, and he grabbed himself in response. She slid her finger under her G-string, then deliberately stuck it in her mouth, sucking it slowly while she gyrated, looking at him all the while, watching him nod his head.

For the next hour and a half, Frankie stayed in the background, drinking beer and watching. Then he arranged for her to give him a lap dance.

"This is weird, giving a lap dance to my brother."

"Half-brother," he interjected.

"In front of other people."

"Nobody knows. I'm just like any other lucky son of a bitch."

Fancy began her routine, removing her flimsy bra but keeping her G-string on. She felt her own wetness, sure it was obvious to the audience. Usually, she enjoyed making guys come in their pants, but this time she didn't want Frankie blowing his load. She knew they would get it on later and she had already decided that she was going to enjoy him as fully as possible. As she rubbed herself sinuously against him, sliding up and down his body, she felt tremendous pride in her body, her serpentine flexibility, the firmness of her belly and — in spite of his wisecrack that morning — the perkiness of her breasts. *Yes, he is a lucky son of a bitch.* She smiled at her brother as she thought how he would feel even luckier later on. She could hardly wait.

Seven

Noreen heard Walter come home around 1:00 in the morning, so when she woke the next morning, she slid out of bed as quietly as possible. It was Saturday, and he had the luxury of sleeping late. She took a hot shower, letting the kinks melt from her body. Fresh and energized, she put on a pot of coffee and went about preparing pancakes and bacon. She smiled, anticipating how happy he would be.

She opened the front door and retrieved the morning paper, inhaling the cold January morning. At 8:00, the street was still quiet. Relaxed and content, Noreen sat down with the paper and her coffee. A knock at the front door startled her.

"Fancy — what a surprise. Come in. I just made coffee. Would you like some?"

Fancy followed her mother into the kitchen and draped her jacket across the back of a chair before sitting down. Noreen set a mug of coffee down in front of her daughter.

"What a wonderful surprise. You haven't been here in such a long time. Did you just get off from work?"

Fancy nodded, adding milk and sugar to her coffee.

"How about something to eat? I was going to make pancakes for Walt, but he's not up yet. Would you like something? Eggs? Toast?"

"No, nothing, thanks. The coffee is fine."

Noreen wasn't sure what to say. Obviously, Fancy had some agenda. She'd just have to wait and find out what it was. She smiled expectantly and sipped at her coffee.

"I saw Frankie yesterday."

"I thought you would. How did it go?"

317

"Good," she said. "It was good. He looks great."

"Yes. He's grown up."

"He told me something." She paused. "He said he's not my brother. Not my full brother."

Noreen narrowed her gaze.

"He said Frank wasn't my father."

Noreen placed her mug carefully back down on the table. "What else did Frankie say?"

"He said Frank told him that you were swingers. That every week, the two of you would go out fucking other people and that's how you got pregnant with me. He said that you and Frank didn't have sex with each other for a year and that Frank couldn't be my father."

Noreen felt the bottom drop out of her soul. She had the sickening, sinking sensation of being in free fall, and clutched the table for support.

"It's true, isn't it?"

Noreen slowly shook her head from side to side.

"Don't lie to me. Don't fucking lie to me. It's true, isn't it? You're a fucking whore and I'm nothing but a bastard."

"No," Noreen whispered, "no, it's not true. That's not the way it was."

"You and Frank weren't fucking all of North Jersey? It's bad enough you were a drunk — you were a whore too?"

"No," Noreen said more strongly.

"Yes, we're both whores. I turned out just like you. Aren't you proud?"

"Stop it. You have to listen to me."

"Listen to what? More lies?"

"No. No more lies. What Frankie said is partly true. But part of what he told you is wrong."

Fancy sat back and folded her arms across her chest. "All right, then. Go ahead. Tell me."

Noreen's throat felt dry. She licked her lips. God, a gin and tonic or a cold beer — please. She took a can of diet soda out of the fridge and looked back at her daughter. "You want one? I don't have any alcohol in the house."

Fancy nodded.

"It's true that Frank and I didn't have as much sex during that year as we had up to then." She hung her head and glanced away. "In some ways, that was a blessing. Your father could be rough. But it's not true that we didn't have sex at all. He might be your father, but without a DNA test there's no way to be sure. He never denied being your father, even though I always wondered."

"I don't want him to be my father. It's better if he wasn't."

Noreen was confused. "I don't understand. A moment ago you seemed incensed that he wasn't your father. Now you're upset because he could be?"

Fancy threw up her hands. "I know. It's all fucked up. I'm all fucked up."

"Honey, you know I never would have engaged in that if your father hadn't made me. It's not something I ever would have done on my own."

Fancy turned away, then got up and paced to the front window. "I kind of hoped you might have fallen in love with someone."

"Yes, that would have been better, wouldn't it? For both of us."

"I hate Frank so much. When Frankie told me that I had a different father, part of me was glad. I wanted to believe I wasn't his, that I had no connection to him at all."

"Listen, you asked me what happened and I'm telling you the truth. You're a grown woman now. It's time we both started being more straight with each other. Why don't we get a DNA test? We'll get you and Frankie tested and then we'll know."

Fancy nodded.

"Can I ask you a question? Why did you say that we're both whores? Neither one of us is a whore."

Fancy's lower lip began to tremble. The logjam was breaking and all that had been stored up began to pour through.

"Because I am! I am," she cried.

"Honey," Noreen went to her daughter. Fancy let herself be embraced by her mother. "What makes you say such a thing?"

In a flood of tears, Fancy confessed to working as a dancer in strip clubs and often having sex with the customers after closing. "I've been doing it for so long," she blubbered, "I don't think anything of it anymore. It seems to be the only thing I'm good at. At least it's the only thing anyone is interested in."

Noreen's head spun. How could this be? How was it possible for her to be so ignorant of the reality around her? Could she trust any of her thoughts or convictions? Did she even know herself?

"What do you mean, you've been doing it for so long?"

Fancy looked at her mother, her brows furrowing. "You really don't know, do you?"

"Know what, honey?"

"About Dad. About Frank. Why do you think I hated him so much?"

"Because he was a rotten bastard .... Oh my God! No. Frances, you're not telling me ...."

Fancy lowered her head.

"Honey, no. Oh God."

"Do you remember the dog we had? Emma?" Fancy sobbed.

"Of course I do — the cute little mutt that ran away. You loved her so much.

We all did."

"She didn't run away."

"What are you talking about? What does Emma have to do with anything?"

"The first time Frank made me have sex with him, I was 12 years old. And afterward, he told me that if I so much as whispered a word to anyone, he would kill me. I was 12 years old. He was my father. He held me tight by the hair. He pushed his face right into mine. Then, he took a pistol from a holster he had on his ankle and he put it in my mouth. I can still taste the metal. And he stared me right in the eye and asked me if I believed he would kill me if I told. Then he pointed the gun at Emma and he pulled the trigger."

"No!" Noreen screamed. How could this be? She imagined the dog being shot, visualized blood spattering, the dog yowling, her little daughter terrified. No! It was too much! What she was hearing could not possibly be real.

"Mommy, can you believe it? The fucking bastard shot Emma. He shot my goddamned dog. He killed her. He shot her right in the head. Then he turned back to me, smiling, and he said that he would kill me and you just like that if I ever told."

Noreen was in shock. She wondered if she were going insane, if she were imagining all of this, if it were a dream. This wasn't actually be happening, was it? This couldn't be real. She managed only to stare at her daughter wordlessly, in stunned disbelief.

"My God," was all she managed to utter, the words barely escaping her lips. Finally, she turned to her daughter, forcing herself to speak, forcing herself to stay in touch with what was happening.

"And he continued to have sex with you after that?"

"At least a couple of times a week. He made me do everything."

"Intercourse?" Noreen whispered.

"Yes, Mom, he fucked me — including in my butt."

"Oh my God. You poor — I never knew." *How could I have known? Who would have thought? Is a mother supposed to consider such possibilities? Is she actually supposed to wonder if her husband is fucking their daughter?*

"I should have known."

"Mom."

Dazed, Noreen returned her attention to her daughter.

"What?"

"He was also doing it to Frankie."

Noreen wanted to smile in spite of herself. Such a serious accusation, and yet preposterous. "Your father wasn't gay, Fancy. That's one thing no one could accuse him off."

"It's true. He started having sex with Frankie when he was about 12."

"How can you say that? How do you know?"

"Because Frankie told me. When we were kids. He told me what Dad did to him. He'd come crying to me about it. He made Frankie take it up his butt."

"Oh God!"

Fancy was relentless. "Same as he did to me." She looked at her mother knowingly and saw her flustered, looking away in embarrassment. "You know what I'm saying is true."

"But why would Frankie tell you?"

"Because," she stammered, "we were having sex with each other."

"You and Frankie?"

Fancy slumped back into the sofa, sobbing. It was too much for Noreen to absorb. How could all of this have happened without her knowing? How could she have been so disconnected? So irrelevant?

"Jesus Christ," she mumbled, "if I don't drink now, I never will."

They both heard Walter coming down the stairs.

"Please don't tell him," Fancy begged, "at least not now, not while I'm here."

Noreen nodded.

"I thought I heard voices," Walter said, reaching the bottom of the stairs. He looked at Fancy's tear streaked face, Noreen's pale expression. "What's going on?" he asked. "

"We were just having a heart to heart. Girl talk."

He looked at Fran and raised his eyebrows. "Anything I should be aware of?"

"No," said Noreen, "at least, not now."

Noreen, her eyes brimming, glanced at her daughter and then back at Walt.

"I'm sorry, Walt, but I need to spend more time alone with my daughter. I think she and I need to go out for breakfast."

She turned back to Fancy. "That'd be all right with you, wouldn't it? Should we do that?"

Fancy, still sniffing and wiping her eyes and nose, nodded.

"That's what we'll do then." She turned to Walt, standing there in his robe and pajamas, barefoot. "Coffee is made. It's on the counter. I'll see you later, OK?"

"I guess so." He gave his wife a hug when she got up.

Noreen drove to the Penrose Diner. She thought of going to Gabe's but she really didn't like the place and right now she needed someplace comfortable. Seated in a booth, Noreen spoke first.

"Fancy, I'm still numb from what you've told me. I knew that I'd failed you as a mother. I've always felt so guilty about that — at least, when I was sober I felt guilty about it. But now," she shook her head incredulously, "what I felt badly about was just the tip of the iceberg. There was so much in your life I was oblivious to."

"I couldn't tell you."

"Oh, honey, I understand. I can't count how many times that son of a bitch threatened to kill me. And I knew he was capable of it."

Fancy stared at her wide-eyed. The waitress brought two glasses of ice water.

"Mom, there is one more thing I think you should know. Something that happened about two years ago."

"What else can there be? I've just heard it all."

"Not quite."

"Well?"

"About two years ago, I was working a club here in the city."

"A strip club?"

"Yeah. And guess who walked in?"

Noreen's face went blank.

"I can't imagine."

"Walter."

"What? My Walter?"

"I didn't recognize him at first. He was with a couple of other men. But after a while, while I was hanging at the bar, he came over to talk to me."

In her own mind, Noreen was devising scenarios that would explain this. Walter, in a sex club?

"He bought me a drink," Fancy said slowly.

Noreen began to feel queasy.

"After a while, he asked me if I'd do a lap dance for him."

"He what? Oh no," she moaned. "No, no."

"I'm sorry, Mom. That's why I never told you. That's why I've avoided coming over to the house. I told him there was no way I was going to do a lap dance for my stepfather. It was just too gross."

"What happened when you said you wouldn't dance for him?"

"Actually, he agreed that he shouldn't have asked. He apologized and blamed it on having had too much to drink. I asked him not to tell you that he saw me and he laughed. We both agreed not to tell. Then he went back to his friends."

"Can I tell him that you told me?"

"I guess so. As long as we're letting it all hang out."

"I hope that's all. Do you have anything else to tell me?"

For the first time, Fancy smiled. It was a pretty smile, and Noreen melted at the sight of it. "No, she said. Not now, anyway."

They left the diner and emerged into the glare of bright mid-morning sunlight. Noreen was surprised she felt as calm as she did. She knew she'd have to deal with the aftershocks of Fancy's revelations for some time, perhaps the rest of her life, but for now she felt calm.

They talked some more during the ride to Fancy's apartment. When they arrived, Noreen turned to her daughter. "You know, I've been looking into going back to school to become an English teacher."

"That's awesome."

"If I can do it at my age, there's no reason you can't think of preparing for something you'd really like to do."

"I know, Mom. Actually, I've been thinking of giving up the dancing."

"Good. You're a grown woman and I don't want to tell you what to do. I just want you to know that if you decide on school or something, I'm willing to help you. OK? It's been a long time since I felt this close to you," Noreen said softly as they embraced. "It's good to tear down walls. Thank you for having the courage to confront me."

Fancy pulled back a bit and smiled at her mother. "I had every intention of really letting you have it. I never thought we'd end up feeling closer."

"No, I didn't think it would turn out this way either. But I'm really glad it did. I'm getting a second chance with you. I don't want to lose you again. Let's not let that happen, OK?"

As she drove away, Noreen made the decision to attend an AA meeting before returning home to confront Walter.

Fancy climbed the stairway to her apartment in a more thoughtful mood than usual. She felt an atypical lightness reminiscent of joy, even though ugly memories still filled her head. As she unlocked the door, she heard music playing from the bedroom radio. "Louis, I'm home," she shouted down the hallway.

She found him in bed, dressed in a sexy nightgown and blond wig, a porn magazine in his hands.

"I've been waiting for you," he said, annoyance in his voice.

"I went to see my mother."

"No shit? You? Went to see your mother?"

"Yeah. Is that a crime or something?"

"Hey, I'm a big fan of family values. I'm just surprised, that's all. When was the last time you paid mommy a visit? When she got married?"

"Yeah, well, I had to check out some stuff with her."

"Like is she drunk yet?"

Fancy tossed her purse on the dresser and stripped off her tee shirt and jeans. She climbed into bed with Louis.

"Other stuff. Family stuff."

"Family secrets?"

"Yeah, sort of. I don't want to talk about it just yet."

Louis put aside his magazine and pulled her to him.

"And how's my mommy this morning?"

"Your mommy is very tired, Louis."

"Oh, oh, I think mommy is angry. I think Lou has been naughty and mommy is going to give Lou a spanking. Hmmm?"

"Not this morning, please. I've been up all night."

"Making lots of money fucking strangers so we can buy our dream house?"

"Come on, you know it's work for me."

"Don't give me that. I need what I need."

"And what is it you need this morning?"

"Mommy's baby needs a spanking and an enema. Am I going to get it? I have to be at work in two hours."

Fancy sighed. She thought about Frankie's offer and her mother's comments about a new start. School. She could get her GED. She could get a regular job, marry a normal guy. Or, she could go to Idaho with Frankie and start fresh where no one knew anything about her or her past. That gave her pause.

"OK," she conceded, "a spanking for my big bad baby and then an enema. But I have to tell you, I'm not sure how much longer I can keep doing this."

He sat up to take off his nightgown. "Spanky now, talky tomorrow."

When Noreen returned from her meeting, Walt was in the living room watching a football game, his feet on the coffee table and a bowl of chips by his side.

"Hi," he said. "That must have been some heart-to-heart the two of you had. You've been gone for hours."

"I went to a meeting afterward," she said, hanging her coat up. "I'd like to talk to you, if that's all right?"

Walt made a face. "This is a playoff game, hon, leading up to the Superbowl. Can it wait?"

"Not really.

Brows furrowed, Walt clicked off the TV. "All right," he said, "what's up?"

Noreen sat down on the sofa and took a deep breath. "Fancy told me you saw her dance. About two years ago."

"Yeah?"

"You say that very nonchalantly."

"How am I supposed to say it?"

"I was surprised to hear you were at a strip club. I never dreamed you'd go to a place like that."

Walt took a swig from the can of soda that was on the table next to him. He had a smirk on his face. "I'm surprised that you're surprised. Why shouldn't I go to a strip club?"

"I'm not saying that you shouldn't go, only that I'm surprised. You've never expressed any interest in anything like that — at least, not to me."

"Noreen, what do you expect? That I'm going to tell you, gee, hon, I'm going out this evening to see some naked women dance? What do you think your reaction would be to that?"

"I wouldn't like it. I don't see why you have to go outside for some cheap thrills. It's not like I've ever refused you."

"Christ, is that what this is actually about? Are you jealous?"

"Well, if you love me and I'm able to satisfy you, why would you have to look at other women?"

"Christ, I don't fucking believe we're having this conversation. First of all, that was while you were in rehab. You were away for a month, drying out. Do you remember?"

Noreen's eyes blurred with tears.

"You were gone for three weeks by then. I guess I felt horny. So when some friends suggested going out for a few drinks, we ended up at one of those so-called gentlemen's clubs, down on Columbus Boulevard. It was just a night out. It was the only time I've gone to a place like that."

Noreen thought about what he said. She could understand that, being horny and missing her and enjoying a night out with the boys. It didn't sound unreasonable.

"So tell me why you asked Fancy to give you a lap dance."

Walter closed his eyes for a moment. "I'm sorry. I was out of line on that, totally out of line. I apologized to her at the time. I don't know if she told you that. I had a few too many and I guess I got carried away by the atmosphere. I haven't felt comfortable around her ever since. I guess part of me was afraid she'd tell you. I really felt ashamed of myself. As a matter of fact, I haven't had that much to drink since then. I don't like it when my judgment gets impaired like that. I'm sorry you found out. I hope she understood."

"Well she hasn't forgotten. It creeped her out. That's why she told me. She wanted to get everything out, so there wouldn't be anything between us anymore."

"What else did she tell you?"

Noreen paused. "She told me that Frank had sexually abused her."

"What? That bastard had sex with his own daughter?"

"That's why she was so freaked out when you approached her that way. It crossed a line."

"But I didn't proposition her. I asked her to dance. That's what she does."

"Jesus, Walter, don't be so obtuse. You just admitted it was wrong. Don't go defending it now."

They both sat in silence.

"Walter, I need to know. Did you go there looking to get laid?"

"What? You think I went there to have sex with Fancy?"

"No. Just to get laid. Is that why you went there? You said you were horny."

"No," he said, "I didn't even think of that. It was just a few drinks with my friends. Sure, I got turned on, but I never thought of having sex with anyone there. I figured when I got home, I might, you know, jerk off or something, but that was about it."

Noreen looked at her husband steadily.

"Is that something you do often? Jerk off?"

Walt flushed in embarrassment.

"I'm serious, Walter. We've often gone for two or three weeks without making love. But you're telling me that one time you were horny enough to go to a strip club and then masturbate at home?"

Walter took a deep breath and looked around the room. "Why are we having this conversation now?"

"Maybe we should have had it before."

"I don't think so. I don't think you should be asking me this stuff."

"So you do masturbate."

"I didn't say that."

"No, you didn't. But you're being evasive enough for me to put two and two together. I'm not stupid, Walter."

"OK," he said, an embarrassed grin on his face, "yeah, I jerk off sometimes."

"Why?"

"Why do you think? Because I'm horny and you're not interested and I need some relief. Christ, Noreen, give me a break."

"Who said I'm not interested?"

"Well," he drawled, "like when you're in rehab, or maybe sick or something."

"You mean when I was drunk." Noreen tried to think back. "But I never refused you. I never said no."

"Maybe not. But there were other ways you'd let me know you weren't interested. You'd pass out, or you'd pick a fight, or get that look on your face."

"I'm sorry. I had no idea I put you off like that."

"Why do you think we'd go weeks, even more, without making love?"

She looked him straight in the eye. "Because I thought you weren't interested."

"What? You thought I wasn't interested?" He was incredulous.

"That's how it seemed," she said. "To be honest, I've wondered why you didn't approach me more often. I would have liked to make love more often, but I didn't want to push it on you if you weren't interested."

"You're serious? I can't fucking believe this! You're telling me that you would have enjoyed having sex more often?"

"Yes," she said, nodding her head, "of course."

Walt shook his head in disbelief.

"But even when we did make love, you weren't all that responsive. I mean, can you honestly say that you enjoy our lovemaking?"

"Yes I do. Very much."

Walt raised his eyebrows.

"I do," she insisted.

"If you say so," he allowed.

Noreen looked at him questioningly. "You couldn't tell?"

"To be honest with you — no, I didn't. I always felt like you were just tolerating it, like it was a responsibility. I never thought you really enjoyed sex or had any enthusiasm for it, at least with me. I guess I appreciated that you were willing to make yourself available occasionally, but afterward I always felt like I'd done something shameful — like I'd taken advantage of you."

Noreen got up from her chair and went to her husband. She kissed him full on the lips and stroked his face.

"I'm sorry. I guess I'm still finding out how damaging my drinking has been to the people I love. I knew some things, like your having to clean up after me or my not being able to go out to dinner with you because I was an obnoxious drunk. But I didn't realize I'd hurt you this way too. Walt, I love you so much and I'm grateful you are who you are. I'm ashamed that I haven't been able to make you feel loved. I'm looking forward so much to going away together. It'll be a second honeymoon."

Walt closed his eyes. "I love you too."

Happily humming, Noreen set about preparing a special dinner for her husband. She felt unburdened for the first time in ages. The difficult confrontations with her daughter and her husband had led to some long-overdue resolutions. The phone interrupted her thoughts.

"Noreen?" she heard her friend's voice. "It's Linda. I'm glad I got you. Are you alone?"

"No, Walt's watching a ball game. I'm making dinner. What's up?"

"Oh, Nor, I've been struggling with myself all day. I have some difficult news to tell you."

Noreen sat down. "What's the matter?" Her friend hesitated on the other end. "Linda?"

"I'm here. You remember, I told you about the man I'm seeing?"

"Of course. What about him? Is he going to get a divorce?"

"No," she said quickly, "nothing like that." She paused. "Last night we went to Jersey for dinner. He doesn't want to take a chance that somebody will see him here in Philly."

"OK ...."

"After dinner we went to a motel. I mean, we could have come back here to my place, but it was exciting, you know — a motel, water bed, mirrors, porn movies."

"I had no idea. You'll have to give me the name of that place." She imagined taking Walt there as a surprise. Just thinking about it was exciting.

"While my friend was registering, a car pulled up alongside with a couple in it," Linda said tentatively. "I thought the car was familiar, so I took a closer look. Noreen, I'm so sorry to tell you ..."

Noreen's first thought was Fancy.

"It was Walter."

"What?" Noreen lowered her voice. "Linda, are you sure?" She heard the tears in her friend's voice when she answered.

"Noreen, I didn't know if I should tell you or not. I've been a mess all day, debating with myself. I even went to a meeting and talked about it, in the abstract of course, I would never use your name, but that didn't help. People came down on both sides. Finally, I decided you had to know."

"Linda, are you absolutely sure it was Walter?"

She heard Linda sniffling. "Yes, I'm absolutely positive. I watched him go inside. Later, around midnight, I looked for his car. I took down the license plate." Linda repeated the number. It was Walter's car.

"Who was he with?" Noreen asked.

"She looked younger, maybe 30, short blonde hair."

Noreen deflated.

"Noreen? Do you want me to come over?"

"No. Not now. I'm not sure yet what I'm going to do."

Drained of emotion, she hung up the phone and sat in silence, a dishtowel still in her lap. What to do? Her brain told her to stomp into the living room, turn off the TV, and confront her husband right then and there. But her body was weak and drained. What she really needed was a drink. She pushed herself up from the chair and went to the doorway of the living room.

"Do me a favor? When the timer goes off, turn off the oven and take out the apple crisp."

"You made apple crisp?"

"Just for you," she said. "I'm going upstairs to rest a bit. I'll be down later."

"OK, no hurry. The game will be on for another hour or so."

With great effort, she climbed the stairs to their bedroom and eased herself onto the bed as if she were a delicate piece of china, easily shattered. How had she come to this? How could so many things have gone so completely wrong? As a child she had always wanted to become a teacher. She and her girlfriends used to play school on the front stoop. She could still be a teacher, couldn't she?

Noreen shook her head. How was she going to become a teacher? Be real. If her marriage fell apart, she didn't even know how she'd support herself. How could Walt do this to her? Was there anything she could trust? Believe in? And Frank, her own husband raping her children — and her not knowing! How could she be so oblivious? Tears spilled from the corners of her eyes and her chest constricted as she began to sob. Damn! Damn, damn, damn. Why was this happening?

But even as Noreen asked the question, she knew the answer. Booze. It had made her a no-show as a parent and as a wife. She had been an apparition, living life through an alcoholic haze. If she hadn't managed to kill herself the way her mother had, she had succeeded in obliterating her life and her relationships. No wonder Frank treated her like shit and her son ran away from home. No wonder Walter had gone looking for someone else. She mourned for her lost life, for the mother she had never been, for the love she had never given or received. Alcohol would numb that grief — but would also punish and destroy. She wanted it — and feared it. Was she really ready to die?

Noreen imagined Walter finding her dead body. She pictured his relief, the call to his lover, their next rendezvous, the bitch moving into her house, and the two of them making love on the very bed where she was lying right this minute. That bastard! Noreen realized then that if she drowned herself in alcohol, it wouldn't accomplish a damn thing. She'd get no postmortem satisfaction from it. Walter would not be left standing alone at her grave punishing himself with remorse and guilt. He'd be cavorting with a young blonde.

Noreen forced herself to sit upright on the edge of the bed. *I've fucked up. Now that I'm sober, I'm paying the price for the past 30 years. Everything is coming home to roost at the same time. Every act does have its consequence, doesn't it? This is what bad karma is all about.*

She stood up. Went into the bathroom and washed her face and hands. She stared at her reflection in the mirror. Put on mascara and eyeliner. Brushed her hair. *Now. It's time.*

In the kitchen, she set the table for dinner. She lit a candle and made sure to put the au jus from the roast into the gravy boat with the little ladle. When Walt came to the table, the little touches weren't lost on him. Finally, she served the coffee and the apple crisp a la mode and Walt wallowed in his contentment. He would have mooed or purred if he could. Instead, he belched and grinned happily. Noreen forced a smile.

"Walt, I was thinking about our conversation this afternoon, about your having gone to that strip club where Fancy was working."

Walt looked up warily from his coffee mug. "Yeah?"

"I was really surprised by some of the things you said, that you thought I didn't enjoy sex with you, that I didn't like you to touch me."

Walt waited for her to continue.

"I guess whenever I thought about our sex life, I remembered back when we were first dating. I guess I thought we were pretty hot then, making love on the living room floor and everything. Remember?"

Walt got a twinkle in his eye. "Of course I remember. We were hot shit then. I used to tell you that you were the best lay I'd ever had. I felt lucky to end up with you."

"Yes. I remember how flattered I was when you said that. It's why I was so surprised you thought I had changed so drastically."

Walt shifted in his chair.

She looked at him evenly, studying him. She saw how uncomfortable he was, and smiled to ease his anxiety.

"It's only now that I've been sober for almost two months that I'm finding out what I was like when I was drunk." She paused for a moment. "This morning, Fancy really gave me an earful." She shook her head in disgust. "The things that went on around me that I was oblivious to. I just wasn't there." She looked at Walt directly, fixing her eyes upon his. "I'm sorry I wasn't there for you either, Walt. I didn't know. I didn't realize."

"It's OK, hon. That's all behind us now. That's history."

"No, it's not behind us, Walt. It lives with us. It's not just part of our history, it's part of our present too. You must wonder if I'm going to relapse, when I'm going to dive back into a bottle."

Walt pursed his lips. "No," he said, "I've got full confidence in you. I know you'll make it."

She laughed. "Walter, how can you not wonder? And worry? Do you have any idea how many times each day I want to take a drink? I don't care what it is as long as it's alcohol. Beer, wine, gin, vodka, it doesn't make any difference. Every time something happens I want a drink — to soothe myself, or to celebrate, or to help me relax, or to get me going. Do you have any idea what I'm going through?"

"I know it's got to be tough for you."

"Tough? Walter, I'm hanging out in the fourth ring of hell here. And you aren't worried about my relapsing? You aren't concerned that someday when you come home from work you won't find me lying in my own piss on the kitchen floor?"

"Well, of course, it's occurred to me. But I don't dwell on it. You're sober now. I have confidence in you. I'm not worried about a relapse. It's not going to happen. I know it."

Noreen looked at him. "Then tell me, Walter, why are you fucking another woman?"

"Wha ...?"

"I asked why you're fucking another woman?"

Walt searched the table in front of him. He tried to respond but his brain short-circuited.

"The blonde? The Jersey motel last night? Walt, please be honest with me. I know you were there. I'm asking why."

She got up and poured herself another mug of coffee and offered the pot to him. He nodded and she refilled his mug. Then she sat down and settled back on her chair, communicating clearly that she was ready to hear him out.

Walt sat silently for what seemed an eternity. Silence accumulated in the room like carbon dioxide until finally the need for oxygen became so great that he opened his mouth and gasped.

"You weren't supposed to find out. I never wanted to hurt you. Her name is Gloria. She used to work at the bank. She's separated from her husband. I gave her a ride home one day. That's how it started."

"How long have you been seeing her?"

"About 18 months."

I've been in rehab three times in the last 18 months. She'd never gone more than 30 days sober at any one time. In the midst of one of her binges she'd totaled her car. It hadn't been a good year and a half.

"Do you love her?"

"I don't know. I like her. She's a nice person."

Noreen wanted to make a crack about how such nice person could be willing to screw somebody else's husband, but then she remembered her friend Linda.

"And now, she's the best lay you ever had."

At first Walter shrugged, but then he nodded.

"So you've been seeing this woman for 18 months — this nice, good woman — and lying to me the whole time, even during these past two months when I've been sober, and you have all the confidence in the world that I'll stay that way!" Her voice had risen, cresting a wave of hurt and indignation.

Walt avoided her eyes.

"Where do we go from here, Walter? What's next?"

He was unprepared for the question. Finally he said simply, "I don't know. I haven't thought about it."

"You haven't thought about it? Walter, you've been having an affair for a year and a half and you haven't thought about where you want things to end up? You've just been following your dick for all this time, letting it lead you around like a dog on a leash?"

He didn't respond.

"What does Gloria want?"

"I guess she'd like it if I got divorced and married her."

"Uh huh," Noreen uttered. "And what are your thoughts about that?"

"Well, to be honest, there were times when you were drinking that I thought about it. But then you'd be sober for a little while and I'd begin to hope that we could work things out. You know, Noreen, sometimes it got pretty bad. Life sucks when you're drunk."

He looked around the kitchen, indicating their dinner, the candle, the dessert dishes. "I can't remember the last time you did something like this. So yeah, sometimes I thought I don't want to spend the rest of my life this way. Maybe I should call it quits. I could do a lot worse than end up with Gloria. But then there'd be times when you were sober. You're different when you're sober. You're a different woman. Then I'd think maybe if I hang in, we can make it."

"You have to make a decision, Walter. You can't have it both ways."

"I know that. What I want is for you to stay sober and for us to stay together. I guess I've been hanging on to Gloria as a kind of insurance."

"I'm sure she doesn't appreciate that anymore than I do."

"I know. She's been getting a little impatient lately."

"So?"

"Like I said. If you're going to stay sober, then I want to stay."

"And if I slip up?"

"Nor, I just don't think I can do that anymore. That roller coaster ride is killing me. I've never complained. I was always there to help you." His eyes glistened. "But it's been hard. Coming home, never knowing what I'd find. This past week has been great, but I don't know if I can hang in through another relapse. Besides, another relapse will kill you."

Flashing back to her last stay at the hospital, Noreen relived the stern warnings from her physicians. She recalled how terrified she'd been at the prospect of dying — not unlike her mother — from her addiction. She shook her head in self-disgust and looked up at her husband.

"Well I'm sober now, Walter. I intend to stay sober, but it's an hour-to-hour battle. I can't give you any guarantees. If you stay, you have to stop seeing Gloria. If you stay, I think we should get some counseling. But you can't stay with me unless you agree to both of those parameters."

"That makes sense."

"Not so fast. I want you to think about it. I've got to get my act together for me — not for you. Whether you stay or go, I've still got to do my own work. I love you and I know that a lot of this is my fault, but you've got to take responsibility for your own weakness. You've got to decide what you want. So think about it."

She got up from the table and picked up her mug and then his to take to the sink, but she stopped midway and put his mug back down. She took his face in her hand and looked at him, then kissed his forehead and picked up his mug again. Walt remained sitting at the table for a few minutes while Noreen loaded the dishwasher. Then he got up and withdrew into the living room.

Noreen picked up the phone and slumped down at the kitchen table.

"Linda, it's me."

"Hi, hon. What happened?"

"Walter and I just had a difficult discussion and I could use a meeting. I was wondering if you're available or if you're going out with your friend."

Linda gave a deep-throated laugh. "Honey, you don't know much about going out with a married man, do you?" She paused suddenly, realizing what she was saying. "I'm sorry. I wasn't thinking. Sure, I'm available. Saturday nights are reserved for wives, is all I meant."

"I understand. Can I come by your place now?"

Noreen hung up and took a deep breath before getting up and walking purposefully into the living room. She sat down on the sofa and cocked her head toward Walt. He looked at her sadly.

"I'm sorry," he said softly.

"I know. Me too. I need to go to a meeting now. It probably won't hurt for you to have some time alone, either. Walt, if you decide to stay, we'll do the best we can. But if you decide to leave, you need to know that I'll be OK. You'll see. Anyway," she said, getting up and smoothing her skirt, "I'll be back later."

Eight

——◦/◦/◦——

Fancy was talking up a good-looking beefy guy when she felt a hand on her ass. She whirled around, ready to insult the creep — and found herself face to face with Frankie, a lascivious twinkle in his eyes.

"Hey," he said lightly, "can I buy you a drink?"

"Maybe later," she rebuffed him.

Frankie got himself a beer and drifted along the bar, watching the dancers.

Later, while she was on stage, she spotted him getting a lap dance from one of the other girls, and was surprised at her own jealous reaction *He better not go banging somebody else*. She focused her attention on the hot guy she had spoken with earlier. If Frankie was trying to make her jealous, well, two could play at that.

At closing time, a couple of men were hanging around Fancy, but Frankie nudged them aside.

"Sorry, guys, but I have to take my sister home."

In his car, she turned to him.

"What the hell was that all about — getting a lap dance from Dawn?"

"So you did notice," he said slyly. "I wasn't sure. I just wanted to get you hot, that's all. You know, get your juices flowing."

"Fuck you."

"Oh yeah?" he said, sliding his hand between her legs.

"Umm, that's more like it," she said, putting both of her hands into his crotch. "So where we going to do it? Here in your car?"

"Like some horny teenager? No, there's a motel just down the road."

Later, when they were resting, Frankie lit up a joint.

"I was hoping you'd show up tonight," she said.

"Never doubt me, Fran."

"Why not? I had no reason to trust you for the past six years."

"I've explained all that. It's over now."

"It's hard to forget, Frankie. We were like this once before. Then you split and I never heard from you. That doesn't exactly inspire trust."

"Come on, cut me a break. With Frank out of the picture, it's a whole new start for us." He took a deep inhale from the joint and leaned close to her face.

"Have you thought about it? Coming out to Idaho with me?"

Fancy reached up and pulled him closer. "Yes, I thought about it."

He waited for her to continue.

"I want us to get DNA tests first. I want to make sure we're not full brother and sister."

"Fran, what fucking difference does it make? Besides, I told you — there's no way that Frank is your father. No way."

"I know what you said, but I want to make sure."

"What difference does it make?"

"I don't know. It just does. It wouldn't feel right, getting married, having a family, if we're full brother and sister."

Frankie rolled onto his back and took a long drag on the joint.

"I don't fucking understand you. Here we are in a motel, but you won't come live with me unless we get a DNA test?"

"It doesn't have to make sense to you. It makes sense to me. It's one thing if we're just fooling around. It's another thing if we're going to raise a family together. That's just the way it is. I'm sorry if it puts a crimp in your plans."

Frankie stared at the ceiling. "How long does it take to do?"

"I don't know. On TV they have the results right away, but I heard it can take a few weeks."

"Fran, I can't wait around here a few weeks. I've got to get back. I have a couple of Indians watching the place for me, caring for the horses, but I can't stay away that long. Come back with me and then we'll get the tests done."

"Or I can stay here and get my test done."

Frankie thought for a moment and shook his head. "What if you decide not to leave Louis. Then what? Am I supposed to travel all the way back across the country to fuck your brains out to persuade you to come with me?"

She smiled coyly. "Would that be such a hardship?"

"I'm serious. I love you, Fran. I want to spend the rest of my life with you. Don't you want that? Don't you want to have a normal life?" He took hit and passed the joint to her.

Fancy took one last inhale and leaned over to put it out in the ashtray. He pulled her down onto him, taking her breast into his mouth.

"Come on, Frankie, quit it," she said, pulling herself away from him. "I can't just walk away from Louis."

"The creep is messed up."

"And you're not? And me? Look at us. I'm a stripper. I'm one step removed from being a prostitute, for Christ's sake. We both do way too many drugs. Neither one of us even has a high school education. And you — you haven't had the balls to tell me what you and Frank have been doing all these years. And don't fucking tell me it was anything legal, because I know better."

"Oh you do, huh?"

"You better fucking believe it." She looked over on the bedside table. "You got another joint or something?"

"Got a pint of bourbon in the car."

"You want to get it?"

"The keys are in my pocket. You get it."

Fancy gave him a dirty look, then got out of bed. She put her coat on over her naked body and slipped her boots on. She purposely left the room door open. When she came back, she had the bottle in her hand.

"Thanks for freezing my balls off," he said.

"If you were a gentleman, you would have volunteered to get it."

"Only I ain't no gentleman."

She crawled onto the bed and kneeled astride him. Pulling the covers off, she poured some bourbon onto his awakening penis. "Now, this is what I call a nightcap," she said, taking him into her mouth.

Frank started to moan as she brought him to a full erection. Then she stopped and rolled onto her back.

"Why'd you stop?"

"We're not done talking."

"You cock teaser."

"Seriously, Frankie, if we're fully related, I don't think I can move out there and live with you. We'll end up having idiots and hemophiliacs for children. So there's no way I'm going with you unless I know for sure that Frank wasn't my father."

"Fran," he said, leaning over and kissing her nipple. "I already told you. Frank swore it wasn't possible."

"But Mom said it was."

"You talked to her?"

"Of course."

Frankie pulled the covers up over his chilled body and took another swallow from the bottle. Then he waved his arm as if dismissing everything she'd said. "Well, what does she know? She was so drunk all the time, she probably didn't even know her own name."

"She's sober now, and she remembers."

"What did you expect? Of course she'd deny it. So would I if I were her."

"No, Frankie, she didn't deny it. She admitted to the wife swapping."

"No way."

"Seriously. But she said she and Frank continued to have sex too, so he could still be my father. Listen, I don't want him to be my father. And if he's not, I'll go with you. I love you. But if we're brother and sister, then, I'm sorry, I just can't do it."

Frankie rubbed his face and rolled away from her. "Fuck off," he said, pushing himself up.

"What?" she demanded.

"I can't fucking believe you'd rather stay with that baby freak than go out west with me and start a new life together."

"That's not what I said."

"You'd rather believe that whore than believe me."

"She's our mother, Frankie."

"She's not my mother. She's to blame for everything, for the fucked up losers we are."

"It's not all her fault."

"She was never a mother to you," he persisted.

"She was as much of a mother as he let her be."

"Why are you siding with her now?"

"I'm just trying to be fair."

"Fair?" he shouted. "When was she fair with us? What did she ever do for us? When did she ever protect us?"

"Don't blame it all on her. Dad was the one who handed out the punishments, not her."

"And she never protected us from him, did she?"

"Who could? Do you really think she could have stopped him from fucking you in the ass?"

"Or you."

"Or me. Do you think she could have stopped him from beating us? You told me that, even though you're a grown man, you couldn't stop him yourself."

"You don't understand."

"What don't I understand? That son of a bitch fucker lived to hurt. Nobody could have stopped him."

"She could have done something if she really wanted to. If she hadn't been a drunk."

"Frankie, he made you beat me! Don't you remember?"

"There was nothing I could do about that then. I was just a kid. I had to do it."

"That's what I'm saying. I know how much you loved me, and you did it anyway — because he made you."

"I was just a kid, Fran. I couldn't go up against him. How can you blame me for that?"

"I'm not blaming you. I'm just saying that nobody could have stopped him. It was him, not her."

Frankie picked up the bottle and took a swallow. "Maybe it wasn't all her fault. But it wasn't all his, either. He's not the monster she makes him out to be."

"Frankie, she didn't make him out to be a monster. His own actions did that."

He took another sip from the bottle. "You didn't know him the way I did."

"Thank God."

He glanced at her. "That's enough. I don't want to hear anymore."

"Fine." She got up and started putting her clothes on.

"What are you doing?"

"What the fuck does it look like? I'm tired. I need to get home."

"Already? It's not even 4:00 yet." He took another sip and smiled leeringly at her. "We have time for a quickie."

"I'm not in the mood, Frankie. Let's go. We're done here."

Church bells woke Fancy from a deep sleep. Groggily, she hauled herself out of bed to pee. On her way back to bed she glanced at the clock: 8:00. A mental image of herself as a little girl in church on Sunday morning, calm and peaceful, flickered in her mind, but the thought of getting dressed and walking to church on a cold winter morning was so repellent that she closed her eyes and dropped back into the warm bed. Lou's heavy body created a gully that she rolled down into, snuggling up against his bear-like frame, feeling safely warm and cozy.

Lou had the day off, so they had the luxury of sleeping late. It was almost 11:00 when he wrapped his arm around her. "Good morning, pussycat," he whispered into her ear.

Fancy became aware of a slight headache. She was still hung over from last night.

"You had another late night. Somebody special?"

Fancy closed her eyes. *Christ, first thing in the morning. I can't deal with this.* She turned her head saw Lou's brown eyes looking at her inquisitively.

"Lou, I just woke up. Can't we wait? You know, take a shower or some-thing?"

"Hey, I'm just asking."

She turned and looked out the window. It was gray and overcast, but at least it wasn't snowing.

When she came out of the bathroom, Lou was taking off his nightgown. She smiled at the familiar sight — Lou was big and brawny and hairy and his penchant for lingerie was so incongruous that it struck her as funny. She never saw it as perverted, the way she viewed the spankings and enemas. She saw it as an expression of the sweet and nurturing side of him.

"If you want," she offered, "I can buy you a new nightgown this week. That one is a little the worse for wear."

"I know," he said, "but I still love it. It's so sensual. I love how it feels on my body, don't you?"

"Yeah, silk is really soft. Maybe I should buy myself one too."

"You can wear mine if you want," he said, holding up his extra large gown, and they both laughed. Lou took his shower and they smoked a joint before going for brunch.

An hour later, they sat back on their booth benches, enjoying another cup of coffee.

"So," he began, "somebody special come into your life?"

"Yeah, my brother's in town."

"Your brother? Christ," he exhaled, "I forgot you had a brother. I can't re-member the last time you mentioned him."

"He was out west with my father."

Lou thought for a moment, then looked at her curiously. "Wasn't your father a gangster or something?"

"Kind of, yeah." Fancy wanted to avoid eye contact, but forced herself to look at Lou. "He was wanted for shooting somebody in a stickup."

"And your brother was with him?"

"Yeah, for the past six years. But my father died and my brother came back."

"The cops don't want him for anything?"

"Not that I know of."

Lou shook his head. "So he's back to stay?"

"No. They had a small ranch out west. He raises horses. He's got to get back there soon."

"So you're glad to see him again, huh?"

"Yeah, it's good to see him. We were real tight before he left."

"You want to do something special with him while he's here? Maybe we should take him out to dinner or something. He's your brother. I'd like to meet him. I met your mom."

Fancy grimaced. "Nooo, I don't think so," she said. "I don't think you two would hit it off."

Lou studied her. "What did you tell him about me? Did you tell him about my thing? Jesus Christ, Fancy, that's supposed to be private. I don't expect you to go blabbing about that."

"No, Lou, I didn't say anything about that, I swear. I hardly said anything about you at all, other than that you're good to me and I care about you."

Lou glared at her.

"No," she continued, "it's just that he's sort of jealous."

"What the hell has he got to be jealous about? He's your brother." Louis leaned back and spread out his huge arms. "Help me out here, babe. What are you saying?"

Fancy leaned across the table, lowering her voice.

"He came back to Philly to get me — to take me back out west with him."

"To live together?"

"Yeah," she said, a little too defiantly.

Lou scrutinized her. "What exactly does that mean?" He leaned forward. "You two, you do it with each other?"

"He's not my full brother," she said defensively.

"Oh," Lou said, nodding, "I guess that's all right then. 'Cause I was beginning to think you had some sick fucking thing going, but now it's OK. He's only your half-brother."

"It's no sicker than what you do, Lou."

Lou rolled his eyes. "So what's the bottom line here? What does it mean that this brother of yours is here in Philly?"

"Like I said. He wants me to go back with him."

"And are you planning to go?"

Fancy heaved a big sigh and her eyes welled up. "I don't know. Part of me wants to. It would mean a new start, getting away from dancing, drugs. Starting over."

"With a criminal. Who's your brother."

"We understand each other, Lou."

"And we don't?" He looked at her imploringly. "Babe, I can't make it without you. You know that. Who else is going to put up with my stuff? And who else is going to let you fuck around the way you do?"

"But I don't want to do that anymore, Lou. I don't."

"Then don't!" he shouted. Lowering his voice, he continued. "If you want to change your life, then change it. I don't make you strip. I don't make you sell your body. You want to do something different, then do it. Here. With me. I'll support you in whatever you want to do. Tell me and we'll do it."

"It's not that easy."

"Whatever it is, you think it's going to be easier out west, without any friends around? Without somebody who knows you and loves you?"

"I'd have Frankie."

"Frances, he's a criminal. He's bound to get arrested at some point. Listen, I've got a few years on you. I'm almost as old as your mother is, for shit's sake. You ain't even 21 yet. I'm telling you, you're making the mistake of a lifetime if you go with him. It'll be nothing but heartache. And I'm not just saying that because I need you and want you. I'm saying it for your own benefit. I don't want anything bad to happen to you. You're a jewel, Fancy, like a fucking diamond or something. Don't do this to yourself. If you don't want to stay with me, then at least let me help you get settled into something new."

"You don't understand. I love him. Ever since we were kids, the only thing I ever wanted was to be older so I could marry him."

"Jesus."

"It's true. I love you too, but it's not the same. I'm sorry. You know I care about you."

They sat in silence for a few minutes and then Lou asked, "When are you going?"

Fancy leaned forward and raked her fingers through her hair. "I don't know." She laughed suddenly. "I still might not go with him."

Lou looked at her searchingly. She explained about the DNA tests.

"If he doesn't do it, I'm not going with him."

"And if it turns out Frank is your father?"

She pouted and played with her teaspoon. "Then I can't do it. Part of it is, I don't want any kid of mine getting Frank's genes. It'd be bad enough having one parent passing on Frank's shit."

"I didn't know you wanted kids."

"I don't know what the fuck I want. I just know I'm not happy with my life the way it is. The idea of breaking out, doing something normal, appeals to me."

"I hear you, but running away, living in the woods or the mountains or whatever, marrying your brother — who's a fucking criminal, for God's sake — that's not normal. You want normal? Get your GED. Get a normal job. Stop stuffing all of Philly up your pussy. Get straight."

"You should talk."

"Yeah, I know. But I've got a normal job making decent money and prospects for advancement. And my sexual interests don't hurt anybody. I'm not a wanted felon. And I did try to get straight. A few times."

Lou looked at her. "For you, I'd try again. I would."

He reached across the table and took her hand. "I need you," he said. "I don't know if I can make it without you in my life."

"I know," she said and raised his hand to her lips.

Nine

Through squinty eyes, Noreen read the clock and was surprised she'd slept so well. *I must have been emotionally exhausted.* Walter had been asleep when she returned home last night. After the meeting, she had gone back to Linda's and they sat talking late into the night.

Now she wondered what she would do if Walter awoke and wanted to make love. Did she want to? She was surprised that part of her did. Even if it was going to be goodbye, one-for-the- road. If he hadn't made up his mind, then maybe she could show him she could still be hot and passionate. On the other hand, she didn't want to get into a competition with that Gloria broad. *I don't want him that way.* But if there was going to be some kind of reconciliation, a new beginning, then she didn't want to miss the opportunity.

Noreen quietly got up, went to the bathroom, brushed her teeth, and came back to the bedroom. She found Walter sitting on the edge of the bed.

"Oh," she said, surprised, "I didn't realize you were awake."

"I went to bed early last night," he mumbled.

He walked stiffly to the bathroom. Noreen watched, feeling disheartened, then slipped on her sweatpants and a sweatshirt and went downstairs to make breakfast. When Walt came down, they ate in what felt like a formal silence.

"How was your meeting last night?" he asked.

"Helpful," she said.

"Good," he replied absently.

"How about you? What did you do?"

"Nothing much," he said, "I watched a little TV, but there really wasn't anything on. So I went up early."

Walt took a deep breath and leaned forward. "I thought about what we talked about, about us."

"I hoped you would."

"Look, I know you can't give me any guarantees — I mean about staying sober." His voice trailed off.

She watched him struggle for words and the courage to say them. Holding her breath, she waited for the news she didn't want to hear. A sinking sensation enveloped her, as if the bottom of her world was dropping out. She didn't want him to see her pain. He was the one who deserved to be punished.

Finally, he looked up. "I'm sorry, but I just can't take the chance. Like I said last night, this has been hell for me. All these years I've been hoping you'd make it — and each time you relapsed, it's taken something out of me. This isn't what I signed on for when we got married. I had no idea how pervasive your drinking problem was." He sat back and turned up his hands. "I just can't open myself up to that anymore. I'm 50 years old. I don't want to spend the rest of my life holding my breath and hoping."

"So now that I'm sober, you want a divorce? Is that it?"

"You're sober *now*. But there's no guarantee you'll stay this way. It's not even two months yet."

"It's longer than I've ever gone before."

"It's not long enough to make me feel secure."

"But if you didn't have Gloria to run to, you'd probably stay, right?"

"I don't know. If it wasn't Gloria, it'd probably be somebody else. She's not the cause of all this. Things have been going downhill since we got married. You were drinking. I was unhappy. The sex was mediocre."

"So it's all my fault?"

"I didn't say that."

"That's funny — that's what I just heard. I was a drunk. I made you unhappy. I didn't turn you on anymore."

"Well, if that's what it was ..."

Noreen fought to control the sobs pushing up into her chest, ready to burst out. "You're right," she admitted. "It probably was all my fault. And maybe you're right, if it hadn't been Gloria, it would have been somebody else."

She looked up briefly before averting her eyes again. "I guess what really pisses me off is that all this is happening now. It would have served me right if you walked out while I was stupid drunk. Retribution? Self-preservation? But now that I'm sober for almost two months and finally getting my act together, making plans to go back to school, working my program, starting psychotherapy — now that I'm on track, that's when you decide to pull the rug out from under me. From us. What a fucking cruel thing to do, Walter. Your sense of timing really sucks. You know that? I may be a drunk, but you're a real shit."

The outburst destroyed her composure and she gave in to the overwhelming despair. Silently, she sought refuge upstairs, alone in their bedroom.

Walt continued to sit at the kitchen table. After a few moments, he pulled his handkerchief from his back pocket and blew his nose and dabbed at his eyes. Then he got up and put the dishes in the dishwasher. He looked around the kitchen and living room and glanced at the stairs. Then he put on a jacket and drove away.

Noreen heard him leave. Gloria would probably be relieved that he was finally free of the alcoholic wife whose apparent lack of interest drove him away. Lying on the bed, surveying the room, Noreen realized that he would be entitled to half of their belongings. She wondered what furniture he might want. She should keep the bedroom set and the kitchenware. Walt would want the TV, which was no loss to her. *We'll just have to work it out.*

Her eyes drifted to the closet. She wondered how much extra space she'd have if he moved his stuff out. Pushing aside his suits and shirts, she was surprised at all the room his belongings took up. *Jesus, he's got more clothes than I do.* She pulled over a chair to inspect some old boxes on the shelf, and was shocked to find a bottle of vodka stashed way up high. Noreen didn't remember putting it there, but had no doubt that she had. For a long time, she'd been in the habit of hiding booze all over the house, in her attempt to outwit Walt's efforts to keep her sober.

She stepped down from the chair, holding the bottle in her hands. The memory of its taste was almost visceral and the sensation made her head spin. Quickly she put the bottle down, unwilling to risk the contamination. But its presence there on the floor was mesmerizing, tantalizing. Through an act of sheer determination, she forced herself out of the room and down the stairs. There had to be a meeting going on somewhere in the city.

Frankie was already sitting at the bar when Fancy came in, her cheeks flushed red from exertion and cold. Frankie ordered her a beer.

"I told Lou about us," she said quickly.

"Jesus, I don't believe you."

"What? If I end up going with you, he has a right to know what's going on."

"Jesus, Fran, you have to learn to hold your cards a little closer. You went and told Ma what we talked about, and you tell Louis every fucking thing."

"Well, yeah. Why not?"

Frankie threw up his hands. "Because it's none of their goddamned business, that's why! You stupid cunt. Jesus, I don't fucking believe you."

"Well, excuse me," she said. "I didn't mean to upset your day. I just thought he had a right to know what might be going down."

Frankie lowered his head and caressed his beer bottle, finally taking a long swallow.

"So what'd the sick baby have to say?" he asked.

"He's upset. What do you think? He doesn't want me to go. He really cares about me."

Frankie rolled his eyes. "He's a fucking baby. You want a baby? We'll make a baby. Jesus."

Fancy furrowed her brows and stared at him as if seeing him in a new light.

"You're mean," she said. "You know that? You're a real mean prick."

"Because I don't have any respect for that creepy faggot you're sponging off of! Look, I don't have a problem with you letting a guy pay half the rent. That's common sense. But I don't understand your reluctance to leap at the chance of a lifetime. Why are you hanging on to this nothing pile of shit? I don't understand."

Fancy lifted her chin and stared down the length of her nose at her older brother. She felt a strange sense of haughty superiority. He had always been the leader, the superior, the better informed, the more knowledgeable. But for the first time, she felt like she'd drawn abreast of him — and maybe, a step ahead.

"No, you really don't, do you? You really have no idea what he and I have built up over these past three years. He's been good to me. He takes care of me. So he's got a fetish or two. Who hasn't? You should hear some of the sick shit I put up with almost every night. He's a good person, Frankie — so no, I don't want to hurt him. And I won't." She paused to let the veiled threat sink in. "And you haven't told me if you're going to get that test done."

Frankie lowered his eyes and glared at his sister. Stalling, he went to the bar to order two more bottles and slid one across the table to her.

"I'll take the damn test. But I can't hang around here for the results and I won't go back without you. Come with me. We'll get tested out there. You'll get a chance to see the place, how wonderful it is. If you don't like it and you decide you don't want to stay, you can come back. What am I going to do? Tie you to a tree?"

"You'll do that? You'll take the test and if it comes out that we're fully related, I can come back?"

"Of course you can come back. Christ, Fran, you're a grown woman. You've been on your own for four years. Don't you know yet that you can make up your own mind?"

"Of course I do. It's just that …"

"What?"

"I didn't think you'd let me go once I was there."

"You're a piece of work, you know that? Listen, we've loved each other forever, right? I want you to be happy. This test is bullshit as far as I'm concerned. I already know how it's going to come out. But if you don't love it out there, I'll be shocked. Even this time of year, with the snow. Fran, it's so soft and powdery, not like snow out here. It's beautiful and quiet, the pine trees and the deer and elk."

Fancy looked at him and smiled. "You make it sound beautiful."

"It is beautiful. And together it'll be even better."

"I had a girlfriend go on the Internet for me and look up the DNA test. We can send away for a kit and the results come back in a week."

"There you go. We can go out there and within a week you'll know what I know. Then it's just a matter of whether you want to stay and be happy in paradise or whether you're fucked up enough to prefer to come back to this shithole."

"You're sure?"

Frankie shook his head. "Don't fucking go pushing your luck. I said so, didn't I?"

"OK," she said, tentatively. "I can tell Lou I'm only going for a visit, to check it out."

"Good. I'll get tickets tomorrow."

"Frankie, could you buy a return ticket for me now, so I'll have it just in case?"

Frankie sighed in exasperation. "Jesus, Fran, I'm paying your way out there. I'll pay for the goddamned test. But the tickets are nonrefundable. If I buy you a return ticket, which is a few hundred bucks, and you don't use it — which I don't think you will — then it's just a fucking waste of money. Fran, I'm so certain that you're going to love it out there and want to stay that I promise you, if you really want to come back, then I'll pay for the ticket. But I don't want to do it ahead of time. You understand?"

"But you promise, if I want to come back, you'll buy the ticket?"

Frankie crossed his heart and held up his right hand.

"OK," she said. She thought for a moment, "How about Wednesday? This way, I can go to work tomorrow night and tell them I'm taking a week off. And I'll have all day Tuesday to get ready."

"Cool," he said, clinking her beer bottle with his, "Wednesday it is. Fran, you've made me the happiest man in the world. It's a dream come true, us being together again."

"I hope so. This is such a big step for me, leaving everything. I tell you, Frankie, it's scary as hell."

"Don't worry. There's nothing to be scared of. You'll see."

Noreen emerged from her AA meeting into a cold, gray afternoon. Still feeling shaky, she called Linda but got her voicemail. Beginning to feel desperate, she called Fancy.

"Fancy? It's me. I'm here in Center City. I was wondering if you're free, if we could get together."

"Sure," she replied, "I'm down here too. I just bought a sweatshirt and a pair of wool socks."

Relieved, she made plans to meet her daughter at a nearby coffee shop.

"I'm glad you were available," Noreen began. "I'm feeling a little shaky today."

"Where's Walter?"

Noreen smiled wanly. "That's why I'm feeling shaky." She reached into her purse for a tissue and blew her nose. "I found out last night that he's been having an affair for the past year and a half. Can you believe it? I had no idea. They say a woman knows, but I had no idea. None at all."

"What a prick. I never liked him. What's going to happen? You guys going to split up?"

She told Fancy about her conversation with Walter, the demands she had laid down and his concerns that she'd relapse again.

"It reminded me of the conversation you and I had. In two weeks I'll be turning 46 and I'm finding out what a complete failure I've been my whole life." She shook her head in disbelief. "Now that I'm sober, I have some clarity about how oblivious I've been. I was a ghost. I could see you when you were growing up, but I wasn't there. I was no support to you at all."

"Mom, that's all in the past."

"No, let me finish. It was the same with Walt. I didn't know it until last night, but I wasn't there for him either. I didn't make him feel loved and wanted, just like you didn't feel loved or wanted. No wonder he found somebody else to love him and make him feel like a man."

"I always knew you loved me."

"You did?" Noreen asked in surprise.

Fancy gave a short laugh. "Yeah, I did. Not that it was much use. I couldn't count on you for anything and eventually, I learned to ignore you. But the way you'd look at me or hold me, I could tell. I still wished you were a better mom, but I knew. It was different with Dad. I never felt like he cared about anything or anybody — only what he wanted, when he wanted it. God, I'm so fucking glad he's dead. I hope he burns in hell."

Noreen nodded and reached across the table for Fancy's hand.

"I have some news too," Fancy admitted to her mother. "I'm going out west with Frankie."

"You're what?" Noreen was flabbergasted. "You can't be serious."

Fancy slumped in her chair. "I thought you'd be excited for me. If it works out, I'll be out of the sex business. I thought you'd be glad."

"I don't understand. How can you go with Frankie? He has no job, nothing."

"He does — he and Frank had a place in Idaho, a ranch. They raised horses."

"He told you that?"

Fancy nodded excitedly.

"And you believe him?"

"Why wouldn't I? He described it — the mountains, the pine trees, the soft powdery snow."

"Fancy, do you even know where Idaho is?"

"Who cares? I'll find out when I get there."

Noreen stared at her questioningly.

"Frankie came back here to get me. We love each other. If the DNA test proves Frank's not my father …" her voice trailed off.

"And if Frank wasn't your father, then what?"

Fancy shrugged. "Then maybe I'll stay."

Noreen wanted to throttle her. "Let's take this one step at a time. I'm a little confused by all of this. Frankie told me that he had no place to go, that he was staying in a hostel here in Philly until he could get a job, maybe settle down here. Was that just a story?"

"I guess so. For some reason, he didn't want you to know his plans."

"So he has no intention of getting a job and staying here?"

"I don't think so."

"Why would he lie about that?"

"I honestly don't know."

"And what about Frank being dead?"

"That part is true."

"How do you know?"

"Mom, I wouldn't be going if there was a chance in hell that Dad is alive."

"What about Louis?"

Fancy looked down at the table.

"You're just going to leave him?"

"I told Louis about me and Frankie. We're leaving on Wednesday. I'll tell Louis that I'm going out for a visit and I'll probably be back in a week or so. That's how long it takes to get the DNA results. That'll give me enough time to see if

I like it."

"And if you like it and if Frank's not your father, then you'll stay there with your brother?"

"Half-brother," she corrected.

"Fancy, half-brother or full brother, it doesn't make any difference. It's still wrong and you know it."

"What have we ever done that wasn't wrong? So people say it's wrong. Who cares? It doesn't change how we feel about each other."

Noreen took a deep breath. Her daughter had a point. Who was she to be moralistic?

"Did Frankie tell you how they've survived all these years?"

Fancy made a face that communicated a resigned *no.*

"Aren't you curious? You know what kind of scum Frank was. Don't you want to know who Frankie is now? He's no longer the 16-year-old boy you thought you loved. Aren't you afraid he might have become more like Frank?"

"Of course I am. We just haven't had time to talk about all that stuff yet. But when I'm out there, I'll have time to figure everything out."

"Don't you think you should have those discussions now, before you leave? Fancy, you have no idea what you might be getting into. I'm afraid for you."

"Mom," she said, reaching across the table to touch her mother's hand, "don't worry. I'll be fine. Look, it's all set up. Frankie is buying the tickets and I know how to take care of myself, believe me. Relax."

Noreen sat back and sipped her coffee. *Could anybody have stopped me from marrying Frank? From going off with him that first night and bringing him home after being out all night?* She saw that Fancy was not to be dissuaded. She had her mind made up. She was young, immature, and had only a narrow and perverted perspective from which to view the world. There was no way Fancy would be able to see beyond her passion, and lecturing her wasn't going to help one bit.

"OK," she said, "I can see that you're going to do this, but humor me for a moment, all right?"

"Sure."

"Let's imagine you're out there in Idaho and something happens, something unforeseen and you need to get help right away. Maybe you're socked in by a blizzard or something."

"OK."

"How are you going to call for help? The telephone lines might be down. He might not have any neighbors. Do you know for sure that your cellphone will work out there?"

Fancy raised her eyebrows. "I just assumed it would."

"Well, I know almost nothing about these things, but I know they don't work everywhere. I want you to promise me two things."

"OK," she said.

"First, find out if your phone will work out there and if it doesn't, get one that will. I'll pay for it if it's necessary."

"I promise. I'll look into it today."

"Thank you. The second is, don't let Frankie know you have it. I know you trust him and you believe everything is going to be fine — and I hope you're right. But if you need anything, I want you to have a way of contacting me or the police or whoever. You understand?" Tears were in her eyes as she pleaded with her daughter.

"Yeah, I understand. That's cool. I can do that."

Noreen was determined to be as good a mother as she could, even if it was late in the game. "Now, do you have enough money?"

"I've got plenty of money," she assured her mother. "I've got a savings account."

"How much are you taking with you?"

"I don't know, I hadn't thought about it." After a moment, she asked, "How much do you think I should take? Frankie said he'd buy me a return ticket if I wanted to come back."

Noreen gave her daughter a cynical look.

"Again, just in case, I'd bring $500, not larger than $50s, and a credit card — and don't let Frankie know you have that either. It's only in case of an emergency."

"You're beginning to make me nervous. You and Louis are so worried. You don't think I should trust Frankie at all."

"There's no harm in being cautious. Now, when you arrive at the airport, will you call and let me and Louis know you've landed safely?"

"I'm not stupid, Ma. I see where this is going. If you have to send the police to rescue me, they'll know where to start looking."

"Louis is going to worry about you as much as I will," Noreen said. "Don't leave us hanging. We both need to know you're all right."

"I understand. I'll call. Don't worry."

Noreen studied her daughter. Although the face had changed, she could still see remnants of the little girl running after her big brother. She remembered their exuberance, their wild, non-stop energy. And she recalled a wily cunning about Frankie that made her uneasy. She often had the feeling — although nothing she could put her finger on — that he was getting away with something. It was easier to get close to Fancy, and the guilt of that reality persisted even now. Once Frank effectively prohibited her from having an active role in raising

Frankie, an emotional distance grew until she felt no connection to him at all.

Driving home, Noreen realized that even though she was concerned about Fancy, she was basking in their newfound closeness. *And I didn't think about Walt or booze the whole time.* That brought a smile to her face.

Linda called just as Noreen walked into her house. Noreen told her about Walt's decision to leave and about her afternoon with Fancy.

"I can't believe it, Lin, that she's impetuous enough to run away with him like that. She thinks she's in love. I don't think she has any idea of how sick this whole thing is. And I can't get rid of the feeling that somehow I'm responsible."

Linda reassured her that Fancy and Frankie were adults and had to assume responsibility for their own behavior. Then she suggested that maybe Noreen could call the police to see if there was a warrant out for Frankie's arrest.

Noreen was in the kitchen reading the Sunday paper when she heard the front door open.

Walter.

He looked at her tentatively. "We should talk, Nor."

Is that what we should be doing? Talking? About everything we did wrong, about all our missed chances. Lost opportunities.

"I don't want to go raking the coals, Walt. What's done is done. I'm not interested in a post-mortem. Our marriage is dead. We killed it."

Walter nodded. "But we do have to talk about what's next for both of us."

Noreen stared at him coldly. "All right, tell me your plans. I assume you'll move in with Gloria."

"Noreen, this was my house before we got married. I lived here for 15 years. Why should I move out?"

"Why? You carry on an affair for a year and a half, you fuck around, you want a divorce, and I'm the one who has to move out? So you can move that 'nice person' into my bed? You son of a bitch! You fuck!"

"Calm down. Hear me out."

Noreen crossed her arms and looked away. Walt spoke softly to her. "I know that under the law you're entitled to half of everything we own and that certainly includes the house. I'm willing to buy you out, pay you your share of what it's worth."

Even as she stewed, she heard logic and fairness in what he proposed. She stole a glance and saw the sincerity on his face. She hated to give him any credit, but he was being respectful. Noreen realized this was all very real. Her marriage was at an end. She recognized that she had nurtured a slim hope that they could put it back together again, but she now understood: The marriage was a corpse and the house a mausoleum. She had participated in the murder and now it was time to plan the burial.

"I'll call a lawyer tomorrow and we'll do whatever we have to do," she said flatly.

"Thank you," Walter said. He offered some suggestions of how they might divide the furniture and agreed that he'd have to pay her alimony. "I'll stay with Gloria until you get a place and I'll continue to pay the bills until we have a final agreement, but I think it would be helpful if you could move out as soon as possible."

Suddenly Noreen felt herself filling with sorrow. The finality of it. The profound sadness, the guilt and remorse, the grieving for what was and what might have been. Total desolation.

"I'll go upstairs to pack some things," he said. "If it's all right with you, I'll take both of our suitcases." He looked at her questioningly.

Their suitcases, the ones they had so much fun buying when they started traveling together. Only two trips so far: Vegas and Florida. The Caribbean would have been their third. So much for plans. She felt that familiar urge and remembered the bottle of vodka lying on the bed.

"Let me go upstairs first and go to the bathroom and put a couple of things away and then I'll go to a meeting. I don't want to be here to watch you pack up and leave."

She had an image of watching him carrying suitcases out the front door. She thought of her neighbors getting an eyeful, having lots to gossip about. Noreen licked her lips. They were chapped and her throat felt dry. Only her eyes were wet. She went upstairs and put the bottle in one of her drawers, then left for a meeting.

Ten

Noreen woke at 2:00 in the morning. The room was dark and chilly. Hoping to drift back to sleep, she was plagued by images of her son. Sitting across the table at the diner, his handsome features reminiscent of his father, the soulful eyes, the boyish smile. How could she not have seen what was going on between her children? *If Frances was 12 and Frankie Jr. was 14, then I was only 37. God, to have obliterated myself so completely by that age.* Yet, even as she reproached herself, she knew that Frank had played a major role in grinding her down into nothingness, barely a shadow. And yes, she was complicit in her own destruction.

What was Frankie really like? He must have some redeeming qualities. If Fancy was so in love with him, there must be some goodness, some hope? Maybe, after she called the police in the morning, she'd find out he had no criminal past. Maybe everything would turn out all right. And what if Frank wasn't Fancy's father? Maybe that did make a difference.

In the morning, Noreen dressed to brave the gray, blustery day. Snow flurries swirled as she climbed the steps to the police station, cigarette butts and wind-blown papers underfoot. Glancing around the gloomy lobby, she saw three or four officers lounging at their desks behind a big glass window. Noreen approached and a young officer spoke to her through a speaker in the glass.

"My son came back into town a few days ago. He's been gone for six years." Nerves building, she wasn't sure how to proceed. The officer's cool professional attitude didn't help her to feel more at ease. In another life, long ago, she had gone to the police to report Frank for domestic violence, but was frightened out of it.

"Anyway," she continued, "he spent those six years with his father, Frank

Petrillo Sr., who is still wanted, I think, for an armed robbery." She paused and took a breath. "I'm afraid that my son, who's 22 now, may have also been involved in some criminal activity. Is there any information you can give me?"

"I'm sorry, ma'am, but we're not allowed to do that. Your son is an adult now and I can't provide any information on him."

"You can't? But suppose he's wanted for some violent crime? You can't ..."
He shook his head.

"No, ma'am. I'm sorry. The only way I could look him up would be if he were standing right here within my grasp. Then, if I looked him up and there was an outstanding warrant, I could arrest him. But without his being right here, I'm not permitted to look him up."

Noreen hung her head in despair. She had been sure the police could tell her if Frankie was wanted or dangerous, so she could warn Fancy, stop her. Now what could she do? She felt like a lost child, unsure of where to turn.

"You can try a private investigator," the officer told her.

She sighed in resignation and turned away. A private investigator. Where would she find a reputable one? They had such sleazy reputations. When she got home, she decided to call Walter. Maybe the bank had occasion to use a private investigator. Even though he was leaving her — or rather, kicking her out — she was sure he'd be willing to help if he could.

Monday morning Fancy woke to the smell of coffee and bacon. Lou was making breakfast for her. She felt bad leaving him, even if it might only be for a week. But she didn't really think it would turn out that way. She expected to stay in Idaho with Frankie. She pictured it: snow-capped mountains, flawless blue skies, green pine trees, horses running through meadows of grass and wild flowers. It would be paradise, just like he said.

She yawned and stretched, rubbing her hands over her body. She liked how her body felt, firm and smooth. She caressed her breasts, appreciating how solid they were, how responsive her nipples were. She was excited by the idea of seeing Frankie again tonight. And in 48 hours or so she'd be on a plane. Actually flying. Both excited and nervous, she was grateful that Frankie would be with her to show her what to do.

Lou came into the room wearing a heavy terrycloth robe over his nightgown, his favorite blond wig on his head.

"Good morning, sleepyhead. Your breakfast awaits."

"It's so nice to have a wife who takes such good care of me," she said.

"Well, don't forget it. A good wife is hard to find."

Louis stood in the doorway, spatula in hand, staring at her naked body as she made her way to the bathroom.

At their Formica table, she let Lou serve her — juice, coffee, toast, scrambled eggs, and bacon.

They ate in silence, then Fancy spoke. "I've decided to go to Idaho with my brother."

He sat back on his chair and his body drooped. Fancy heard the air go out of him, as if he'd been punched.

"When are you leaving?" he managed to ask, unable to look at her.

"Wednesday," she said, keeping her tone light.

He lowered his head again and wiped at the corner of his eye with a finger. Then he picked up his dishes and dropped them in the sink with a clatter. Fancy startled at the sharp, crashing sound. Bracing himself against the sink, Lou tore the wig from his head and threw it on the floor. Fancy's eyes welled up. She knew it would be like this. Hurting Lou was the one thing she hadn't wanted to do — and yet here she was.

"It's only for a visit," she said weakly. "I'll be back in a week. I promise." Her lip quivered and she began to cry.

"Yeah. Sure," he mumbled, without turning.

"I will," she repeated, more urgently. "I swear it."

Lou's broad back expanded as he took a deep breath.

"Don't," he whispered. "Don't say things you don't mean. Please."

"I'm so sorry. I am. I don't mean to hurt you. Really."

He went into the bathroom and closed the door. Fancy sat alone at the table. Eventually, she picked the broken shards out of the sink and dropped them into the garbage. How many more things would she be responsible for breaking?

When Lou emerged from the bathroom, Fancy rose to embrace him. His body stiffened. He mumbled some unintelligible words and then got dressed, leaving with only a perfunctory "see ya." The door closed behind him and it was the end of the world. What could she do? Bring Lou with her? Despite his brawny size, she could envision Frankie beating the crap out of him. And Frankie would do that, wouldn't he? He could and he would. Frankie did have that mean streak in him. But he could be sweet and loving too.

When Noreen returned home after the disappointing trip to the police station, she called Walter at the bank. His secretary said he was busy and that she would take a message for him. He called back in a half-hour and she told him what she was trying to do.

"The police can't do anything, but they said I could get a private investigator."

Walter interrupted her. "Noreen, I'm sorry, but I simply cannot talk to you about this now. I'll drop by the house after work and we'll talk about it then."

"Walter …" but he hung up.

The prick. She felt like calling him back, but knew she'd be blocked by his secretary and there was no sense yelling at her. She'd just have to wait until 5:30.

Noreen spent the rest of the afternoon in a meeting and talking to Linda. She longed to talk to her therapist as well, but her appointment wasn't until Thursday and Fancy would be gone by then.

At 5:30, his car pulled up. Noreen expected him to ring or knock, but instead, he let himself in, peeled off his hat and gloves, and removed his coat. *Just make yourself right at home, why don't you?*

"Thank you for coming," she began.

"Sure," he mumbled, "now what's this business about a private investigator?"

Noreen explained her quest to find out if Frankie was a criminal. "I'm concerned about Fancy. I don't trust him. Even as a little boy, there was something about him. He was never a normal child. I need to find out if he's ever actually done anything bad."

"Then what are you planning to do? Send the cops after him?"

"At least I can warn her. At least I can tell her the truth. She's so blinded by her passion for him, some sentimental notion that theirs is the love of the ages, that she can't see what she's doing."

"All right," he said, "when I get in tomorrow, I'll see what I can do. Maybe we have somebody on retainer. I'll look into it."

"Thank you, Walter. I appreciate it. I feel like I just got her back into my life. I don't want to lose her again."

"Listen," he said, "I have a favor to ask you too."

"What's that?" she asked warily.

He hesitated. "Gloria's place is a little snug. I'm living out of the suitcases there."

He saw her eyebrows flare up.

"I know. It's my own doing. I'm just saying, I'll appreciate it if you can be expeditious in finding a place and moving out."

Noreen's jaw dropped. "Christ, Walter, you've been gone — what? Less than 24 hours and already you're complaining that I'm not moving fast enough?"

"I know you need time. It's just that …"

"Things are a little snug."

"Yeah," he said, "I'm just saying, it'd be a favor if you didn't put it off, you know?"

"OK," she said, "you'll be expeditious and I will be too. Agreed?"

"Agreed."

Frankie showed up after midnight to drive Fancy home, but he made a detour.

"I wanted you to see where I'm staying," he told her. "And I bought you a present."

Fancy scanned the spacious room. There was no denying it was first class, but she'd been in fancy hotel suites before. Still, she was impressed that her brother could afford this. She spotted a new suitcase on the bed along with some wrapped presents, but was distracted by a knock on the door.

"Room service?" she cried.

"Why not? It's practically our last night on the town. Why not live it up? I got us some champagne."

"You had it all arranged?"

"Don't be so surprised. Nothing is too good for us. I've been waiting six years for this. It's time to celebrate."

Fancy felt overwhelmed. He was doting on her. It wasn't just their sexual passion — he really cared about her happiness. She turned to hug him and before she knew it, his hand was on her ass, pressing her to him, grinding his pelvis into hers.

"Whoa," she said, disengaging from him, "don't I get to open my presents first?"

"Sure," he laughed, giving her ass a squeeze, "you do that and I'll open the champagne."

Fancy wasn't used to receiving presents, especially ones wrapped so elegantly. The first box contained winter boots.

"You'll need those where we're going," Frankie said knowingly. "These are the best. They'll keep your feet warm and dry no matter what."

He poured two glasses. "To us," he said, "forever."

"To us," she repeated, "forever and ever." She untied fancy ribbons and opened package after package — a shearling vest, sexy pajamas, thermal underwear. She put all of her new goodies into the new suitcase to bring home.

Home. She banished the thought of Louis from her mind. Nothing could interfere with feeling wonderful. She and Frankie drank more champagne and made love. Louis was still asleep when she got in, and he left before she awoke in the morning.

Fancy spent Tuesday preparing for her trip. One concern was where to hide a stash of Lou's pills in her suitcase, afraid that her luggage might be inspected at the airport. Following her mother's advice, she purchased a cellphone that would work in Idaho — assuming she was within range of a transmission tower. She also withdrew some cash from her account and found a hiding place. After lunch, she called her mother to say goodbye.

"I sure hope you know what you're doing," Noreen said gravely.

"Don't worry, I'll be fine. I got a new cellphone, like you suggested, so I can call you from there."

Noreen asked for the number. "I want to hear from you as soon as you land. Do you know what flight you're taking?"

"I don't know the flight number. Frankie has the tickets, but we have to be at the airport real early."

"Do you know what airline you're flying on?"

"Sorry, Mom. Frankie might have told me, but all those names sound the same to me. I'm letting him handle everything. But I'll call you as soon as we land. I promise."

"You're spending tonight with Frankie?"

"Yeah, since we have to leave so early in the morning, it'll be a lot easier."

"How did Louis take the news that you're leaving?"

"I told him I'm only going out for a visit, so he's fine with that."

"I'm sure he's going to worry, so please give him a call too. OK?"

"Of course. Are you kidding? He'd die if I didn't call him."

Noreen hadn't said anything about her efforts to discover if Frankie had any warrants out for his arrest. She knew that would only upset her daughter. At least she had her daughter's cellphone number. And how many airports could there be in Idaho, anyway? Still when they had said goodbye, she had a feeling of doom. Maybe she was just being an overly anxious mother making up for years of neglect, but she had a nagging dread that she might never see her daughter again.

On impulse, she called Walter at work. Voicemail. *Christ, wasn't he ever at his desk?* Finally, at 6:00 that evening, when he hadn't returned her call, she put her coat on and went to a meeting.

Later that night, Noreen sat curled up on her sofa. The TV was on, but her thoughts were elsewhere. Concerned about her daughter, she was furious that Walter had not lived up to his promise. She decided to take her own sweet time looking for an apartment. Screw him!

Just then, the phone rang.

"Noreen, it's me, Walt."

"Well," she drawled, "a voice from my past."

"I'm sorry I couldn't get back to you earlier today."

"Are you?" she said sarcastically.

"Yes, I am," he insisted. "I had business to take care of and I just got back. But I promised you I'd look into that private investigator business and I did."

"Thank you for being so expeditious."

"Anyway, there's a firm in New York that our main office keeps on retainer. If you want, I can give you the name. I'm sure they're reputable and can do the job easily enough."

"You might as well. It's a little like closing the door after the horses have left the barn, but yeah, give me their name and number."

After giving her the information, Walter asked her how she was holding up.

"To tell you the truth, Walter, I'm so upset about Fancy that I haven't spent two seconds dwelling on what a shit you are." She imagined him grimacing. "Don't worry," she said, "I won't forget about getting a lawyer and finding a place to live. Probably, it'll do me good to have something to keep me busy so I don't think about it too much."

There was an awkward silence that seemed to stretch on. Finally, Walter wished her luck and said goodbye.

Eleven

After hardly sleeping, Frankie and Fancy left the hotel Wednesday morning and took a cab to Philadelphia International Airport. Fancy wore her new silk long underwear under her outfit, as well as her new boots and shearling vest. The airport was unfamiliar and exciting, but also bewildering and chaotic — long lines, cars, taxis, vans, limousines, piles of luggage, tugging children. At security she had to take off her shoes and jacket, and empty all her pockets.

She held Frankie's hand as he led her through the maze of corridors. At their gate, she studied the television screen that displayed the flight information: a mishmash of numbers and symbols that made her eyes glaze over. A sign behind the lectern said: Northwest Flight 685 to Minneapolis.

"Frankie, look at that sign. Are we in the right place?"

Frankie smiled and put his arm around her. "That's just our first stop. You don't think they have a direct flight straight to Idaho, do you?"

His remark made her feel stupid.

The hour passed quickly as she observed the other travelers. There were so many ugly people: girls with blotchy skin and frizzy hair, guys with no chin or a huge nose. She felt proud to be with Frankie. She was sure they made a handsome couple and that people were envious. And old people! Older than her mother or even Walter, old enough to be her grandparents — if she'd had any. Others were returning from vacations all over the world. She could tell from their tan faces and the souvenirs they carried. She asked Frankie where else he had flown.

"Mostly around the west," he said. "Usually we would drive. Frank had a big-ass Cadillac. But sometimes we'd fly to California or Seattle or Vancouver — that's in Canada — or down to Texas or Mexico."

"Wow!" she said, impressed at her brother's level of sophistication. She felt keenly aware of how small her own world had been, where going to Atlantic City was a major trip.

"So what were you and Frank doing that you traveled so much?"

"For a while, Frank got back into liquor sales," Frankie said casually. "He had to use a different name of course, but getting new identities was never a problem. Then he was in commercial real estate for a while, and then oil and mineral rights. Then, about a year and a half ago, he won this ranch in a poker game in Vegas."

Frankie laughed at the recollection. "We've been there ever since, until he died. Winning that ranch was the best thing that ever happened. It's so peaceful and real. You know what I mean? There's no bullshit. There's no con, no lying, nothing false. Just the horses and the weather and the clean air. No pollution. No horns honking. Just stillness."

"I'm sure it's beautiful, but it sounds like it could get a little bit boring. What do you do for excitement?"

"Go hunting," he said simply, "or fishing, or ride a horse up into the hills, or read, watch TV, go to the bar just down the road a bit. Drink, listen to the jukebox, shoot pool, dance."

Fancy thought about that. She didn't want to feel like a prisoner out in the wilderness. She was a city girl — being a Girl Scout had never been on her list of priorities.

"Tell me about the ranch," she said, snuggling up to him.

"Well, let's see. We have the main house. It's a big, two-story log cabin with a wide porch around three sides. In the living room, there's a big stone fireplace, but we also have a wood stove to heat the house. Chopping firewood is another major pastime," he said, laughing. "Downstairs, there's a living room and kitchen. There are lots of windows so the sun comes in all day long and you can see the mountains all around us. Even in the summer, there's snow on the tops of some of them. The deer come right up to the house sometimes."

Fancy was wide-eyed.

"Upstairs, there are three bedrooms and a big, big bathroom. You'd be amazed how warm and snug these log cabins can be. It's more comfortable than a regular house."

"What about the property?"

"Well, there's the barn and stables. We have six of our own horses and we board another half dozen or so. So there's always work to do, mucking out their stalls and feeding them."

"Sounds like great fun," she said, wrinkling up her nose. *Cleaning out stalls? I don't think so. Chopping firewood?*

Frankie saw her look of disgust. "Don't worry about the work. I'm not expecting you to break your back. I've got a few guys from the local reservation who do all of that and are glad to have the opportunity to earn a few bucks. Besides, they're great with the horses." He grew pensive for a moment. "Maybe that's one of the things I love about it, Fran. I just took to the horses. It's like I've got a natural talent with them or something. For the first time, I felt like this is what I was born to do."

Fancy thought about that. She was happy he'd found something that made him feel whole. *The only thing I seem to be good at is sucking cocks. But maybe there's still hope. Maybe this new beginning will give me a chance to find something that makes me feel good about myself.*

A woman at the lectern was making an announcement, but Fancy had trouble deciphering the garbled words. Frankie picked up his bag and stood up. "We'll be boarding in a couple of minutes," he said.

Soon the plane slowly backed away from the gate and sat on runway, idling. Then the engines roared and the whole plane began to shudder and vibrate. She stole a glance at Frankie and, for the first time, she felt nervous. Suddenly she was thrust back into her seat as the plane raced down the runway. When she looked at the hangers some distance away, it didn't look like they were moving that fast, but then she saw the runway rapidly disappearing under the plane. Smoothly, silently, they left the ground as if simply stepping up into the air. The front of the plane veered up at a steep angle and she had to strain to lean forward to look down at the city sprawling outward as far as she could see. After a few minutes they were above the clouds — above the clouds! — and nothing more could be seen of the city they had left.

Frankie held her hand. "You have no idea how happy I am to be bringing you home with me, to be able to see you every day, go to sleep with you next to me, wake up with you in my bed. I love you so much."

Fancy grinned. "I love you too. I always have."

The thought of them being entwined on a daily basis was delightful to her too, but her excitement was tinged with a hint of worry. She'd never been much of a homemaker; Lou had actually seen to most of that. The idea of having her own home with Frankie appealed to her, but she wondered what he might expect of her in the way of cooking or cleaning — not exactly her strong suit. And the ranch itself might be visually spectacular, but she wasn't sure if she'd take to living in the boonies.

"Frankie, how far is the ranch from the nearest town or city?"

"There's a little village, where the bar is that I told you about, just a couple of miles down the road. I mean, you could walk there in 30 or 40 minutes, which I've done plenty of times. There must be half a dozen small towns within 20 miles or so, and the nearest big city is probably a little over 60 miles. Don't worry about it. You're not going to be isolated. Civilization is just over the mountain, that's all. You'll see," he said, patting her hand, "you're going to love it."

Noreen woke in a panic. In her dream, Frances was a little girl, alone in the woods and being chased by a tiger. She ran screaming "Mommy, Mommy," but Noreen was thwarted at every turn in her attempts to rescue her daughter. *It seemed so real.* She lay in bed, her heart racing. *Well, it doesn't take a shrink to figure out what that's all about.*

About 8:30, Linda called to see how she was doing. Noreen told her about the investigative firm Walter found for her.

"I'm waiting until 9:00 to see if I can find out anything, although, even if I do, she's already out there with him."

"Hopefully, all your worrying will be for nothing," Linda said optimistically. "Maybe the worst will be that she discovers her childhood fantasy doesn't stack up in the light of day and she'll be home again before you know it."

"Wouldn't that be nice," Noreen said wryly.

They made plans to meet for lunch and to go to a women's meeting in the afternoon.

Noreen poured herself a mug of coffee and dialed the investigative firm in New York. After being on hold for a minute, a man named Matthew Garrett got on the line. She explained what she hoped to accomplish and he assured her he'd be able to help. He asked for all the information she had on both her ex-husband and her son, as well as a physical description of both Fancy and Frankie. Mr. Garrett thanked her and said he'd call her back as soon as he had anything at all.

Noreen felt relieved, as if Mr. Garrett would make everything all right. Whatever he found out would give her a sense of clarity and resolution. Maybe everything would be fine, as Linda and others had suggested. But even if Frankie was wanted for some horrible crime, she'd be able to contact Fancy on her cellphone. Noreen felt lighter than she had in days.

They were in the air only a short while when the flight attendants started serving drinks and snacks. Frankie ordered a vodka on the rocks for each of them. Fancy was grateful. She'd taken some of Lou's pills early that morning but now she felt a little antsy. The drink would take the edge off. With the first sip, she remembered sneaking drinks when she was still in fifth grade. She leaned back and looked out at the endless cloud layer below her. She didn't know what all the fuss was about flying. It was boring. She glanced at Frankie. He'd already drained his drink and was reclining back, his eyes closed. He looked so sweet and boyish.

As a boy he'd had a thin and hairless body. She remembered thinking he was cute. They had always been close and she had always admired and loved him. Then, one time when they were playing a game together, he suddenly put his hand in her crotch. The next thing she knew, he had taken off his clothes and was undressing her. She recalled how he had wanted to stick his boner into her butt and she had to show him how to fuck her the right way, the way Daddy did. She had almost been glad that her father had introduced her to sex because now she knew how to make Frankie happy, to make him love her forever. She glanced over at him. And here he was, back in her life and all hers. Fancy could hardly contain her joy.

From time to time, thoughts of Louis popped into her mind, but she was determined not to dwell on him. *He'll be fine. He only wants someone to spank him and pump shit up his ass.* But images of him that last morning kept slipping back into her mind and she felt sad in spite of herself. When they landed she'd definitely call her mom and Louis. It was the least she could do.

Noreen and Linda were sitting in the Penrose Diner when it started to snow. Over the course of their lunch, it became heavier and steadier.

"The main thing I want to know," Linda was saying, "is how you're doing with your sobriety."

"I'm OK, Lin, honest. I mean, I think about it all the time. I get angry at Walter and want to take a drink just to spite him, as if it would actually hurt him." She shook her head at the absurdity of her thinking. "Then I realize it would only confirm for him that he made the right decision. And I imagine his little whore saying 'I told you so, Walter.' That makes me all the more determined. I won't let them win. I'm not going to be the loser. But then I think of Fancy, flying out to Idaho to live with her brother. Christ, I must have been really fucked up to raise a son and daughter who think incest is the best thing since white bread."

"Noreen ..."

"I know. It wasn't just me, maybe not even mostly me. Still they're my kids and as adults they don't see anything wrong with what they're doing. It's crazy. Then I wonder what kind of crap Frankie Jr. might have been mixed up in these past six years with that psycho father of his, and I start worrying what he might do to her. I keep remembering how he used to beat the tar out of her when they were younger."

"Unfortunately, they're adults. There may not be anything you can do about it."

"Right, so I need to stop thinking about it. I need to hide, blur it all out. I'm drinking so much soda and coffee lately, trying to drown my urge for booze, I feel like I'm going to float away." She sighed. "But so far, I've been able to stay sober."

"I'm proud of you, Nor. This past week has been hell. You haven't even been out of the hospital two weeks yet and look at all you've had to put up with. To tell you the truth, I'm in awe. I'm impressed by your determination. You're a hell of an inspiration. I've been sober for over 10 years and I don't know if I could handle all that you have these past 10 days."

Noreen blushed. "Thanks. That means a lot coming from you. You have no idea how much help you are to me."

Linda turned to look out of the window. "Look at the snow coming down. If we're going to make that meeting, we should get going."

A soft bell rang and the pilot informed the passengers and flight attendants that they would be landing soon. Frankie told her to set her watch back an hour. Central Time. It was just mid-morning, yet she felt like she'd been up all day.

After they had collected their luggage, he led her out into the freezing air toward the long-term parking lot.

"What are we going outside for?" she asked, confused.

"We're spending the night with a friend of mine. He wanted me to pick up something for him in Philly and bring it to him. He left his truck here so we could drive out. We'll spend the night at his place and tomorrow he'll drive us back to the airport."

"Jesus, Frankie, I thought we'd be in Idaho today. After all your talking, I can't wait to see the ranch. Our ranch."

"I wanted to surprise you. I figured it would be an extra treat for you to see a little bit of Minnesota."

They headed for a rusted-out pickup truck and Frankie brushed snow off windshield. He retrieved a key from a magnetic box under the fender and started it up.

"Christ, it's fucking cold. I hope this heater works," she said, shivering.

"Give it time to warm up," he said. "Relax. We'll stop for lunch in an hour or so."

"OK," she answered, "I'm getting hungry."

As they left the parking lot, she remembered her promise to call her mother and Louis. *Maybe when we stop for lunch.* Frankie drove through downtown Minneapolis, and she marveled at the skywalks, which allowed people to walk from one building to another without having to go into the cold. Then he found the interstate and they headed north.

They stopped for lunch about an hour north of Minneapolis. Fancy was starved. While waiting for their order, Frankie went to the john and she took out her cellphone and noticed with dismay that the battery was completely dead. She looked up to find Frank standing over her.

"Who are you calling?"

"I promised Mom I'd call her when we landed, but my cellphone battery is dead. I'll go get a charger," she said, starting to get up.

"Wait," Frankie said, reaching across the table to restrain her. "When we get to my friend's, you can use his phone. Believe me, it's no problem."

Noreen was sitting in an AA meeting when she felt her phone vibrate. She looked to see who it was and felt a surge of excitement when she saw the New York number. She hurried from the room to answer.

"Mrs. Beckmeyer?

"Yes, Mr. Garrett?"

"I have some preliminary news for you."

"What have you found out?"

"I don't have anything on your son, Frank Petrillo Jr., yet. I'm still checking, but so far there are no outstanding warrants for his arrest. However, there are a number of listings for your ex-husband, including the one from Pennsylvania. Mostly, he's wanted as a suspect in a number of scams and forgeries throughout the whole western part of the country. But he's also wanted for questioning in a couple of hold-ups and a possible rape."

Noreen closed her eyes. *Oh, no.*

Matt Garrett continued. "Your ex used a number of aliases and I'm checking out those names as well. It's possible your son went by an alias as well. One other bit of bad news: In two of the hold-ups and in the rape, there was a second, unidentified white male accompanying the suspect. It's possible your son was an accomplice."

"It's what I was afraid of," she sighed.

"I'll continue to check out these aliases as well as search county courthouses for bench warrants that haven't been included in the national database. I'll let you know what I find out."

She thanked him and hung up. Sitting limply on a bench in the hallway, surrounded by wet coats, boots, and umbrellas, she felt an arm around her shoulder. Suddenly Noreen's eyes filled up and she buried her head in Linda's shoulder.

"That was the private investigator," she said at last, still trying to catch her breath. "Frank is wanted for questioning all over the west — fraud, scams mostly, but also for armed robbery and," her voice grew unsteady, "rape and assault."

Linda said nothing.

"There was a second man with him, probably Frankie. It had to be. Frank would never trust anyone else. God, Linda, rape and assault and armed robbery? Who knows what else they've done? I've got to try to reach Fancy."

Noreen clutched her phone in her hand the whole time. She looked up Fancy's new cellphone number. No answer. She left a voicemail. "Fancy, I've got some bad news. It's about Frankie. There are warrants out for Frank's arrest. Fancy, it looks like they both are wanted for rape and assault and armed robbery. Please be very careful and call me as soon as you can. I love you."

Driving north into the Minnesota woods, Fancy was surprised to see so many signs with French names. She commented on it to Frankie, but he just shrugged.

What a sourpuss, can't drive and talk at the same time? She leaned over and turned the radio on, but all she got was static. "Christ, what a shithole this place is. I'd sure as hell hate to be stuck out here. Just a bunch of dead trees. Doesn't anybody live out here?"

"It is pretty isolated up here," he acknowledged. "Lots of hunting and fishing, but not too much of anything else. There's not much farming, the soil's not so hot. Hardly anybody lives up here."

"We have much further to go?"

Frankie looked at the odometer. "About another 150 miles. It'll probably take us about another two and a half, three hours. We should get to Snake's place about 4:00 or so. It'll still be light."

"That's your friend's name? Snake? How'd he get a name like that?"

Frankie laughed. "He did it the old-fashioned way. He earned it!"

Despite herself, she got caught up in the contagion of Frankie's fit of laughing.

"What did he do?"

Frankie laughed and shook his head. "He's just evil. What can I say? The name suits him."

"That's fucking great. You bring me a couple of hundred miles into the wilderness, the middle of nowhere, to some crazy freak with the name of Snake? How fucking romantic. I'm glad it's only for one night. I can tell you, Frankie, this is not the way I pictured Minnesota and it's not the way I pictured our first night out here together."

In part, she had in mind an illustrated book she had read as a little girl about an Indian named Hiawatha and the land of Gitcheegoomee that was filled with pint-sized Indian children and Walt Disney animals like Bambi and Thumper — not this endless gray stretch of dark woods. *Three more hours, Christ!* She curled up and tried to sleep.

When Fancy woke up, they were turning onto a two-lane highway. They passed an occasional dairy farm or rundown gas station, but otherwise, it was the end of the world — uninhabited and uninhabitable.

"Where the fuck are we?"

"About another 35 miles, I figure. We should be there in under an hour," he said, flicking her a smile.

"I have to pee," she said. "Can we pull over?"

"You're going to just squat down by the side of the road?"

"Why not?" she asked. "There's nobody crazy enough to be out here except us. Who's going to see?"

"You're right," he admitted and pulled over. "I've got to go too."

He pulled over and they both got out. Frankie lofted his stream out into the snow, while Fancy pulled her pants below her knees and made a steaming yellow puddle below her.

"Christ," she exclaimed, "it's freaking cold. Don't let your dick freeze off or I'm going back to Philly for sure."

Back in the truck they rode in relative silence. The sky slowly turned a darker gray and the depth of the snow along the sides of the road gradually deepened. Fancy dreaded the ride back to Minneapolis the next day — especially if they had to squeeze three people onto the seat, one of them an evil creep named Snake.

She shuddered to wonder what was so bad about this asshole that her own brother avoided telling her anything about him. Frankie passed an abandoned gas station and, after a couple more miles, pulled off onto a rutted dirt road. He crept along, the two of them being jostled about. Fancy thought that if it weren't for the seat belt, she might be thrown out of the truck.

"Jesus," she said, "where are you taking me, Frankie? Is there much more of this?"

"Don't worry," he said, "it's only another couple of miles along this road."

"Has this guy got bad breath or something, that the rest of the world stuck him way out here away from civilization?"

"Actually, Snake has a meth factory."

"What? He makes speed?"

Frankie smiled. Fancy thought about it. Speed! They could load up on the stuff. "No shit?"

"No shit," he said, "he's got quite a set-up. Only about 50 miles from the Canadian border. There's nobody around for miles and miles, as you've seen. He makes meth and he has a still where he makes some great whiskey and he grows a little pot in the summer. He's doing all right."

"So we're planning on getting high tonight?"

Frankie smiled again, but he kept his eyes on the rutted road in front of him and both hands on the steering wheel.

"I thought you'd be pleased," he said.

"Well, it does compensate," she said. *Christ, to live in this hellhole, you'd have to be high all the time.*

After another few miles, Frankie stopped the truck and went to the side of the road. She watched him approach a metal gate, which he unlocked and swung aside. Then, getting back into the cab, he turned onto a lane hardly wide enough to accommodate the truck. After locking the gate behind him, he drove along the winding trail for about 15 minutes until she saw three old beat-up trailers and a dilapidated two-story house. He parked next to an old sedan half covered in snow.

They climbed out of the truck into the darkening gloom. A light was on in one of the trailers, but everything else was dark. The air was damp and cold, as if it would soon snow. She was surprised that they had electricity way out here. She had never seen anything so isolated. The only sound was their footsteps in the frozen snow.

"This is it," said Frankie. "The end of the trail."

Fancy gazed at her surroundings. It looked abandoned, haunted. The stillness, the emptiness was eerie, as if everything had died. The only sign of life was the dim light in the trailer.

"Where's your friend?" she asked tensely.

"Probably in the trailer. Why don't you go on and I'll get our stuff from the truck."

"You want me to help?"

"No, you go on. I've got it."

Reluctantly, Fancy started toward the trailer, grateful that there were no dogs or animals of any kind. Tracks led between the lighted trailer and the other two, but the snow around the house seemed undisturbed. In the growing dusk, the house looked rundown and abandoned. As she approached the trailer, a shadow moved behind the curtained door. Slowly it opened and she saw the outline of a tall, thin man. Fancy looked back and noticed Frankie taking their suitcases from the bed of the pickup.

The man waited for her to approach, so she walked up the trampled path leading to his open door.

"Hi," she said, "I'm Fancy, Frankie's sister."

"Yes," he said, his voice full of amusement, "I know who you are." He flicked a switch and the light over the door went on. Fancy looked up into a gaunt and bewhiskered face.

"You're ... Snake?"

The tall man made a deep, whiskey-throated, raspy sound. "Frankie likes to call me Snake. But you, sweetheart, you don't have to call me that."

Fancy heard Frankie crunching up behind her in the snow, carrying a suitcase in each hand. She deliberately waited for him. There was something about this old geezer's familiarity with her that made her feel uncomfortable. She wanted Frankie with her.

"So," Frankie said, "you two have made the introductions?"

"Not completely, my boy," said the man. "I've been waiting for you. But now that we're all together again, Frances, I want to welcome you to our home."

At first, Fancy thought Snake was just being hospitable, but then it dawned on her. She looked at Frankie, her eyes wide in disbelief, searching for reassurance. The old man was laughing. What a great joke they had played on her. Why wasn't she laughing? She looked back up at the man, past the unkempt beard and unruly hair, into the cold, sardonic, laughing eyes.

"You!" she shouted, turning back to Frankie.

"Come on in, Frances, your brother and I have been waiting for a long time. We've both missed your sweet body. Haven't we, son?"

Twelve

On Friday, Noreen received another call from Matt Garrett. He still had not found any record of warrants out for Frank Jr. However, there were two tickets for Wednesday morning's Northwest flight to Minneapolis in the name of Francis Petrillo Jr. and Frances Petrillo. But the trail ended in Minneapolis. There was no trace of them after that. Matt said he was checking rental cars and public transport, to see if he could locate them. Also, he found no death record for Frank Petrillo Sr., or any of his known aliases.

Noreen hung up, dread now enveloping her. Fancy had been gone for two days and neither she nor Louis had heard from her. Now, the trail led to Minneapolis. Why Minneapolis? She checked her voicemail obsessively, but there were no messages. What had happened?

Noreen stared across the kitchen table at the bottle of vodka as if gazing upon it would yield wisdom or insight. Certainly not hope. Nothing good could come from that bottle. If it stood for anything, it stood for self-centeredness and self-loathing. Noreen smiled at that. Self-loathing and self-indulgence, the Pisces of depression. She was depressed. That had been confirmed yesterday by Dr. Brown. At Tomasina's suggestion, a psychiatrist had prescribed an anti-depressant. That was supposed to make her feel OK about her life? That was supposed to erase the pain that came with remembering what kind of mother she had been? What kind of a wife to Walter? What kind of a foster daughter she'd been? Answering sincere efforts at love with deceit and stealing?

Today was her 60th day sober. Would she finish the day that way? Did it matter? Was there any reason to continue the fight? She wondered if her fate had been sealed at birth. Maybe she was destined to die like her mother had, imploding on self-loathing, with all her inner, putrid rottenness oozing out of her. Maybe that was an appropriate and fitting ending.

The phone rang.

"Mrs. Noreen Beckmeyer?"

"Yes."

A detective on the Philadelphia police force asked if she was the mother of Miss Frances Petrillo, also known as Fancy Petrillo.

Her heart stopped beating.

"Yes."

"We're trying to locate your daughter. Her roommate, Mr. Louis Ukowicz, died of a drug overdose. He left a note for your daughter, an apparent suicide note. Do you know where she is?"

"No," said Noreen, stunned. *Louis killed himself?* "She left with her brother on Wednesday morning. Apparently they went to Minneapolis. I've reported her missing. Her brother is a wanted criminal."

She felt the tears welling up in her eyes, the sobs building in her chest, the loosening mucous in her nose. *Funny how the body wants to empty itself out at a time like this. Perhaps I should take a good shit too.*

"If it's all right with you, I'd like to come over and ask you a few questions," the detective said.

"Can you bring the note with you? I'd like to see it. Maybe you can tell me more about how he died, in case I hear from my daughter."

And in that moment, Noreen knew she'd never talk to her daughter again. She was as good as dead, just like Louis.

The bottle on the table stared back at her. *Well, maybe after the detective leaves.* Upstairs in the bathroom, she regarded herself in the mirror. In two days, she'd aged 10 years. When was the last time she had showered? *Yesterday. I showered yesterday.*

Noreen was slipping into sweats when the detective arrived. He asked her about Frances and Louis. She told him everything she knew. He told her about the bowl of pills at the bedside, about Louis' body dressed in a nightgown and wig. Did she know anything about that? Noreen shook her head. No, she didn't know anything about that. Finally, he showed her the note.

"I have to keep it," he said, "but you can make a copy of it if you need to."

She read the note. It was addressed to Fancy and at the bottom it gave Noreen's name as Fancy's mother and her phone number. In his simple hand, he told Fancy he loved her, that he knew she'd never be back and he couldn't imagine life without her. That was all. He had been alone in the world. Fancy was his only connection and she had cut the cord on him.

Thirteen

Fancy lay in bed at the back of what was now her trailer. She huddled under the blankets, chilly despite the kerosene heater. The radio was playing some stupid cowboy music on the only station she could get, but at least it was company of a sort, better than nothing. Sometimes Frank or Frankie brought her meth or weed. She'd been here a week. Frankie had apologized for his deception, but he didn't actually think what he'd done was so bad.

"I really love you," he said. "I thought you'd be glad to see him after all these years. He's your father. I didn't think you'd mind."

Hadn't Frankie heard her at all? Even now, when she'd complain to him about Frank treating her like property, forcing himself on her just the way he used to, he acted as though he didn't really believe her.

"Come on, Fran, you were born for sex. Don't deny it. You love it. Sure, it's better with you and me than with anybody else. But I know you. A cock's a cock. It don't matter whose it is. If you could take on all those horny bastards in those dives you worked, you can handle Frank with no problem."

So the week had passed with her servicing Frank Sr. — in addition to Frankie — knowing better than to put up too much resistance. Just lie back and be quiet. If necessary, think of something or someone else — although actually, she had gotten off a few times.

From the moment she'd stepped into Frank's trailer, she'd been plotting her escape. But they'd confiscated her boots and heavy clothing, and all she had were jeans, light socks, tee shirts, and a couple of light sweaters. Frank and Frankie had taken her cellphone, her money, and her credit cards. There was no way she could go into the woods with all that snow, the freezing temperatures — and the possibility of wolves and bears — and survive.

Besides, she knew that if she tried and failed, Frank would beat the shit out of her. He might even kill her. He told her as much that first night.

"We're awfully glad to have you here with us," he said. "But don't go getting any ideas of having the run of the place. Unless one of us is with you, you'll stay in your trailer. Get me?" He looked at her hard. "One step out of line and you're finished."

Since then, she'd only been out of her trailer to go to Frank's, where they ate. Each time one of them had been with her, giving her boots and a jacket to make the trip and then taking them away when she got back to her little trailer.

She'd thought of playing her brother against their father, but she now knew she couldn't trust Frankie as far as she could throw him. Sometimes Frank would leave to meet his contacts and sell the meth. Sometimes he'd send Frankie to buy supplies. When that happened, Frank was usually in the third trailer cooking up the meth. It seemed that her best chance would be when she was alone with one of them. But best chance at what? If she tried to disable one of them and escape, she'd better do it right or else she was dead.

On the other hand, Fancy was not confident that if she were a good little girl, everything would turn out roses. From snatches of conversation, she had the impression that with spring, they might change locations and move on — and she wasn't sure she was in their plans. She feared Frank might kill her. She wished she could talk to Louis or her mother. Why hadn't she listened to them?

Fancy heard the door open and looked down the short passageway. The heavy footstep told her it was Frank, even before she saw him. He turned and latched the door from the inside and then stood for a moment surveying the small kitchenette, the four-person booth that could be quickly changed into a bed. When his eyes met hers, he raised his eyebrows.

"Well?" he said.

"Well what?" she countered.

"Come on, Frances. It's almost lunchtime and you've still got your clothes on? Is that any way to treat your one and only pops?"

"I'm sorry. I didn't know you were coming, pardon the expression."

Frank stood in the doorway, a smirk on his wild-haired face. "Just for being a smartass, that's where you're going to get it." He started to remove his jacket and gloves. "Come on, honeybunch. Assume the position and let's get this over with. I've got things to do."

Fancy bit her lip, lifting her sweater over her head and sitting back on the bed to remove her jeans. She left her socks on. Her father kicked off his boots and dropped his jeans to the floor. Fancy turned onto her stomach and raised her butt into the air. Despite herself, she got aroused and almost out of habit let out a few moans. *Make him happy.* She allowed herself to move responsively to his thrusting. He came fast and withdrew from her, wiping himself or her butt.

"Don't tell me you didn't get off," he said gruffly.

"Of course I did. You always make me come. You know that."

Frank looked at her sideways as he pulled on his jeans. "Well, you're just going to have to remember how good it is, 'cause I'll be gone for a couple of days and you'll have to make do with your dipshit brother."

Fancy looked at him questioningly as she wiped herself with the sheet.

"Don't get too nosy. I've just got some business to take care of. You be a good girl and be waiting for me when I get back."

"When're you leaving?"

"Now," he said, putting on his boots, "try not to miss me too much."

She heard the door being locked from outside and watched Frank drive away in the sedan. Frankie was the only one who drove the pickup. It was a stick shift. Damn. But even if she could drive it, how would she get past the locked gate? Frankie had the keys. There had to be a way.

Later that afternoon, Frankie came to her trailer. He brought heavy clothing for her escorted trip to the main trailer for dinner. As Fancy pulled on her boots, she whined to Frankie, "Jesus, you'd think you'd bring me out once in a while instead of keeping me cooped up like a prisoner. I'm bored as hell."

"Yeah, that's all I'd have to do — take you out of here and then lose you someplace. Frank would have my head."

"He wouldn't have to know. Christ, even if we went for a burger, anything. There's got to be someplace around here we could go."

Frankie nodded and walked back toward the door. "Come on," he said, "hurry it."

Fancy put on her jacket and scarf. Frankie didn't bother locking her trailer after they left. Trudging through the snow, Fancy took note once again of where everything was. She entered the big trailer. It was brighter and smelled of men and mustiness. But it was bigger and warmer.

"What's for din-din, pasta or cereal?" she asked.

"I made pasta last night."

"Why don't you let me cook for a change?"

"You? You don't know how to cook. That fat fairy did all the cooking for you."

"No he didn't. I cooked some."

Frankie smirked as he took cereal out of the cupboard.

"I'm serious, Frankie. Let me cook us some eggs. I'm tired of fucking cereal."

He hesitated and gave her a look. "OK, just this once. And no word to Frank about this."

She jumped up from the booth and approached the stove before he had a chance to change his mind.

"And no funny business," he warned as she shouldered him aside and gave him a big smile.

"Of course not, honey," she cooed. But the little fridge contained only the remnants of a loaf of bread, some margarine, a half-filled container of powdered milk, and a few cans of beer.

"Shit!"

"What?"

"No eggs. Nothing. Christ, didn't anybody ever teach you how to food shop?"

"That's hot. What did Mom ever have in the fridge besides beer?"

"That's not true. She wasn't near that bad. Besides, she drank vodka and she kept it in the freezer."

They both laughed.

"Come on, Frankie, you've got to be hungry for something besides cereal and pasta. Shit, even rice and beans sounds like a fucking feast. Come on, let's go someplace and get something decent."

Frankie got up from the booth and reached for a couple of cereal bowls.

"You're wasting my time," he said. "No fucking way I take you out of here." He shoved her aside and poured cereal into the bowls.

"Then, at least go get something. Go by yourself. I'm going nuts, Frankie, and don't tell me it's not getting to you. Don't tell me your mouth doesn't water for pizza or a cheeseburger or some fried chicken. Come on, Frankie. Even Frank would be glad to eat something different for a change."

She saw him hesitating, unsure.

"You think you're a smartass, don't you? Get me out of here and then you take off. But that's not the way it's going to be."

"Don't be a jerk. Where could I go? Even if I could break out of here, do I look like Nanook of the North? There's bears and wolves out there. Do I look that stupid to you?"

"Even so, you're not staying in here. You're going back where you belong until I get back."

"Of course," she smiled. "Can I take this bowl of cereal with me?" she said, indicating one of the bowls he'd just filled. "I'm starving. When you come back, I'll have the strength to fuck your brains out."

Once she was inside, he locked the trailer and she saw him head down the narrow access road in the truck. It was 5:00 and almost dark. She knew he'd be gone at least an hour and a half.

Using the thin edge of the cereal spoon as a screwdriver, she tried to unscrew the handle to the trailer door. It was slow work. There was only enough room to turn the screw a tiny bit, not even a quarter turn each time. In her haste, the spoon slipped out of the screw head and she had to slow down and remind herself to press harder.

It took over a half-hour to loosen the three screws that held the handle to the door. Still, the door did not immediately swing open. She used the handle of the spoon as a lever to pry the door open. It moved a fraction of an inch. Not enough. Then, with the spoon still serving as a lever, she kicked the door right at that spot. After a series of forceful blows, the door burst open.

Fancy stood in the doorway and breathed in the cold air. It smelled like freedom. She filled her lungs and exhaled with relief. For the first time since she'd arrived, she had her boots and hat and gloves and jacket and was alone, outside, no longer confined.

Now, what to do first? It was almost completely dark and she'd have less than an hour before Frankie returned.

Fancy had fantasized about this moment many times. She raced through the snow to the third trailer, where Frank had his meth lab. It was unlocked, as she thought it would be. Entering the trailer, she turned on the light and saw the array of paraphernalia: beakers, chemicals, old car batteries. She turned on both gas burners full force. In a few minutes, the trailer would be filled with gas fumes and any small spark would set it off.

She took a quick look around for a supply of the crystals, but didn't see any. Frank must have taken it all with him to sell. *Oh well, maybe it's time to kick the habit anyway.* Then she saw a flashlight and stuck it into her jacket pocket, along with a pack of matches, before going out. She shut the door and raced back to her own trailer to turn on the gas stove, and did the same to Frank and Frankie's trailer. Propane fumes filled the air in the entire compound. Hesitating for a brief moment, she ran to Frank's bedroom at the rear of the trailer and set fire to one of the dirty sheets on the disheveled bed, taking another one with her.

Fancy returned to her own trailer. *Interesting that I've begun to think of it as mine.* She ripped the sheet in two, jammed half into the door, and lit it with a match. Then she raced back to the lab, placed the other half of the sheet under the front door, and set it ablaze. Racing to the abandoned house, she tried to disguise her tracks in the snow, sweeping branches behind her. She hoped that in the darkness, her tracks wouldn't be visible and Frankie would assume she had run away. Where she could, she shook tree branches so that snow would fall onto the path she had taken.

She had just reached the house when she heard a series of explosions. All three trailers were ablaze. The trailer that had served as the lab erupted in a huge yellow ball of flame. But amidst the exhiliration, the satisfying revenge quickly turned to fear and panic at what her father and brother would do to her now if they caught her.

Frantically turning her attention back to the house, she found a cellar window and kicked in the rotting frame. She lowered herself into the darkness and pulled the window closed behind her. With the flashlight shining around the abandoned cellar, she looked for the stairs leading to the first floor. The old stone basement was cold and musty, strewn with piles of old lumber, rusted tools, and molding furniture. Huge spider webs hung from the low ceiling.

Against one wall, she spotted a pile of clothes. Something about it drew her attention and she cautiously crept closer. Fancy jumped back so suddenly that she fell down. The clothes covered two corpses, apparently a man and a woman. The flesh and organs had disintegrated or been eaten by insects. Nothing was left but bones and dried skin.

Aside from the shock, she was surprised that the skeletons didn't evoke more fear or horror in her. They looked surprisingly benign, like a fake prop in a Halloween haunted house attraction. She wondered briefly who they were, but then felt anxious about time and went back to her task.

As she climbed the stairs, she kept the flashlight partly shielded by her hand. At the top, she pushed the door open and entered the old farmhouse kitchen. Light from the blazing trailers filled the room with flickering shadows. Large, moist flakes had begun to fall outside, and she briefly worried that the snow would put out the fires. She wanted Frank and Frankie to lose everything. Fear and panic rose again in her stomach. *First, find a place to hide, in case Frankie looks for me here in the house.*

Fancy was still exploring the first floor when she saw the lights outside. Cautiously, she looked out a window and saw Frankie's pickup bouncing up the access road. She watched him speed up to the trailers and jump out. Saw his arms flail, heard his voice call her name. It sounded far away, muffled by the snow and the crackling flames. She saw him spin around and around, searching. She worried that he might come toward the house looking for her, but he didn't. He just stood there, shaking his head, looking from one burning trailer to another, periodically calling her name. She could tell he didn't expect her to answer.

She watched as he slowly, reluctantly, climbed back into his pickup. He turned it around and headed back down the access trail. He was going. There would be no reason for him to come back. She knew Frank would blame him and he couldn't risk that confrontation. She was safe. Although — maybe he was going to get Frank. It was possible Frank would want to see for himself that everything was really destroyed, but that probably wouldn't be for hours

She had no idea where Frank went to sell his meth, but he was always gone for at least two days. Maybe she could sleep for a while, then strike out and reach the main road by morning. Maybe she'd be able to catch a ride, get to the police and notify her mother. Maybe it would be OK.

Fancy crouched in what used to be a pantry. Pulling the door closed behind her, she curled up on the floor. She was awakened by heavy pounding, which at first sounded like thunder. Then she recognized the heavy footsteps echoing in the empty house. She held her breath. The sound came closer. She shrank into herself. The door burst open and a light shined into her face. Reflexively, she squinted and put up her arm in front of her face.

"Jesus Christ," said a voice. "What are you doing here?"

"Frankie?"

"I thought you were dead or something. Jesus, what the hell happened here?"

"I saw you drive away."

"Yeah." He took the light out of her eyes and squatted next to her. "I had to come back and look for you," he said. "I was worried about you. I couldn't figure out what happened. Did somebody raid the place? How did you get out?"

Fancy clasped her arms around him and pulled him to her. "Some men came. I heard voices. The next thing I know, things were blowing up. I put the mattress around me. I'm not sure what happened. I must have been unconscious. I woke up and the trailer was burning. I barely got out. I guess the door had blown open. And then I hid in here."

He rubbed her back. "It's OK. Everything's all right now. I've got the truck. Let's get out of here." He helped her to her feet, grabbing a burlap sack lying on the floor under the shelves. Fancy saw that the fires were glowing softly now under the falling snow. She guessed she'd slept for a couple of hours.

"Come on," he urged, "the snow is piling up."

Fancy allowed herself to be pulled along as they exited the house and marched through the snow to Frankie's pickup.

"Did you get us something to eat?" she asked.

Frankie looked at her incredulously. "You can think of food at a time like this? Don't you realize we just lost everything? Whoever did this is going to pay. Believe me. You can count on it."

Fancy stared at him dumbly as she watched him climb into the truck.

"Come on!" he yelled. "Get your damn ass in the truck. We've got to get out of here." Obediently, Fancy climbed into the passenger side and Frankie started down the access road.

"So, if you saw me when I was up here before, why didn't you come out and show yourself, huh?"

Fancy's mind raced and she recalled watching him spinning in circles of frustration and calling her name out.

"I must have been dazed. I thought I heard someone calling my name. By the time I got to a window to look out, you were already driving away. I called to you but, of course, you couldn't hear me."

Without taking his eyes off the road, Frankie nodded.

"How did you get into the house?"

"I knocked in a cellar window," she said, glancing up at him.

"Yeah," he said, half to himself. "I was wondering why there were no footsteps in the snow leading up to the front door. I didn't expect to find you in there."

Fancy thought for a moment. "But weren't you looking for me? I thought you said that's why you came back again."

Frankie shot her a glance. "Sure. Why else? I just didn't really expect to find you. I thought that either you'd be off in the woods, frozen somewhere, or eaten by wolves — or else maybe they'd taken you."

"Who?"

"Whoever raided us."

Fancy looked at him stupidly. He was being too flip about this.

Frankie drove right through the open gate. Although it registered with her, she wasn't sure if it meant anything, just that it was different. If she remembered correctly, Frankie was now heading toward the main road — if you could call it that. The truck was still confined to the ruts in the road and Frankie tried to maintain some speed to avoid getting stuck in the snow. They drove in ominous silence. She had expected him to be full of questions. Maybe she should be talking more. Maybe her silence was incriminating.

"So who would have done this, raided us like that? I could have been killed."

Frankie didn't answer immediately, didn't take his eyes off the road. "I don't know. Somebody had it in for us, that's for sure. But it'll be all right. We were going to move in the spring anyway. Frank got all of our meth out, so we'll be OK."

"Where is Frank?"

"He went off to sell our supply. Where'd you think he was?"

"I don't know." She thought for a moment. "Is that where we're going? To meet Frank?"

Frankie got a big grin on his face. "Well, if that's what you want to do. I kind of had something else in mind." He stole a quick glance at her.

"Like what?"

"Suppose you and me just take off?"

She looked at him, dumbfounded.

"I really feel like a shit for lying to you — that whole story about a horse ranch in Idaho. It's just that, it's something I've dreamed about so much it was real to me. Now we can do it. I've got the money. We can get out of this life and really start over."

"You really mean it?"

"Look in the bag," he said, gesturing to the sack he had thrown behind his seat.

Fancy reached behind the seat and hauled the heavy bag onto her lap. Even in the near dark, she could see it was filled with money.

"I don't understand," she said.

"It's our stash, our savings. It's what we've been doing this past couple of years."

"How much is there?"

"I don't know. Maybe three-quarters of a mil. Enough for us to get started."

"What about Frank?"

"What about him? He'll have the cash from this sale. When he gets back to-morrow, he'll find everything destroyed and the two of us gone. He's going to blame us anyway, so we might as well take the money and run."

"You'd do that? I mean, we can really go away, just the two of us and never see him again?"

"That's what I'm saying."

"I never thought you'd do it. I didn't think you'd ever cross him."

Their dirt road came to an end and Frankie pulled onto pavement. There were a few inches of snow on the ground, but the pickup rode through it with-out much trouble. A few miles down the road, they came to an abandoned gas station and she was surprised when Frankie turned the truck into the empty lot, plowing through the snow. Then she saw the car, covered with a layer of snow. Her heart sank. She looked at her brother, but he had his eyes on the man in the car.

In a flash, Fancy jammed her foot down on top of Frankie's and propelled the truck forward. He tried to turn the wheel, but she held it straight. Smashing straight into the driver's side of the car, she heard glass shattering and the dull crumple of metal. The impact sent her into the dashboard and Frankie's head cracked against the windshield. There was a surprising silence.

Then Frankie grabbed her arm. "You fucking little bitch."

"Let go of me," she screamed, clawing at his arm, twisting to break his grip. She managed to open her door and fell out onto the snowy ground. Scrambling to her feet, she ran back to the road. Maybe someone would see her. Someone would pass by. She heard Frankie calling her, but she didn't stop. She heard a crack and felt a sting in her leg — and suddenly she was down. Her hand came away from the back of her thigh red and sticky.

She tried to get up, but fear and pain paralyzed her. Crawling toward the road, her vision blurred. She tried to scramble to her feet, but slipped and fell. Another crack sounded, and Fancy collapsed breathless into the snow. She surrendered to fatigue and helplessness — too tired, too scared to care. Two more shots and then silence. She closed her eyes, resigned to the idea of dying.

Footsteps in the snow. It didn't matter who it was. She had no more hope.

"I don't know what you and sonny boy thought you were doing, but the two of you are either incredibly stupid or incredibly unlucky."

Fancy felt his foot in her side, pushing at her, turning her over. She rolled onto her back and stared up at her father. He stood above her, a gun in one hand and the burlap bag in the other.

"Frankie was supposed to meet me here with this," he said, indicating the bag of money. "He told me what you did to our little compound. I don't know how you managed to pull it off, but I'll give you credit for it. I guess he got lucky and found you when he went back for our rainy-day fund. Is that when he got the idea to kill me and run off with you and the loot?" Frank shook his head. "Well, the idiot got his just reward."

"You killed him? You killed Frankie?"

Frank laughed. "Of course I killed him. You think I'd let him try to murder me and let him live? Are you crazy as well as stupid?"

"Then you killed him for nothing."

Frank cocked his head in puzzlement.

"He didn't try to kill you. He wasn't double-crossing you. He was bringing the money — and me — to you. He could have taken me away. He didn't have to come here. He chose you over me. I steered the truck into you, not him."

Frank thought for a moment and then shrugged.

"Oh well, I still have the money," he said. Then he pointed the gun at her head and pulled the trigger.

Fourteen

Three days later, Noreen received a phone call from Matthew Garrett.

"I just received word from the Minnesota State Police. I think they may have found your son and your daughter."

"Oh, thank God," she gasped. "Where?"

"They found the bodies of a young man and a young woman up in northern Minnesota. The male had a number of identifications on him that matched the aliases your son and ex-husband used. The physical description of the female matches that of your daughter."

Noreen sank onto the kitchen chair. "Oh," she said. "Oh God."

"I'm sorry," he said. "The State Police contacted me because I'd left my number with them when I was looking for her. You'll have to go out there to ID the bodies."

"I understand," she said. "How did they die?"

"They were both shot. I suspect your ex-husband did it. They found a burned meth lab a few miles from where the bodies were discovered. There were remnants of some female clothing in one of the trailers. It looks like she could have been there, perhaps as a prisoner of some kind. I don't know."

"Yes," Noreen said, "they would have been capable of doing that."

Noreen wanted to lay her head on the table and go to sleep, never to wake. If a drink had been handy, she just might have taken it. It had turned out worse than she had feared. She had suspected Frank might turn up in the picture. She never fully believed Frankie was operating on his own. And now that bastard had succeeded in destroying her whole family. *Well, he did that a long time ago, didn't he.*

But he wasn't going to destroy her too. Not if she could help it. Numbly, Noreen reached for the phone and dialed Linda's number. She left a message.

Noreen remained slouched at the kitchen table for a long time. Eventually, it got dark. *If I smoked, I'd have a cigarette. If I believed in God, I'd pray. But now, there's nothing for me to do.*

The phone rang. Hearing Linda's voice was a relief and a release. She was still sobbing when Linda burst into the house 20 minutes later. Noreen let herself be comforted into silence. Linda still had not spoken.

Noreen slowly pulled herself back from Linda's embrace and wiped her eyes.

"I'll make coffee," Linda said, "then you can tell me all about it."